Also by Nigel McCrery

SILENT WITNESS
STRANGE SCREAMS OF DEATH

NIGEL McCRERY

THE SPIDER'S WEB

POCKET
B O O K S

LONDON · SYDNEY · NEW YORK · TOKYO · SINGAPORE · TORONTO

First published in Great Britain by Simon & Schuster UK Ltd, 1998
This edition first published by Pocket Books, 1999
An imprint of Simon & Schuster UK Ltd
A Viacom Company

Simon & Schuster Ltd
Africa House
64–78 Kingsway
London WC2B 6AH

Simon & Schuster Australia
Sydney

A CIP catalogue record for this book is available from the British Library.

ISBN 0-671-01595-8

1 3 5 7 9 10 8 6 4 2

Printed and bound in Great Britain by
Caledonian International Book Manufacturing, Glasgow

THE SPIDER'S WEB

PROLOGUE

PROLOGUE

THE MOON STOOD HIGH ABOVE THE FLAT EAST ANGLIAN landscape. Like a giant blue lantern it hung, isolated against the wide Norfolk sky. Its searching silvery beams penetrated the thick, December darkness and reflected off the crisp, sharp frost which had settled like a white cloak over the landscape bringing beauty to the wretched decay of winter.

Jack Falconer moved his large body slowly and purposefully through the woodlands which covered the ancient slopes of Herdan Hill. Jack had poached the area for over twenty years, following generations of his forebears. Although it wasn't a good living, it was adequate enough for his needs, with a little left over for a rainy day. He considered the local game to be his by right of ancient custom. Why should any man, no matter how rich, be able to lay claim to the land just because he had a few extra shillings in his pocket? Jack believed that the land belonged to those who tended it, and he had tended it well for many years. He reached his final trap and paused for a moment. Staring through his own steaming breath, he took time to look out across the level countryside. Even in the dark, with only the moon to act as his lantern, it was a grand sight. Who needed fancy pictures, he pondered, when you had God's beauty all around you? Gazing up towards the clear night sky he tried to make out some of the more obvious constellations.

Herdan Hill was one of the few high points in the county and stood out like an ominous carbuncle against its flat surroundings. Now, in the depths of winter, it was a lonely, desolate place visited by few. During the summer months, however, the place was swarming with picnickers and walkers, all there to admire the views and spend a few hours away from the pressures of city life. Because it was the only high point for miles the hill was steeped in myths; mainly, as is normal in Norfolk, to do with the devil and satanic worship. This was where, according to local legend, the devil was supposed to rise from hell, to walk abroad amongst the people causing mischief. There had been a church at the top of the hill once, the remnants of which could still be seen, and black masses were reputed to have been celebrated within its sacred confines. It had been deconsecrated many years before and had eventually fallen into ruin. The steep climb, it would seem, was too much even for Old Nick himself. Jack chuckled. The stories were all nonsense, of course, but more interesting than believing the hill was merely an anomalous blip on an otherwise featureless landscape.

He had started to set his last trap when the flash of a car's headlamps, appearing unexpectedly over the brow of the hill, startled him. Instinctively, Jack threw himself to the floor and rolled quickly under the nearest frost-covered bush. He lay there for a moment scarcely daring to breathe, fearful of being discovered. He needn't have worried. Wrapped tightly in his green and brown combat fatigues, with his dark woolly hat pulled low over his head and face, he blended in perfectly with his dank, leafy surroundings. Jack had the capacity, practised over many years, to lie perfectly still for long periods of time. He was even able to control his breathing, so the rising vapours from his breath didn't betray his position. 'Patience,' his father had always taught him 'is the very meat of poaching.'

He glanced at his watch – it was one-thirty. He was surprised to see anyone on the hill at that time of the morning. No one, he considered, save the police or a game warden, would be daft enough to chance climbing the steep icy road at that time of the night. He peered out carefully through a small clearing in the hawthorn bush to see if he could distinguish the driver. It wasn't the police, he was sure of that. Wrong kind of car, a Metro, and besides, it was far too cold for them, they'd be tucked up somewhere warm with mugs of tea in their hands. It might still be a warden though, he pondered. He waited as the car began to move slowly down the hill, picking up speed as the incline steepened, its accelerating tyres crushing the frosty road surface into blackened tread patterns as it went. Although the car continued to pick up speed, there wasn't a sound from the engine. Jack deduced that the driver must have the car in neutral.

As the car sped silently past the trees and bushes which lined and edged the road, the intrusive light from the fluorescent moon forced its way through the naked branches of the densely packed wood and into the car's darkened interior. It picked out the driver's face in flickering rays of cold light, illuminating it for a moment before it melted back into the car's shadows. Although he only glimpsed the driver's youthful features, Jack Falconer still experienced an incomprehensible sense of foreboding. There was something terribly wrong. He wasn't sure why, but a tremor of unease and anticipation ran through him, holding him rigidly to the spot and suspending his icy breath inside his throat. As he continued to watch the car it neared the sharp right-hand bend that twisted awkwardly back on itself before disappearing deeper into the overhanging woodland. Jack realized almost at once that the vehicle was going too fast to have any chance of negotiating such a sharp turn. Even under normal driving conditions the bend was hazardous and had to be taken with care, but with black ice freezing and smoothing the tarmacked road, it was an almost impossible manoeuvre. The car's young driver either hadn't seen the bend, or had simply lost control by the time he reached it. Whatever the reason, there was no visible reaction to the impending danger. Jack felt like jumping to his feet and screaming a warning, but instead found himself transfixed, mesmerized by the fast-approaching disaster.

Finally, the small Metro careered off the road, jumping slightly as it bounced off the grassy verge before crashing headlong into a large and ancient oak tree. The sound of crushed metal and splintering glass filled the air for a few seconds before being replaced by an intense and ominous silence. For an instant, everything was still, even the chilling wind seemed to have disappeared. The spectacle of a car smashing itself violently against a tree shocked even a hard-bitten character like Jack Falconer. After a few moments he'd recovered enough to force himself to his feet and he began to move resolutely towards the wreckage. He wasn't quite sure what he could do even when he reached it, but felt compelled to take some action. Almost as soon as he had started running towards the crumpled mass of white and silver metal, however, it exploded with an enormous roar and erupted into a great ball of red and orange flame, lighting up the night sky and melting the surrounding frost.

The force of the explosion blew Jack off his feet, throwing him backwards through the air before dumping his body on top of the bush under which he had just been hiding. Struggling for breath, he rolled of the bush and scrambled back to his feet, staring with disbelief into the roaring inferno that engulfed the car. If there had been any chance to help the driver before, that opportunity was gone. Jack stood trying to peer through the gaps in the smoke and flames, searching for any signs of life. For an instant he thought he could make out the dark outline of a figure. He only saw the shape for an instant silhouetted against the effulgent flames, before it disappeared once more into the plumes of black smoke that surrounded and obliterated the vehicle. Forgetting his own security for once, Jack called out, 'You there, can you hear me? Can you get out?'

His voice was lost, however, beneath the crackling and bellowing of the burning car. Jack strained his eyes, searching through the darkness, but there was nothing. If there had been anyone they were surely dead now. He began to think the figure had been an illusion created by the strange shadows that now crept through the woods like black fingers before the raging fire.

Despite the flames, Jack began to move towards the car again, using his hands to protect his face. As he got closer however he suddenly and inexplicably sensed danger. He stopped immediately, his instincts keeping him rooted to the spot. Jack had learnt to trust his instincts over the years and only challenged them reluctantly. Unsettled by this sensation Jack continued to search the area warily, his eyes darting in all directions and his ears straining for any unusual or unaccountable sounds. There was nothing, yet he still sensed that he was surrounded by some evil. The poacher had become the prey and despite the cold sweat oozed from every pore, before dribbling like tears across his face. Finally, Jack Falconer's giant frame turned quickly and ran blindly back through the woods, smashing down anything that got in his way and leaving the unseen and dangerous entity far behind.

1

LIKE THOUSANDS OF WORSHIPPERS BEFORE THEM, THE
VOICES OF St Mary's Church choir crept and crawled across
the church's crumbling masonry, their psalms and hymns
etching themselves into the building's ancient symbolism
leaving faint echoes of their Christian devotions and praise
behind. As the choirmaster held his thin wooden baton
above his head instructing his attentive company to hold
the final note, Sam's voice finally reached the very peak of
its range. Then, as calmly as he had begun, the conductor
gently lowered his hands ordering them to stop. He looked
up and smiled along the expectant faces.

'I think we're there, ladies and gentlemen. I think we're
there. Well done.' Concerned frowns turned to contented
smiles and general mutterings of satisfaction reverberated
around the small but enthusiastic band of singers. Although
only a small church choir, they still took their music very
seriously.

Loud applause from the back of the church indicated that
the Reverend Andrews had also been listening to their
efforts and was clearly delighted by them. Peter Andrews

7

had only been in the parish of Sowerby a year but had already made his mark. Still reasonably young, he was fresh-faced and enthusiastic and seemed to be everywhere at once, raising money, organizing plays, attending social gatherings, and reorganizing the young mothers group. Despite his years he had been a military padre and served in the Gulf as well as several inner-city parishes around the country, not as relaxing as Sowerby. Resurrecting the defunct church choir had been his idea and, despite a shaky start, the numbers had grown slowly until there were between twelve and fifteen regular and enthusiastic members. It had been he who had persuaded Sam to take part, even giving her a rather embarrassing audition. Although Sam's vocal range was poor, he had recruited her anyway; telling her that practice would improve her potential.

He had also decided to make a video film entitled *A year in the life of an English village*. To this end he had enlisted one of the locals, Edmond Moore, to help with the project. Many in the village thought Edmond an odd choice considering he'd lived in the village for even less time than the Reverend. Quiet and reserved, he didn't mix well and knew little of the village's people and traditions, but Peter Andrews considered that this was a good way to 'introduce him to the village' and made Edmond both his cameraman and sound operator. The fact that all the video equipment also belonged to Edmond was not lost on the congregation, however. Sam wasn't sure about Edmond Moore either. There was something about him that didn't sit right in her mind and she always felt uncomfortable in his presence.

Andrews hoped to show the film at the village hall the following summer, charging people a small admission fee to watch. He then planned to sell copies of the video to local residents who had taken some part in the film or to visitors with an interest in English parish life. To this end, he had made sure he had shots of just about everyone in the small East Anglian hamlet, as well as a good few from outside it. The money raised was to go towards a more economical, and effective, heating system for the church. Sam for one thought it a worthwhile project. Although she enjoyed being a member of the choir, finding that the weekly ritual both soothed and relaxed her, during the winter months it was like performing in a giant fridge. The church's prehistoric brickwork held in as much cold as it kept out, maintaining the temperature inside St Mary's well below freezing. In an attempt to save money, the boiler was not turned on until early on Sunday morning and switched off again after the evening service. Consequently, the entire choir sang wrapped tightly in thick jumpers and coats, many with brightly coloured woollen hats pulled firmly down over their ears. On particularly cold evenings Sam would watch, amused, as the steam from a dozen voices rose rhythmically and in tune with the music before drifting, like incense from a High Mass, towards the roof and disappearing amongst the dark oak rafters.

St Mary's no longer had its own vicar, and had to share the Reverend Andrews with four other parishes. However, this number would soon be reduced to three, as falling congregations and a lack of funds meant that St Cuthbert's in Newfield would soon have to close. Five hundred years of worship ended as an economic expedience to the men in grey suits, who had played speculative games with church money and lost. Subsequently there was now only one service during the week – to which people seldom came in winter because of the icy conditions – and two on Sundays which were still surprisingly well attended. Since forcing herself into Ely Cathedral some years previously, the

spiritual side of Sam's life had become increasingly
important to her. The sudden and violent death of her father
and the scientific realities of her occupation as a pathologist had, for many years, made her question and reject all
things religious and ethereal. Strangely, the same cold
clinical analysis which made her reject the supernatural
eventually led her to return to it.

Sam had seen more death than most and knew how cold
and impersonal it could be. Death, without compromises or
agreements, took away everything and replaced it with
nothing. Although Sam was convinced that she could read
the personality of a corpse from the lines and structure of its
face, she also observed that in death the very essence of a
person's being had been removed. That essence, call it the
soul, which defines individuality disappeared like a morning
haze before the July sun. Sam no longer believed so strongly
that life ended just because the body had ceased functioning,
but increasingly felt that perhaps death was only another step
towards a different level of consciousness.

The choir dispersed quickly and began to make their way
home, eager for their cozy armchairs and a warm fire.
During the spring and summer they would often linger and
talk, or make their way to a local pub for a few drinks. Sam
found it a pleasant change from the normal hospital chatter
and rumour. The Reverend Andrews waited by the door,
thanking each member in turn for coming out on such an
inhospitable evening while Edmond Moore filmed the
procession. When Sam finally reached him, his smile
seemed to broaden.

'Well done, Sam. You see my faith in you was well
founded.'

Sam smiled back politely.

'Let's hope I can hold out until Sunday's service.'

Andrews nodded.

'Of course you will, God will see to that.'

Sam gave him a speculative smile and made her way out of the church. Turning right and following the gravelled path to the back of the church she quickly found herself standing in front of her mother's grave. Crouching down by the small marble headstone, she ran her fingers along the smooth edges of her mother's name and began to reminisce. Christmas had been her parents' favourite time and most of Sam's childhood memories seemed to be based around the Yuletide holiday. If memories were an intrinsic measure of a person's life, then Sam considered that hers had been a good one, and both parents had played an immeasurably important part in that. The anger she had felt towards her mother for so many years had finally ended with her death. It was only then that she had felt any sense of compassion or remorse. Crying had been important then. Like exorcising a dark spirit from her soul so that she could finally be at peace with her mother's memory. A different form of anger consumed her now. An anger born out of a sense of loss and wasted years. Life, she knew, was far too short to hold feelings of bitterness for long. She wished that instead of spending most of her life being angry, she had tried to be more forgiving. Now, like most orphaned children, Sam felt sad and alone. She was suddenly envious of her sister Wyn's relationship with her mother. Sam had never really been close to anyone apart from her father and perhaps Tom Adams, and even that had ended on a sour note. She had always been too busy making her way in the world to spend time on relationships. Now she wondered if it wasn't too late. Having Wyn and her nephew Ricky living at the cottage helped. It was like making amends for years of neglect. And although she knew it was only her conscience pricking her, Sam was still determined to remain close to them at least. She imagined her own headstone for a moment: 'Here lies Sam Ryan, spinster of this parish'.

Sam breathed out purposefully; she really was feeling sorry for herself.

Her thoughts were suddenly interrupted by a voice at her shoulder.

'Wordsworth, isn't it?'

This unexpected intrusion into her private thoughts made Sam jump. She turned to see Eric Chambers standing by her side.

'The inscription on your mother's memorial, *"A slumber did my spirit seal"*. Wordsworth?'

Sam nodded. 'I hadn't realized you were so well read, Eric.'

He smiled at her.

'I'm not, I looked it up. *"I had no human fears, She seemed a thing that could not feel the touch of earthly years."* '

Sam felt slightly confused by this revelation.

'Why the interest?'

'Don't get too much poetry on the memorials these days. Everything seems so regimented, uninteresting, bland. They'll be digging up the stones and putting them around the edge of the cemetery next I expect.' He shook his head disapprovingly and continued, 'Breath of fresh air to see something interesting on a memorial. The Michaelmas daisies are a picture, too.'

Sam had planted several of these beautiful autumnal flowers around her mother's grave. They had been her favourites and they were now in full and radiant bloom. Sam smiled her appreciation at Eric as they began to walk back along the path together towards the small car park behind the church.

Eric Chambers was known locally as the 'Colonel'.

Despite having known him for a number of years Sam wasn't quite sure why, and didn't like to ask. She assumed it was something to do with his general outlook and bearing. Eric's views, like his clothes, were rather worn and old fashioned, but good for a few years yet. A confirmed bachelor, in his seventies, he looked ten years younger, and was certainly fitter than his years allowed. He lived alone in the small cottage he had been brought up in, surrounded by family heirlooms and bric-a-brac that aged and gathered dust together with their owner. Despite this, however, he did not appear to be as sad or lonely as might be supposed and filled his days with a wide array of projects and jobs. As well as being the churchwarden and choirmaster, he also taught music and, uncharacteristically, computer studies at several of the local clubs and colleges. He had even managed to teach the Reverend Andrews how to use a computer, helping to transfer all the parish records and accounts on to a series of floppy disks, and was determined to introduce him to the mysteries of the Internet next.

He was fond of saying, especially to his pupils, churchmen included, 'I might be getting on a bit, but my mind and outlook are still young.'

Sam agreed with him. Village life, she pondered, wouldn't be the same without the Eric Chambers of this world to organize it. His greatest asset, as far as Sam was concerned, however, was his cottage garden. Small and magnificently coloured, its scents were intoxicating. Sam had visited the garden the previous summer and been overwhelmed by its design and diversity. Eric also seemed to know every flower in the garden by name and to remember when and why they had been planted. It was like a floral biography of his life. He had generously given her various cuttings, which now thrived in a corner of her own efflorescent creation.

'My mother's buried just over there.' He pointed towards the far side of the cemetery. 'Simple plot, no moving sentiments or poetry I'm afraid, but a pleasant place under the yew tree.'

Sam nodded her understanding.

'What about your father?'

Eric shook his head.

'No idea what happened to him. Old story, I'm afraid. Left when I was young, ran off with a local girl, never saw either of them again.'

Sam looked at him sympathetically. 'I'm sorry.'

'I'm not. A bad lot, according to my mother. Wasn't the first time it had happened, only this time he decided not to come back with his tail between his legs. We muddled on.' He coughed uncomfortably and changed the subject. 'I understand you're dealing with the death of Simon Vickers?'

Sam stared across at him, confused for a moment.

'The young man killed in the car crash on Herdan Hill.'

Sam finally realized who he was talking about. 'No, I'm not, Trevor Stuart's dealing with it.'

Eric seemed surprised by this unexpected revelation.

'But I thought you were the county's Forensic Pathologist?'

'I am, well, one of them anyway. Trevor's the other.'

Eric nodded his understanding. 'Oh, I see. Terrible business. Simon used to come to one of my computer clubs, he was quite brilliant. Had an outstanding future ahead of him. Such a waste. I was surprised when I found out the facts. Never seemed the kind to get involved in stealing cars. But then I suppose you can never really tell.'

Sam shook her head, sadly. 'No, I suppose not.'

'Do they know how he died yet?'

Sam shrugged, not really wanting to pass comment on

something she knew nothing about. 'The inquest's tomorrow morning it's bound to be in the evening paper.'

Eric nodded, clearly dissatisfied with Sam's reply. He coughed awkwardly again.

'Multiple injuries I should think. Just hope he didn't suffer.'

He suddenly stiffened and looked up towards the stars, scanning them for a moment before returning to the subject. 'You know, dead before the fire started.'

He was still fishing for the information and Sam didn't like to disappoint him, but her reply was still non-committal.

'I don't suppose he'd have known much about it.'

Eric nodded, finally satisfied with Sam's reply.

'Good, good. It's the family our thoughts should go out to then. It's always the living that suffer most. The dead, they're out of it, but the living,' he shrugged, 'their grieving goes on forever.'

Sam looked across at him, concerned about the apparent depths of his own feelings.

'Forever?'

Forever seemed such a depressingly long time and Sam had hoped that her own grieving might ease soon. But Eric seemed so positive.

'Oh yes. As time passes it gets easier to live with, of course, but you never stop grieving and remembering. I'll probably still be missing my mother when I'm on my own deathbed. No one's hand to hold if you know what I mean?'

Sam nodded. Despite his busy life, Eric was still a lonely soul.

'Funny thing really, I was only up there the other week with the Reverend Andrews looking at the old church.'

Sam was puzzled.

'Why?'

'He's thinking of reconsecrating it using it for festivals and the like. Try and stop some of the silly stories they tell about the hill, and church as well.'

'Sounds like a very good idea.'

Sam just hoped she wouldn't have to sing up there in the winter. They finally reached the church gate that led into the car park.

'See you next week, then?'

Eric nodded. 'Certainly you will, I never miss. You could set your alarm by me.'

He nodded politely and strode off. After a few steps he stopped and looked back. 'How are those cuttings of mine doing by the way?'

'Beautifully. You'll have to come and have a look in the spring.'

He waved his stick in acceptance of her invitation and disappeared into the night.

Sam stamped her feet down hard onto the cold concrete steps in front of the coroner's court, in a vain effort to increase the circulation to her legs and ankles. The temperature hadn't risen much above freezing all morning and Sam hadn't dressed for it. She had lived in the county long enough to know it was the coldest place in England during the winter. The icy winds raced unhindered from the Siberian plains across Norfolk's featureless landscape, freezing everything and everybody that was unlucky enough to get in its path. Even Ely, a place she normally loved, looked cold and uninviting. She watched interested as council workmen attached Christmas decorations to the lamps and walls but even this cheery sight failed to raise her spirits. Sam would normally have had several layers of clothes wrapped tightly around her body, with a pair of thick leather boots covering her legs and feet; East Anglian winters had put an end to any notion of vanity she may have had long ago. However, as Trevor Stuart had invited her to a lunchtime recital in Ely Cathedral followed by lunch at one of the better local hotels, Sam felt she had to make an effort. She'd slipped on a short black dress, black tights, and court shoes. Over this she had wrapped her smart, black, woollen coat. Even this normally reliable garment, however, was unable to stave off the cutting chill. Her inappropriate dress would have mattered little if Trevor had been on time.

The inquest on Simon Vickers was obviously not as straightforward as he had anticipated. Sam could have taken advantage of her position and made herself comfortable inside the centrally heated courtroom, but she made it a point never to attend inquests unless she was personally involved with them. She was far too opinionated to be a mere bystander and had to suppress the desire to become involved in every case she heard, especially when some relevant scientific point was either misinterpreted or incorrectly challenged. Sam was aware of the importance of giving evidence. She'd seen too many important cases fall because the evidence was either ill-prepared or not presented properly. Your work could be as expert or as clever as you liked, but if you couldn't convince a court or a coroner, then all those hours of dedicated effort would be a complete waste of time.

She glanced at her watch, twelve-fifteen, the concert had already begun. Like a small child unable to get her own way, she stamped her feet down hard on the concrete floor, venting her annoyance at her friend's lateness. At last, the sound of hushed chattering voices inside the building told her the case was over and the court was finally clearing. As she watched, the usual array of people emerged: police, press, and coroner's officers. The hushed voices were quickly replaced, however, by the sound of intense and desperate weeping. A woman's cries echoed along dark panelled passages and high-ceilinged courtrooms before bursting forth onto the street and being carried away by the cold December wind. For Sam, the fanfare of grief was a familiar sound, but one she never quite got used to.

A middle-aged couple finally emerged through the court's large oak doors. They were being comforted by a third man whom Sam recognized as John Gordon, a local and very capable solicitor who Sam herself had crossed swords with a time or two, and not always successfully. She suddenly felt sorry for Trevor. Gordon spoke quietly to the couple for a few moments before shaking hands gently and moving off. As he left, the man turned back to his wife and pulled her closer to him. Her head hung in a sort of humiliated shame between his shoulder and chin, from where she sobbed uncontrollably. Sam was struck by the haggard look on the man's face. He looked tired and dark shadows were drawn long and intensely beneath his eyes. His pain was etched into every line and crease of his face. Sam had seen people age overnight as mental anguish took its physical toll. Looking through his grief, Sam estimated that the man was only in his late forties, although he looked ten years older. Sam's observations were interrupted by the arrival of Trevor Stuart.

'When you're ready, we're already late.'

Sam glared at him for a moment, unappreciative of his sarcastic tone. As they began to descend the steps, Sam glanced back towards the couple. The man caught her eye and scanned her face for answers to questions that she just didn't have. Sam jerked her head away quickly, feeling embarrassed and awkward, and made her way towards the giant cathedral which now hovered imposingly above her.

*

The concert had been more interesting than Sam had anticipated. The East Anglian Philharmonic was not noted as being one of the country's great orchestras, but it was very capable and had a broad repertoire. They had begun with Barber's *Adagio for Strings*, which Sam loved, and concluded with Mozart's Symphonies numbers 40 and 41, which relaxed her sufficiently to enjoy her forthcoming lunch. For such a small place the White Lamb hotel and restaurant was impressive. It had a first-class menu prepared by one of the finest chefs in the district as well as ten romantically appointed bedrooms which included veiled four-poster beds and Victorian bathrooms. Sam had brought Tom here on a couple of special occasions and even he had been impressed by the arrangements.

On arrival, they were escorted to a table at the far side of the restaurant. It was, fortunately, close to a radiator. Sam had never really warmed up since her long wait outside the court for Trevor and sitting in the draughty interior of the ancient cathedral hadn't helped. She slipped off her shoes and ran her freezing feet up and down the inside edge of the radiator. She had always suffered from cold feet. Even as a child chilblains had been the bane of her life. Her father would spend hours in the evening rubbing her feet and warming them up. Sam felt sure that it was those periods of intimacy which brought her closer to him. Tom, when they were still together, had tried to emulate her father's efforts a few times but it was never quite as effective.

They ordered their food carefully and, as they both had the remainder of the day off, decided to splash out on a bottle of quality wine. As the first course arrived, Sam stopped the idle chitchat about the orchestra's performance and indulged her curiosity about the incidents outside the courthouse earlier.

'I take it they were the parents outside the court?'

'Which ones?'

'The ones who looked desperate, the woman was crying?'

'Oh, them.'

There was an edge to his voice when he realized who Sam was referring to. 'Yes, they're the boy's parents. They're the ones who caused all the problems.'

'What problems?'

'Brought in their own solicitor to examine the evidence. God knows why, it was clear-cut enough.'

'What was the verdict?'

'Accidental death, only verdict it could have been.'

'Circumstances?'

Sam had suddenly become clinical and inquisitive. Trevor had seen her in these moods too often to try and divert her attention. He had learnt that it was far easier to appease Sam rather than meet her head on.

'Went out for the evening, apparently to meet a friend, but instead of that he got drunk, stole a car and crashed it into a tree on Herdan Hill.'

'So why were his parents concerned enough to get their own solicitor?'

'As far as they were concerned their little lad would never have done a thing like that. You know the type: their little boy didn't drink, didn't drive, was honest and trustworthy.'

'Perhaps they though he was.'

Trevor scowled, unconvinced. 'I wouldn't mind, but he already had an NCR number so they must have had some idea what he was like.'

It was the second time Sam had heard that opinion expressed in less than twenty-four hours. She persisted with her questions.

'What were his convictions for?'

Trevor shrugged. 'Violence, what else.'

'So you're convinced of his guilt then?'

'I'm a pathologist. I don't express opinions, I deal in facts and prepare reports.'

'Since when did you stop expressing opinions?'

'Okay, if that's what you want. I think that parents don't always know as much about their children or their activities as they think they do. Pick up any paper, any day of the week, and there will be a story just like this one staring you in the face.'

'You don't sound very sympathetic.'

'Frankly, Sam, I'm not. If they go out to rob and steal, as far as I'm concerned they deserve everything they get.'

Sam looked across at him slightly shocked. 'Even death?'

'That's the chance they take. At least this time it was the culprit and not some poor innocent bystander.'

'Any problems with the PM?'

'None. Multiple injuries consistent with a head-on car crash. Almost certainly dead before the flames got to him and he was three or four times over the limit. Bloody fool.'

'Badly burnt?'

'Bad enough. Made the PM more difficult. You know what it's like, you've done plenty yourself.'

Sam nodded.

'Now that your curiosity has been satisfied, can we get back to the reason I invited you out for this rather expensive lunch?'

'So there is an ulterior motive?'

Trevor looked up at her, 'Can't a friend and colleague take his partner out occasionally without arousing her suspicions about his motivations?'

Sam smiled at his hurt expression. 'Clearly, my suspicions were completely founded.'

'Always the clever one.' He paused for a moment then blurted it out. 'I'm thinking of getting married again.'

Sam wasn't so much shocked by this revelation as fascinated. Little that Trevor did these days surprised her.

'So where did you meet this one, Mothercare?'

Trevor frowned at her. 'She's a radiographer at the Park actually.'

'Not the tall blonde one, Claire, is it?'

Trevor felt uncomfortable at Sam's astuteness and nodded awkwardly. 'Emily, actually, and yes it is.'

Sam shook her head. The radiographers were considered some of the most desirable women in the hospital. Something to do with the look of purity their short white coats gave them, Sam supposed.

'And how old is she?'

Trevor looked down into his soup, embarrassed to meet Sam's disapproving gaze.

'Twenty-four, but years older than that in maturity and experience.' Trevor realized he was floundering.

'She'd have to be. So when's the happy day?'

'June. We thought we'd get married in the summer. Hoping to use Trinity Chapel, me being an old boy and all.'

'Very romantic. And the honeymoon . . . Club Eighteen-Thirty?'

Trevor's sense of humour was quickly evaporating under Sam's sarcastic onslaught.

'I invited you to lunch for a bit of advice and to ask you to be my best man, er, wom . . . person, not to be the comic turn.'

The invitation took the wind out of Sam's sails, and she was both flattered and surprised, 'I don't know what to say. Isn't a man suppose to do that, a brother, best friend?'

He smiled across at her.

'You are my best friend, Sam.'

Sam became more earnest. 'Look, I'm sorry if I sound like your aunt but are you sure you're doing the right thing?'

As the waiters removed the first course and replaced it with the second, Trevor shook his head. 'Of course I'm not sure, but I'd like to try.'

'There's over twenty years' difference.'

'So?'

'So a lot of people could get hurt here, including you. What do her parents think for a start?'

'Only her mum left, dad died a few years ago, and I seem to have charmed her all right.'

'You've probably got more in common.'

Sam finally put her knife and fork down and looked despairingly across at him, 'Well you seem to have made your mind up.'

'Minds, it takes two to tango.'

Sam looked at him for a moment, searching for her decision. Despite his many failings she liked Trevor. Over the years he'd been a good friend and confidant and got her out of many a pickle. She finally nodded. 'Yes, I'd love to be your best man, person.'

Trevor's face lit up and he leaned across the table and kissed her. 'You were always that, Sam.'

Trevor's compliment made Sam flush. Noticing, he lightened the moment. 'Just don't lose the ring.'

Sam shook her head and smiled broadly, 'I won't. Promise.'

It had started snowing by the time Sam began her journey home. The small white flakes of ice were being thrown in all directions by an icy wind that couldn't seem to make its mind up which way to blow. They clung to Sam's windscreen for a moment before crawling across the glass and being wiped away. As she drove away from the small market town Sam glanced back towards the cathedral. Dark grey clouds had rolled in from the east and hovered ominously above the immense building. The cathedral stood out vividly against the dark, snow-filled sky. Sam didn't like snow; it froze her feet and chilled her through. It was all right on Christmas cards, but that was about it. She did find it a great leveller though, making everything from the dirtiest streets to the muddiest fields look white, crisp and fresh. By the time she was turning off the main road and climbing the dirt track towards her cottage the snow was falling in large flurries and the ground was already covered. Sam was glad that the farmer, who owned the right of way to her cottage, had finally decided to repair the track and fill in the increasing number of potholes that seemed to appear daily. Sam was also pleased that she had traded in her saloon car for the four-wheel drive Range Rover she was now driving. Trevor had been convinced it was just another fashion accessory but he was wrong. Given the area's uncertain weather conditions and the inhospitable places she was often compelled to visit, Sam had found it indispensable.

Although Trevor and his forthcoming marriage were preying on her mind they weren't the only things that were troubling her. For some reason she was finding it difficult to shake off the image of the dead boy's father outside the coroner's court. His look of despair and hopelessness haunted her. She had seen and felt more than her fair share of sadness, both personally and professionally, and thought she was tough enough to deal with anything by now, but the boy's father had managed to reveal a flaw in her long-established defences. Finally, turning off the track, Sam heard the gravel on her front path crunch reassuringly beneath the wheels. Locking her car and pulling the hood of her coat over her head Sam made for the front door, but then thought better of it. Instead, she decided to walk to the back of the house and check Eric's cuttings.

During the winter the garden was a drab and uninteresting place but still needed plenty of work to prepare it for the spring and summer. With the coming of winter many of the smells that Sam relied upon to calm her paranoia no longer floated through the air, filling her nose and mind with their stimulating aromas. It was a time of concern, sometimes verging on panic, as she was no longer able to get the daily fix her garden offered. So many of her colleagues, including Trevor, had already lost their sense of smell and, along with it, much of their taste and she couldn't imagine how they coped. It wasn't, as so many seemed to think, the smells from the bodies that caused the damage to the olfactory senses. Although unpleasant, they were natural enough and no worse than some of the manure she had covered her garden with over the years. It was the damned chemicals that pathologists used which killed off the nerve endings. It was a slow unnoticed process that damaged without hurt and caused years of pain.

She looked up into the clear night sky, observing a small dot of light that seemed to travel through the constellations, adding an odd and unexpected dimension to each of them before moving on to the next. Sam thought it was a shooting star when she first saw it, but later realized it was one of many satellites that littered the upper atmosphere. After a few moments her attention returned to Earth and she opened the greenhouse door. She had been propagating Eric's plants inside the greenhouse since he'd presented them to her some months before. She had hoped to get them planted before the winter set in but had never quite got around to it. Given the current conditions it was probably for the best, otherwise they would almost certainly have perished by now. She stepped inside the greenhouse and closed the door quickly behind her before switching on the small electric light. The interior was illuminated at once and Sam looked along the shelves of plants and flowers trying desperately to remember where she had stored Eric's. She hadn't had a chance to examine them for a while and couldn't help feeling it would be extremely embarrassing if Eric did visit and discovered his precious cuttings were no more.

Walking along the shelves slowly she eventually discovered them halfway along the greenhouse looking green and healthy; they had grown several inches. Relieved she crouched down to examine the flowers of an Amaryllis belladonna 'Hathor' which she had been protecting in the heated greenhouse. This spectacular bulb had extended its flowering time to reward her with its beautifully fragrant pure white flowers. Breathing in deeply, she sucked in the flower's famous aroma to the back of her nose. It was then that she noticed. She knew the smell of this Amaryllis well enough and although it was still there, its aroma wasn't as strong as she had expected. Holding the flower even closer to her nose she breathed in deeply again. Still the aroma was weaker than usual. It might just be, she hoped, that the flower was finally fading and so its scent was following suit. She stood up again and, leaving the greenhouse, walked across the garden to where a magnificent Mahonia 'Charity' was in full flower, a plant whose smell was strong and unmistakable. She drew a branch towards herself and breathed in deeply again. Although she could distinguish the smell it wasn't as pungent as she knew it should have been. Sam felt as if someone had kicked her in the stomach. She became nauseous and tears forced themselves down her cheeks. Breathing deeply, Sam tried hard to keep her emotions under control. Her greatest fear was finally being realized. It wasn't completely unexpected, for some time now smells, and even tastes, had lacked their usual crispness. Her mind had just switched into denial and she kept putting off the inevitable, blaming everything from colds to hay fever for her problems. Now she would just have to face up to it, there were no more excuses left. Her most precious senses were dissolving before her eyes and there was little, if anything, that anyone could do to stop it.

Stepping back onto her snow-covered path she scanned her beloved garden and wondered whether her relationship with it would remain the same. She felt like a sighted person who had suddenly gone blind and wondered if she would be able to memorize smells as people tried to memorize colour. Calming a little, she started to think rationally about what was happening to her. Firstly, she would need to know how much damage had already been done, and how long it was likely to be before her sense of smell disappeared completely. She'd have to give Edward Cross a call at the Ear, Nose and Throat department at the Park Hospital and make an urgent appointment to see him. In her heart she really didn't want to know, but it would, at least, give her an idea of how long she had left, so she could plan any future strategies, although short of giving up her job she hadn't got a clue what they would be. The snow was falling heavily now, covering both the garden and herself. Pulling herself together, she made her way back down the garden path towards the inviting lights outside her cottage.

Eric Chambers stood inside the small porch that protected the front door to his house and shook his waxed coat vigorously. The melting droplets of snow and ice flew in all directions, as if he were a wet dog drying itself. When he'd shaken the worst off he opened it up and hung it over the back of an old wicker chair that sat permanently in the corner of the small outbuilding to slowly dry off. Before entering his warm, dry, hall he rubbed his two dogs equally vigorously with an old towel. Satisfied they were both dry and clean he opened the front door and let the yapping animals into the house.

The cold had chilled him through and he was ready for a hot drink. He had considered something a little stronger, but wanted to keep a clear head for the work ahead. Putting the kettle on the range to boil, he retired to the sitting room and stared out across his shrouded garden. The entire place was covered in a thick layer of snow that spread evenly across everything without a blemish. Only the bird tables were clear because of the wide wooden roofs he had fixed over them the summer before. With food scarce, birds suffered in weather like this and he liked to look after them. Probably why he hated cats so much.

His eye was drawn without thinking to the large Rhododendron bush that flourished in the far right-hand corner of the garden. It was one of the oldest plants on display and when in bloom, one of the most spectacular. It had to be kept under strict control, of course, but as long as you kept an eye on it things were fine. It always made him smile when he looked at it. Not out of any sense of pride but because of the terrible secret it held. People always thought they knew good old reliable Eric, stalwart of the community. They had even nicknamed him the 'Colonel', because he was so reliable. He enjoyed having a secret, being different from the man they all thought he was. Sam Ryan had once told him that his garden was full of surprises and secrets; if only she knew how many secrets the garden really contained. He chuckled to himself and wondered what she and, for that matter, the village, would say when the terrible truth was finally revealed. Perhaps he would leave a full confession together with his will. Wouldn't matter then, but it would certainly shake the community up a little. With luck, it would make them question their own smug and secure existence and force them to look over their shoulders for a year or two. He poured himself a large mug of tea before wandering over to his computer and switching it on. As the screen lit up he typed in his code name and began to search his precious Internet.

Sam let herself in through the back door, kicking off her snow-covered shoes before hanging up her cold, wet coat. The house was in darkness, and everyone appeared to have retired for the evening. Sam was grateful for that. She turned on the kitchen light and, walking across to the small kitchen mirror wiped away the dark lines of mascara that were streaked black across her face. After a few moments, and with the worst washed clear from her face Sam left the kitchen, turned off the light and started to make her way up the stairs to bed. As she did she noticed a small line of light creeping from beneath her study door. Making her way across to the door she carefully put her ear to it before gently pushing it open and looking inside. Ricky was sitting at her desk staring blankly into the computer screen while stamping out instructions sharply and professionally onto the keyboard.

'You're up late.'

Ricky turned and looked at his aunt. 'Depends how old you are.'

'What?'

'If you're nineteen it's early, if you're thirty-something then, yes, I guess it's late.'

Sam frowned at him.

'Don't mind me using your computer do you? Only it helps with the course I'm doing and besides, I didn't think you would be needing it at this time of night.'

Ricky, on Sam's advice and after many years of nagging, had finally enrolled himself on a part-time computer course, although he remained working at McDonalds during the day.

Sam shook her head. 'No, I don't mind, as long as you ask first and don't try to access my private files.'

Ricky looked back at the screen. 'As if. Even if I did I wouldn't understand a bloody word.'

Sam walked across to his side.

'What are you up to anyway.'

'Searching through the Web pages to see if I can find any bargains.'

Sam shook her head. 'Shopping by computer, there'll be no point going out soon.'

'There'll always be sex.'

'I'm sure they're working on that as we speak.'

He smiled up at her. 'I hope so, save me using all those corny chat-up lines.'

Sam crouched down and examined what appeared to be a very small desktop notebook computer. It was about the size of a filofax but had its own screen. It was attached to the back of her computer by means of a long grey connector.

'What's this?'

Ricky looked across at her. 'I hadn't realized you were that far behind with your computer studies.'

Sam didn't respond to the comment. 'Just tell me what it is.'

'It's a PDA.'

'Which stands for?'

'Personal digital assistant.'

Sam knew he was trying to impress and intimidate her with his techno speak, but she wasn't being drawn.

'So what does it do?'

'It's a sort of hi-tech notebook. You can write or draw

pictures onto it and then transfer them into the mother unit where the writing comes out all neatly typed. Might be the end of the secretary.'

That should worry Jean, Sam thought. She picked it up and carefully examined it.

'Looks expensive.'

Ricky leaned over and took it off her, putting it back on top of the desk.

'It is.'

'McDonalds must be paying well.'

'I saved up and managed to find a cheap one.'

'Where?'

'On the Web.'

Sam redirected her attentions to the computer screen. 'What are you looking for?'

'Scanner. Should be able to find a cheap one if my source is still trading.'

'Who would your source be?'

'Can't tell you that, top secret. Well I suppose I could but then I'd have to kill you.'

'Charming.'

'Only joking. It's a company that seems to be able to undercut just about everybody else by at least fifty per cent. Not bad eh?'

Sam nodded. 'Not bad at all. Are you sure their equipment is legitimate. Didn't fall off the back of a lorry or anything?'

'Didn't see any damage on the PDA.'

'Stop being clever. You know what I mean. I don't want Tom Adams around here looking for you.'

'Make a change from looking for you.'

'Ricky!'

'Yes, I'm quite sure they're legitimate. Lots of people use them.'

'So who are they?'

'They're HTTP, colon, forward slash, forward slash, WWW, dot, Bee dot, CO dot, UK, forward slash, PDA, forward slash.'

'Catchy name. So how do you contact these, forward slash, people?'

Ricky smiled broadly at her.

'You use a search engine to find your Web pages. Then you type in the kind of thing your looking for like, 'scanner buying' and with a bit of luck you'll find what you need.'

'Then what?'

'They'll normally supply a Web form, you just fill that out, send it down the line and wait to see if they can fulfil the order.'

'How do you pay?'

'Credit card if you've got one.'

'Which you haven't.'

'I normally pay cash.'

'The company's local then?'

Ricky nodded. 'Something like that.'

'Well, just remember what I told you about Tom Adams, I wasn't joking.'

Ricky shrugged. 'I told you, I'm a big boy now.'

Sam looked at him sceptically.

'We'll see, and don't be on it all night.'

Ricky smiled up at her, his gaze lingering slightly longer then normal.

'Are you okay?'

'Yes, of course I am, why shouldn't I be?'

Ricky blinked. 'No reason. I won't be long.'

Sam nodded and left the room feeling embarrassed and slightly stupid. Her efforts to hide her earlier distress had clearly failed.

2

THE VIDEO CAMERAS ATTACHED HIGH ONTO THE CON-
crete walls of the multistorey car park followed Sam's
Range Rover as it twisted its way slowly through the
hospital's dark and narrow car park. As she finally
manoeuvred into her reserved space and parked, the camera
nearest to her whirred into life and zoomed in to examine
the vehicle's numberplate. Satisfied, the unseen controller
moved the camera back to its original position. Although
the introduction of video cameras and increased overhead
lighting and had improved the car park's security and
brightened its dismal interior, Sam still felt uneasy every
time she was obliged to park there. Despite the hospital's
best efforts there were still dark corners which were
impossible to penetrate with the naked eye and they
continued to nudge Sam's darkest nightmares.

She fingered her personal attack alarm to reassure
herself, keeping her thumb over the panic button as she
locked her car and walked across to the lift. She wasn't
entirely convinced by these alarms, and was not sure how
much notice people would take even if she did activate it.

Probably as much notice as they took of car alarms. Still, she mused, if she had to, she could always hit an attacker with it. Sam was in favour of the legalization of CS gas or other noxious spray, so that women might really be able to protect themselves without fear of prosecution. The lift took a few moments to reach the chosen floor. When it did, the doors opened to reveal a long, brightly lit and busy hallway. She reached her office door quickly and entered. Jean, Sam's secretary, was perched behind her desk typing up Sam's hardly legible handwritten PM reports on her computer. Sam guessed she had probably been there for some hours already, catching up on the backlog of work which had mounted up over the past few months.

'Morning, Jean.'

Jean looked up at her boss, her stern features breaking naturally into a wide smile. 'Morning, Doctor Ryan, coffee?'

Sam nodded desperately. Despite being Sam's secretary and friend for many years Jean would not be talked out of her formal approach. She always called Sam 'Doctor' even when they occasionally went for a quite lunch time drink. Sam had given up trying to change their relationship and now just accepted that as far as Jean was concerned she would always be 'Doctor', and that was it. Jean was the product of another age, an age where formality, like thick blue stockings, were vital to the wellbeing of the hospital and the state, and she was far too set in her ways to change now.

'Please, and make it a strong one.'

'Heavy night?'

Sam shook her head. 'No, not really, just a bad one. I kept dreaming the same dream over and over.'

Sam was used to the occasional alarming dream, they came with the job. But normally these dreams were vague

THE SPIDER'S WEB

and poorly remembered, their themes being varied and elusive. This one, however, persisted, waking her and disturbing her sleep patterns. Jean's interest was aroused.

'Any tall dark handsome strangers involved?'

'I think I would have remembered if there had been. Besides, they don't look quite as inviting lying on a mortuary slab.'

'So what was it about then?' Jan persisted.

'That's the odd thing,' Sam frowned. 'It disturbed me a great deal but I can't remember it in any detail, just flashes, and the more I try to focus on it, the further it fades.'

Jean shook her head.

'Then how do you know it was the same dream?'

Sam shrugged.

'I'm not sure, I just do.'

'Something's bothering you,' said Jean sympathetically. 'I think I'd better make it a very strong coffee.'

Sam nodded her agreement before pushing her way into the main office and being confronted with a tall, young and handsome man working energetically on her computer.

'Mornin, luv, be finished in a minute, sorry to hold you up.'

Jean was by Sam's side in a trice. 'Sorry, Doctor Ryan, I forgot. They're installing some sort of new program into the hospital computers, I'm afraid there's going to be a bit of disruption for the next few days.'

Sam sighed and nodded her understanding before walking across to her desk and throwing her briefcase onto the floor. As she did the man stood.

'There, that should do for now.'

Sam looked at him. 'Can I use it now?'

'No, sorry luv, not for a few hours yet, but we should be back on line by the end of the day.'

Sam hated the expression 'Luv' but let it go for the

moment. As he disappeared through the door she slumped into her high-backed chair and eyed the large pile of paperwork which, as usual, spilled over the top of her in-tray. She found the thought of working her way through it a daunting one, but knew it had to be done. As she began to examine the first report Jean knocked and made her way into the office, a steaming cup of coffee in her right hand. Sam looked up.

'Thanks Jean.'

'He was handsome wasn't he?' said Jean, putting the mug down by the side of Sam's desk.

Sam answered without looking up. 'Who?'

'Who, indeed. The young man that came to do the computer, he was good-looking.'

'Really, I didn't notice,' Sam shrugged. 'He was just in the way.'

Jean realized she was getting nowhere so returned to her more formal duties.

'Do you want to go through your diary and phone calls now?'

'Not unless there's a major emergency. We'll go through them this afternoon, after lunch. If I don't get stuck into this lot, things will be said in high places.'

Jean smiled her agreement and left the office leaving Sam to concentrate.

Once engrossed in her work, time slipped by unnoticed. When the commotion began outside her office Sam looked up at the wall clock. It was noon, and she had been working for over three hours. Despite the thick oak door between her office and Jean's, Sam could clearly hear Jean's raised and firm tones, protesting to some unseen person that 'the doctor is busy,' and 'you'll have to have an appointment.' Finally the door flew open and Jean appeared. She was red faced and flustered, which was unusual in itself.

'There are two people,' she sneered the word, 'outside, who are insisting on seeing you.'

Sam strained her neck in an attempt to look into Jean's office but could only see the couple's backs. Sam indicated to Jean to shut the door.

'Who are they?'

Sam was not used to people barging into her office and demanding a meeting. In fact with the exception of the occasional pushy police officer and Trevor Stuart of course, she couldn't remember it ever having happened before.

'They are very rude.'

Sam raised her eyebrow impatiently.

'Mr and Mrs Vickers. They don't have an appointment, and won't even tell me what they want to see you about. Shall I call security and have them removed?'

Vickers, Vickers. Sam knew the name but couldn't place it. Then it came to her. They were the couple she'd seen outside the coroner's court the previous day, the man whose face had haunted her ever since. Then Sam remembered, it had been he, Mr Vickers, whom she had been dreaming about the evening before. His haunted face slipping in and out of her subconscious like some half-seen spectre. Sam closed the open file in front of her and threw it back into the in-tray.

'Send them in.'

Jean looked slightly surprised at Sam's request.

'Are you sure, I mean . . .'

Sam looked at her and sighed deeply, bringing the debate to an end. Jean turned and, with a disapproving sniff, did as she was bid.

'Would you like to come this way please, doctor *will* see you after all.'

She led them into her office. As they entered, Sam rose from her chair and began to cross the office to greet them.

It was strange seeing them here, these people who had troubled her so much, who now looked ordinary and unremarkable. They really were the kind of people you would pass in the street or sit opposite on a train, without even registering their existence. Perhaps it was that ordinariness that made them so memorable when they were at the peak of their emotions. Mr Vickers was tall, about six feet or six feet one tall. He was slim with piercing green eyes and a crop of dark brown hair, which was tinged with grey, and receding at the front. He wore a dark blue two-piece suit covered with a shabby brown mackintosh. His wife was shorter than he by several inches and of a much heavier build. She was well, but conservatively, dressed in a tweed jacket, long dark skirt and brown knee-length boots. Dark shadows hung like sacks beneath her eyes, aging her face prematurely, masking the beauty that revealed itself in her self-conscious smile. As they entered the office Sam noticed that Mrs Vickers grabbed her husband's hand for support and squeezed it so tight that his knuckles lost their colour and whitened. Sam held out her hand and Mr Vickers took it.

'I'm Doctor Samantha Ryan, pleased to meet you.'

Sam tried to sound calm and reassuring, especially after their encounter with the formidable Jean. She directed them across her office to the chairs opposite her desk.

'Would you like some tea or coffee?'

The woman looked across at her husband nervously as if even this level of decision-making was difficult for her to cope with. Mr Vickers took his answer from his wife's eyes.

'Tea, if that's okay, milk but no sugar.'

'That's fine.'

Sam looked across at Jean who was still eyeing the Vickers with a mixture of suspicion and annoyance.

'Could you attend to that, please, Jean?'

For a moment Jean didn't respond but remained staring across at the couple who had dared to invade her domain without an invitation.

'Jean!'

This time Jean looked up and with another of her infamous sniffs, left the room, closing the door with undue firmness behind her. Sam resumed her seat and put on her best reassuring smile.

'So, what is it I can do for you?'

After glancing at his wife to make sure that it was all right, Mr Vickers began.

'We're both sorry to be bothering you like this but I'm afraid we've become a bit desperate, and not being the kind of people who usually get involved in this sort of thing we weren't sure of the etiquette. If we're causing you problems we could make an appointment like your secretary said. Only we're that upset we just wanted someone to listen to what we've got to say.'

Sam nodded.

'Well, now's your chance.'

Mr Vickers looked across at his wife again before continuing. 'It was our solicitor, Mr Gordon, who suggested that we should come and see you . . .'

Sam cut in. 'Why didn't he contact me, he certainly knows the etiquettes?'

'He said it might come better from us,' Mr Vickers shrugged.

The emotional approach, Sam pondered, very clever if not a little underhand. She nodded encouragement, and allowed him to continue.

'We're the parents of Simon Vickers.'

Sam nodded. 'I know, I saw you outside the coroner's court. I'm very sorry.'

'Well, you see, that's why we're here. What they said in the coroner's court, it was all wrong. Simon just wouldn't have done anything like that. He was more interested in his computer than he was in cars.'

Mrs Vickers cut in, 'And he didn't drink, we know he didn't.'

'He hated cars,' Mr Vickers continued. 'He said they destroyed the atmosphere, poisoned people. Even made us buy a car that only used lead-free petrol. He just wasn't the type.'

'People do all sorts of things that even those closest to them don't know about,' said Sam, leaning back in he chair. She was trying to professional but could sense the slowly rising emotion in the tone of Mr Vickers's voice.

'Don't get us wrong, we're not saying Simon was a saint, far from it, he was a typical teenager. But we were very close, always had been, almost from the moment he was born. He was our only child, all we had. We didn't put restrictions on him and he was always honest with us. It was an understanding we had. It had always worked fine.'

'People change.'

Mrs Vickers cut in again with an emphatic, 'Not Simon.'

Her eyes filled with tears. She wiped them with a small embroidered handkerchief, which she removed from her sleeve.

'If he'd been knocked down by a car, or involved in an air crash then we could have accepted that,' her husband said.

Sam cut in this time. 'But not at the wheel of a stolen car?'

'No,' Mr Vickers shook his head firmly. 'As I said, he would never have had anything to do with cars, his own or anyone else's. It was all we could do to get him off his bike and into the back of ours. All we want is the truth, Doctor

Ryan, once we've got that we can get on with our grieving and our lives.'

'I don't see what I can do that the police and the coroner's court haven't already done.'

'Mr Gordon says you are very good at getting to the truth and if there is any doubt, any at all, then you'd be able to find it.'

Sam was flattered. She had done several defence jobs for Peters, Walton and Gordon in the past and had been fairly successful, although Trevor still seemed to be their first choice. All boys together, she thought, still unsure why John Gordon hadn't bothered contacting her himself.

'What is it you'd like me to do?'

'A second PM. We'd like a another opinion about our son's death.'

Sam suddenly realized why John Gordon hadn't approached her directly. Trevor had carried out the first PM and, considering their long-standing relationship with Trevor which they clearly didn't want to spoil, it would be easier all round if the approach came directly from the parents.

Sam returned to the point. 'On what grounds?'

Mr Vickers glanced at his wife again before answering.

'The court's verdict was wrong, we know it was. We don't believe that Simon was killed in an accident the way the court said.'

'How do you think he was killed, then?'

'We've no idea, that's why we were hoping you might look into the case. We've delayed the funeral.'

'We're willing to pay,' Mrs Vickers interrupted again.

Mr Vickers nodded his agreement. 'We wouldn't expect you to do it for free. We're not rich people, you understand Doctor Ryan, but we have got a bit put by and with Simon gone there's nothing much else to spend it on.'

'What if my findings don't differ?'

'Then we'll know we've done all we can and that will be an end to it.'

Sam leant back in her chair examining their desperate faces line by line. She finally made up her mind.

'I'm not willing to conduct a second PM at this time . . .'

The couple immediately looked crestfallen so Sam explained quickly. 'What I will do, however, is examine all the relevant documentation and reports, and if I find anything that I'm not convinced by I'll conduct the second PM for you.'

'That's all we're asking, Doctor Ryan, a second opinion. We just want to know, one way or the other.'

'How much is it likely to cost?' Mrs Vickers asked nervously.

'Let me read the reports first, after that we'll see.'

Jean entered with the tea and laid it down on the table while Sam contemplated how she was going to broach the subject with Trevor.

The death of his friend had affected Dominic Parr far more than he had expected. He hadn't appreciated just how close they'd become until Simon wasn't there any more and now he missed him. Simon had been the outgoing one, the man with all the good ideas. Dominic had always been quieter, more subdued, introverted his teacher had once told him. Despite this Simon never made him feel like a trainspotter but shared his passion for computers and the Internet. He encouraged and flattered Dominic, even, at times, admired him for the work he had done. Often Dominic would solve problems or become involved in projects just to please Simon, knowing that he would be able to bask in the praise he'd never really got from his parents. He wasn't even sure they liked him, and if they did, they certainly didn't understand him like Simon did. They just wanted him to go out and get some mundane job, with mundane people, and live in their mundane world. As long as it was safe, with a pension at the end, that was all right by them. Christ, what did they know! He wasn't like that, not deep down. Despite his inadequacies he liked to have exciting and interesting people around him, and Simon was as exciting and as interesting as they came.

He had wondered for a while if he loved him. He would lie in bed pondering this question over and over. Even peeking under the sheets at times to see if the thought of his friend aroused him, but it didn't. Eventually he came to the conclusion that he probably did love Simon, but not in any physical way. They were above all that, their friendship was on a different plane, and was more important than the mere physical, with all its problems and petty jealousies. Although it was an emotional attachment it was also a practical one, with the two of them coming together to form a whole, and that whole was dedicated to expanding their minds through the Network. They'd invented their own language, a sort of Enigma code, so they could send messages to each other without fear of others being able to decipher them.

The one thing that kept turning over and over in Dominic's mind was why? Why had Simon done it, what was he trying to prove? No matter how he tried to rationalize it, he couldn't. It all seemed too insane. What he was going to do without Simon, he really had no idea. He had never been in this situation before and could not begin to cope with his emotions. They had had such great plans for the future and there was still so much to do, but who was he going to share it all with now? What would life be like without Simon? Would there even be a life without him? Dominic had, for a time at least, contemplated killing himself but he was far too much of a coward for that, and no matter how grim life might appear it was still life. He finally decided that all his work should be dedicated to Simon's memory so that people didn't forget him or his genius. He sat down by his desk and switched on his machine. He had a particular job to do and hadn't really had time before. He was going to wait until after Simon's funeral but for some reason it had been delayed and there was no longer a firm date. This delay had forced him to make the announcement over the Network to all their friends, known and unknown, as well as anyone else who might log into his personal memorial.

It was late afternoon by the time Sam arrived at Doctor Cross's clinic. One of the few perks of the job was being able to see a specialist almost at a moment's notice. She made her way to reception and was directed from there to his private office. Cross was expecting her. Sam didn't know him well, they'd met at various social functions and he'd attended one of her lectures and complimented her on it, but that was about all. He was one of the best consultants in the ENT department and the Park had been lucky to get him. She knocked gently on his door.

'Come in Sam.'

She opened the door and peered in. The consulting room was probably twice as large as hers, with half of it set aside as an office and the other half turned into a plush examination room. Closing the door quietly behind her, Sam strode into the room.

'Thanks for seeing me at such short notice, Edward.' He smiled across at her.

'You sounded so desperate I don't think I really had a choice.'

'Did I really sound that awful?' Sam grimaced.

He nodded. 'I'm afraid so. Shall we get on?'

Slipping off her coat, Sam made herself as comfortable as possible in the old-fashioned metal chair in the centre of his room. He picked up his nasal speculum from a small metal tray and commenced his examination.

The whole procedure took about half an hour and was even more thorough than Sam had expected. When he had finished, he still wanted her to go for both an X-ray and CT scan. He ushered Sam across to his desk. She didn't have to wait long for his prognosis.

'I'm afraid your nose is a bit of a mess.'

'How much of a mess?'

'A lot. Far too many polyps that I can see to do you any good and probably a good many more that I can't see. The damage is already pretty widespread, Sam.'

'Is it irreversible?'

Cross nodded. 'Afraid so. There's another negative aspect to all this as well.'

Sam felt her heart sink further.

'There's a strong likelihood that it will affect your sense of taste, too.'

She knew one complemented the other, and the thought of losing both made her despair.

'So that's it, there's nothing I can do?'

Cross's previously serious face began to relax a little. 'Oh, there's plenty you can do. How's your sense of smell at the moment?'

Sam shrugged. 'It's still there, just not as strong, it's a bit like smelling something through a cloth.'

'Taste?'

Sam hadn't noticed any change there at all and shook her head. 'Nothing that I'm aware of.'

Cross nodded knowingly.

'If you want to keep what's left of your senses intact,

then you'll have to stop the pathology and perhaps move to a different branch of medicine.'

The shock of Cross's statement and the matter-of-fact way in which he presented it shook Sam to her very core. The room suddenly seemed to become darker and close in around her. Holding on tight to her reason she began to question his judgement.

'Surely there's no need to give up pathology completely. I mean, if I made sure I stuck to all the health and safety rules and regulations, took a bit more care, then . . .'

Cross cut her short and shook his head.

'No. It might delay it, give you a little extra time. But that cloth in front of your face you mentioned would become thicker until finally there was nothing.' He paused for a moment, giving Sam time to take in what he'd just said. 'You have a simple but stark choice to make. Give up pathology or give up your sense of smell.'

'How long have I got to make up my mind?'

Cross shook his head again.

'Not long. The damage will get worse every time you perform a PM, no matter how careful you are, until finally it will reach a point of no return.'

'It's not all that bad, Sam.' He looked across at her understandingly. 'There are a dozen other fields of medicine in which you could shine. Christ, this department is short of good people and it's worthwhile work.'

Sam stared into his face.

'I came into the profession to be a pathologist, I've never considered, and will never consider, doing anything else.'

'Perhaps you could stay within the profession but in a different capacity. What about teaching? God alone knows there's a massive shortage of well-qualified people to teach the next generation of blunderers what to do with a sharpened scalpel.'

'No. You know what they say: those that can, do, those that can't teach.'

Cross looked at her sympathetically.

'Look, all this must have come as quite a shock. Why don't you take a few days off and consider your options. It's not the end of the world, just a change of direction, and in a few years' time you'll be enjoying your new-found role as much as you enjoyed pathology. Christ, I wanted to be a brain surgeon, I was crestfallen when I realized I wasn't going to make it! Now I spend most of my time looking up people's noses and enjoying every moment.'

Despite Cross's assurances Sam had stopped listening. She stood and made her way across to the door. 'Thanks for the examination Edward. If you send your bill to Jean I'll make sure it's paid promptly.'

'Fee be dammed, it was the very least I could do for a colleague, especially one as talented as you.'

Sam nodded her thanks.

'I'd also like this kept quiet, the fewer people that know the better for now. Not sure I can cope with all the advice right now.'

'I understand,' Cross nodded.

Sam turned and left his consulting rooms. She had intended to make her way back to her office to try and finish off the pile of paperwork but after this she just didn't have the energy. She knew she had a lot of hard thinking to do and needed some time on her own to get over the shock, clear her head, and consider her options.

Although there was a strong desire within Sam to go straight home and sulk, she didn't. Instead, she decided to risk the snow and ice and make her way to the top of Herdan Hill to examine the scene of the accident. She didn't usually visit scenes after the body had been removed, but thought in this case it was worth the effort. The gritters had been out and the road was largely free of snow and ice. After reaching the brow of the hill and passing the *Keep in Low Gear* warning sign, she made her way slowly down the other side before parking in a small dirt pull-in by the side of the road. She'd stopped in the same spot the previous summer when she had come for a picnic with Wyn, her sister. The sun was out then and the hill bustled with people.

Buttoning her coat up to the collar and arranging her dark woolly hat around her face and neck, she stepped out of her car. Herdan Hill was one of the few high points in the area and offered superb views across the countryside towards the sea. Standing on the edge of the slope she let the cool breezes run over her face, allowing a thousand assorted smells to drift aimlessly though her nose and throat. Sam wondered how much longer she would be able to detect and discern those smells and wondered again whether she would still have a memory of them when they were gone. The snowy white landscape seemed to go on for miles before vanishing into the distant landscape. Only the dark roads and walls stood out. They crisscrossed the countryside, breaking up the perfectly smooth surface like shattered glass. For one of the few times in her life Sam experienced almost complete silence. No one else would have been stupid enough to try and climb Herdan Hill in this weather, and she realized she was probably the only person for miles. The snow absorbed and muffled any other sounds and gave the area an almost eerie peace.

Tucking her hands beneath her arms Sam began to walk along the road towards the scene of the crash. As she did, her options ran through her mind. She couldn't really imagine herself doing any other kind of work but pathology, but, at the same time, she didn't particularly relish the idea of losing both her sense of smell and taste. Perhaps, she considered, she should seek a second opinion. Maybe Cross was being too careful and was only considering the worst possible scenario. But then perhaps she was clutching at straws. She'd gone to Cross in the first place because he was the best and she knew he hadn't exaggerated or made a mistake. The ball was firmly back in her court and she hadn't a clue which way to hit it.

Sam finally reached her destination, a large blackened oak tree. It stood out starkly like a festering sore against the virgin white snow. A grim monument to Simon's last moments. Perched up against the side of the tree were two bunches of flowers. One was clearly from a florist, an elaborate arrangement of imported greenhouse flowers in a cellophane bag whilst the other was just a simple collection of greenery and a few winter flowers, such as could have been gathered from a garden, held together with a brown elastic band. Sam crouched down in the snow and examined the card attached to the large tribute. This one was from Simon's parents and the card carried what Sam supposed was an original sentiment from his parents as she did not recognize it as an extract from a poem: 'Just one more look oh Lord, just one more touch. To hold him in the evening or kiss his cheek at night.' Sam was surprised not to recognize it.

The second bunch was anonymous with no card or tribute to indicate who it was from. Sam admired them for a moment, before turning back to the road which she instinctively searched for any evidence left from the accident. Despite searching the area carefully, however, there was nothing. No brake marks and no indication of the inevitable skidding as the driver fought to try and keep control of the vehicle before the final and deadly impact. It was a vain hope, of course, as about four weeks had passed since the crash, making it highly unlikely that she would find anything significant at this stage. Sam found it difficult to believe that Simon wouldn't have reacted at all before leaving the road and the initial accident investigation should have discovered what evidence there was to find. The weather around the time of the accident had been poor so some evidence might have been destroyed, but burnt rubber and signs of skidding weren't removed easily and even heavy falls of snow would not have obliterated all such signs.

As her eyes continued to scan the road it pondered on the fact that evidence which would have been expected but which was not present held as much significance as that which was discovered. Sam made a mental note to check on which traffic officer dealt with the accident.

'I hope you're not thinking about stealing them, they took me a long time to find.'

Sam spun around, both shocked and surprised at the invasion of her privacy. Standing in front of her was a tall, shabbily dressed man who looked as if he hadn't shaved in weeks. He was well built with an aging tweed jacket, worn corduroy trousers and a dirty cap pulled tightly over his head, and wore the largest pair of Wellington boots Sam could ever remember seeing. More alarming, however, was the double-barrelled shotgun he carried across his arm. Sam remained silent for a moment, desperately trying to determine where he could have come from. One moment she had been on her own and the next, he'd appeared like some kind of woodland ghost. She glanced around quickly, searching for escape routes and judging the distance between herself and her car. He spoke again, as if reading Sam's thoughts.

'Sorry, lass, I've frightened you.'

Sam remained silent. He certainly had frightened her and

she didn't want to admit it, although it must have been clear from her demeanour.

'Well, if it makes you feel any better, you frightened me as well.'

Sam's courage began to return. 'What are you doing here?'

He smiled down at her.

'Me job, lass.'

'And what's that?'

His smile remained but seemed to grow wider. 'Shall we call it Country Gentleman.'

Sam guessed it was just a polite way of saying poacher.

'Bit cold even for that kind of work, isn't it?'

He gave her a cheeky smile. 'Ah well, that's me job isn't it? If I don't work, I don't eat. Now you know about me what about you? What are you doing here. Not stealing the flowers, I hope.'

He patted his shotgun menacingly as he said it and Sam found herself becoming nervous and defensive again.

'No, I was just admiring them. I'm a doctor.'

It wasn't entirely true, but for some reason she didn't want to tell him what she really did.

'A doctor, is it?' He eyed her sceptically 'Well, you've come a bit late to help this poor young soul. I thought you were just another gawper, we've had a few of those since the killing. Bloody neck-craners. Thought people would have had better things to do with their time, wouldn't you?'

Sam looked back at the tree. She was a voyeur of death but had never considered herself to be a gawper before.

'I'm no gawper.'

The man still wasn't satisfied. 'What you doing here then?'

'The view, wanted to see what it looked like with all the snow.'

The poacher nodded and looked out across the countryside. 'It's a grand sight and no mistake, but you took a bit of a risk climbing the hill just for a view.'

'Not really, my car's a four-wheel drive.'

'I bet the young lad wished he'd had a four-wheel drive when he came hurtling down the hill. I think the snow got under his wheels, anyways he lost control and smashed into the tree, poor beggar. Odd thing though, the car never made a sound before it crashed. Made a lot of sound after that mind. He was white as snow as well.'

Sam was puzzled.

'Who?'

'The driver, white as snow. Probably knew what were coming. No way to die, burning. Could have done with that vicar I keep seeing up here.'

'The Reverend Andrews?'

'Not being a churchgoing man I don't know his name. Been poking around the old church. Had someone with him taking pictures.'

'I think he wants to reconsecrate the church.'

'Does he now? Don't know why folks can't let things rest. Always people up here poking around, scaring off the game. It's my bloody living they're upsetting.'

Sam returned quickly to the point.

'You saw the accident then?'

'Oh aye, I saw it all right, put me off me ale for the rest of the day.'

If he was telling the truth he could be an important witness. She decided to test him.

'About three in the morning wasn't it?'

He shook his head. 'Closer to half past one. Want to get your watch looked at.'

He suddenly turned as if bored with the conversation and began to walk back towards the woods. Despite the snow,

Sam quickly caught up with him. She was now convinced he knew something.

'Did you tell the police what you saw?'

He shook his head. 'I have a deal with the police. Jack Falconer don't bother them and they don't bother Jack Falconer, and that's the way I like it.'

'But you're the only witness to an accident where a young boy died.'

He stopped for a moment and picked up several pheasants which lay on the ground.

'Only witness? I weren't the only witness, there were another.'

He suddenly reached out and handed one of the pheasants to Sam. 'Have that, call it compensation for frightening you.'

Sam took it without thinking.

'Who else saw it then?'

The man turned for a moment and his face darkened.

'Didn't really see him, well not clear anyway, just felt him.'

'Felt him? Are you sure, I mean . . .?'

He cut her short. 'I'm sure all right.'

'Haven't you any idea who it might have been?'

He looked at her and his eyes narrowed. 'The devil, that's who missus, the devil.'

With that he turned back and walked quickly into the woods. Sam tried to follow him but by the time she reached the spot where he'd walked into the trees the poacher had vanished. She stopped and listened hard, but there wasn't a sound. He'd disappeared completely.

Sam got back to the cottage late. Kicking the snow off her shoes and picking up Shaw, her cold-looking cat, from the doorstep, she pushed open the large front door and made her way into the welcoming warmth and light of the hallway.

Wyn called through, 'Is that you, Sam?'

Sam made her way out of the hall, through the sitting room and into the kitchen before replying.

'If it's not, you're in real trouble.'

Wyn frowned as Sam gave her a kiss and she held up the pheasant she'd been holding in her hand. 'What do you think?'

'Where the hell did you get that from, knock it down in your car?'

'A friend gave it to me. It's been poached I think. Supposed to taste better aren't they?'

'Who'd have thought it, eminent forensic pathologist a receiver of stolen goods.'

Sam smiled. 'Nobody's perfect. Better eat the evidence quickly then or we might find ourselves doing some "bird" ourselves. On the other hand, I think we're suppose to hang it up until the maggots start to crawl out of its flesh.'

Wyn shook her head despairingly.

'Well you needn't bother hanging it up in this kitchen. Horrible thing.'

Sam made her way into the small wooden conservatory which was attached to the kitchen, and hung the bird on a hook in the corner of the room. When she returned Wyn was poised at the cooker putting the final ingredients into a large pot of stew.

'What's for supper?'

'What do you mean, "what's for supper", can't you smell it?'

The meeting with the poacher on Herdan Hill had made Sam forget about her own problems, but Wyn's question brought them all back. The aroma from one of Wyn's Irish stews was normally unmistakable and floated around the entire house, clinging to everything it touched. She could smell it now that her sister had mentioned it, but wondered if she was really smelling the stew or whether her brain was just telling her what she should be smelling. She sat down at the kitchen table, which had already been laid and gave a deep false sniff.

'Nose isn't too good at the moment, I think I'm starting with a cold. You know what it's like.'

Wyn looked at her for a moment as if she had detected the lie and Sam began to feel uncomfortable. Although they had never really been close as sisters, Wyn always had the uncanny knack of knowing when Sam was either in trouble or lying. Whether she detected Sam's white lie on this occasion Sam couldn't tell. Fortunately Wyn didn't pursue it and Sam was grateful. She would have liked to discuss her problem with her sister and see what she thought, but knew she would only make a fuss and Sam couldn't cope with that right now. She changed the subject.

'No Ricky?'

Wyn shook her head. 'No, he said he'd be back in time for supper but the little bugger hasn't turned up yet.'

'Where's he gone?'

'Shot off on his bike. Gone to that computer club at the church hall.'

The meal was finally ready. Wyn spooned it onto plates and brought it across to the table. The two women began to eat together.

'Ricky seems to have become very interested in computers.'

'About time he was interested in something besides girls and having a good time.'

'He's young, give him a chance.'

'Give him a chance? He's had more chances than a cat.'

Sam smiled across at Shaw who was watching them both from the corner of the room.

'Caught him using my computer last night . . .'

Wyn sat up, concerned. 'Sorry Sam, he told me you said it was okay.'

'It is and I did,' Sam nodded. 'It's just that he seems to be buying himself some rather expensive equipment.'

'Well, I don't know where he's getting the money from. Don't think his job pays that well.'

'That's what I thought.'

Wyn suddenly sat up.

'You don't think he's nicking it, do you?'

Sam shook her head vigorously. 'Absolutely not. But he might be getting the equipment from some rather dodgy sources.'

Wyn nodded across to the pheasant. 'Like aunty, like nephew.'

'It's hardly the same. Anyway it might be worth keeping an eye on him for a while.'

Wyn suddenly flushed with anger. 'Wait till he gets back, I'll . . .'

Sam shook her head.

'Don't do anything. It will only make him withdraw, then we'll get nowhere. Let's just keep an eye on him for a while.'

Wyn nodded in agreement.

'Okay. But if I find out . . .'

The door suddenly flew open and Ricky walked in. Wyn turned to face him thumping her finger down on her watch.

'You're late.'

He joined them quickly at the table.

'I know, sorry.'

Sam looked at him.

'It was good, then.'

Ricky nodded. 'Yes, very. Eric Chambers said to send his best.'

Sam had forgotten that it was one of the many clubs that Eric ran.

'He's on the ball for an old 'un. Managed to get a few students from the university to help as well.'

'Nice to know you still think there's some life left in us old 'uns,' said Wyn, putting his dinner in front of him.

'He brought one oddball along though.'

Sam looked across at him.

'Who was that?'

'Some bloke called Moore, Edward, Edmond, something like that. Do you know him?'

Sam nodded. 'A bit. He's making a film about the village with the vicar. Newcomer. Probably trying to help him mix in a little.'

'Well I wish he'd go and mix somewhere else. He's always staring.'

Sam was interested.

'What, at you?'

'Not just me, most of us, I reckon he's a bit weird.'

'In what way?'

'Don't know, just don't like him around. He's opening a judo club in the village and wants some of us to join, but I don't think he's getting too many takers.'

'What's he like with computers?'

'Seems to know what he's doing. Just that no one likes working with him. That reminds me, can I use your computer again tonight?'

'As long as you're happy to pay the phone bill when it comes in. The Web isn't free you know.'

Ricky grinned.

'No problem. Thanks.'

As Ricky took his first mouth full of food Sam and Wyn looked at each other despairingly.

*

Sam began her morning list with little enthusiasm. There were eighteen bodies, most of them old and most of them having died, for one reason or another, as a result of the cold. Too hot, too cold, and down they went by the dozen only to end up at the wrong end of her scalpel. They were all straightforward enough and she would normally get through them in no time, allowing her the opportunity to catch up with some of the work she'd left behind the day before.

Sam had hoped that sleeping on it would have cleared her mind but she hadn't slept, at least, not properly. She tossed and turned, made herself a drink, and even tried working on her computer but it was no good, the knowledge that she needed to make an urgent and life-changing decision lingered and nothing seemed to divert her attention. Lying on her bed, contemplating the dawn, Sam began to review her odd encounter with the poacher. She had considered ringing Tom Adams and telling him what had happened. On the other hand if she set the police off on his trail there was a good chance of alienating him and she felt he had far more to tell her. Besides, she considered, he wasn't even sure he had seen someone else on the hill that night he just had 'a feeling' and she knew what Tom Adams would make of that. She finally decided she should wait until after the second PM. If she found nothing, as she expected, then she'd forget it. If not, then she would have to reconsider her position.

Sam was sure the poacher didn't live too far from the hill, probably in one of the small villages that surrounded it, so he shouldn't be difficult to find when the time came. If he had seen anything he was more likely to tell her than the police anyway. Besides as far as the police were concerned the case was over, it was an accidental death and their involvement had ended. The fact that Sam's recently discovered witness was a poacher, and would therefore be considered unreliable, would not help any campaign to reopen the investigation. His reference to a second presence on the hill still concerned her, however. Who could it have been? An unknown passenger, a passer-by? But then why hadn't he reported the accident to the police? Perhaps he had, and Sam just wasn't aware of it. More likely it was a trick of the light combined with shock and fear. The poacher was clearly still upset by what he'd witnessed. Even when recounting the story, fear was etched across his face. But then just because a person was frightened didn't mean they were wrong, and he did seem sure about what he'd seen. She would have to get the coroner's report and examine all the statements taken about the accident. The permutations rolled over in Sam's mind until conscious and organized thought began to drift into the confusion of dream as she had finally managed to sleep.

Her thoughts were interrupted by Fred, who pushed a large bowl of formalin onto the table where she was working and lifted the lid ready for immersing some offending organ for later examination. As he did so, the formalin slopped over the edge of the clear plastic bowl and splashed onto the white marble table, showering Sam's green apron and splashing onto her face. Sam immediately spun around at him.

'For God's sake, Fred, don't you ever consider the bloody Health and Safety regulations>' Sam pointed angrily towards a noticeboard. 'If you don't, then they're pinned up over there for all to read, or am I just wasting my time?'

Fred couldn't remember the last time Sam had screamed at him like that, in fact he wasn't sure she ever had before. Health and Safety regulations, except the more important ones, had never been an issue before. He was careful and professional in his job, but adhering meticulously to every dot and comma of the regulations made work much more difficult, especially when you were under pressure as they were. Something had upset Doctor Ryan, though, and although he was determined to find out what he didn't consider this to be a good time.

'Sorry, Doctor Ryan, I'll be more careful in the future.'

Normally his 'sorry for himself' voice would calm the situation but on this occasion it didn't.

'Don't be more careful in the future Fred, just try being a little more professional.'

Her tone was ice cold. Fred's lips pursed and tightened as he bit back his response to this unfounded attack and he returned the lid to the container and removed it from harm's way, letting Sam finish off the list.

Because of Sam's sudden and strict adherence to the Health and Safety Act, the morning list had taken much longer than normal and hadn't helped improve her mood. As she marched down the hall towards her office, Sam realized that she would probably have just about enough time to grab some lunch and catch up with the most recent calls before wading once more through the backlog of paperwork. As she marched past Jean's desk, her secretary got up and, picking up a green file, followed her into the office.

'I just want the phone messages, Jean, nothing else. I haven't got time.'

Jean turned, slightly peeved by Sam's tone. 'As you wish Doctor Ryan.'

She disappeared into her office and returned with Sam's phone messages.

'There are only two . . .'

Sam didn't bother looking up as she pulled the first of several files that were piled up on her desk towards her.

'Good, what are they?'

Her sharpness hadn't disappeared.

'One from Mr Gordon asking for an interview at your earliest convenience . . .'

'He'll be lucky, haven't even had a chance to look at his files yet.'

'Another from Tom Adams asking if you'd ring him back when you can.'

Sam nodded, intrigued by this.

'And finally, Trevor Stuart's secretary has sent the Simon Vickers file over to your office. She's sorry they're late, but most of the hospital's computers still aren't working properly.'

Sam scanned her desk quickly. 'Well, it's not here yet.'

Jean scowled, unimpressed by Sam's current mood.

'It's in my office. I had it in my hand when you dismissed me from the room.'

Sam slumped back into her chair realizing she was being unreasonable.

'Sorry, Jean, bad day.'

Jean nodded. 'So I've been hearing.'

Fred had been quick with his warning, Sam realized.

'I take it you do want the file then?'

'Yes please, and could you get me the coroner's file as well?'

'I've already sent for it. I thought it might come in handy if you're considering taking the case.'

Sam was a little bemused by Jean's knowledge of her thoughts and intentions.

'How did you know I was thinking about it?'

'The door between our offices isn't that thick, doctor.'

Not if you're listening at the keyhole, Sam pondered. Jean left the room for a moment, returning quickly with the relevant file and dropping it unceremoniously on Sam's desk before marching out again without a word. Sam shook her head, she had managed to upset both Jean and Fred today. She wondered who would be next.

As Jean left Sam began to collect her thoughts. She couldn't see the point of arranging a meeting with John Gordon just yet. It would be pointless until after she'd had time to go through Trevor's files, and if she found no inconsistencies there it would be pointless anyway. Tom Adams, on the other hand, was a different matter. She hadn't seen much of him since he returned from the Serial Crimes Squad some months ago. As well as being promoted to Superintendent and deputy head of the county CID he'd also taken control of all major investigations for the county including murder. Sam tried to return his call but he was in court, so she left a message. She'd found herself missing him recently and reminiscing about their previous relationship. It would be good to spend some time with him again. Finally, bringing herself back to reality, she returned to the files. Although she left Simon Vickers's till last, she spent the rest of the afternoon going over it line by line, fearful of missing anything. On the face of it the PM had been very straightforward with few problems. She agreed with all Trevor's procedures and conclusions. Yet, despite this, something bothered her. She didn't know quite what, but there was something wrong. She hoped that she wasn't being influenced by the pleas of Simon's parents or the strange evidence given by the poacher, and tried hard to remain objective and scientific.

Later during the afternoon a copy of the coroner's report arrived. She studied it carefully again, looking for any inconsistencies, but there was nothing obvious. Both Trevor and the coroner had done a good and competent job. Despite this however she could not escape her gut reaction that there was something wrong and she began to feel like the poacher with his irrational feelings of evil. She did discover that the person who reported the accident had seen the fire from one of the roads that by-passed the hill. So neither the poacher nor the other mysterious person, if there ever was one, had done anything about it. The rest of the report summarized the police inquiry and consisted of various statements outlining what had led to the accident and its ultimate outcome. There were also witness statements from the owner of the car, Simon Vickers's parents, and finally from the woman who had reported seeing the flames at the top of Herdan.

Sam scanned through her statement once more trying to fix its contents into her mind. Mrs Claire Sharp had apparently been driving passed Herdan Hill when she had heard and seen the explosion. She timed it at approximately one thirty-five. It had then taken her a further ten minutes to find a phone and call the local police. The police arrived at the scene, together with the fire service, twenty-five minutes later at a quarter past two and put out the fire. Trevor Stuart wasn't called out to the scene but the police surgeon, a Doctor Samuel Hardstaff was. He pronounced life extinct at three twenty-six. Trevor did the PM the following day. Sam sighed, it all seemed very straightforward.

She finally closed the file and walked across to her window. Nothing she had read in any of the reports made her think that Simon Vickers's death had been anything other than a tragic accident. Yet, there was still something. Something that wasn't there or had been missed, like the lack of tyre marks at the scene. If she was ever going to discover what it was, she would have to re-examine the entire case. She sighed deeply, considering the enormity of what she was contemplating. Finally, she walked back to

her desk, tucked the reports inside her briefcase, threw on
her coat and made for the door.

It took Sam about half an hour to get to Cherry Hinton and
find the house she was looking for. Parked smartly on the
driveway was a new Ford Escort, probably the replacement
for the one that had been stolen by Simon Vickers. It was
an ill wind, Sam pondered. She parked her car and marched
up to the front door, ringing the bell long and hard. A few
moments later a large man tucking into a thick-cut
sandwich opened the door. He looked down at her
intimidatingly. Sam smiled up.

'Mr Enright?'

'Who wants to know?'

Sam pulled her identification from her bag awkwardly.

'Doctor Sam Ryan, I'm the county's forensic
pathologist.'

She showed him her identification. He glanced at it,
uninterested, and took another bite out of his sandwich.

'So what's the problem?'

'I'm involved with the case of Simon Vickers, who I
understand is alleged to have stolen your car ...'

'Alleged, that's a good one, he was only found dead at
the wheel of the bloody car having managed to wrap it
around a tree. Little bastard got all he deserved if you ask
me.'

Sam decided she disliked this man intensely, but bit her
tongue and nodded understandingly.

'Would you mind if I asked you a few questions about
the theft?'

He shrugged. 'If you like but I told the police what
happened. Can't add anything.'

He stood in the door as if he were guarding it against an
unwanted intruder. He clearly wasn't going to invite her in.

'Where was the car stolen from?'

'The drive, where the new one is. At least I got something out of it. Although why the hell he picked on my car, God knows. Next door had a better one and faster.'

'Was it locked?'

'Locked it myself. Had one of those new computer locks and alarms on it. Suppose to be impregnable, state of the art. Another waste of bloody money, didn't know a thing about it until the next day.'

'And you're sure it was locked.'

Mr Enright didn't seem to appreciate this question.

'Said so, didn't I?'

'Yes, you did. Can you remember what time you locked it?'

He thought for a moment.

'About half eleven.'

'And when did you realize it was missing?'

He stared at her. 'Stolen you mean.'

'Sorry, stolen.'

'Six-thirty next morning. Made me bloody late for work. Although them next door reckoned they might have heard it being driven off about midnight.'

'What is your neighbour's name?'

'Clements. He runs the local Neighbourhood Watch scheme. Lot of bloody good they are.'

Sam couldn't remember reading his statement. 'Did he give the police this information?'

He shrugged.

'Don't think so, he only told me a couple of days ago and he's supposed to be the local bloody coordinator. Bunch of useless busybodies if you ask me.'

Sam smiled.

'Well, that's it, thank you very much.'

He nodded, took one more mouthful of sandwich and

closed the door in her face. Sam jumped back into her car and pulled away from the house relieved that the interview was over. She got on with most people, but Enright had made her flesh crawl and she was glad to see the back of him. As she made her way back through the darkness towards her cottage, the day's activities played themselves over and over in her head. She scanned over the files, remembering her conversation with Mr and Mrs Vickers and her encounters with the poacher and Enright. Although Sam realized most of the evidence she had was circumstantial and that she was being driven largely by her own gut reactions, which wasn't particularly scientific, too much about the case still troubled her. Why would a boy who apparently didn't drink and hated cars, get drunk and steal one. And where did he learn to break into a well-secured car in the first place? Pulling into her drive Sam finally decided that there were just too many inconsistencies, and, despite the opposition she knew she would face from Trevor and the police, finally resolved to carry out a second PM on Simon Vickers's body.

3

NOW THAT SAM HAD MADE UP HER MIND TO PERFORM the second postmortem examination on Simon Vickers, she knew that the next few days were going to be difficult. When she arrived in her office, Jean was already there.

'Morning, Jean. Sorry about yesterday. I was in a bit of a . . .'

She didn't get chance to finish the sentence as Jean suddenly put a finger up against her lips and indicated towards the office. She beckoned Sam closer and whispered. 'Doctor Stuart's in your office and he doesn't seem very happy.'

Sam winced, it wasn't what she wanted to hear. She had hoped to have a few days to prepare before the inevitable confrontation with Trevor.

Jean continued. 'I've given him a cup of Earl Grey, that should soothe him a little.'

Sam sighed deeply and looked down at her secretary.

'Thanks, Jean.'

'And if that fails, I've got the poker under my desk just in case he turns nasty.'

Sam tried a reassuring smile which failed miserably. Finally, steeling herself, she entered the office. Trevor was standing by the window looking out across the hospital campus, sipping his tea. Sam couldn't help noticing that he looked slightly forlorn. She tried to sound casual.

'Morning Trevor, you're up bright and early.'

For a moment he didn't respond, but continued to stare fixedly out of the large square window contemplating, she supposed, what to say to her.

'Lovely views of the countryside from here,' he said abruptly.

Sam put her briefcase down by the side of her desk and joined him by the window, putting a reassuring arm on his shoulder and following his gaze.

'That's why I chose it. Even more beautiful in the snow, isn't it?'

Trevor nodded and turned to her, looking deeply into her face. 'So, have you made your mind up yet?'

Sam turned and walked back to her desk.

'About what?'

She tried hard to sound matter of fact but it failed to impress.

'Don't bandy words with me Sam. I know Mr and Mrs Vickers visited you yesterday, and that shortly after they left you requested a copy of their son's PM report. It doesn't take a genius to work out what you're considering.'

Sam shrugged.

'So what's your point?'

Trevor could feel himself becoming increasingly annoyed at Sam's flippant attitude. 'Are you going to conduct a second PM?'

Sam had hoped to break the news gently and explain her reasons at the same time. That opportunity had now passed, so she decided to be as forthright as Trevor.

'Yes, yes, I am.'

Trevor shook his head disbelivingly and threw his arms dramatically above his head, 'For Christ's sake, why?'

Sam shrugged. 'Because they asked me to.'

'And you agreed, just like that?'

A sarcastic edge developed in Trevor's tone.

Sam nodded.

'Can't you see what's happening, Sam? Where's that Ryan astuteness we all admire so much?'

Sam was not about to indulge Trevor's sarcastic and sanctimonious lecture and she turned sharply on him.

'So what are they up to, Trevor?'

'Isn't it obvious? They're trying to blame someone. Their precious son, who could do no wrong, has stolen a car and killed himself in it. They just can accept that it was his own fault and are looking to spread the blame around a little.'

Sam frowned. 'They didn't give me that impression. More like two anxious people trying to discover the truth surrounding their son's death.'

Sam picked up her briefcase and began to unpack it onto her desk while Trevor snapped angrily, 'They've got the truth, they just can't face it.'

Sam clicked her briefcase shut, put it on the floor and looked across at him.

'Well, they don't seem to think so.'

Trevor scowled at her and began to pour himself another tea. He held up the square cup.

'Want one?'

Sam shook her head. She didn't feel like being soothed. 'No thanks.'

He began to fill his own mug.

'Think you'll find anything?'

Sam shrugged, she knew it was a loaded question and

answered carefully. 'Shouldn't think so, but it will put their minds at rest.'

Trevor wasn't satisfied with her response.

'So you're not basing your judgement on any lingering doubts you might have, just on some sort of misguided social responsibility?'

'Not entirely, but I suppose it's part of it.'

'Parents, what the hell do they know? Are they qualified?'

'No, but I am, that's why they need my help.'

Trevor gave a short, sarcastic laugh.

'Never quite saw you as a do-gooder, Sam.'

'And I never thought you could be quite so paranoid about your work.'

Trevor was taken aback by the comment.

'I'm not.'

'Then why all the fuss, Trevor? Or are you worried that I might find something?'

'Certainly not. There's nothing left to discover.'

'Then what are you so worried about?'

'I'm not, I . . . I, just don't like people questioning my judgement.'

'Our judgement is questioned every day of the week it's part of the job description.'

Trevor sat down in one of the large chairs opposite Sam's desk and suddenly seemed to calm down.

'Did you find any errors or inconsistencies in my report?'

Sam shook her head. 'No, nothing. Look, no one is questioning your competence, Trevor, especially not me, and I'm almost certain I'll agree with everything in your report, but I'd be failing the department and his parents if I refused their request.'

'So you don't think you're failing me by doing it?'

'No, I don't. For what it's worth, your friend John Gordon advised Simon's parents to come and see me. Probably because he thought there would be less risk of upsetting you that way rather than putting in the request personally.'

Trevor looked up, surprised, as Sam continued, 'The Vickers, despite what you may think of their motives, are determined that a second PM should be carried out.' Sam walked across to where her friend was sitting and put her arms on his shoulders. 'Now, who would you prefer to do it, me, or some outsider, with a company of solicitors paying the bill and determined to find something just to justify the fee?'

Trevor sighed loudly, his mood changing from angry to pathetic.

'When are you going to do it?'

'I've made some space tomorrow.'

Trevor nodded.

'Good, the sooner the better. I'll have to have a quiet word with John Gordon. I'm surprised he's pursuing the matter, he can normally spot a lost cause when he sees one.'

'He's the Vickers' solicitor, perhaps he had no choice.'

'John Gordon not have a choice? That'll be the day.'

Sam had never been happy about Trevor's relationship with Gordon's firm, it was all a bit too cosy for her liking. She changed the subject.

'How are the wedding plans coming along?'

Trevor smiled, his mood changing.

'Very well. Couldn't get permission for the wedding to be held in Trinity Chapel, being divorced and all, but they have said yes to holding the reception in the Old Kitchens, so that's something to look forward to.'

'Has Emily chosen the dress yet?'

'Yes a beautiful cream creation.'

'You've seen it, then?'

'Good God, no! I need all the luck I can get right now, but she described it to me most vividly.'

Sam smiled at him.

'I'm sure it will be a great day.'

Trevor put down his cup, looked at his watch and made for the door.

'Better get on, got the list to finish. You'll let me know as soon as you've finished, won't you?'

'Of course I will.'

Trevor still looked concerned.

'And stop worrying, everything will be fine.'

He gave Sam a broad, false smile and left the room.

Jack Falconer had been living on the edge of his nerves since the night of the crash. He wasn't normally a nervous man, but over the past few weeks things had happened, and, if he was perfectly honest with himself, he was frightened. At first he thought it was just the aftereffects of witnessing the boy's death. That fateful night kept playing itself over and over in his mind. The blank, empty look on the boy's face, the unseen but malevolent presence which pervaded the very air surrounding him, seemed to have etched themselves into his subconscious. He shuddered for a moment and tried to clear his mind. He'd ventured out into the village the following morning to pick up a local paper. He discovered that the boy's name was Simon Vickers and that he was a seventeen-year-old student from one of the local villages. There was a photograph of him on the front page standing with some friends. He hardly recognized the lad, he looked so alive and not at all like the figure he'd seen sitting at the wheel of the car. It was the look in his eyes he remembered most. They were fixed and staring. Like a lamped rabbit, frozen to the spot and unable to react as it awaited its inevitable fate. He shook his head. What a terrible way for a young man to die, there was no justice in the world, none at all. The papers had said it was a tragic accident following the theft of a car. Stupid, stupid, such a waste.

He looked around his cottage straining his ears for any unusual sounds. It wasn't his normal practice. Normally, when you were this far from civilization people didn't bother you and, after all, the cottage had been picked by his grandfather because of its remoteness. Recently though, someone had made it their business to bother him. The 'incidences', as Jack thought of them, began a few days after the crash. They didn't seem important at first, just a feeling, an instinct, but it was hard to dismiss as just fancy. he felt he was being watched, the same impression of malevolence unsettled him. He never saw anyone, but he certainly sensed them and these feelings made him restless, uneasy. Then came the noises. The cottage backed on to a large wood so he was used to strange and unusual sounds, sometimes he welcomed them, a little reminder that despite his isolation he wasn't alone. But these were different, these were human. One night he'd heard someone circling the cottage, searching for a weak spot. He was sure his heart had stopped as he strained his ears and followed their footsteps around his cottage. Examining the surroundings of his cottage the following day in the morning light, it was clear that someone had been there. Whoever it was had been careful, tried hard to cover their tracks, but they weren't as good as they thought and had left plenty of signs – broken twigs, part of a footprint. At least it was human and not cloven, he pondered, so at least he was only dealing with a man and not the supernatural. After that he had begun to take precautions. He slept with his shotgun close by and permanently loaded. Began to examine his cottage from the relative safety of the woods before walking down to it, and stuck strands of his hair to the doors and windows with spittle, checking to see if any were broken before he had the courage to push his own door open. It was a new experience for Jack; normally he was the poacher, but now he felt as if he was the prey.

The rest of Sam's day went by predictably enough. As well as her general list, which was longer than usual due to the continuing cold, she also managed to find time to have one last glance through Trevor's PM report. Despite trying hard to find fault, she could only point to a few punctuation errors. It was clear, precise and seemingly accurate, with nothing obviously missed, overlooked or misinterpreted. For the first time since she had decided to perform the second PM, Sam began to have doubts. Perhaps this time her arrogance really had got the better of her and this was one crusade which wasn't worth fighting. By eight o'clock she'd had enough of reports, and decided to head home. Making her way down to the car park Sam decided she ought to tell the Vickers personally about her decision. Normally she would have done this by phone, but felt that on this occasion a visit would be more appropriate.

It would usually only take about half an hour to travel from the hospital to the Vickers' home in Impington, which was situated a short distance outside Cambridge. However, due to the snow and ice, everything on the road, even at that time of the night, was travelling at a snail's pace and the journey took twice as long. Fifty-five minutes later, Sam was pulling into the smartly kept Gladstone Drive and counting off the house numbers. She eventually arrived outside number twenty-eight and parked. The street, like the estate, was a smart nineteen-sixties creation, built with no imagination and only one design in mind, square. The place was pleasant enough, but Sam couldn't help wondering what wickedness lurked behind the privacy of the neatly hung net curtains.

Sam gave the bell a long hard ring. As she waited several curtains along the street twitched. Neighbourhood Watch at it again, she mused. After a few moments the door opened and Mr Vickers appeared. he looked both pleased and surprised to see her.

'Doctor Ryan, what a surprise. Come in, come in.'

As Sam stepped across the threshold Mr Vickers called through an open door, 'Edna, it's Doctor Ryan!'

He directed her into the sitting room.

'Please go in, you've caught us out a bit, we weren't expecting visitors.'

As Sam walked into the room Mrs Vickers eased herself out of her armchair and stood up. She looked drawn and tired.

'Sorry about the state of the place Doctor Ryan but we weren't expecting . . .'

Sam smiled and reassured her.

'Looks fine to me. It's certainly a lot tidier than my place normally is.'

As she looked around the room Sam noticed a photograph of Simon standing on top of the television. Picking up the silver gilt frame she scanned the face. Smiling back was a fresh-faced handsome boy with a crop of long fair hair and crystal blue eyes. he was surrounded by his friends, all smiling, happy with his life and with the confidence of youth.

'He was a good-looking boy.'

Mrs Vickers almost snatched the frame away from Sam defensively, as if she was worried that she was about to lose her most treasured possession.

'Yes, he was. It was taken a few years ago while he was

on some environmental camp in Devon. it was always our favourite.'

Putting the picture carefully back in its place, she returned her attention to Sam, who decided to get on with it.

'I think you've probably guessed why I'm here.'

They both looked at her expectantly.

'I considered phoning, but thought it might come better if I visited.'

They continued to watch her silently, straining for her decision. Finally Sam blurted it out.

'I've decided to do the second postmortem examination on Simon.'

Mrs Vickers suddenly clutched her husband's hand and squeezed tightly.

'Oh, thank God, thank God.'

Mr Vickers, desperately trying to keep his own emotions under control, stared across at Sam. 'So you think there was something odd about his death?'

'I'm not sure, so I don't want you to get your hopes up too much.'

Mr Vickers persisted, 'Then why are you doing it?'

Sam swallowed hard. 'Because I'm not sure. I do have some vague doubts.'

'What kind of doubts?'

Sam didn't reply, unable to explain the unexplainable. Mrs Vickers came to her rescue.

'We've got what we wanted, Derek, let's just be grateful for that.' She turned back to Sam. 'When will you be doing it?'

'Day after tomorrow. I'll call you as soon as it's over and let you know what happened.'

Mr Vickers, still fighting with his emotions, held his hand out to Sam. She took it. 'Thank you Doctor Ryan, thank you very much. We know you'll get to the truth for us.'

Sam suddenly felt uncomfortable with their unquestioning faith in her ability to find a truth which they felt convinced was waiting to be discovered.

'I know how important this is to you, but please remember it is very unlikely that I will find anything that will contradict Doctor Stuart's report or give the police anything fresh to act on.'

'We realize that,' Mr Vickers nodded, 'but at least we'll have a second opinion and we'll be satisfied then, no matter what the outcome.'

Sam smiled across at the distressed couple, suddenly dreading the next forty-eight hours.

Since her meeting with Trevor, his attitude had changed and instead of the continuing hostility Sam had expected, he had suddenly become very reasonable. Perhaps Sam's notion that it would be better if she conducted the second PM rather than an unknown, and possibly hostile, pathologist had, as she had hoped, hit home. They had been friends since Sam first came to the Park Hospital and although he realized she would not compromise her position by conducting the PM in anything but the most professional manner, he also knew that she would be fair and unbiased, which might not always be the case when the defence was paying the pathologist's costs.

Sam arrived early at the Park to carry out the PM. She had managed to persuade Fred to turn up and assist on the promise of a day off later in the week. It was still dark when she arrived, and the car park was empty. Her footsteps echoed through the isolated building, bouncing off the concrete walls and ceilings before sending strange echoes around the grey interior, making it feel more sinister than usual. Sam made her way quickly to the lift, her eyes scanning this way and that for any signs of danger. She didn't bother going to her main office although she was almost certain that, even at this unearthly time of the morning, Jean would probably be there with a hot mug of coffee at her side, typing out yet another of her PM reports. Sam often wondered if Jean ever went home, or whether she kept some sort of camp bed secreted in the office and never really left. Making her way quickly down to the mortuary Sam was pleased to find that Fred was already there, and was holding a steaming mug of tea. Sam grabbed it appreciatively.

'Thanks Fred.'

He looked surprised. 'Who said it was yours?'

Sam shrugged.

'Sorry, Fred, but I'm desperate.'

'Bad night?'

Sam grimaced agreement.

'Couldn't sleep. I've had a few nights like that recently, too much on my mind, I think.'

'So I've heard.'

Sam stared hard into his face. 'What have you "heard"?'

Fred pressed a finger to his nose.

'I hear that the old sense of smell isn't what it was.'

Sam felt a sudden flash of anger as her private world was suddenly invaded by an outsider. Christ, she thought, if Fred knows, the chances are that the entire hospital does. She calmed herself.

'How did you find out about . . .'

'Hospital drums. You know what it's like around here, nothing's secret for long.'

The hospital's network consisted primarily of the medical secretaries. Being in charge of sending and receiving most of the hospital's letters, there was very little that got past them, and working on the 'now you promise you won't tell anyone else' school of gossip, not many secrets remained so for long.

'I'm sorry about the other day, when I slopped the formalin around. It wasn't very professional,' Fed said apologetically.

Sam smiled at her contrite assistant, her initial anger subsiding. 'No, I'm sorry, I shouldn't have snapped like that.'

'If I'd known, I'd have been more careful.'

'If I'd told you, then perhaps you would have been. But I think as a general rule we all ought to be a bit more mindful of the old Health and Safety regulations. You lost your sense of smell, didn't you, Fred?'

Fred nodded. 'Up until a few years ago I had. Got most of it back now though.'

Sam was surprised and intrigued.

'How? Took the holy waters at Lourdes or something?'

'No, nothing like that, but I have to admit it was a bit of a miracle nevertheless.'

Sam was becoming impatient.

'So what happened?'

'Alternative medicine. Heard about this woman in Chinatown, Madam Wong . . .'

Sam cut in sceptically, 'Last door on the right in the Street of a Thousand Eyes, no doubt.'

Fred gave a short laugh.

'No, seriously, it's true. My sense of smell and taste were completely shot. Everything, even ale, tasted odd.'

'End of life as you know it.'

'Precisely. Anyway, I go to see this Madam Wong and she sorts me out.'

'It all sounds a bit dubious to me. What did she do?'

'Lotions and potions. You know what these Chinese are like.'

Sam was still sceptical and becoming increasingly impatient. 'So what happened?'

Fred sat down on one of the stools and crossed his arms earnestly.

'Well, it was a bit slow to start off with, but my sense of smell and taste gradually began to come back. it was the spicy stuff at first, you know, curries, that sort of stuff. Then, thank God, the ale . . .'

'That must have cheered you up.'

Fred nodded in agreement.

'It did. Then gradually most of it came back.'

'Most?'

'Well it's not all back, I'd say about seventy per cent. Don't get me wrong, I can taste, smell and eat most things . . .' he sniffed the air for a moment, 'especially this place, but nothing is quite as sharp as it was.'

'Like smelling it through a cloth?'

Fred nodded.

'A thin cloth, but yes, that's a good way of looking at it.'

Normally Sam wasn't much for alternative therapies, but, like most people, when desperate enough she would probably be willing to try anything if it helped and she was certainly desperate.

'Have you got Madam Wong's phone number?'

Fred shook his head.

'She's not on the phone, you have to visit her personally. I've got her address if you want it.'

'That would be handy.'

'You can't make appointments, though, you just have to turn up and queue with the rest of us mortals. And I'd be there early if I were you, there's always a decent queue.'

'Thanks Fred.' She looked at her watch. 'I think we'd better get on.'

Fred nodded, put down his mug, and the two of them prepared for the task ahead.

Fred had already prepared Simon Vickers's body. Save for its outline, the blackened and twisted corpse no longer resembled a human being, looking more like a piece of dried out and overdone beef. It contrasted grimly with the white marble slab upon which it lay. Sam slowly scanned what was left of Simon Vickers and for a moment remembered the attractive and vibrant boy she had seen in the photograph when she visited the Vickers' home. She called across, 'Have you got the X-rays Fred?'

'They're by the viewer.'

Sam walked across to them and held each of them up in turn while Fred watched.

'Hell of a lot of damage, Christ it must have been hot.'

Sam nodded.

Fred pointed to numerous light patches that seemed to cover the body. 'What do you reckon they are?'

Sam examined the X-rays.

'Debris, blasted into the body by the impact of the explosion I would think.'

'What kind of debris?'

'Metal, glass, plastic, any hard object that will rip through flesh easily.'

'Doctor Stuart didn't bother removing it all, then.'

Sam shrugged.

'Not all of it, what's the point? He'd have taken some sections out for analysis, but it could take hours to get it all out. Might have done it if it had been a bombing and they wanted to reassemble the device. But car accidents . . .' Sam shrugged. 'Odd, though.'

Fred glanced across at her.

'What is?'

'The positioning of the debris. Most of it has impacted

on the front of the body.'

'What's odd about that?'

'Most car explosions I've dealt with involve the petrol tank. It's normally at the back of the car, so the worst of the debris is in the victim's back.'

'Might have been the fuel injection system. That's at the front.'

Sam continued to look at the X-rays carefully.

'Maybe.'

She finally turned out the light and moved back to Simon Vickers's charred remains. Eyeing each part of the blackened body carefully, Sam assessed the various difficulties presented by the postmortem examination. The body, as the X-rays had shown, was covered in small pieces of debris, which had been blown into the body as the car exploded before being welded into the soft tissue by the heat from the fire to become an integral part of Simon Vickers's body. In parts, the layers of tissue and muscle had been completely destroyed, exposing the blackened skeleton beneath. Both legs beneath the knees were missing, as was much of the right arm. His lips and mouth had also been burnt away exposing his surprisingly well-preserved teeth and leaving him with a fixed and grisly smile. The teeth were always difficult to destroy. Even when everything else had been consumed, the teeth tended to remain, leaving clues to the identity of the victim and occasionally leading to the arrest of a suspect. Sam pulled the microphone which hovered above her head into position, and began to dictate:

'Six thirty am, Monday 15th December 1997. Second postmortem examination on Simon Vickers. A white male, seventeen years of age and in previous good health. he is five feet eleven inches tall and eleven stone, six pounds in weight.'

Fred passed Sam the scalpel and she began her work in earnest.

Eric Chambers finally reached the top of the hill that overlooked Sam's cottage. He stopped for a moment to take in the panoramic views which the climb offered him. Everything looked so fresh and clean. He loved the view but hadn't seen it cloaked in the fabric of winter for many years. In these conditions he would normally have taken his car but there was something about today which had tempted him out and so he had made the effort. The dogs seemed to appreciate it, too. By road it was five or six miles, but trekking across the fields halved the distance. There were rights of way all the way to the cottage, and the surrounding countryside was quite wonderful. Sam had certainly chosen to live in one of the finest locations in the county. Despite his love of the countryside, he knew that at certain times of the year it could take on a harsh, even unpleasant appearance, but when the snow fell, which it often did in East Anglia, even when other areas were enjoying mild temperatures, the scenery became spectacular. Snow at Christmas always cheered him, it was so perfectly in keeping with the season. He pulled a handkerchief from his pocket and wiped the end of his wet nose before calling out to his dogs who were vainly trying to dig out a rabbit burrow.

'Monty, Rommel, here, come on. Not much further.'

The dogs left their precious hole obediently and, with tails wagging, scurried off down the hill leaving their dark paw tracks in the snow behind them. Pulling his woollen scarf tighter around his neck, Eric Chambers pushed his walking stick into the snow and strode off in pursuit.

Twenty minutes of hard walking finally brought Eric to Sam's back gate. Pushing it open he ushered his dogs through and followed, closing the gate securely behind him. The normally rich and fragrant garden was completely covered in a carpet of ice and snow. Making his way down the path to the back door he peered in through the window to see if he could spot any signs of life; there was nothing. Picking up his stick he knocked firmly on the door with his silver-topped handle. He'd only called on the off chance that either Sam or her sister, whom he had never met, would be in. There was no reply, and he was beginning to prepare himself for the cold walk home when Wyn suddenly appeared at the door.

'Can I help you?'

Eric Chambers removed his hat.

'I'm terribly sorry to bother you, but is Doctor Ryan in?'

'No, sorry, she's at work. I'm not expecting her home until late.'

'Oh I see.' He paused for a moment, unsure what to say next. Then, replacing his hat, 'Would you be good enough to tell her that Eric Chambers popped around? I live in the next village.'

Wyn nodded.

'Can I tell her what it's about?'

'Nothing important, just came to see how a couple of my plants were doing.' He indicated to the garden with his stick. 'Silly time to come really, but there you are.'

'Are you the gentleman who runs the computer club at the church hall?'

'Yes that's right,' Eric nodded.

'I'm Ricky's mother, Sam's sister.'

'Of course, sorry, I wasn't sure . . .'

'If I was the cleaner?'

Eric began to look awkward and uncomfortable.

'It's all right, plenty of people think that, and I suppose I am in a way.'

'Bright boy Ricky, should go far,' said Eric, going on the offensive. 'Genius on the Web.'

Wyn found herself warming to him. He didn't seem dangerous but he did look cold. 'Like some tea before you walk back?'

Eric didn't want to appear too keen, but was delighted to have the chance to sit down with a warming drink.

'If it's no trouble, old bones and all that.'

Wyn stood back from the doorway and gestured him into the cottage. 'If it was any trouble I wouldn't have asked. You can leave those two urchins in the porch, though.' She indicated to Eric's two dogs.

'Quite so, quite so, I'm sure they'll be very happy to stay out here. Rommel, Monty, stay, stay.'

The two dogs looked confused, but finally settled down together in the corner of the conservatory. Wyn ushered Eric through the kitchen and into the warmth of the sitting room.

Sam had taken her time over Simon Vickers' PM, checking and rechecking everything slowly and meticulously. Every observation noted in Trevor's report was correct, but despite that, she was becoming increasingly aware that in one fundamental area Trevor had been completely wrong. Simon Vickers hadn't died as a result of a car accident, he'd been murdered. Sam knew if she were going to stick her neck out and not get it chopped off, she would have to be certain of her facts. It was fortunate that she made her discovery at an early stage during the postmortem examination and, after making her final observations, Sam returned to the exposed neck. The hyoid bone had definitely been snapped, whether directly by external pressure or by the use of a ligature she couldn't be certain, but the injury certainly hadn't been caused by accident.

Sam had dealt with hundreds of deaths resulting from car accidents, but never once had she discovered a broken hyoid. Even when the body was subjected to a sudden and sharp impact or exposed to the intense heat of a fire, the hyoid bone tended to stay intact. Despite considering other explanations the only hypothesis Sam could reasonably make was that Simon Vickers had been strangled. Like most pathologists, Sam liked to have more than one piece of evidence to present, it made it easier to convince the sceptics. However, because of the state of the body, this proved impossible. All the characteristic signs, such as damage to the cartilage of the trachea, bruising and other injuries to the throat and tongue, as well as damage to the thyroid and crocoid cartilages, were no longer evident, having been consumed by the fire. Sam called across to Fed, who was preparing some of the larger pieces of debris Sam had dug out of Simon Vickers's body.

'Fred, have you ever dealt with a car accident where the hyoid bone was broken?'

Fred wandered across the mortuary and examined Simon Vickers's neck.

'No never, doesn't mean it's impossible, though, surely?'

'Unusual, though.'

Fred shook his head. 'Unusual doesn't mean impossible, you know what this game's like . . .'

'Never say never, never say always.'

Fred smiled and nodded.

'Right.'

Looking down at the exposed section of Simon Vickers's neck, Fred examined the hyoid bone for himself. He might not have been qualified, but experience made him a knowledgeable assistant. 'All the same, you're right, it is unusual.'

Sam stood away from the body for a moment and, looking down at it, tried to assess the implications of what she was about to announce. Finally, realizing there was nothing else she could do, she turned to Fed.

'I think you'd better call the police. I'm pretty sure we've got a murder on our hands.'

Fred looked surprised for a moment and didn't move, also realizing the enormity of Sam's last statement.

'Are you positive?'

Sam nodded.

'Unfortunately, yes.'

Fred headed for the door. As he reached it, however, he stopped and turned back to Sam.

'Shall I let Doctor Stuart know as well?'

Sam shook her head. 'No, I'll do that.'

Fred looked at her sympathetically for moment then turned and disappeared out of the room. Sam returned to the body. What she needed now was time, time to try and consider the best way to explain to Trevor. No matter which way she did it, Sam knew it wasn't going to be easy.

It didn't take long for Tom Adams and his team to arrive at the mortuary. Sam hadn't bothered changing and had spent her time in the mortuary office going over both Trevor's and the coroner's report, desperately searching for something that might help corroborate her findings. Fred announced their arrival.

'Superintendent Adams and Inspector White, Doctor.'

Sam looked up as the two men strode into her office.

'Tom, Chalky.'

They sat down on the two hard chairs at the far side of the office and made themselves comfortable. Tom looked across at Sam and gave her a broad smile. Although their work still brought them into contact, their once close relationship had long since ended. Sam liked to flatter herself that Tom would love to carry on where they left off, and, occasionally, if she were honest with herself, so would she. Adams came immediately to the point.

'So Sam, what have you got for us this time?'

'Murder.'

Adams seemed unperturbed by Sam's revelation. He'd almost guessed as much when he got the call. Sam wasn't a time waster and would only call him in if she considered it vital.

'I take it we are talking about Simon Vickers?'

Sam nodded. 'Yes.'

'I thought the cause of death had all been sorted out at the inquest. Accidental, wasn't it?'

'Coroners can make mistakes.'

'And Trevor?'

'Pathologists too.'

Adams remained silent for a moment trying to assess Sam's resolve then said, 'Okay, you'd better tell us what you've discovered.'

'As you may or may not know, Simon Vickers' family are unhappy with the findings of both the police and coroner's court . . .'

'I'd heard rumours.'

'As a result of this dissatisfaction they asked me to conduct a second postmortem examination, which I agreed to do. I carried out the PM this morning, and I am now convinced that Simon Vickers did not die in a car accident, but was in fact murdered, and probably placed in the car after his death to make it appear like an accident.'

Chalky White glanced sceptically across at his boss. Adams caught the glance but knew Sam too well to ignore anything that she said.

'How have you come to that conclusion, when nobody

else has?'

'The hyoid bone in his neck was broken.'

White interrupted her, still sceptical. 'So were a lot of other bones, what makes the hyoid so special?'

Adams glanced across at him.

'It's the one normally broken when a person is strangled. Isn't that right Doctor Ryan?'

Sam nodded. 'Glad to see you've been taking some note of the things you've seen over the years.'

Adams smiled quietly at her patronizing tone.

'So you think Simon Vickers was strangled? But couldn't it have been broken in the impact. Most of the rest of him was.'

Sam shook her head. 'In all the years I've been a pathologist, I have never seen the hyoid bone broken in this kind of an accident. I have, however, been involved in a number of murders involving manual or ligature strangulation where the hyoid has been broken in much the same way.'

'Was there any other evidence that might support your findings?'

'No, the fire had caused too much damage.'

'Are you *sure* that the hyoid bone couldn't have been broken in the accident? I understand it was a bad one.'

Sam shrugged.

'There's always a chance, but surely we're dealing with probabilities here, and the probabilities of the hyoid being broken by the accident are very small.'

'But it's not impossible?' White interrupted.

'Improbable, I've never seen one.'

'Not impossible, then?' said Tom.

Sam frowned. 'The circumstances would have to be very unusual.'

'I think they were.' Although Tom had learnt to trust

89

Sam's instincts over the years, command brought with it additional responsibilities, and he began to behave increasingly like his old boss, Farmer. Had he become more cautious, or was he just more responsible? In truth, he wasn't sure himself. However, he still felt he had to explain.

'I can't justify opening a major murder inquiry on that kind of evidence. Do you have any idea of how much it would cost?'

Sam shook her head. 'What price justice, eh?'

'I'd aim that kind of flippant remark at the ratepayers of this county and see what they've got to say about it,' said Tom, nettled by Sam's sarcasm. 'If you want me to direct resources and cash at something like this you're going to have to come up with a bit more than just a broken bone. Besides, if it was so important, why didn't Trevor point it out in his report?'

'I don't know, he must have missed it.'

'Or thought it so unimportant in the general mess he had to deal with that he didn't bother mentioning it.'

Sam could feel herself on the defensive and it began to annoy her.

'I doubt that.'

'When, and if, you get a bit more, then let me know and perhaps I'll be more responsive, but until then I can see no reason to start a murder inquiry.'

Sam remained seated. She considered again mentioning her meeting with the poacher, but still decided it would create more problems than it would solve.

'What about the fact that he didn't like cars?'

White looked at her. 'Says who?'

'His parents. He hated cars. He was a bit of a eco-warrior. So why would a boy who hated cars steal one?'

White shook his head.

'Parents don't know everything about their kids. They think they do, but they don't.'

'And Cherry Hinton is miles from Impington, why cycle miles to steal a car when there must have been plenty of available vehicles on his own estate?'

'Divert attention away from himself. You know what they say, never do it in your own backyard.'

'Why about bypassing all the car's sophisticated security system? That wasn't the work of an amateur.'

'Who said he was an amateur?' asked White. 'Got form, hadn't he?'

'For a minor assault once, and that was whilst taking part in a demonstration against the growing supremacy of the car.'

'Look, just because we hadn't nicked him for it before, doesn't mean he wasn't bang at it. There's hundreds of them out there we've never nicked, probably never will, but that doesn't mean they're not real villains.'

Adams cut in. 'Sam, parents always think the best of their children. If they don't it's an admission they have failed and that's hard to live with. Are you aware of everything that Ricky does when he's out and about?'

'He's my nephew, not my son.'

'Don't split hairs, you know what I'm talking about. I'm not saying they're bad parents, I'm sure they're not. I'm just pointing out that you can't monitor your children's activities twenty-four hours a day.'

Sam shook her head, still unconvinced. 'You're wrong.'

Adams was unsympathetic.

'Who knows, maybe I am. But then maybe you are. All I do know is that I have to deal in facts, because if I don't it will be my head on the block not yours, and at the moment you don't have enough to make me even consider mounting the scaffold.'

Sam threw her arms up in a gesture of despair. Adams stood, followed faithfully by Inspector White. Sam looked at Adams.

'Who was the traffic officer that dealt with the accident?'

Adams thought for a moment.

'Brian Williams. You'll find him at the traffic wing. He's a very experienced sergeant so be careful what you say.'

Sam nodded.

'I just want a peek at the accident report, that's all.'

Adams shrugged.

'That's up to him. But knowing you I'm sure you'll smooth-talk it out of him.'

As Adams turned to leave, Sam stood.

'Was there anything else?'

Adams looked confused.

'You rang earlier.'

'Personal, I'll call you this evening.'

Sam nodded her understanding and watched as the two detectives left the room. She realized that although she was convinced about Simon Vickers's murder, convincing others, even Adams, was not going to be easy.

4

As usual, it was late by the time Sam arrived home. With her normal workload increasing yearly, taking on extra cases was always difficult, especially one like Simon Vickers's. Despite the additional pressures, however, the abnormal silence drew Sam like moth to a bright light. Her peculiarity of mind needed to be indulged regularly, and the mere routine of her profession was never abstract enough to satisfy her. For Sam, there was nothing like the strange and unusual to focus her thoughts. Engaging the vehicle's four-wheel drive, she began to climb the dirt track that ultimately led to her cottage. Although it had finally stopped snowing the air was still thin, and the ice had compacted hard across the ground. As Sam turned into her drive she could hear the ice crack beneath the weight of her heavy wheels. As she stepped out of her vehicle the expected security light failed to flicker on. Sam sighed, this was another of life's minor irritants. Now she would have to remember that it needed dealing with and it would be another of those jobs she just never seemed to get around to.

She locked her car and began to make her way towards the cottage. Just before opening the front door she looked up towards the clear night sky. The wide open Norfolk skies and brilliantly clear atmosphere were the two features Sam most loved about the county. The isolation of the cottage also freed it from most types of light pollution, giving her a lucid and unrestricted view of the night sky. During the summer she would often lie in her garden looking up into the darkness, and examine the clearly visible constellations which scattered themselves across the sky twinkling down at her like a vast, sequined gown. Occasionally, she would spot the orange tail of a shooting star as it flashed across the heavens to oblivion. Occasionally she had seen a meteor shower plunging white with heat through the atmosphere. Sam had spent hours watching the comet Hale-Bopp as it moved slowly across the sky, its immense, hazy tail making it distinctive amongst the other stars. She had even bought a telescope to try and get a better look. It was a wonderful sight and one she knew she was sharing with the rest of the world; it made her feel very insignificant.

Guided by the light from the moon, Sam searched frantically for her door keys. Finally discovering them secreted in one of the bag's numerous side-pockets, she unlocked the door and made her way towards the front room. Wyn was sitting on the settee reading a magazine in the light of a small side lamp. She looked up as Sam entered the room.

'You're late.'

'Sorry, but you know what it's like.'

Wyn returned to her magazine and attempted to adopt an air of indifference.

'Well, your dinner's been in the oven for hours, probably burnt to a cinder.'

Sam threw her coat over a chair and dropped her

briefcase on the floor.

'Sorry, Wyn, it's been a messy day. I'll grab a sandwich later.'

'It beats me how you ever manage to keep that figure of yours.'

Sam collapsed into the armchair opposite her sister. 'Nervous energy and gardening.'

Wyn looked up. 'Talking about gardening, I had a friend of yours around today.'

Sam became interested.

'Tom?'

Wyn gave her a knowing smile.

'Still hankering after the policeman, are we?'

Sam suddenly felt awkward. 'No, just that he's been trying to get hold of me and. . .'

Wyn cut in, 'I'm sure he has.'

Sam found herself looking away from her sister and blushing.

'Anyway it wasn't your amorous policeman, it was Eric.'

'Eric Chambers?'

Wyn nodded. 'Yea, nice man. Came to see some cuttings he'd given you last summer, wanted to know how they were getting on.'

'They're in the greenhouse, they seem to be doing fine. I'm surprised he didn't wait until the spring. Did he stay long?'

'A while. I could hardly turn him away after he'd walked so far to see you.'

Sam shook her head.

'Walked! They'll find him frozen to death in a field one day. I think his mind wants what his body can't offer.'

'Don't we all. He seemed very concerned about that case you're dealing with.'

'Simon Vickers?'

'Asked a lot of questions about him.'

'He used to be one of his pupils.'

'Yes, he said. He used to come to the meetings at the church hall.'

'Where Ricky goes?'

Wyn nodded.

'Funny, he never said anything.'

'You know the young, nothing matters but them.'

'Bit harsh, Wyn, but you would have thought he'd have said something.'

'Anyway,' Wyn continued, 'I've got something to ask you. Would you mind terribly if Ricky and I spent Christmas with aunty Maude in Harrogate this year? Only she's asked us to go up, feeling a bit lonely I think.'

Aunt Maude was her mother's sister and had been on her own since the death of her husband five years earlier. She was too frail to travel so if they wanted to keep in touch, a trip north was necessary. Although Sam didn't relish the idea of spending Christmas on her own, she really didn't see what else she could say.

'Of course I don't mind. I'm sure Maude will be delighted. When are you going?'

'Christmas Eve, and back on New Year's Day.' Wyn could see the concern in her sister's eyes. 'Why don't you come with us? It's only for a few days.'

Sam shook her head, 'I'm too busy.'

'As usual.'

Sam put her arms up in despair. 'Well I am, but you go, I'll be fine.'

A loud knock on the door stopped any further conversation. Wyn walked down the corridor and opened the door cautiously.

'Hello, Wyn, long time no see.'

Tom Adams's smiling face looked down at her.

'Well, talk of the devil.'

Adams leaned down and kissed her on the cheek.

'Thought my ears were burning. Is Sam in?'

Wyn looked at him, mock-despairingly.

'And there was I thinking it was me you'd come to see. She's in the kitchen.'

Wyn directed him down the corridor and into the room. Sam called out to her sister as Tom entered.

'Who is it, Wyn? I . . . Oh hello Tom, what a nice, if not completely unexpected, surprise.'

He crossed the room and kissed her.

'Well I'm glad you still think it's a nice surprise, Sam.'

Wyn, picked up the kettle and made her way across to the sink, filling it from the tap before depositing it onto the glowing hob. As she did Tom made his way across to the pheasant hanging from a small kitchen hook in the corner of the room. He prodded it gently making the carcass swing.

'Where did you get this, Sam, didn't know they were in season yet? Hope you haven't turned to poaching.'

Wyn stared desperately at her sister. Sam was equal to it.

'Found it dead by the side of the road. Seemed a shame to waste it so I brought it home. That's okay isn't it?'

Adams nodded.

'Think so. When's the PM?'

Sam smiled innocently at him before making her way across to the kitchen table and sitting down. Adams followed.

'So, what can be that urgent it brings you all the way out here on a freezing December night?'

'Do I need a reason?'

'No, but as you've been trying to reach me for the last couple of days, you don't have to be Sherlock Holmes to suspect there's more to it than an exchange of Christmas cards.'

He gave her a sharp half-grin.

'Originally it was to invite you out for dinner…'

'And now?'

'I'd still like to take you to dinner, but I was also wondering how much further you were going to push the Vickers case.'

'I see. I'm going to "push it" until you're convinced that Simon Vickers was murdered and didn't die in a car accident.'

'Don't you ever admit you might be wrong?'

Sam grinned. 'Sometimes, but I'm not in this case.'

Adams shook his head. He knew there was little point trying to persuade her to drop the case. 'If it makes you feel any better send me what you've got and I'll take another look, but don't hold your breath.'

Sam was pleased that Tom wasn't being completely intransigent about her theory.

'It'll take a day or two. Most of our computers are down at the moment. Some sort of reprogramming going on.'

Adams smiled. 'That's fine. Ours are down too. It must be something in the air. What about Saturday night?'

'I don't think my report will be ready by then, I…'

Adams looked at her despairingly. 'For dinner.'

'Oh sorry, yes, that sounds fine, thank you.'

'Pick you up about eight?'

Sam nodded.

'Lovely.'

As Adams stood to go Sam looked up at him. 'I haven't told Trevor yet, he's been away in London. I'd like to be the one that explains if you don't mind.'

'That'll be fine. Good luck, I think you'll need it.'

Sam winced. She knew he was right.

*

Sam decided to see Trevor as soon as possible to discuss her findings with him. She had tried to ring him the previous evening, but only managed to leave a message on his answerphone. Even now, as she made her way to their rendezvous, she wasn't sure that Trevor would respond to her message to see her for breakfast. She had decided not to meet in the formality of the hospital but had selected Travers, a smart restaurant by the edge of the river Cam behind Magdalene Bridge. As she crossed Trinity Bridge, she nodded politely to the porter who guarded the entrance to New Court, parked in the last available space next to a shabby and ancient black Mercedes. Making her way into the cloistered protection of Nevile's Court and then through the oak-panelled exterior of the Great Hall before emerging into the splendor of Great Court. Sam had never seen the court covered in snow before. It was truly magnificent, and made even the college's ancient stonework look fresh. With the students on holiday, the only marks which spoilt the pureness of the image were those of the Fellows' feet which crisscrossed the court as they exercised their ancient rights to traverse the court by way of the snow-obscured lawns. This was an act forbidden to undergraduates and other such unworthy individuals, who were compelled to remain firmly upon the paths. Making her way down the steps Sam followed the path around the edge of the snow-covered lawns and towards Great Gate. Once through it she turned left onto Trinity Street and then left again towards Magdalene Bridge and the restaurant, finally arriving at Travers cold, damp and hungry.

Although she was late, Trevor hadn't arrived and she was grateful for that. Slipping off her damp coat she selected a table at the far side of the restaurant which overlooked the river, and made herself comfortable. Almost as soon as she had relaxed, a young and pretty waitress was by her side, notebook in hand, to take her order. For now, at least, she just ordered coffee. As the waitress retreated to collect her order, Sam looked out of the window towards Magdalene College and Bridge. A punt containing three thickly wrapped Japanese tourists glided under the bridge towards her, determined to make the most of the 'Cambridge Experience' even under the most atrocious of conditions. As it was pushed past her window, Sam's thoughts wandered along the river with it. Despite running the matter through her mind continually, she still wasn't sure how she was going to approach the subject with Trevor. Come straight out with it, or dance around the idea for a while in the hope that he might pick up her hints. Before she had time to make up her mind, a familiar voice invaded her thoughts.

'Morning Sam, sorry I'm late, traffic. As soon as the weather changes everything stops. Thought we would have been used to it by now wouldn't you?'

Sam smiled across at him sympathetically.

'Don't worry, I've only just got here myself. I wasn't sure you'd picked up my message.'

'Why shouldn't I?'

'Oh, I don't know thought you might be paying court to Emily, I know what you young couples are like.'

Sam's attempt to keep the mood light failed.

'Shall we get to the point, Sam?'

'Coffee first?'

Trevor nodded. 'Black.'

'Like your mood?'

Trevor gave her a short sarcastic smile. Having noted the arrival of her companion, the waitress returned. Trevor took a cursory glance at the menu and put it down.

'Just coffee, please.'

He looked across at Sam.

'I've ordered, thank you.'

The waitress retreated to prepare the order and Trevor returned to the subject.

'So, you think that Simon Vickers was murdered?'

Sam remained silent for a moment, surprised and confused at Trevor's revelation. Still, she pondered, it stopped her debate on how she was going to tell him.

'Yes. Who told you?'

'Does it matter?'

Sam's previous calm began to desert her and she felt her hackles rise at Trevor's attitude.

'Yes, actually it does.'

'Well, if you have to know, the police called me last night and outlined your findings.' The sarcastic tone in Trevor's voice was becoming more pronounced.

'What did they tell you?'

'What you would expect really. You'd conducted the second PM as a result of which you decided Vickers had been murdered, strangled I understand, and therefore my findings were wrong and yours right. Is that about it?'

'That's not quite what I said.'

'Isn't it?'

'No.'

'Then what did you say, Sam? Do tell.'

If Trevor hadn't been such an old and established friend she'd have walked out. As it was she felt compelled to keep her calm.

'His hyoid bone was broken.'

Sam had hoped this revelation might change Trevor's mood but it didn't.

'So were most of his bones as I remember. Bones get broken in accidents, that's the way it is. I thought you would have known that, Sam.'

Sam shook her head. 'Not the hyoid. At least, I've never seen one broken under these conditions, I doubt you have either.'

He shrugged.

'Maybe not, but it doesn't mean it couldn't happen.'

'The only time I've ever seen it is in cases of strangulation, which means that there is a strong possibility that Simon wasn't killed as a result of the accident, but was murdered. Surely it's worth a further examination if nothing else.'

Trevor wasn't impressed.

'I'm sorry, Sam, but I can't accept that.'

'Did you notice the injury during your original PM?'

'I can't remember, it was some time ago. I've conducted a few more since then.'

'It's just that there was no mention of it in your report.'

'Perhaps I thought it so unimportant I didn't bother to note it.'

Sam's previous control was beginning to desert her. 'Oh come off it, Trevor. If you'd noticed that the hyoid bone had been snapped there is no way you'd have failed to mention it.'

Trevor's face seemed to suddenly grow dark. In all the years Sam had known him she could never remember seeing Trevor look quite so angry.

'Are you calling me incompetent?'

There was an edge to his voice that unnerved, even slightly frightened Sam, but she persisted.

'No, Trevor, I'm not calling you incompetent, but I'm saying that on this occasion you might have missed something. We all do occasionally.'

'Even you?'

'All of us.'

Trevor suddenly shot to his feet, his face red with rage.

'I missed nothing, and if you think I'm going to be another sacrifice on the altar of your arrogance then you can think again!'

For a moment Sam was shocked. 'Trevor, this is getting us nowhere, let's just talk it out and come to some mutual conclusion.'

Trevor pulled his wallet from his pocket angrily and threw a five pound note onto the table.

'Keep the change.'

His voice curled with anger and sarcasm. He turned and stormed out of the restaurant. Sam, who had tried to stay calm, collapsed back into her seat exhausted. She avoided the stare of the other diners whose eyes were suddenly fixed on her table.

The encounter with Trevor hadn't gone quite as planned. Instead of getting him on her side, she had managed to alienate him completely. Although, in truth, she doubted that however she had handled it the result would have been different. She was still angry at Tom Adams for contacting Trevor and forewarning him of their meeting, especially after she had specifically asked him not to. Trevor must have been brooding on it all night. After he had stormed out, Sam didn't linger at the restaurant, but paid the bill quickly, leaving Trevor's five pounds as a large tip. At least the waitress seemed delighted with the outcome, which was more than she was.

Sam followed her route back to New Court and from there made her way towards Impington and the home of Mr and Mrs Vickers. She had considered phoning them after she had completed the PM but felt they at least deserved to be informed in person. She just hoped that Tom Adams or one of his squad hadn't already passed on the information. Pulling up outside their house Sam climbed out of her

Range Rover and made her way to the front door, knocking loudly on the PVC frame. For a while nothing happened, and Sam began to wish she had phoned first to check they were in. Just as she was preparing to leave, the door swung open and Mr Vickers appeared.

'Doctor Ryan. Sorry, I was clearing the snow in the garden.'

He examined her earnest face.

'You've got some news, then?'

'Yes.'

Mr Vickers didn't move, but remained staring at her, searching her face for information and waiting for her to give up her news on the doorstep. Sam had no intention of being quite so public.

'Can I come in?'

Sam's request broke Mr Vickers's concentration and he stood to one side. 'Of course you can, sorry, but we've been a bit eager for news.'

Sam made her way into the sitting room where she expected to find Mrs Vickers waiting. The room was empty.

'Mrs Vickers not around?'

'No, she's just popped out to do a bit of shopping, she'll not be long. Please sit down.'

Sam positioned herself in the armchair opposite the television where the picture of the young and attractive Simon Vickers stared out at her demandingly. Mr Vickers sat on the edge of the settee and waited impatiently for her report. Sam could feel his tension.

'What I've got to say might be difficult for you and your wife. Shall we wait for her so I can tell you together?'

Mr Vickers shook his head.

'No, I'd rather you told me now, Edna needs to be told in a certain way, bit of delicacy, if you know what I mean?'

Sam did and accepted what he said. She got on with it.

'I think Simon was murdered.'

Mr Vickers stared into her face for a moment trying to take in the enormity of what she had just said. Then he looked across at his son's photograph.

'Told you we'd get justice, Simon. I'll not let you down twice.'

His mood was strangely mixed. Although it was what he had been hoping for he didn't really want to know, as if the knowledge finally killed any hope that it was all a terrible dream from which he would wake at any moment. He turned to face Sam, tears rolling down his cheeks.

'Sorry, bit of a shock you understand. Its all been so bloody awful. Have you got children, Doctor Ryan?'

Sam shook her head. 'No.'

'You see, when they're born, it's like having a contract. They give you enormous pleasure and you promise to look after them, care for them, provide them with the best chance to have a good life. I didn't keep my side of the contract, I let him down, failed to protect him. All I can do now is try and make amends, but I'm not sure I ever will.'

'You didn't let anyone down. He wasn't a child anymore, he was a young man, and you have to let go some time, they have to learn to be their own person. There was nothing you could have done. There is only one person responsible for the death of your son and that's whoever killed him.'

Sam wasn't convinced she was getting through but hoped it helped. Crying must have been difficult, especially for a man of Mr Vickers' generation. He was brought up in an age when showing any emotion was considered a weakness. Her own father, who would have been only a little older, had he lived, was just the same, and although Sam knew that he loved her, he very seldom said it. Even as her mother lay on her deathbed, Sam knew it was the one thing that still bothered her.

NIGEL McCRERY

Sometimes things needed to be said, not necessarily for our own good but for the good of others. Sam had inherited her father's outward lack of emotion, and was convinced it was a factor in her own inability to conduct a lasting relationship. She had tried to change, but finally surrendered to the inevitable, and accepted that it was as much part of her personality as was the desire to be a pathologist.

'How did he die?'

This was the hardest part of all.

'He was strangled.'

'It would have been quick, then. I mean, he wouldn't have suffered or anything?'

'No, he wouldn't have suffered, it would have been very quick,' Sam lied.

In truth, she had no idea how long Simon would have suffered. That depended on the mind of the person strangling him. It might have been quick, but then again it might not have been. It was a strange and sad situation, that the only solace Mr Vickers could now take was in the hope that his son's death had not been a painful one.

'What brought you to that conclusion? I mean, they said he was a bit of a mess, after the fire. I think that's why the police wouldn't let us see him.'

'The hyoid bone in his neck was broken.'

'It couldn't have been broken during the accident then?'

Sam shook her head. 'No. He was definitely strangled.'

He glanced back to the photograph of his dead son.

'So what happens now? I take it the police get involved again?'

This was an awkward one for Sam and she knew she'd have to tread gently.

'They aren't convinced by my findings yet.'

Mr Vickers looked surprised. 'What do you mean they're not convinced? You told them what you'd found, didn't you,

106

how can they argue with that, you're the expert?'

Sam shrugged.

'I'm afraid they can. They feel they need more evidence before they can commence a full-scale and expensive murder inquiry.'

'That's ridiculous, his neck was broken, he was strangled, it couldn't have happened any other way. What more do they need, for God's sake? I mean, if they're not going to take your word for it, what's the point in you doing the PMs?'

He was right, what was the point? Sam tried to justify the unjustifiable.

'Murder inquiries can take quite a chunk out of the police budget, I think they like to be a hundred and ten per cent sure before they take any action.'

Mr Vickers shook his head.

'My son's life calculated in a ledger by some faceless police authority as an economic risk. Is that all he was worth?' He collapsed, rather than sat, back on the settee. 'Well at least now we know for sure, that's something I suppose.' He looked across at Sam. 'Thank you for your efforts, Doctor Ryan, thank you very much.'

Sam could almost feel his despair.

'You'll let me have your bill, won't you?'

'That won't be necessary.'

'We don't want charity, Doctor Ryan, we've always paid our way, owe nobody anything. I'd like it to stay that way.'

'It doesn't have to end like this you know, we can fight them.'

'Fight the police? I doubt it.'

'With your permission, I'd like to make a few more inquiries into your son's death, see if I can't dig up enough additional evidence to try and persuade the police to change their minds.'

'I can't see the police being very happy about that. Won't you get yourself into trouble?'

'Probably, but it won't be the first time and I doubt it will be the last.'

'Well if you're sure, of course you've got our permission.'

Sam decided she should qualify her intentions.

'You must understand Mr Vickers...'

'Derek, my name's Derek,' he interrupted. 'Seems silly to be so formal now.'

Sam nodded.

'Derek, you and your wife must understand that I can't guarantee to find any more evidence, I'm working on my own. I have very few resources and very little time. All I can promise is that I'll do my best, but I might not get very far.'

Derek Vickers smiled, albeit painfully. 'Your best is all we can ask, you've already done more than enough for us, doctor, and it's greatly appreciated. Is there anything we can do?'

Sam was mildly amused at the way Mr Vickers spoke on behalf of his missing wife. She wondered whether she would ever experience the trust and closeness which allowed one partner to speak for another with complete confidence.

'A couple of things, actually.'

Mr Vickers was all attention.

'Firstly, can you write down everything that happened on the night Simon went missing? Don't leave anything out, no matter how trivial it might seem to you.'

'No problem, it's not a night I'll forget in a hurry.'

Sam smiled gently. 'No, I don't suppose it is. I'd also like a list of all his friends, former girl friends, people he might have met recently, even people he's mentioned but perhaps you've never met.'

'He only had one friend, that he seemed close to, anyway.'

'Who was that?'

'Dominic…'

'Dominic Parr?'

Mr Vickers nodded, surprised. 'How do you know Dominic?'

'I don't. A friend of mine used to teach your son, he mentioned that Dominic was a friend of his. Wouldn't happen to have his address, would you?'

'Milton somewhere. I'll find it for you.'

'There's no great urgency. Ring me when you've got it.'

'Either Dominic was around here or Simon was around there. Lived in each other's pockets most of the time. Haven't seem him since Simon died though. Thought he'd have popped around to see us wouldn't you?'

Sam smiled at him sympathetically.

'I'd also like to know about any school trips or holidays that Simon took over the past year as well as any clubs or organizations he belonged to. Also, anything that might have happened recently, which you thought, even in retrospect, might have been a little unusual.'

Mr Vickers nodded enthusiastically.

'No problem, but it might take a day or two.'

'That's fine, I'd rather you took your time and didn't miss anything. Finally, would you mind if I took a look a quick look at Simon's room?'

Mr Vickers nodded. 'Of course you can, if you think it will help.'

Simon's room was large and remarkably tidy for a teenager's. Although there was the usual array of posters and pictures around the walls with the exception of a large poster showing Guns 'n' Roses in concert and another of

Cambridge United FC, the majority were based around environmental issues. The one dominating feature of the room, however, was Simon's computer. A large and expensive looking object.

'Powerful looking machine.'

Mr Vickers nodded. 'One of the best on the market, or so Simon said. I don't know too much about these things.'

'Did he buy it himself?'

'No. He didn't have too much money just the bit we gave him and his Saturday job. We bought it for his last birthday, he was pretty pleased with it.'

Sam smiled and toyed with the keyboard.

'It was a very generous gift. Was he on the Net?'

'Oh yes. We had it installed for him at the same time. He spent hours contacting people and printing off information.'

'That must have been a bit pricey?'

Mr Vickers shrugged. 'We had a separate line put in and he paid all his own bills. So to be honest I don't know how much it cost.'

'I thought you said he didn't have too much cash?'

'Seemed to have enough to pay his phone bill, he never came to us for anything extra anyway.'

'Where did he work?'

'McDonalds, the one in town.'

Sam looked up.

'Odd place for an environmentalist to work.'

'He needed the money, I guess.'

Sam nodded, unconvinced.

'My nephew works there as well. They must have known each other.'

'He only worked there on a Saturday and the occasional Sunday if they were short.'

'Ricky's full time I'm afraid.'

'It's a job, and they're still hard enough to come by.'

Sam was touched by his diplomacy. 'I'd like to have a quick look through some of Simon's computer files if that's okay and take a few photographs of his room?'

He nodded nervously.

'I suppose so, if you think it's relevant.'

'I do.'

While Mr Vickers watched anxiously, Sam quickly scanned the room deciding on her shots. She took photographs of his posters, computer, bookshelves, in fact anything that took her interest, no matter how vague. She paid particular note of the long, hand-drawn poster Simon had pinned up next to his computer. It was covered in drawings of various animals and insects from a cat to a fly. Under some there were people's first names while others were just left blank. Under a drawing of a giant fly Sam saw Simon's name, under a large bee was the name Dominic which she assumed was Dominic Parr, but the one that concerned her most was a large monster-like ant with the name 'Ricky' penned underneath. She took several close up shots of both the fly and bee, finishing off her roll of film with numerous photographs of the ant. Dropping her camera back inside her bag she sat down by the computer and turned the machine on. The message screen appeared after a few moments. The computer immediately displayed the Windows messaging service informing the user that they had three outstanding messages waiting to be read. Moving the mouse around quickly, she tried to gain access to the message server, when a small square board appeared demanding the password. Sam collapsed back into the chair. She should have guessed there would be a security code to protect the files. If the system was anything like hers then she would have three chances to get it right after which the computer would automatically close itself down. It would probably be a six figure sequence so the possibilities ran into the thousands and she had no idea where to begin. Sam stared hard into the screen trying to will the information out of it. Finally, sitting forward she typed in FLY123 and waited. The message came back quickly, 'incorrect code, please try again.' Sam realized that realistically she had no chance of hitting upon the correct code. She turned to Derek Vickers.

'Any idea what Simon's access code was?'

'Sorry, Doctor Ryan, I've got no idea. As I said, not my sort of thing.'

Sam persisted. 'Don't suppose you know whether Simon kept a codebook?'

Mr Vickers frowned.

'I don't think so, kept most things in his head, he was clever like that. Bit of a photographic memory. It might be worth asking Dominic, though. If anyone would know he would.'

Sam nodded thoughtfully.

'In that case I'd better have his address now, after all.'

Derek Vickers disappeared, giving Sam a few moments to have one last look for anything resembling a codebook but there was nothing. He returned quickly.

'57 Colton Road, Milton. Here, I've written it down for you. Phone number's on there as well. I found this, too, forgotten we'd got it actually, don't know if it will be any good.'

He handed Sam a small neat sketchpad, which she opened and flicked through. The pages consisted of numerous drawings of animals and insects. On the front page was a rather disturbing drawing of a fly. The fly was caught in an immense web, which had spun itself tightly around the small insect's body holding it fast to the lattice screen. Moving slowly towards the trapped creature was an immense black spider with large crimson fangs. Under it

Simon had written, 'You pull and fight but there is no escape and your end is inevitable.' It was the stuff of nightmares and contrasted sharply with the rest of the drawings inside the sketchpad.

Sam looked across Mr Vickers. 'Can I hang onto this?'

Mr Vickers looked unsure.

'I'll look after it. I'll take a copy when I get back to work and return the original.'

He nodded. 'Okay but as soon as you can, the wife doesn't like anything of Simon's moved if you understand what I mean.'

'Of course. Well, I think that's it for now, don't forget to let me have that list of his friends, and the statements. Remember, take your time and make it accurate. It might be important.'

'I won't miss a thing.'

'There is one last thing?'

Mr Vickers looked at her expectantly.

'What time did Simon go out the night he died?'

'Midnight.'

'Are you sure? Seems rather late.'

'He always went out late, bit of an owl was Simon. Normally back by two, though.'

'How do you know that?'

'I'm a parent.' He stopped himself for a moment. 'Was, anyway, couldn't sleep until he was in. You know, fussy father.'

Sam could feel herself getting caught up in the emotion of the moment again and moved on quickly.

'Was he on foot?'

'No, he took his bike, he went everywhere on it.'

Sam nodded, finally satisfied. As she reached the front door Mrs Vickers returned with the shopping. Seeing Sam emerge from the house she suddenly became anxious.

'Doctor Ryan, what on earth are you doing here? Is there any news?'

Sam wasn't sure what to say and looked back at Mr Vickers for help.

'Its all right, Edna, I'll explain inside.' Putting his arm gently around her shoulder, he guided her into the house, 'Come on love, come and have a cup of tea, I'll can tell you all about it then.'

As Sam unlocked the driver's door to her Range Rover, a loud piercing scream emanated from the house. Sam recognized the passion behind it. There was never an easy way to pass on that kind of message, she thought.

Eric Chambers blew out hard as he pushed his brush firmly into the snow, moving it slowly from the street and into the gutter. He didn't really know why he was bothering, nobody else in the road seemed to be. There was a time when it was almost a disgrace to leave the snow piled up in the street outside your own cottage. Still, there was a time when many things were different. Time and people moved on, and not always for the best. A call from the opposite pavement suddenly attracted his attention.

'Eric!'

He looked up and stared across the road. He'd already recognized the voice and knew who it was without looking at him. With a brief wave the Reverend Andrews crossed the frozen road in company with his morose sound and camera man, Edmond Moore.

'It's good to see that not all the community spirit has gone out of the village. These pavements are treacherous.'

Eric eyed Moore's camera suspiciously.

'You're not going to film me brushing away the snow, are you? There must be more interesting things to take pictures of.'

Andrews looked at his assistant.

'Have we got plenty of shots of the village in the snow Edmond?'

He nodded wearily. 'Yes, reverend.'

'What about people sweeping it away?'

'Sweeping it, throwing it, rolling in it, coming up and down hills on it.'

'Good, good. In that case, no, Eric, your big chance for stardom will have to wait. But you can make a couple of weary travellers a warming drink.'

Eric hadn't quite finished sweeping but there was a determination in the reverend's voice that told Eric it was a lost cause.

'Perhaps we can talk about the Bishop's concert at the same time.'

Eric looked at him in surprise. 'What concert?'

The Reverend Andrews put his arm around his shoulder.

'Did I not tell you about that? Well, all the more reason to talk a while.'

He looked back at Edmond Moore. 'Have we got any shots of people drinking tea?'

Moore looked at him despairingly; Andrews took the hint.

'Perhaps we should pass on that one.' He returned his attentions to Eric. 'Look, Eric, if you're really busy I can let myself in and make the tea while you finish up here. I take it you keep the key in the same place?'

Eric stopped sweeping and leaned on his brush.

'Well you're clearly not going to leave me in peace until you get one, so let's get the kettle on.'

He called to his two dogs, who were running happily up and down the road, kicking up the snow and jumping around each other like a couple of puppies.

'Monty, Rommel, come on, teatime.'

The two dogs obeyed at once and ran back down the cottage path, barking contentedly, towards the door, closely followed by the Reverend Andrews, Eric and Edmond Moore.

Once inside, Eric directed them into the sitting room while he made his way to the kitchen and put the kettle on. Eric was a man of habit and disliked surprises, or anything else that disturbed his daily routine for that matter. Occasionally, however, even he had to accede to events. As the kettle came to the boil a chilling wind suddenly blew through the kitchen. It was clear to Eric that one of his two guests had, for some reason, opened a window, and let the heat out of the once warm room. Pouring the tea and balancing the mugs on a tray he made his way back into the sitting room. To his surprise it wasn't a window that had been opened, but the patio doors at the far end of the room. He looked across at Moore.

'Who the hell opened them?'

Moore, who was examining a rather fine porcelain figure which sat majestically on top of one of Eric's cabinets, didn't even bother looking up.

'The reverend. Something about some plant you've got that he'd like some cuttings from.'

Eric put down the tray and rushed to the doors. Staring out towards the back of his garden he noticed the Reverend Andrews crouching down by the Rhododendron bush and brushing away the snow from the bottom of it. Eric strode out into the garden, his heart pounding and flushed with anger. He knew he mustn't make too much of a scene and was trying desperately to keep himself calm and under control.

'Can I ask you what the hell you're doing, reverend?'

Andrews stood and looked across at his parishioner, surprised at his aggression. Although he hadn't been in the village long and was certainly unsure how Eric regarded him, he had never seen him lose his temper before.

'Sorry, Eric, I didn't mean to cause any offence, I was just looking.'

Eric realized that panic had overtaken him and began to calm down.

'Sorry, reverend, it's a particular favourite of mine and I'm always worried about losing it.'

Andrews smiled.

'You've no need to worry, Eric, I was being very careful. You really do have green fingers. Given the kind of soil you've got here, this bush shouldn't stand an earthly. How do you do it?'

Eric shook his head briskly, dismissing the compliment and eager to change the subject.

'No idea, you'd need to ask my mother, she put it in years and years ago. All I do is keep the thing trimmed really. It's a beautiful sight in the spring, though.'

The reverend looked suitably impressed. 'She must have been a fine gardener, your mother. I've been trying to grow one for years. Lost cause, I'm afraid.'

Eric forced a short smile as the vicar continued. 'Mind if I take some soil samples, Eric? Might give me the answers I've been looking for.'

'Not at the moment, reverend, it's not a good time. I'll bring you some round later when the snow's cleared a bit.'

'Well, as long as that's a promise I'll leave it for now, but I'm jealous, Eric.'

Eric Chambers changed the subject.

'Your tea's getting cold, reverend, and I want to hear about this Bishop's concert, see if I can help.'

Andrews smiled up at him. 'Right you are Eric, let's go in.'

*

Dominic Parr lived on the Berwick Estate in Milton. It was a small, compact estate that lacked both charm and character. Sam parked outside the house and made her way towards the front door. She rang the doorbell firmly and waited. After a few moments she tried again, this time letting the bell ring longer. Putting her ear close to the door she strained her ears for any sign of life but there was nothing. Exploring the side of the house she found it barred by a large brown wooden gate. As she retreated back towards her car, she glanced up towards the front bedroom window and saw one of the curtains move as if being dropped back into position by an unseen hand. She continued to stare at the window but there was no further movement. As she began to climb back into her car she noticed a middle-aged woman turn suddenly from the street and onto the house's driveway. She was carrying two heavy plastic shopping bags and seemed to stagger more than walk. As she put one of the bags down and rummaged through her purse for the front door key, Sam walked over and spoke.

'Mrs Parr?'

The woman turned and eyed Sam suspiciously. 'Who wants to know?'

'Sorry, I'm Doctor Ryan, Doctor Samantha Ryan from the Park Hospital.'

'I didn't call you out, sure you've got the right address?'

'I've come to see your son, Dominic.'

'Is he ill?'

'It's nothing like that, I'm a pathologist.'

She eyed Sam even more suspiciously. 'Are you sure you've got the right house? Dominic was all right when I left, I've only been gone half an hour.'

'No, I'm investigating the death of a friend of his, Simon Vickers. I thought Dominic might be able to help.'

Mrs Parr's voice deepened menacingly.

'I don't want my son mixed up in anything like that. He has his problems but he wouldn't go around stealing cars.'

'He won't be, I'm just finishing off the inquiry, you know, dotting the "i"s and crossing the "t"s.'

Mrs Parr wasn't convinced but opened the door nevertheless.

'Suppose you'd better come in then.'

Sam followed her into the hall. As soon as Mrs Parr was in the house she screamed out her son's name.

'Dominic, you've got a visitor!'

'I'm not sure he's in, I rang a couple of times and . . .'

Mrs Parr dumped the two heavy bags on top of the kitchen table before returning to the bottom of the stairs.

'He's in all right, just can't be bothered to answer the bloody door, lazy little sod. Dominic, if you're not down here in thirty seconds I'll come up there and drag you down!'

They waited. Suddenly, a slim, pasty-faced boy in his late teens appeared at the top of the stairs.

'There's a pathologist here wants to ask you a few questions!'

Dominic only came halfway down the stairs and seemed reluctant to venture any further. Probably keeping out of range of his mother's hand, Sam pondered. His eyes darted nervously between his mother and Sam. Mrs Parr looked at Sam.

'Well, here he is, you can ask what you like now.'

Sam wasn't sure what kind of a response she was going to get with Mrs Parr eyeing her nervous son.

'I wonder if it would be possible to see Dominic on his own. I've a few embarrassing questions to ask him, and, you know what teenage boys are like about these sorts of things.'

'Whatever you like.' She looked up at her son. 'Make

119

sure you answer all the doctor's questions, otherwise I'll have something to say about it.'

Sam nodded her thanks at Mrs Parr who returned to the kitchen and started to unpack her bag.

'Shall we have a chat in your room?'

Dominic nodded and Sam followed him up the stairs.

Entering the room Sam was struck by how similar it was to Simon's. Although smaller and more compact Dominic had similar posters, wallpaper and bed covers. At the centre of the room, against the outside wall, was a large desktop computer, which was surround by expensive-looking equipment. Stuck against the side of the computer was a small, yellow sticky label with a picture of a bee, similar to the one she'd seen in Simon's room. There was only one chair in the room, so Sam perched herself on the edge of the bed while Dominic stood at the opposite side of the room, his hands in his pockets, swaying nervously from side to side. He spoke for the first time.

'Are you the police?'

Sam shook her head. 'Why, are you expecting them?'

'Not really, but you look like the police.'

Sam felt quite insulted by this observation. The last thing she thought she looked like was a policewoman.

'No, I'm not the police. Like your mum said, I'm a pathologist.'

He shrugged. 'Same thing.'

'No, nothing like the same thing.'

'So you've nothing to do with the police, then?'

'I work with them sometimes, that's all.'

Dominic didn't look convinced. Sam continued, 'I did the second postmortem examination on Simon. That's what I've come to talk to you about.'

Dominic watched her but remained silent.

'You see, I think Simon was murdered.'

Dominic stopped his swaying and stared at her in disbelief. He looked genuinely shocked.

'Murdered? I thought it was an accident, that he was killed in that car crash.'

'So did everyone else but he wasn't. It looks as though he was strangled.'

Dominic began to become agitated. 'If he was murdered why aren't the police here?'

'They will be,' Sam lied, 'but there's a few questions I'd like to ask you first.'

He began swaying again.

'Like what?'

'Like what happened the night Simon died?'

He shrugged again. 'Don't know, he never turned up.'

'You were supposed to be meeting up then?'

Dominic nodded.

'Yea, he'd got a new scanner and wanted me to see it, see if I wanted one, like.'

'Sounds expensive, you must have a good job.'

'Not really, just stacking shelves, but Simon could get the stuff cheap so I could just about cover it.'

'Where did he get it from?'

Dominic shrugged. 'Don't know, didn't say.'

'And you didn't ask?'

'No, why should I? It was cheap.'

Sam indicated to his computer.

'Looks like you've got a lot of kit here, must be worth a bit.'

'Computer's secondhand, it's Simon's old one. He got me the rest of the stuff at a lot less than it costs in the shops.'

'It still has to be paid for. What did you do, save up?'

'Yea, that's right, saved up.'

'You must be a good saver.'

Dominic nodded. 'Nothing else to spend my money on.'

Sam returned to the point.

'Did Simon tell you he wasn't coming?'

Dominic shook his head.

'Has he let you down before?'

'Couple of times...'

'But he normally lets you know?'

'Normally. I thought he must be ill or something.'

'Didn't you bother ringing him to see where he was?'

'No. We don't use the phone, just send messages between our computers. More interesting that way. Anyway what's the point? I was going to see him at college the next day, he'd have explained then.'

'What time did you expect him?'

'Some time after twelve, normal time.'

'That's late.'

'Web sites are clearer late at night, easier to use.'

Sam nodded. 'When did you find out he'd been killed?'

'When I got back from college. When he wasn't there. Like I said I just thought he was ill or something. I checked my messages but there was nothing so I sent him a couple to see if he would respond like, but he didn't.' That explained two of the messages, Sam thought.

Dominic continued, 'Then the nosy old cow from next door comes around saying she's heard this report on the radio that Simon's dead. I didn't believe her at first, she's always saying things that aren't true. I knew Simon was no thief, he couldn't even drive a car, never mind nick one. I cycled around to his house...'

'Mr Vickers said he hadn't seen you since Simon's death.'

'I didn't go in. There was this police car outside the house and that was enough.'

'What do you think about the idea of him being

murdered?'

'Makes more sense I suppose, although who would want to kill Simon? Everyone liked him. I know that's the kind of thing that people say when someone kicks it, but it's still true.'

'Didn't he have any enemies?'

'No, none that I know of anyway. Like I said, everyone liked him. He was all right, easy to get on with.'

'But he was your friend.'

'Yea, he was.' Dominic seemed proud of the fact.

'You knew him well then?'

He nodded. 'Yea, well enough.'

'Do you think he was capable of stealing a car?'

Dominic shook his head firmly.

'No, I don't think so. He hated the bloody things, that's why we went everywhere on our bikes.'

'When I was at Simon's house I tried to have a look at some of his messages but I couldn't get into his files because they're protected by a password. I don't suppose you know what that password is do you? It's very important.'

Dominic shook his head.

'Sorry, no idea. He kept that kind of thing to himself.'

Sam wasn't sure why, but she knew he was lying. She would have to be careful.

'Any idea what it might have been?'

Dominic shook his head again. 'Haven't a clue.'

'If Simon really was your friend why are you lying to me? You know what Simon's codes are, why won't you tell me?'

He was becoming increasingly nervous again.

'I don't know, honestly I don't. We were friends sure, but he didn't tell me everything.'

'About computers, he did.'

'No, no he didn't. He kept a lot of stuff to himself.'

'Are you going to tell the police the same story when they turn up to question you?'

'Suppose so, why not? It's the truth.'

Sam pulled out the photograph she had taken of the fly inside Simon's room and showed it to the boy.

'Any idea what that's all about?'

He looked at it and handed it straight back. 'It's a fly, it was Simon's Net name.'

Sam was more confused than ever.

'What's his Net name?'

'If you want to talk to someone and don't want them to know who you are, you invent a Net name. You know, a name you can hide behind when you're using the Web. Then, if someone wants to call you, they just send out your Net name and you can pick it up. That's why your Net name has to be special to you.'

Sam began to understand.

'Like an insect?'

'Dominic nodded. 'Yea, that's right, like an insect.'

'Is your Net name the bee?'

He looked at her nervously.

'Yea, that's right. How did you know that?'

Sam handed him the photograph of the bee.

'It matches the one on the side of your computer.' He stared at it for a moment before handing it back to Sam. She held up the picture of the ant next.

'Know who this is?'

He looked at it and shook his head. 'No, no idea.' He handed it back.

'That's odd because Ricky knows you. I saw him putting your Net address on my computer the other day. Does the name Ricky Copson mean anything to you?'

He backtracked quickly.

'Yea I know him, he uses the club, he's okay, cool.'

'But you couldn't remember his net name was Ant?'

'I can now, sorry, just slipped my mind for a minute. So many names stored up there, it's difficult to remember sometimes. How do you know him?'

'I'm his aunt.'

He nodded, even more nervous than before. Sam felt frustrated – he was clearly hiding something but what?

'Who's the Spider?'

At the mention of the Spider, Dominic's colour seemed to drain.

'No idea, never heard of him.'

'That's what you just said about the ant.'

'I know, but I really haven't heard of any Spider.'

'It was one of the drawings Simon kept by his computer. Thought you might know who he was.'

Dominic shook his head vigorously wetting his lips with his tongue.

'Sorry, like I said, I don't.'

Sam leaned forward towards him. 'For someone who was suppose to be close to Simon you don't seem to know very much, do you?'

Dominic swallowed hard.

'He was private about some things. I mean, I would never have thought he'd steal a car, but he did.'

Sam was becoming increasingly annoyed at Dominic's lack of cooperation.

'He didn't seem to tell you much. Odd sort of a friend.'

Dominic didn't answer. Sam produced Simon's sketch-pad and showed him the drawing at the front.

'Can you explain this? Weird drawing, don't you think? Was there something on Simon's mind?'

Dominic swallowed hard. 'Don't know, never seen them before.'

'Stop lying, Dominic, just tell me what you know and I'll

leave you alone.'

'I don't know anything, I don't. It was just another Net name that Simon knew about. He didn't say who he was, just that he was called the Spider.'

'You do know about him then?'

'No, look I forgot, Simon might have mentioned him a couple of times, I can't remember. But he never told me who he was.'

'I wonder what else we can try to make you remember. Was Simon frightened of him?'

'I don't know, he didn't say.'

'I get the impression from this drawing that he was.'

'Perhaps he was, but he didn't tell me.'

'Memory playing tricks with you again is it Dominic? You must have some idea. I can't imagine Simon kept that kind of information to himself.'

'He was Simon's contact not mine. I had nothing to do with him.'

He was becoming increasingly agitated and nervous and Sam wasn't sure whether further questioning would help or just make things worse.

'All right, Dominic, if that's all you've got to say. But remember, just because Simon's dead doesn't mean he doesn't still need your help. If you know something or remember anything later then please call me. Help me catch your friend's killer before he does it again.'

Dominic shrugged. 'I've told you all I can, honest.'

Sam pulled a card from her purse and left it on the edge of the desk.

'If you think of anything else then you can get hold of me on any one of those numbers, okay?'

He didn't respond. Sam was firmer.

'Okay?'

He nodded and picked up her card.

'Okay.'

'I'll expect to hear from you soon, then?'

He didn't move and Sam left the room. Mrs Parr was waiting for her at the bottom of the stairs.

'Helpful, was he?'

Sam nodded. 'Told me all he could I think.'

'Good. He can be an awkward little sod when he wants to be.'

As Sam left, Dominic watched her from his bedroom. As soon as he felt safe again he returned to his computer. Pulling out the floppy disc from the drive he kissed it and dropped it into the top pocket of his jacket. Without knowing it the nosy pathologist had just made him a fortune.

5

Sam PARKED HER CAR BETWEEN TWO WHITE AND RED TRAFFIC cars outside the Cambridge Constabulary's traffic wing. After locking her car she made her way purposefully into the reception and rang the bell marked 'push'. After a few moments a tall, miserable-looking man in late middle age appeared from the office behind the reception desk. From his ill-fitting and stained uniform Sam deduced that he was a civilian operator. These operators were recruited to replace police officers in an administration capacity, thus releasing trained police officers back onto the streets. For the most part they were made up of former police officers subsidizing their pensions with a few years' more work before finally being put out to grass, although Sam dreaded to think which department this sad-looking individual was attached to.

'Can I help you, luv?'

It was the second time someone had called her 'luv' recently. Sam disliked his patronizing tone almost as much as she disliked being called luv, but she needed his help so she forced herself to remain calm.

'I've come to see Sergeant Williams.'

His tone remained monosyllabic and patronizing.

'Is he expecting you, luv?'

Sam finally flared.

'I'm not your luv, so I would appreciate it if you didn't keep calling me it. And yes, he is expecting me.'

The civilian operator remained silent for a moment as if stunned by Sam's outburst, before gathering himself and retreating morosely back into his office. Sam watched him go, and waited. After a few moments the smiling face of Sergeant Williams appeared from the office.

'Doctor Ryan?'

Sam nodded.

'Sergeant Williams. Sorry to keep you waiting.'

He put his hand out and Sam shook it. His bright personality contrasted sharply with that of the previous encounter.

'You haven't, I've only just got here.'

He pulled open the office door and invited Sam through.

'We'll go and see the car shall we? It's on the forecourt, opposite side of the garage, it's only a short walk.'

Sam followed him through the offices and across a large garage before emerging once more into the light. The forecourt was littered with old and damaged cars in various states of decay.

'I think what you're looking for is over here,' said Williams, walking towards the far corner of the yard.

Sam followed him towards a blackened and twisted wreck. The car, if indeed it could still be referred to as such, barely resembled a vehicle. Instead it appeared to Sam as a twisted and grotesque parody, a mirror image of the tragic end to Simon Vickers's promising young life.

'Well, here it is. I'm not sure what you think you can do with it.'

He raised his eyebrows as Sam walked slowly around the car.

'Were you the first on the scene of the accident?'

'Almost, couple of local lads beat me to it.'

'Discover anything wrong with it?'

He shook his head. 'Nothing out of the ordinary, if that's what you mean.'

'What about the brakes and steering?'

He shrugged.

'Couldn't tell really, too much fire damage.'

Sam stopped at the front of the car for a moment.

'How fast was it going when it collided with the tree?'

'About forty.'

'How do you know that if everything was burnt?'

'Wing mirrors.'

Sam looked confused.

'When a car stops as suddenly as this one did, bits of it keep going, like the wing mirrors. They were found about twenty metres in front of the car with no obstructions, which gives the car an approximate speed of around forty mph.'

'And if it was going at thirty?'

'About eight and a half metres.'

Sam smiled at him.

'So it really is all done with mirrors.'

'Something like that.'

She peered through the driver's door into the scorched interior. 'What gear was he in when he crashed?'

'Second.'

'Bit of a low gear for forty miles an hour.'

'Drunks do odd things.'

Sam looked up at him. 'But he wasn't drunk enough not to drop into a low gear like the sign at the top of the hill suggests?'

Williams wasn't impressed.

'Might still have been in a low gear from climbing the hill, like the sign at the bottom of the hill suggests.'

'Car must have been screaming a bit in that low a gear?'

'I'd have thought so. But who was going to hear anything up there at that time of night?'

Sam remembered the poacher's description of the car's total silence as it rolled down the hill prior to the explosion. It just didn't fit the circumstances she had discovered here.

'What about brake and skid marks?'

Williams shook his head.

'There were none.'

'He took no evasive action at all? Didn't he even try and brake?'

'No. He came straight down the hill, hit the edge of the road and crashed headlong into the tree. Must have been over in seconds.'

Sam looked at him quizzically. 'Don't you think that's a bit odd?'

'Not for a double D. Sorry, drunken driver. When you're that pissed you do all sorts of strange things. He might have even lost consciousness. He wouldn't be the first drunk to do that and crash. At least this time he only killed himself and not some other poor sod.'

'What about the tyres, anything worth noting on those?'

Williams shook his head. 'Anything worth examining was destroyed by the fire. Sorry.'

Sam nodded thoughtfully and walked to the back of the car.

'What about the explosion, how did that happen?'

'Like they normally happen. Spilling petrol onto a hot engine finally blows back to the petrol tank and bang. The car used unleaded petrol as well. It's far more flammable.'

Sam was puzzled.

'So the main explosion was at the back of the car?'

'Yes, in the petrol tank, why?'

Sam shrugged.

'No reason.'

She was lying. If the explosion had been at the back of the car then why were all the shrapnel and fibres blasted into the front of Simon's body. With this in mind she changed tack.

'Have you still got the bottle of whisky they found at the scene?'

'No sorry, lab's got it. I've got their number if you want it.'

'No, it's okay, I know where they are.' Sam sighed deeply. 'So you found nothing out of the ordinary at all?'

Williams shook his head again. 'No, should I have done?'

'Maybe, I'm not sure.'

You could try talking to Rebecca Webber.'

'Who's she?'

'One of the county's fire investigation officers. She was at the scene and had a good look at the car.'

'Why?'

'County policy. They always attend fatal fires no matter where they occur.'

'Any idea where I might find her?'

'Fire station might be a good start.'

Sam grinned.

'Thanks, I'll have a chat with her.'

As Sam began to walk back towards the traffic wing she stopped for a moment.

'One last question.'

Williams looked at her expectantly.

'Do you know where Simon Vickers's bike was found?'

'Outside the house where he nicked the car.'

Sam thought for a few seconds.

'This model of car, easy to steal is it?'

'Normally, it's fairly straightforward but this one had some sort of specialist computer locking system on it so I'm surprised it went.'

'What if our thief was some sort of specialist computer operator or programmer?'

Williams shrugged.

'Possibly, but I believe you really would have to know what you were doing.'

Sam nodded in agreement.

'I think our killer does.'

Despite her enthusiasm, Sam knew she couldn't collect all the evidence she needed on her own. If she was to have any chance at all of convincing Tom Adams of her theories then she needed help, and given her current circumstances there was really only one person she could turn to: Marcia Evans. Sam hadn't seen Marcia for a while. She'd talked to her on the phone a couple of times, even managed to arrange a couple of evenings out, but had to cancel them both at the last minute because of work. Turning up now, she considered, might seem a bit cynical, but she really didn't see what other choice she had. Sam just hoped their friendship could stand it. She'd fallen out with enough close friends recently, and was running a bit short of them.

A few minutes after eleven o'clock Sam found herself driving along the tree-lined road leading to the Forensic Science Laboratories at Scrivingdon. Despite the obvious picture postcard attraction of the frost and snow over the landscape, Sam wished the weather would start to warm up. She would be glad to see the back of the snow, even though the thought of a white Christmas was appealing. Unfortunately the cold had brought with it a lot of additional pressures and a thaw might ease some of those. She'd dealt with a teenage death from hypothermia the previous week, and then there were the increased deaths from accidents as well as suicides, which always increased during this season of joy. Unfortunately the weather forecast suggested that the freezing temperatures were set for some days yet.

Passing through the security gate, Sam parked her car in front of the laboratory and made her way inside. She enjoyed her visits to Scrivingdon. She felt like a child let loose in a toyshop. Everywhere she looked, white-coated scientists, their hands protected with tight clear latex gloves, examined a variety of objects from jackets to pants, searching for minute samples and trace elements, trying hard to uncover vital evidence on which rested the hopes and fears of innocent and guilty alike. For many years Scrivingdon had been a Home Office laboratory, and only worked for the police and the authorities. In more recent years it had become semi-independent and now worked for either side on a commercial basis, and forensic science wasn't cheap.

Sam soon found Marcia's room. She knocked and entered. Marcia was standing at the far end of the laboratory taping a pair of green and brown combat trousers. Sam greeted her gently.

'Morning, Marcia, long time no see.'

Marcia turned. 'Good grief, look what the snow has just blown in. Trouble at mill, Doctor Ryan?'

Marcia always became formal and called Sam by her surname when she was annoyed or irritated by her.

'No, not really. I happened to be passing and I thought I'd pop in and see how things were going.'

Marcia returned to her work. 'You live, and work, on the other side of the county. Just passing, I'm sure.'

'Well, you know I had a bit of business to do at the lab and I took the opportunity to see you.'

'Who with?'

'What do you mean?'

'Who in the laboratory did you have "a bit of business" with?'

Sam was stumped. 'Okay, okay, I came to see you. I need your help. Happy now?'

Marcia nodded.

'Yep. Now, are you going to tell me what you want?'

'Only if you'll let me buy you lunch.'

'No bribes, Sam. I haven't seen you for weeks and the first time you manage to drag yourself across here it's because you want something, not to see me.'

'Sorry. I have tried, it's just a matter of time, or the lack of it.'

Marcia glared at her, unconvinced, and grunted.

'Look, let me buy you lunch. We can catch up with all sorts then.'

Marcia stopped working for a moment and stared at her friend.

'I think you'd better tell me what it will cost me first.'

'I'm re-examining the death of a young boy called Simon Vickers.'

'The boy killed on Herdan Hill?'

Sam nodded.

'It was in the paper. It seemed straightforward enough.'

'Well it wasn't, but I'm having problems convincing the police of that.'

'I thought Tom Adams was putty in your hands.'

'So did I. My charms are obviously waning.'

'So what do you want me to do?'

'I can't do it all on my own, I need some help and I don't know anyone else I can trust.'

Marcia returned to her work.

'I'll have to think about it.'

'Well, if you can come, I thought the Dog and Duck at one. If that's all right?'

Marcia looked up. 'That's a bit of a way isn't it?'

'I think it's best we keep any meetings quiet for the moment.'

Marcia suddenly lifted two long strands of hair from the bottom of the trousers she was examining.

'That should do it, let him talk his way out of this one, I don't think.'

Sam walked across to her. 'What have you got?'

'With a bit of luck some hair samples from the scene of a burglary. The owner of these delightful fashion statements, along with two of his mates, burgled no less than fifty homes over two weeks. So far, and with the help of their "concerned" solicitors, they have refused to say a word. If this fibre matches the ones found at the last scene then we've got the little sod.'

'I thought you said there were three of them. What about the other two?'

'Market forces, Sam, market forces. Since we entered the market place our rates have had to go up, and with police budgets being slimmed down all the time, they can only afford to have one garment checked.'

'And the other two?'

'The other two?' She gave a short sarcastic laugh, 'the other two walk.'

'That's ridiculous.'

'No, that's the law. And before you say it, yes, the judicial system is being taken over by accountants and greedy slimy lawyers and no one could give a stuff.'

Sam edged a little closer to her friend.

'There is one other small thing that might be helpful, if

you wouldn't mind doing it.'

'What?' Marcia replied without looking up.

'A whisky bottle was collected from the scene of the accident. I was wondering if you could find it and see what the brand was. It might help if you could let me know if they found anything on it as well.'

Marcia looked at her for a moment, mulling over the request.

'I'll think about it.'

Sam nodded nervously. 'I'll see you at the pub at one then?'

'Maybe.'

Sam turned and left.

Dominic Parr realized he'd have to act quickly. Although Sam's visit had caught him off guard, the fact that the woman pathologist had told him Simon had been murdered was going to be very useful. Play the fool, he pondered, and it's surprising what people tell you. The information had presented opportunities that he had only dreamt of until that moment. Perhaps the best turn his friend had ever done for him was being murdered and not merely killed in some bloody stupid road accident. At last he could break away from the rathole of a house, his nagging stupid mother, and his shit of a life and really live it up a little. With the kind of money he'd get now, he could set himself up for life. Go anywhere, do anything, and all first class. Simon might have been afraid of the Spider, but *he* wasn't, and now it was time for him to pay. All the plans they'd made would be realized after all. Although Simon wouldn't be there in person, he would be in spirit. Still looking after him, even from beyond the grave. It was a bit spooky really, he thought, but then Simon always did say they were friends forever.

The only real threat came from Ricky and his nosy aunt. But Ricky would keep his mouth shut, he'd have to, he was in it almost as deep as Dominic was. For now, however, he needed to plan. Plan everything down to the last detail with no mistakes, slip-ups or stupidity. Although he knew his brain didn't match Simon's, he'd picked up a thing or two from his friend and felt sure he could carry it off. The first place he needed to visit was Simon's parents to get his own hard copy of the messages Doctor Ryan had mentioned. It shouldn't be difficult. He'd just make up some story and they were bound to let him in, especially if he made himself look as tragic as possible. Then, once he'd got it, he'd have to send it down the line to the Spider, with a translation of course, that should shake things up a bit. Once he'd done that, a few more messages making his demands should finally settle matters. He wouldn't be greedy; just enough to see him in luxury for the rest of his life should do it. He chuckled to himself as he visualized his affluent future. He pulled his jacket from the back of the chair and slipped it on. Before leaving the room he took a quick glance at the photograph of Simon he kept above his computer.

'Thanks, Simon, thanks for being my mate, thanks for looking after me.'

He gave the photograph an affectionate stroke with his hand before making his way quickly to the back of his shed to collect his cycle and setting off to the Vickers' home. He'd never felt so alive in his life.

Sam arrived at the Dog and Duck slightly late but despite that there was no sign of Marcia. She decided to have a quick drink and if Marcia hadn't turned up by the time she'd finished, she would make her way back to the Park and think again. She had only just sat down when Marcia suddenly appeared by her side. She waved a thin brown file in Sam's face.

'I think you'd better make mine a double after what I've discovered.'

Sam squeezed her arm with pleasure and gratitude. 'I think I'll make it a triple. Want anything to eat?'

Marcia looked pointedly at her watch. 'No time, sorry, I've the biggest pile of work to catch up with.'

Sam got her drink and returned to her friend, who opened the file and passed Sam the top sheet of paper from it. Sam scanned it quickly. It was the report from the fingerprint expert who had examined the bottle and confirmed that the fingerprints found on the bottle were those of Simon Vickers. Sam looked across at Marcia, who was taking a long drink from her glass.

'How does he know they were Simon's? As I remember he didn't have any fingers left, never mind prints.'

Marcia put her drink down. 'He took some comparisons and eliminations from Simon's bedroom. Twenty-one points of similarity. They're his all right.'

Sam felt slightly stupid at not seeing the obvious. Marcia handed her two photographs of the bottle with the prints highlighted by dusting powder.

'What do you think of that?'

Sam looked at them. 'Simon Vickers's prints on a whisky bottle?'

Marcia smiled.

'Correct. But what's odd about it?'

Sam shrugged and shook her head.

'There's only one set and they're near perfect. If you're drinking from a bottle, and what's more getting drunk, you move your hand around. You don't hold it in one position indefinitely. There should be several sets of prints around the bottle, most of which should almost certainly be smudged.'

Sam knew Marcia was right.

'Why didn't fingerprints pick this up?'

'Gary Portant. He couldn't pick up a cold. He's only interested in picking up his pension and from what I can gather he was only asked to verify whether or not Simon's prints were on the bottle. It wouldn't have occurred to him to investigate any further. There's a couple of other things, too.' She pulled out several close-up photographs of the prints and handed them to Sam.

'Look at the spread patterns on the prints. They're not right.'

Sam concentrated her attention on them but couldn't see a problem.

'When you pick up some sort of weight, like a full bottle of whisky, you have to grip it hard. The harder you grip it the more your fingerprint pattern spreads, they become flatter, rounder, taking in more of the overall print.'

Marcia breathed hard onto the surface of her glass making it steamy, before pressing her fingers hard onto it and showing Sam.

'Look at those, see, very flat, very spread. Now watch.'

She copied her actions on the opposite side of the glass. This time however she touched the glass with her fingers one at a time, 'Now look. There's been very little pressure so the print is longer and thinner. Just like the ones on the bottle. They might be Simon Vickers's prints, but someone else has put them there.'

Sam looked at her and smiled as Marcia continued, 'There's also several unexplained sets of prints on the bottle as well.'

'Our killer?'

Marcia shrugged.

'Maybe. But more likely to be the prints of the person

who sold the bottle in the first place. I don't think our killer's stupid enough to leave his prints behind after engineering such an elaborate murder, do you?'

'We all make mistakes.'

'Well, perhaps you're right at that. The type of whisky's odd as well. Do you know what the brand was?'

Sam shook her head.

'It was Lagavulin, a very old and very expensive malt. Why would a kid who just wants to get pissed buy one of the most expensive whiskies there is? Surely he'd go for the cheapest? Unless he simply grabbed the nearest bottle from his parents' drinks cabinet. And why was it found outside the car?'

Sam smiled and shook her head with admiration as Marcia's face became animated. She raised a glass to her.

'We are so alike. You just can't help yourself, can you? You've discovered an inconsistency and now you have to explore it further. Yes, I wondered about the bottle being outside the car, there seems to be no evidence of scorching or any other damage which might have been sustained in the crash; unless you've an explanation for that? And his parents are teetotallers so he didn't get the whisky from his home.'

'That's it then Sam, you're right, we are dealing with a murder and yes I'm happy to help in any way that I can.'

Sam smiled warmly at her friend. If there was a soul mate for her then Marcia came as close as anyone she knew. They had spent many fulfilling hours over the years discussing the evidence from cases they were working on. They enjoyed many of the same interests and Marcia's gregarious and extrovert nature was a perfect counterfoil for Sam's more reserved and cool approach. Marcia finished her drink and looked across at Sam.

'So, what made you suspect?'

'When I performed the second PM on Simon's body I discovered his hyoid bone had been snapped.'

'So you think he was strangled and the accident staged to try and cover up the crime?'

'It wouldn't be the first time. Remember that bloke who strangled his wife and then put her neck on the railway line to try and make it look like suicide?'

'He got off, didn't he?'

'Yes, but only on a technicality.'

'Why didn't Trevor pick it up?'

Sam shrugged. 'It happens. The body was a bit of a mess after the fire, it's an easy thing to do. The problem with this case has been that everyone seems to have investigated it with preconceptions and they have all concentrated on the obvious and dismissed any signs which might have indicated anything out of the ordinary.'

'What does he think now?'

'He's not talking to me.'

'That bad, eh?'

Sam nodded. 'Worse.'

'I shouldn't worry too much, his male pride's been pricked, that's all, he'll come around.'

'I'm not so sure.'

'I am. For all their equality bullshit they still don't like women showing them up, but they'll just have to get used to the idea because we ain't going away and we're getting better all the time.'

Sam smiled at her friend, glad of her support.

'Are you sure it wasn't broken during the accident?' Marcia continued.

'Positive.'

Marcia leaned back in her chair. 'Whatever happened to "Never say never, never say always"?'

'There are exceptions to all the rules, and this is one of them.'

Marcia knew her old friend well enough not to argue with her on points of pathology.

'What did the police have to say about it?'

'They want more evidence before they will "commit resources". I think that's the current phrase.'

'So, what do you want me to do?'

'I'd like you to visit the crash sight first, see if you can pick anything up, anything that might have been missed.'

'Haven't the Traffic boys already done that?'

'Yes but perhaps not as thoroughly as they might have done, since they thought they were dealing with an accident, not a murder.'

Marcia nodded. 'Okay, I've got a few days' leave left, I'll see what I can do. No promises though, there might be nothing, especially after this weather.'

Sam smiled at her old friend.

'One other thing. When you're there look out for an old poacher.'

Marcia raised her eyebrows.

'He turned up when I was there, seemed to appear from nowhere.'

'Sounds like my boss.'

'He was a witness to the accident but won't come forward, well, not officially, anyway. I think he knows something important, it's just a case of trying to get him to tell us and, more importantly, the police, what he saw.'

'I'll have to use my charms on him.'

'I'd wait until you've seen him before making those kinds of commitments.'

'That bad, eh?'

Sam nodded and Marcia shrugged. 'I'm sure I've had worse.'

Sam looked at her.

'I know you have.'

Marcia's mouth opened in shock before the two women dissolved into giggles.

After some searching Sam managed to find a suitable parking place just outside the main fire station office where the fire investigation team were based. As Sam followed the signs across the car park towards the far side of the building, her eye was drawn towards a new, red BMW Z3 sports car. She didn't know why but she just knew that it belonged to Webber. A bit fast and showy for Sam's taste, but obviously the vehicle of a person that liked to live in the fast lane of life. Sam climbed the long staircase towards the fire investigation team's office, glad that she had stuck to soft drinks in the pub. Marcia had a habit of getting her drunk even when they met for a 'quick one' and she knew she'd need a clear head if she was to gain anything from the afternoon meeting. She was pleased that Rebecca Webber had agreed to see her at such short notice. Sam was sure that she would not have been quite so accommodating had the roles been reversed. She knocked gently on the door marked 'Senior Fire Investigator'.

'Come in.'

Sam pushed the door open to be confronted by a tall, attractive woman in her mid-thirties with long brown hair caught back at the nape of her neck to reveal a very pretty face. She smiled at Sam and put her hand out.

'You must be Doctor Ryan. Pleased to meet you, although given your reputation you feel like an old friend.'

Sam took her hand and shook it gently.

'Thank you, all flattery gratefully accepted.'

'Please sit down.'

She guided her to a chair and sat down opposite, coming to the point at once.

'I understand you're taking another look at the accident on Herdan Hill?'

Sam nodded.

'How did you get on with Brian?'

'He was very helpful.'

'He normally is.'

Sam brought the conversation back to the point.

'Is it normal practice for fire investigation officers to attend car fires?'

'It varies from force to force. But we examine all fatal fires, car or otherwise.'

'As you know I'm not entirely happy that Simon Vickers's death was accidental and I was wondering if...'

'I could help you prove your case?'

Sam nodded. 'Something like that.'

'Sorry, I can't. I went over the car with a fine-tooth comb but didn't find anything out of the ordinary.'

Sam sighed deeply.

'It was a bit of a long shot.'

Webber smiled warmly at her.

'They're sometimes worth taking. Does Tom know what you're up to?'

There was something about the way she said 'Tom' that was warmer than Sam liked, but she put it to the back of her mind for the moment.

'Tom Adams, you mean?'

Rebecca nodded.

'He does, but he's not convinced yet. Wants a bit more evidence.'

'Men always do. Especially Tom.'

Her familiarity with his name increasingly unsettled Sam.

'You know Superintendent Adams well, then?'

'Quite well. We've worked together on a few cases. I've always found him quite receptive, well, once you've persuaded him round to your way of thinking, anyway.'

Sam gave her a half-smile. 'Sounds like you do know him well. Is your husband a fireman?'

'He was.'

'Divorced?'

This was a ridiculous turn of conversation but Sam needed to know.

'From the brigade? Well, sort of. He was killed a couple of years ago on his way to a fire.'

Sam suddenly felt cold.

'I'm sorry.'

'It was a while ago now, I've come to terms with it. What about you?'

'Single, can't find anyone willing to take on my lifestyle.'

'Tom said you were a busy woman. Driven was the word I think he used. Funny isn't it, if men are driven it's okay, but if women are they seem to think there's something wrong with us.'

Sam didn't think the conversation about her sounded very flattering. Besides, she wasn't driven, just professional.

'Well if that's all, I've got the biggest pile of work.'

'Sorry, yes, I've already taken up enough of your time. Thanks for seeing me. And if anything else does come to mind…'

'I'll call you. And don't give up on Tom. Like I said, he takes some persuading but I normally get what I want.'

Sam forced out a smile. As she opened the door, Rebecca Webber called across to her. 'There was one thing.'

Sam turned to face her.

'The explosion, I'm convinced it was at the front of the

car and not at the back where the fuel tank's situated. It's not exceptional but it is unusual. I don't know if that's any help at all.'

Sam nodded.

'Thanks, yes it might be.'

Although she was tired, Sam didn't go straight home. She decided to try a little experiment. First she drove to Simon Vickers's home in Impington and from there made her way by the shortest route to the house of Mr Enright, the owner of the stolen car, at the far side of Cherry Hinton. It took her just over forty minutes. Even allowing for traffic, which hadn't been particularly busy, it must have taken Simon longer, perhaps twice the time. If he left home at twelve the earliest he could have arrived at Enright's house was around one. Then he would have had to break into the car before making his way to Herdan Hill. At least another hour and a quarter. Which would have made it two fifteen. In the meantime he would have had to stop, buy his bottle of whisky, get drunk and then crash the car. Even if he had already bought the bottle and had a drink before he stole the car, there just wasn't enough time. The other fact that was perhaps less compelling but equally as important, was why Simon, if he was as drunk as it appeared, didn't crash before he reached Herdan Hill. The road, especially between Cherry Hinton and Herdan Hill, was particularly bad, with numerous hairpin and sharp bends. Why hadn't Simon lost control on one of those, especially given the state of the roads that night? How had he got so far unscathed? Perhaps at last she had an argument which would impress Tom Adams.

Sam arrived home feeling both alarmed and pleased. Alarmed at the possible relationship between Rebecca

Webber and Tom and pleased because the inquiry did seem to be moving forward. She had not only managed to get the support of both the parents but, more importantly, Marcia as well, despite having neglected her friend for months. Pulling onto her drive Sam spotted Tom Adams's large blue Rover parked in her usual place under the security lamp. He hadn't had it long and was very proud of it. As she climbed out of the car she wondered what he wanted. It was a bit soon even for Tom to have discovered Sam's clandestine inquires into the Simon Vickers case. She let herself in and made her way quickly into the sitting room. She needn't have worried, Tom and Wyn were standing by a very tall Christmas tree, which they had secured into an old tin bucket, and were busy decorating. Wyn looked across at her and, picking up a large glass of red wine from the top of the fireplace raised it to her.

'Merry Christmas, Sam.'

Tom followed suit.

'Yes, Merry Christmas.'

Sam put down her case and walked across to them. 'Nice tree.'

Wyn indicated Adams. 'Tom bought it, he tells me buying a live tree is a bit of a tradition in this house. He's brought a few presents as well.'

'Not to be opened until Christmas,' said Tom, giving Sam a severe glance.

Sam stood admiring the tree.

'Where did you get it?'

'I picked it up from the Forestry Commission place in Telford, remember?'

Sam did. Had it really been a year since they went together to collect the last tree? It had been a clear, fresh morning when they'd mixed with numerous other people all vying for the best-shaped tree. It was funny, really, there were dozens of trees, yet everyone seemed to want the same one, and there was a bit of a feeding frenzy. As a local brass band played carols and the WRVS served hot coffee and mince pies, Tom eventually found one that they both liked. It had been close though, someone else was holding it up when they first spotted it, and they were forced to hover around in the hope that it would be put down again. The trouble was, several other people also had their eye on the tree, so when it was eventually dropped, Tom had to be very quick off the mark and beat a rather angry-looking woman by a whisker.

'I was worried that you might already have one.' Tom's voice brought Sam back to reality.

'No, haven't had time.'

'Too busy involving yourself in the Simon Vickers case, I expect?'

Sam realized he was only fishing for information.

'Somebody has to. By the way, was it you that told Trevor I'd agreed to do the second PM after I specifically asked you not to?'

Tom shook his head. 'No, it was Chalky, I'm afraid. Sorry. I've spoken to him; it won't happen again.'

'Who's he got it in for, me or my theories?'

'Both, I think. He's a bit old fashioned.'

'Old fashioned, he's a sexist pig. He's really caused me problems.'

Tom nodded, 'Yes, well I'm sure he has, he's not the most diplomatic of men, but he's still a good copper.'

Tom was loyal, sometimes to the point of distraction, but Sam admired him for it nevertheless. Wyn suddenly broke in. 'Fancy a glass of plonk?'

Adams looked across at her and smiled.

'I'd love one, thanks.'

Wyn nodded and glanced across at her sister. 'Good

excuse to open another bottle of your best red.'

With that Wyn disappeared into the kitchen and Sam turned her attention back to Tom, who was sipping from his glass.

'Drinking on duty, officer, tut, tut, whatever next?'

Tom put the glass down. 'It's my day off, we do get them occasionally you know.'

Sam changed the subject.

'I was talking to a friend of yours today.'

Tom looked interested.

'Rebecca Webber?'

Tom flushed as he replied. 'Oh yes, the fire investigations officer. We've worked on a few cases in the past. Nice woman.'

'Yes she seemed very nice. Spoke well of you.'

'Did she?'

'She tells me that with enough hard work you can be persuaded to do anything.'

Tom remained silent but continued to look awkward.

'There's nothing going on there I ought to know about is there?'

He shook his head earnestly.

'No, nothing, just a professional relationship like many others.'

He looked at Sam and raised his eyebrows.

'I thought she was very attractive.'

'Yes, I suppose she is.'

He changed the topic quickly.

'I missed you today, wasn't quite the same picking the tree on my own. Too many memories, I think.'

The sleight of hand was extremely obvious.

'I'm surprised you were on your own.'

Tom wouldn't be drawn any further.

'Are we still on for Saturday?'

Sam reappeared from the side of the tree.

'Yes, we're still on for Saturday.'

'Good, then I'll pick you up at eight.'

'I'll look forward to it.'

Sam was desperate to tell him what she had discovered, but held back for the moment. She knew she wouldn't get too many more opportunities to convince him of her case, and wanted as much ammunition as she could muster before commencing her final onslaught.

Wyn entered the room with a fresh bottle of wine and filled all their glasses. Raising her own glass she looked at her two companions.

'To us, a very merry Christmas.'

Tom and Sam glanced briefly at each other, then raised their glasses in response.

'Merry Christmas.'

As the laboratory wasn't busy and her pending cases were bland and uninteresting, Marcia decided to book the rest of the week off. She waited until after the rush hour before travelling to Herdan Hill to have a look at the crash site. Her car, an ancient and seldom serviced Ford Escort estate, struggled to reach the top of the hill and then spluttered uncertainly like an exhausted fell runner. She found the scene quickly, the charred bark of the tree and the small floral memorial clearly marking the spot. She parked up in the small gravelled car park by the wooden viewing gallery and moved around to the back of the car. Although the sun peeped out for a moment the wind was still bitingly cold, and easily cut through the several layers of clothes she had wrapped around herself. She hoped that the freezing conditions wouldn't affect her car too much. She didn't fancy the long and steep walk back to the road and as no one else would be stupid enough to climb the Hill in the current conditions the chances of thumbing a lift from a passing motorist were slim. Still, she thought, she could always freewheel it down to the road. The thought cheered her as she opened the car's boot and exchanged her smart town shoes for a pair of practical rubber wellingtons, picked up her murder bag and the long search stick which she had 'borrowed' from a Special Operations man, and made her way to the scene.

The memorial was quite touching, with flowers from the boy's family and friends, plus several anonymous bunches of wild and cultivated plants. Most of the bunches were past their best, even the ones from relatives, people clearly found it difficult and even dangerous to climb the hill at this time of the year and had made the journey only once. The one exception to this was a small bunch of African Violets, which had obviously been left recently and were still in full bloom. Marcia crouched down and admired their vivid colours.

As she did so she thought she heard something or someone move in the bushes behind her. She turned quickly, but there was nothing. Marcia shrugged mentally, probably an animal she pondered. Removing a small but quality camera from her bag, she began to photograph the scene and surrounding area. She took pictures of the roads, the tree, in fact anything that took her fancy or which she thought might be of interest later. Finally, changing the film, she panned the camera along the road from the top of the hill, past the crash scene before following the road as it disappeared through the trees and down the hill. This gave her an overall panoramic view of the scene. She would have examined the skid patterns next, but there weren't any. She wasn't entirely surprised to find nothing; even if there had been any to start with, the recent weather would have destroyed most, if not all of them. She crouched down for a better look but there

153

wasn't a mark. Nothing to indicate that he had skidded or braked before leaving the road and hitting the tree.

She looked back along the road. It was steep, probably a one in five incline, with a sharp bend to the right. The driver must have seen the bend even at night. Still, he was drunk, she thought, perhaps that was it, didn't see it until the last moment, bang. Returning to the side of the road she began to poke around in the foliage with her search stick for any debris that might have been missed by previous sweeps. Although she came across small pieces of glass from the car's shattered windscreen, which she dropped carefully into a clear plastic exhibit bag, there was very little else. It was when she got very close to the tree that she noticed an odd smell: chemicals. It was vaguely familiar but she couldn't place it. She put her nose close to the charred and blackened bark and breathed in deeply. It was stronger now, but try as she might, the source of the odour escaped her. Taking a scalpel and exhibit bag she scraped samples of the bark into it. Then, just to make sure, she cut away a large section of the bark and dropped that into her murder bag as well. Marcia was slightly disappointed with her limited findings and annoyed with herself that she hadn't been able to place the smell.

As she snapped her bag shut something caught her attention. It was nothing obvious, just a small flash of light that she saw out of the corner of her eye for an instant before it disappeared. She stopped and slowly scanned the bark of the tree. As she did the sun caught the object again, and Marcia finally managed to locate it. Something was embedded high up in the trunk just below the first layer of branches. Marcia looked around for some means to climb up but there was nothing.

'Want a hand, lass?'

Jack Falconer's deep disembodied voice made Marcia

jump. She spun around quickly pushing her stick in front of her like a spear for protection. Staring down at her was Jack Falconer's large, scruffy frame. She wasn't sure what to do; she was on her own in the middle of nowhere with a large powerful-looking man bearing down on her. Although he hadn't harmed Sam, that didn't necessarily mean he wasn't dangerous. It was probably the bunch of wild flowers she noticed Jack was clutching that calmed her down. Marcia couldn't imagine any attacker, no matter how bizarre, bringing his victim flowers before he committed some gross act. She looked down at them and tried to appear light-hearted.

'For me?'

He didn't see the funny side and shook his head, nodding towards the tree.

'No, for the lad, I'm looking after things until the weather picks up and his parents can come and freshen up the flowers.'

He walked past her and put the flowers down with the rest. Sam hadn't exaggerated. He was tall, ugly and very smelly. Marcia was surprised she hadn't smelt him before she saw him.

'Are you anything to do with that doctor woman that was here before?'

'Doctor Ryan?'

'Yea, think that was her name. Interested in the crash.'

'Yes, I'm helping her out. She said you saw the accident.'

He stood up and faced her. 'I saw it all right. Don't think it was any accident, though. Told her that.'

'What do you think happened then?'

He shrugged.

'Not sure, but it were no accident.'

'Have you told the police?'

He shook his head. 'Like I told your doctor friend, they don't bother me and I don't bother them. I prefer it that way.'

Marcia was becoming increasingly intrigued.

'So what makes you think it wasn't an accident?'

'He weren't moving, like a rabbit caught in a lamp he were, frozen. Living things always move, trees, grass, people. Even when you're sleeping you're still moving, but not he. His eyes were open, like, but he couldn't see nothing, I'm sure of that.'

'Might have been drunk or something?'

'No. I've seen a lot of dead things in my time, and he looked no better than any of them.'

Although Marcia believed him, she wondered what Tom Adams and the coroner would make of him. Not much, if she was any judge. Despite her concerns, however, Marcia decided to try and persuade him.

'Look, I realize you might not get on with the police but I really think...'

'No chance, lass, me and them walk different sides of the line.'

He changed the subject. 'What was it you were looking at when I was watching you?'

She wondered just how long he'd been there.

'There's something embedded in the tree and I wanted to pull it out. It might be important, but I can't reach.' She pointed towards it.

'I can see it, want a leg up?'

Falconer bent down linked his hands together and Marcia stepped into them. As she did he straightened up and pushed her high into the lower branches of the tree. Stretching both her body and arms she finally managed to reach the object and pull it free before Falconer lowered her gently back to the ground. Once on the floor she ran her hands over the object gently, trying to determine what it was. It was metal of some sort and very jagged, like a piece of shrapnel. Marcia was certain it had come from the car. Falconer glanced over her shoulder.

'What do you reckon it is?'

'Shrapnel from the car, I expect, blown into the tree when the car exploded. I'll have it analysed and we'll soon know.'

A sudden and unexpected rustling from the bushes at the far side of the road made Jack stand up abruptly and grip his shotgun tightly. His face became deep and alert as his eyes struggled to see through the dense foliage that led into the woods. Marcia thought he looked frightened.

'Are you okay?'

He glanced at her quickly without replying before backing slowly away from her, his head moving from side to side as if searching for someone or something. Marcia followed his stare but could see nothing. Suddenly he turned and ran, smashing through the trees and undergrowth like a man in a panic.

'Hang on, wait, I haven't finished, where can I find you, where…?' Marcia called after him.

Before she had time to finish he had disappeared from sight. She searched through the bushes and trees to see if she could spot what had frightened him, but there was nothing. Everything appeared to be as calm and as natural as when she had arrived. Finally, crouching down and opening her exhibit bag, she dropped both the bark and the grey charred piece of metal inside, clicking it shut quickly and returning to her car.

Sam was determined to take Fred's advice and visit Madam Wong in London, despite her scepticism. Although she found alternative remedies interesting, they had yet to prove their real worth to the more conventional world of medicine. Sam wasn't entirely convinced by their lotion and potion approach but she was desperate, and desperate people will clutch at any straw.

Arriving in Soho she found a parking spot on Dean Street and parked. Walking past both Blacks and the Groucho club, she entered Chinatown and located Madam Wong's shop. It wasn't difficult to find and was distinguished by the long queue which had formed outside. She hesitated, wondering whether it was worth the wait. Then, deciding that as she was there it would be ridiculous to leave, she joined the back of the queue. After about an hour, by which time there were only two more people in front of her, the woman who had been queuing immediately behind her suddenly spoke.

'Been before have you?'

Sam turned to face a small, shabbily dressed woman in her late sixties or early seventies. She shook her head and replied awkwardly, 'No, first time.'

'She's very good you know, Madam Wong. Don't trust foreigners as a rule, but she's very good. Only does noses, though. If there's anything else wrong with you you'll have to go elsewhere.'

Sam nodded reassuringly. 'It is my nose.'

'Good, you should be all right then. Do you know, I haven't queued like this since the war. Used to enjoy queuing then, got to know people. People had time for you in those days, no one's got time any more. Spoke to a woman on the tube the other day, she looked at me as if I were a mugger. Me, a mugger, at my age? Sense of smell been gone long, has it?'

'It's not entirely…'

The elderly woman didn't let her finish but broke in again quickly.

'Mine's been gone for twenty years, used to work with chemicals, I think that's what did it. Went to see my doctor, fat lot of good he was, so I came here. She's sorting me out okay.'

'You got your senses back?'

'About three-quarters, helluva lot better than nothing. She reckoned there was already too much damage for a full recovery. All those chemicals, you see, no insurance in them days, neither.'

Sam finally reached the entrance and turned her attention to the Chinese woman sitting by the side of the door.

'Twenty-five pounds please.'

Her words were short and to the point. The fee was twenty-five pounds. No cheques and certainly no credit cards were accepted. Sam paid up and the woman dropped the money into one of the desk drawers.

'Name?'

'Samantha Ryan.'

She wrote it into a large ledger that seemed to cover the front of the desk.

'Where from?'

'Cambridge.'

After she had finished writing she handed Sam what looked like an old raffle ticket, carefully noting the number and entering it by her name. She ushered her inside the shop.

The entrance hall was dark and gloomy and smelt strongly of pungent but unrecognizable substances. After a few minutes another Chinese woman appeared in the hall and directed Sam through one of the doors. The contrast was immediate. The room was large and bright with several large windows and whitewashed walls. Around the walls were numerous shelves, all of which contained dozens of jars in different colours and sizes. In the centre were two large, comfortable wicker chairs and the floor was covered in a patchwork of brightly coloured rugs. Madam Wong sat at the far side of the room behind a large oak desk, which was covered in papers, books and jars, and not entirely unlike her own desk at work. The one thing that really struck Sam, however, was the lack of a computer. She couldn't remember the last time she had seen an office or a doctor's surgery without one. As she entered the room, Madam Wong stood and walked across to her, smiling broadly and holding out her hand.

'Samantha, I'm very pleased to meet you. Please sit.'

She guided Sam to one of the wicker chairs and then sat in front of her. There was something warm and welcoming about Madam Wong that made her relax and feel at ease. She took Sam's right hand gently and examined it closely before exchanging it for the left.

'You are a healer, yet I see death all around you,' she said, looking into Sam's face quizzically.

'I'm a pathologist.'

Madam Wong nodded slowly. She then moved her hands up to Sam's neck and head, feeling every lump and bump on her scalp before examining her eyes, nose, mouth and tongue, nodding and making short notes as she went along. Sam strained to see what she was writing but it was all in Chinese. When she had finished, Madam Wong sat back in her seat.

'I would like you to provide samples of urine, blood and saliva. Do you have any objections?'

Sam couldn't see what good the examination or the samples would do for her condition, but decided not to question Madam Wong too deeply and await the results. Sam shook her head, 'Not at all, but I would prefer to take the blood sample myself with my own equipment.'

Madam Wong did not appear to be insulted, but after she reassured Sam that her equipment was of the highest standards, supplied by a major wholesaler and that needles and syringes were never used twice, Sam agreed to supply a blood sample using them.

Madam Wong rang a small brass bell on her table and the Chinese woman who had initially ushered her in appeared again and directed her to another room where the various samples were taken. When she had finished, Sam was asked to return at four o'clock for the results and was shown out of a side door.

Marcia wasn't easily put off and wanted far more information out of Jack Falconer than he had been willing to give. She also wanted an explanation for his odd behaviour on Herdan Hill. Checking her map she ringed several nearby villages; if he was a local poacher he wouldn't live far from his patch. Once she'd tracked him down to his lair he wouldn't get rid of her quite so easily the next time. As she entered each village she did the usual checks: Post Office, local pub, paper shop and the village police house if it had one. The first two villages yielded nothing and Marcia was beginning to doubt her theory when she finally arrived at the Post Office in Market Dayton. There Marcia was greeted by a very sweet and co-operative postmistress who recognized the poacher's description at once.

'You'll be wanting Jack Falconer. What's he been up to this time. That man could find trouble in a village full of angels.' She shook her head. 'He's not a bad man you understand, we've all had a few bits off Jack in the past.' She winked at Marcia knowingly. 'Just can't seem to live without trouble.' She gave a chuckle and then beckoned Marcia outside. Once on the street she directed Marcia to the far side of the village. 'You'll find his cottage about five miles outside the village. It's at the top end of a dirt track on your right. You can't miss it.'

Marcia thanked her and set off in pursuit of her prey.

She saw the smoke shortly after she left the village and at first couldn't quite work out where it was coming from, but it seemed to be across the same route she was taking. As she turned off the road and began to drive along an unkept farm track, she realized she was heading straight for it. After half a mile she found Jack Falconer's cottage. It was ablaze, with smoke and fire pouring from the thatched roof and billowing through the windows. Marcia jumped out of her car and, pushing her way through the gate, ran across to the cottage, unsure what she could do but compelled to take some form of action. She had no idea if Jack Falconer would be in there. She called out.

'Mr Falconer can you hear me? Mr Falconer!'

She ran around to the back of the cottage, shielding her face from the increasing heat. The entire cottage was now engulfed in flames and Marcia felt sure that if there was anyone inside they would almost certainly be dead by now. A sudden and painful scream from inside the inferno forced Marcia to reconsider. Throwing her jacket over her head to provide some kind of protection from the heat, she forced herself towards the back door, kicking at it desperately as she tried to force it open and screaming at the unseen person inside.

'Mr Falconer, over here, over here!'

Marcia wasn't quite sure which came next, the explosion or the feeling of flying through the air. All she really remembered was the door suddenly bursting open and fire pouring through the vacant space enveloping her in a ball of flame, before the force of the flying door, which had been blown off its hinges, picked her up and threw her smouldering form onto the overgrown garden.

Sam arrived back at the shop at four and was shown straight

in to Madam Wong's consulting room. She sat back in the wicker chair and Madam Wong came immediately to the point.

'The nerves leading to your olfactory bulb have been damaged especially the part relating to your sense of smell. To try and repair this damage we have to correct some of your body's imbalances. To do this we have to restore several elements. The first thing we discovered was a lack of Magnesium and Zinc in your system, these omissions have disturbed your body's natural energy flows.'

Sam listened intently and somewhat sceptically as Madam Wong continued, 'To correct these energy flows we are going to supplement your body with some trace elements together with herbal and homeopathic compositions.' She produced four different-coloured bottles from a drawer just behind her chair.

'You are to take one of these each day.'

Sam took the first bottle and nodded.

'The first one, in the red bottle, is a magnesium supplement, the second in the blue bottle is a zinc supplement. The other two in the green bottles, which are to be taken twice a day, are herbal compositions especially prepared for your body and condition. It will take a little while to work so be patient.'

Sam examined the last two bottles and the phrase 'Just because it's Chinese doesn't mean it won't kill you' flashed uncomfortably through her mind.

'How long is "a while"?'

A few weeks, maybe a month.'

'Will the tablets last that long?'

'Oh yes, I have given you plenty.'

Sam was still sceptical.

'How much extra do I owe you for these tablets?'

Madam Wong shook her head. 'Nothing, it's all included

within your consultation fee.'

'And if it doesn't work?'

'Then please return and we will try again for no extra charge but I think you will be pleased with what you have.'

Sam finally stood and shook her hand.

'Thank you for your time and trouble, it's appreciated.'

'It is only trouble if you do nothing with the medicine I have given you. It won't kill you, you know.'

She suddenly felt slightly embarrassed, as if Madam Wong had been reading her mind.

'I will. To be honest, I have little choice.'

'We all have choices, different paths are offered to us. We must try to take the right ones. It is not always easy.'

Sam took one last look at Madam Wong's smiling and confident face. It put her at ease and unsettled her all at the same time; it was as if she were staring through her mortal body and into her very soul. Sam turned quickly and left the surgery, closing the door firmly behind her.

Sam arrived home several hours later exhausted and stressed. Kicking off her shoes she went straight upstairs and threw herself onto the bed. She fell asleep instantly. She wasn't sure what time it was when the persistent ringing of the phone finally wakened her with a start. It was still dark. As she groped for the handset Sam managed to knock her bedside lamp onto the floor. Cursing, she finally found the receiver and pulled it under the covers with her. When she wasn't on call, she would normally turn the phone off and let the answering machine take all her messages, but in her exhausted state she had managed to forget. Her voice was tired and weak.

'Hello, Doctor Ryan.'

The voice on the other end was brisk, professional, and she knew at once it was the police.

'Sorry to bother you ma'am but we've discovered a body in the Cam and were wondering if you could attend?'

'I'm on holiday, Doctor Stuart's on call.'

'Yes ma'am, but I'm afraid he's already committed on another call. Superintendent Adams sends his compliments and he says he'll make it up to you.'

'Where's the body?'

'Opposite Trinity College's boathouse, it's still in the water I understand.'

'Has the police surgeon been out to it yet?'

'Been and gone, I understand.'

Sam sighed long and hard.

'Okay, I'll be there as soon as I can.'

Sam almost threw the phone back onto the receiver before lifting the covers away from her naked body. She glanced across at the clock, it was five thirty in the morning. The last thing in the world she wanted right now was to view a body in a frozen river. She staggered towards the bathroom hoping a shower might revive her.

It was just over an hour before Sam finally arrived at the boathouse. The scene didn't seem as confused as normal, and there were few people about. She parked her car, grabbed her bag and made her way over to the edge of the bank where Tom Adams was standing. He looked around as she arrived.

'Sorry to call you out, Sam.'

Sam ignored his apology and made her way to the riverbank.

'What have we got?'

'Drowning, looks like an accident. Went in a bit further upstream and the current dragged him down here.'

'So what am I doing here, the police surgeon could have dealt with this.'

'Local wino reported seeing him thrown in, so the local

plods decided to play it safe and call me out.'

'And you decided to pass the good news down the line?'

Tom smiled. 'Something like that. My guess is the victim was high on something and decided to test out the ice for a prank. Happens every year. Bloody students think they know it all and they know nothing.'

'What about the wino's evidence?'

'Not what you'd call a reliable witness, so I'm not sure.' He pulled the collar of his coat tighter around his neck.

'Where's the body?'

Tom stood to one side and pointed a few metres downstream from where they stood. Stepping over to the spot, Sam could see the body of a young man lying just below the surface of the ice. Nearby the ice was cracked and broken with a small hole smashed into it. Sam knelt down and examined the hole.

'I thought you said he went in further upriver?'

Adams nodded. 'He did.'

'Then what's this hole doing here?'

'PC Plod had a go at getting him out, he was doing okay until he dropped his truncheon in the river, daft sod.'

Sam began to brush the shattered surface ice away from over the body to get a better look at the victim.

'I'm not certain what you want me to do while he's still in there.'

Adams crouched down by her side. 'We didn't want to move him until you arrived.'

'Well, I'm certainly not going to get in there with him.'

As Sam cleared the ice, the body began to look oddly familiar. The face was blurred under the ice and difficult to see, but she was certain. She continued to smooth out the ice with her frozen fingers in an attempt to get a better view of the features. When she'd finished, Sam pushed her face close to the ice, peering hard through the frozen water until finally she managed to focus on the obscured face.

'Oh my God!'

Sam pushed herself backward on to the riverbank stumbling and falling as she did so. Tom managed to catch hold of her arm and pull her to her feet.

'What the hell's wrong?'

Sam crossed her arms defensively and looked back towards the river.

'It's Dominic Parr.'

Tom Adams looked across at her, confused.

'He was Simon Vickers's best friend.'

6

SAM COULD DO LITTLE BUT WAIT AND WATCH WHILE THE
police divers tried to free Dominic's pale and frozen body
from the icy river. It wasn't an easy job; although the ice
around the top of the body was thick and compact, the
temperature below the body was increasing and the ice had
begun to thaw. Consequently the currents were trying to
push the body further downstream while the ice, to which
it had become attached, tried to hold it in place. Sam
couldn't stop looking at the remains. Stuck under the ice,
he looked like a grotesque rag doll which had been
abandoned by a child. Sam wondered if she had played an
inadvertent part in his death. Perhaps it had simply been a
tragic accident, but perhaps she had put too much pressure
on him, upset him and led him to suicide. However, if the
witness were to be believed, and her instincts nudged her in
that direction, perhaps he too had been murdered. All she
knew for sure was that she had to remain objective and
thorough and let the science dictate her conclusions.

Extra holes had to be cut into the ice to allow police
divers room to hold the body in position while it was

carefully prised free. Due to the freezing water, the police frogmen had to work in relays of ten minutes to prevent the penetrating cold from chilling their bodies to a dangerous level. While they were still working, Sam took the opportunity to take the water temperature, entering the measurement into her notebook before taking and recording the air temperature as well. Finally, after almost an hour, Dominic's lifeless body was finally pulled out of the river. The divers carried it quickly to where the black plastic body bag had been laid on the ground. Sam walked across to him. She crouched down and looked into his face. He was deathly pale, making the blue tingeing around his mouth stand out vividly. His eyes were half open and stared blankly outwards. Sam spoke into her dictaphone.

'Riverbank by the side of the Cam, opposite the Trinity boathouse. Oh six-fifteen, 19th December 1997. I am examining the body of a white male, in his late teens, believed to be that of Dominic Parr.'

She felt his neck and moved his arms gently.

'Although there are early signs of rigor mortis it hasn't yet developed and may have been slowed by the freezing temperature of the water.'

She looked up at Tom Adams who had joined her by the body.

'What time did the witness think he went into the water?'

Tom was silent for a moment. 'About eleven. But he also told us that he was thrown in by someone whose description was uncannily similar to that of Frankenstein's monster. So, as you can appreciate, we're not looking at him as a particularly reliable witness.'

'But doesn't that, combined with the fact that he was Simon Vickers's best friend, cause you any moment of doubt? Bit of a coincidence, don't you think?'

Tom exhaled loudly and shook his head.

'We haven't established that Simon Vickers was murdered yet, and even if he was, as far as I'm aware, Dominic Parr wasn't a witness, nor was he associated with it in any way. So motive could be a bit of a problem here. You and your theories, Sam.'

'It's not a theory. I just don't believe in these kinds of coincidences.'

Tom crouched down by her side. 'When did you give him the card?' He held it, wet and crumpled, in his hand.

'Yesterday.'

'Why?'

'I thought he was hiding something. I thought if I gave him my card and some time to think he might decide to tell me what he knew.'

'What did you say to him?'

'I asked him if he knew anything about the night Simon died.'

'And did he?'

Sam nodded. 'Yes, I think he did.'

'You *think*. What did he say?'

'Nothing specific,' she shrugged. 'But like I said, he knew far more than he was saying.'

'So you put him under a bit of pressure?'

'No, there was no pressure, I just asked him about Simon. I'm not a policeman.'

'No, Sam, you're not and you shouldn't have even been talking to him.'

'What else could I do, give up? You want evidence, I'm trying to find it. It's as simple as that.'

'All you're doing, Sam, is taking a series of unconnected circumstances and manipulating them to fit a particular theory.'

Sam was annoyed at Tom's continuing negative approach. She was desperate to tell him what Marcia had discovered but dared not in case she got her friend into trouble. She needed some new evidence so that Tom couldn't wriggle out of doing something. Christ, she thought, she was beginning to sound like him.

'Sounds like police basic training to me. Short of videoing one of the murders I'm not sure what more I can do.'

'Give me some considered evidence, that's what you can do.'

'We might have a serial killer on the loose and you want "considered evidence". Christ, Tom, there was a time…'

'Serial killer? Come off it Sam, this is Cambridge, not New bloody York.'

'How can you say that after you've just come off the Serial Crime Squad?'

'I can say that because the one thing that I did learn on the squad was that killers like that are few and far between and not very likely to pop up in Cambridge.'

'Oh, that's all right, then. So nothing bad ever happens in Cambridge.'

'Now you're being stupid.'

'And you're being blind. What's happened to you Tom? Where's the old gut feeling, your intuition?'

'So, what do you think it was then?'

Sam stared at him angrily. 'Murder, that's what I think it was, murder.'

'You really have a taste for the spectacular, don't you? What about suicide, considered that? He's just lost his best, perhaps only, friend, he's depressed, he jumps in. It happens every day. It couldn't be that you're feeling the slightest bit guilty that your interview with him might have pushed him over the edge?'

Sam turned to face him. 'No!'

She was vehement in her denial but he might have

guessed her fear that she had in some degree contributed to the poor boy's death. Had she pushed Dominic over the edge with her revelation about his friend's murder? In truth she couldn't be sure, but the guilt bore down on her heavily. Sam remained silent, letting Tom continue.

'Like I said before, Sam, provide me with enough evidence and I'll see what I can do, otherwise, as far as I'm concerned, all we've got at the moment is an accidental death. You know as well as I do that in the majority of cases, the most obvious and simple explanation is likely to be the correct one.'

Sam turned away from him in disgust and continued her examination. She examined the front of Dominic's body, searching for any signs of violence. She next examined his hands for cadaveric spasm, the involuntary clenching of the hands as the victim drowns. Often clues could be found squeezed between the victim's fingers as they made their desperate bid for life. On this occasion, however, the hands were clear. She looked up at one of the police frogmen who had gathered around her, forming, it seemed to her, the protective turrets of a castle around the body of the boy they had struggled so long and hard to release.

'Could you turn him over, please?'

The police diver did as he was bid and Sam quickly examined Dominic's back and neck. Again, they all seemed clear and free from any obvious signs of violence. Sam felt oddly disappointed with this. She had been hoping that there would be something immediately obvious, like a knife wound or other signs of violence which would support her case. When she had finished Sam nodded to the diver who rolled him onto his back and she continued with her notes.

'There are no obvious signs of violence, and at the present time it appears to be a case of drowning, although this will have to be confirmed at the PM.'

She packed her dictaphone away and stood. One of the divers looked across at her.

'Okay to pack him and stack him, doctor?'

Sam hated these odd police sayings, but remained silent and nodded. The diver crouched down and he began to pull the black plastic sheeting around Dominic's body before pulling the zip up tight and helping carry it to the undertaker's wagon, which had arrived like a hungry vulture half an hour previously. Ambulances wouldn't normally turn out if the victim had already been pronounced dead at the scene and a call system for undertakers was used to move the body to the mortuary. Sam was always surprised how much money there was in undertaking.

With Dominic's remains on their way to the mortuary Sam returned to the river. Despite the hour, a small crowd of onlookers had already gathered on the opposite bank. As Sam stared across at them she noticed a short dark man standing close to the edge of the bank with a video camera glued tightly to his right eye. As Sam watched he slowly moved the camera away from his face; it was Edmond Moore. When he spotted Sam watching him he looked across at her and nodded expressionlessly before turning and disappearing through the assembling crowd. Sam wondered what he was doing there at that time of the morning, armed with his video camera, and she couldn't help wondering why other people's misfortune held such a fascination. Pushing thoughts of Moore to one side for the moment, she picked up a large stick from the side of the riverbank and began to hit the hardened river. Adams watched for a moment before joining her.

'Relieving your tensions?'

Sam, already out of breath from her efforts, finally threw her stick back onto the bank and turned to Adams.

'Too thick.'

Adams looked confused, unsure whether she was referring to him or the ice.

'The ice, it's too thick, he couldn't have gone through it. Well, not without help anyway.'

Adams looked across the frozen river.

'The thickness varies in different parts of the river. It might be thinner upstream where he went in. He was just unlucky, stepped on a thin bit and couldn't get out.'

'Even if he was on his own, he's a strong fit lad, he should have at least made some effort to pull himself out.'

'Come off it, Sam, not even our divers lasted long before they were frozen through. These things happen every year, you should know that better than most.'

'The divers were standing still. He'd have been fighting, struggling to get himself out.'

Tom shook his head. 'And that would make two of you clutching at straws.'

She ignored him.

'Where do you think he went in?'

'If our wino's right, about quarter of a mile upstream. There is a hole a few feet from the bank.'

'Have you had it photographed?'

'No, it didn't seem worth it, but if you think it's important?'

Sam nodded. 'Yes I do.'

'Consider it done.'

Sam snapped her bag open and retrieved a small glass sample bottle. Unscrewing the top she crouched down by the river and filled it with water before recapping, drying and labelling it. Tom watched her carefully.

'What are you doing?'

'I'm going to check the diatoms.'

'What?'

'Small organisms found in the water. They vary from place to place so with a bit of luck, if he did drown, by examining the different kinds of diatoms in the water in his lungs, I should be able to pinpoint exactly where he went into the water. If you'll show me where you think he went in I'd like to take some samples from there as well, if that's okay.'

'Fine by me. Just follow the riverbank, you can't miss it, one of my lads should be there.'

As Sam began to make her way along the bank Tom shouted after her. 'If you do find anything "dodgy" during the PM, don't forget to let me have a copy of the report.'

'If I find anything "dodgy" you'll be the first to know.'

Sam arrived shortly after Dominic Parr's body reached the mortuary. She was keen to get on and hopeful that she might discover something that would help convince Tom Adams of her theories. Fred was already there, changed and preparing the mortuary for its latest case. He realized it must be more than just a drowning from the tone of Doctor Ryan's voice when she rang her instructions through to him. There wasn't normally so much urgency with an accidental death, it sounded more like she was dealing with a murder, yet she couldn't be, because the normal police and scientific support teams that usually follow a murder inquiry just weren't around.

Sam entered the room as the black body bag was laid on the mortuary slab. Fred looked up at her.

'Do you want me to open the bag, doctor?'

'Just hang on a second.'

While Fred waited, Sam collected a camera from her small mortuary office and loaded it with a roll of film. When she had finished she turned to Fred.

'Okay, Fred, when you're ready.'

Fred looked at her for a moment without moving until Sam brought the camera down from her eye.

'Is there a problem, Fred?'

'Yes Doctor Ryan, there is. I have the distinct impression that you're not telling me something. And as the senior technician in this mortuary I think I ought to know what it is before the PM proceeds.'

Sam pondered his request for a moment.

'I think we might be dealing with another murder and I also think that Dominic Parr, the young man hidden inside the black body bag, might be a victim of the same person that killed Simon Vickers.'

Fred looked shocked at Sam's revelation.

'So where are the police and the rest of them?'

Sam shrugged. 'They are not convinced yet, that's what we're here for, to find evidence to convince them. As far as you and I are concerned Fred, Dominic is a murder victim, and as far as its possible, we'll treat him as such, okay?'

'Whatever you like Doctor Ryan, I just hope you know what you're doing.'

Sam smiled at him.

'Trust me. Shall we get on?'

Fred nodded and began to unzip the bag while Sam took all the appropriate photographs. As soon as the body had been revealed they reversed their roles and while Sam removed Dominic's clothing Fred took the photographs. Once outside his cold river tomb, rigor mortis had developed quickly and made the job of removing the clothes from the stiffening limbs much more difficult. As each item was peeled away Sam searched it, emptying the pockets of all objects before handing them to Fred, who dropped them into clear plastic exhibit bags. Each item would have to be air dried before the bags could be sealed. This procedure stopped shrinkage and thus an altered relationship between the position of any wound on the body and any corresponding rip or tear on the clothing. After his shirt had been removed only his socks were left. Fred pulled off the right sock, followed by the left. As the second sock came away from Dominic's white and wrinkled foot, an object that had been concealed inside it clattered onto the sterile floor beneath the dissecting table. Sam crouched down and picked it up, holding it in front of her face. It was a plastic floppy disk. Fred leaned across her shoulder.

'Odd place to keep a computer disk.'

Sam nodded. 'Yes, it is, isn't it? He certainly didn't want anyone finding it.'

Turning the small square disk around in her hand she tried to read the information on the front, but the ink had run, making the writing illegible. Fred held out a small exhibit bag for the disk and Sam dropped it inside.

'Let's hope we can dry it out a bit.'

'You'll be lucky.'

As Fred began to move across the mortuary towards the other exhibits Sam called after him.

'Don't put it with the rest of his property, just stick it on my desk would you? I'd like to see if I can get anything out of it when it's dry.'

Fred nodded his understanding and put the disk to one side. Dominic's body now lay naked across the marble slab. Once the body had dried sufficiently, Fred started taping the skin methodically as Sam watched.

'You'd make a first class SOCO, Fred.'

'What and work in all those cold wet fields? No thanks, Doctor Ryan, I'm happy as I am.'

Once the body had been taped, and the debris collected, Sam combed through the body hair with a fine postmortem comb to drag out any clues that might have remained fastened to the head or body hair. Samples of blood, urine and cerebro-spinal fluid were then extracted before Sam began to take swabs from the mouth, nose, penis and finally anus. As Sam took the anal swab she noticed a tearing to the outside walls of the anus. Closer examination also revealed bruising and other small lacerations.

'Sexual intercourse appears to have taken place between Dominic Parr and an unknown third party before death. The injuries to the anal region lead me to believe that sex was not with consent, and that Dominic may have been raped before entering the water.'

Fred passed her the scalpel.

'I'm going to have to cut further into the area to establish the depth of the injuries.' Dissecting upward was always difficult and Sam took her time. 'The injuries extend some four to five inches along the passage. I am going to take samples from these areas for examination.' Sam knew that good quality samples would be important. She needed to establish whether Dominic had regular anal intercourse or not, an important point when trying to establish rape. Old scarring, if any, would show this. Blood samples could also be important in establishing whether a person was actively homosexual or not and these would have to be examined closely. Sam next took anal swabs. Due to the time the body had spent in the water however, there was little chance of recovering any worthwhile swabs for blood or DNA analysis, but she had been lucky before, so it was an important procedure.

Once all the preliminary work had been completed, Sam began the full examination.

'Postmortem on Dominic Parr oh eight forty-five. Friday 19th December 1997. He is a white male, nineteen years of age. He weighs nine stone six pounds and is five feet eight inches in height.

'He appears well nourished and there are no obvious

signs of external injuries. There is fine white foam formed in both his mouth and nostrils, probably caused by a mixture of air, water and mucus. Fred, can you take samples?'

Sam stood back while Fred leaned over the body and took several samples from both the mouth and the nose. This kind of frothing from the mouth and nose was common in cases of drowning, and taking samples was vital if the laboratories were later to check for any signs of poisoning. When Fred had finished, Sam moved back to the body.

'The skin on both the hands and the soles of the feet is white and wrinkled, caused by the body's prolonged submersion in water. His fingers and nails appear normal, with no signs of damage.'

Fingers and nails were often damaged and injured as the victims tried to pull themselves from the water. Sam turned to Fred and showed him Dominic's hands.

'What do you make of those, Fred?'

Fred examined them quickly.

'They seem fine.'

Sam nodded her agreement.

'Yes, they do, don't they? That's what's wrong. I would have expected to find cuts, broken nails, lacerations to the hands as he struggled to pull himself out, but there's nothing. His hands are smooth, undamaged, nails intact. Odd, don't you think?'

Fred nodded.

'Very.'

Sam next examined the ears, looking for the conspicuous haemorrhaging which is caused by changes in barometric pressure, and is one of the classic indications of drowning. She glanced across at Fred, who had already produced a scalpel from the tray. He handed it to Sam as she began the slow and methodical process of examining the body of Dominic Parr.

As Sam cut deeply into the body, exposing the chest and abdomen, the lungs tried to force themselves through the lengthening slit like giant expanding sponges. She glanced at them and noted the familiar purple blotches that covered the organs. Grepitus, the hyperinflation of the lungs, and the odd blotching was typical of drowning cases and confirmed that it was drowning, and not cardiac inhibition, which had been the cause of Dominic Parr's death. Often the shock of the body entering the water, especially if it is extremely cold, can bring on a reflex cardiac arrest causing death before the victim becomes submerged. Fred then took samples of water from Dominic's stomach and oesophagus, as well as samples of oedema from the lungs. Debris, such as algae and weed from the point of drowning, are often found in these samples, as well as the microscopic diatoms. The distribution of diatoms is another good indicator of the cause of death. As the water enters the body, and while the blood is still circulating, these diatoms will be distributed around the body, finding their way into the victim's organs and bone marrow, clearly indicating that a victim drowned, rather than being dead before entering the water. The diatoms can be collected from the organs removed during autopsy by dissolving the organ tissue with a strong mineral acid. The acid-resistant silica shells of the diatoms are left behind and these can then be observed under a microscope. With over fifteen thousand species of diatoms, it is possible, with considerable accuracy in some cases, to pinpoint almost exactly where and when a person went into the water. As soon as Fred had finished taking his samples Sam gave her instructions.

'Get those analysed as quickly as you can, please, Fred. I want to check them as soon as possible.'

Fred nodded and put the samples carefully into a laboratory tray. Sam continued. 'There are small ulcers inside the stomach indicating that the deceased was also suffering from hypothermia at the time of his death almost certainly brought on by the freezing water.'

As Fred watched, Sam moved along the body an inch at a time. He knew it was going to be a long morning.

As soon as the PM was finished, Fred sent off the various samples before beginning the task of stitching Dominic Parr back together again. Sam locked herself in her office and began to write up her notes. Despite going through them slowly and methodically she could find nothing that indicated that he had been murdered. The fact that he may have been raped might help, but then she'd seen similar injuries on people who had consented to sex. She knew she would have to be sure before Tom Adams would take any action. There were no other signs of external or internal injuries that couldn't quite properly be explained by the circumstances surrounding Dominic's drowning. There were certainly no signs of strangulation, head wounds, or other signs of violent assault on the body. Unless the labs came up with something, she'd drawn a blank. Yet it seemed extraordinary that Simon Vickers's friend, and potentially an important witness, had died so soon after Simon's own death and Sam's visit. A knock on the office door distracted her. As she turned, Fred put his head around the door.

'Made you a coffee, thought you might need one.'

He handed it to Sam who took it gratefully. 'All stitched up?'

'Almost, don't suppose he'll go anywhere while I have a quick break.'

Fred sat down opposite her. 'By the look on your face you're not making much headway with the case?'

Sam shook her head. 'No, it looks like I might be dealing with a coincidence after all.'

'Even though you think he was raped?'

Sam shrugged.

'But was he? Might have just been involved in some violent sex act, it didn't have to be without his consent.'

'Odd, though.'

'Odd won't make Tom Adams start an inquiry.'

Fred sipped carefully from the edge of his mug and looked thoughtfully at Sam's computer screen. 'There was one thing that puzzled me a little when you were cutting him up.'

Fred was never one for technical speak, despite having received high grades in his professional exams.

'What was that?'

'Remember the injuries to the muscles over the scapula?'

Sam nodded.

'Almost certainly done when he was struggling to get himself out of the water.'

Fred gave her a knowing smile. 'If that was the case then why weren't his fingers and nails torn and injured like you said. If he put up that much of a fight they were almost sure to be, weren't they?'

Sam sat perfectly still for a moment, while Fred continued. 'Remember that death in police custody case we dealt with last year?'

Sam nodded.

'Well, the victim, the one we found in the cell, had similar injuries to his arms and shoulder. Caused through having his arms forced up behind his back too far. I'm sorry if this sounds a bit far-fetched but if his arms were forced up his back, then he would be in the perfect position for sex and perhaps with his head pushed down under the water. Let's be honest, he was a puny-looking lad, unlikely to have put up that much of a fight if he was being held, right?'

Sam pondered what Fred had just told her. Then she sprang to her feet and grabbed his face, kissing him hard on the cheek.

'Why the hell didn't I see it?'

'You're too close to the case, happens sometimes.'

Sam smiled broadly at her assistant. 'I owe you one, Fred.'

With that she ran out of the mortuary and towards the lifts. Fred watched her go before looking back at the still full mug of steaming coffee.

'Too much caffeine again.'

He chuckled to himself and made his way back into the mortuary to finish stitching up Dominic Parr's body.

Before the fire brigade had time to arrive the Great Oak had already exploded, blowing off its branches and allowing the flames to penetrate to its very core. The small memorial that had been placed at the base of its trunk was quickly incinerated and turned to blackened ash, which the fire-storm blew out over Herdan Hill. The other trees surrounding the Oak were already ablaze and threatening to destroy the woodland on the entire Hill. Despite the ferocity of the blaze, when the fire brigade finally arrived they quickly brought the flames under control and after a few hours only the dampening down remained to be done. Although the fire was bad it wasn't extensive and the wood would soon recover; the Oak on the other hand, was almost completely destroyed. Leading fire fighter Stan Johnson picked up what was left of a large petrol can and examined it before turning to the charred and still smouldering stump of the tree. It seemed such a shame that after five hundred years a few kids with a box of matches and a can of petrol could destroy such a magnificent object.

*

Sam didn't have to wait long for Tom Adams to arrive. She'd kept her message purposefully vague in the hope of drawing Tom out quickly and the plan had clearly worked. Jean announced him.

'Superintendent Adams.'

Jean always had a knowing way in her tone and a certain look on her face when she introduced Tom, which had began to irritate Sam. She had confronted Jean about it but she had denied all knowledge and failed to stop. Sam finally gave up and had to accept the irritation quietly. Tom strode across the room and sat down in the chair opposite Sam's desk.

'Got your message. So, has he got a broken neck too?'

Sam picked up his sarcastic tone at once but ignored it and smiled broadly.

'Not quite, but there are some serious irregularities.'

'Irregularities, now there's an interesting word. Are you trying to tell me he wasn't drowned?'

Sam shook her head.

'He was drowned all right, no doubt about that, all the classic signs are there but it wasn't an accident or suicide. He was held under the water by his arms until he drowned, and I believe he may have been raped before being killed.'

Tom looked at her despairingly.

'And your evidence?'

'There was serious tearing and bruising to the anus and damage to the muscles over his scapula…' Sam indicated to the area on her own body.

'Like you said at the scene, he was probably trying to fight his way out of the ice, I don't see what that proves.'

Sam continued. 'But his hands and nails, which, given the circumstances, I would have also expected to have been injured, show no signs of damage. The two just aren't consistent.'

Tom remained thoughtful for a moment.

'But surely he could have got the injures at any time? Doesn't have to have been during a struggle. Who knows what he got up to. Fell off his bike, sports injury…'

'I don't think he played much sport.'

'It doesn't matter, Sam, the point is there are a hundred and one ways he could have received those injuries.'

'And why do you think there were no signs of damage to his hands?'

'Perhaps it wasn't an accident. Perhaps he did commit suicide, then he wouldn't have wanted to get out.'

'And the injuries around his anus?'

'Okay, I'll make enquiries about that, but it might just be that he was gay.'

Sam sighed angrily. 'What happened to you, Tom?'

'Rank happened to me. Responsibility happened to me. Does that answer your question?'

Jean's sudden appearance in the room changed the increasingly hostile atmosphere. She glanced from Sam to Tom Adams.

'Sorry to bother you, Doctor Ryan, but Doctor Stuart's here.'

Sam looked across the room at her secretary.

'Can't it wait? I'm rather busy right now.'

'It's not you he wants to see, it's Superintendent Adams.'

Before Jean had a chance to say any more, Trevor Stuart entered the room.

'I'm sorry to intrude, but it would be handy if I could have a word with both of you.'

Sam nodded towards Jean and she left. Trevor Stuart crossed the room and sat next to Tom. Sam eyed him nervously, waiting for the professional assassination to come.

'Two things.' He turned to Adams. 'The old man you

found in the burnt out cottage yesterday, it's definitely murder. He was strangled, probably with some sort of ligature. I would think the fire was then started with the purpose of covering up the crime.'

Tom looked surprised. 'Are you sure?'

'It's his favourite question,' Sam interjected.

'Yes I'm quite sure. His hyoid bone is broken.'

Trevor then turned his attention to Sam. 'I owe you an apology. If it hadn't been for you spotting the broken hyoid on Simon Vickers, I'd have missed it this time as well. Sometimes old dogs don't want to learn new tricks. My pride had been pricked and I acted like a bloody fool. Sorry.'

For a moment Sam was lost for words. Then she smiled across at her colleague, relieved that their dispute was over at last.

'As I said, we've all missed things. It could have happened to any of us.'

Trevor turned back to Tom.

'In view of this finding I am left with no choice but to concur with Doctor Ryan's views, and it is now also my opinion that Simon Vickers was murdered and not accidentally killed in the car crash as my original report indicated.'

Sam had never heard her partner be so formal before. She knew what he was saying must be hurting but he did it all the same. Tom Adams looked at them both.

'You're the best double act since Laurel and Hardy, do you know that?'

They both continued to stare at him silently.

'Okay, okay, I'll take another look at the circumstances. I'll put Chalky and a DC on it for a few days. If they come up with anything I'll open the case on Simon and Dominic. Satisfied?'

'And the cost?'

'I can hide it inside the poacher's murder for now.'

The word 'poacher' startled Sam. 'What poacher's this?'

'Old boy called Jack Falconer, lived just outside Middle Fen, back end of Herdan Hill. Been a pain in the arse for years. One of the first people I nicked when I was a young PC. Looks like someone's poached him now.'

'Jack Falconer? I know him, he witnessed the crash. He told me about it.'

'I didn't know there was a witness,' Tom said, eyes narrowed.

'He wouldn't come forward, well not officially anyway.'

'But you sweet-talked him?'

'No, he just wasn't frightened of me.' Tom scowled at her, but she continued. 'I found him, or rather he found me, when I was examining the crash scene. He told me he didn't think it was an accident, either.'

'So what was his theory?'

Sam knew the next line was going to make her appear stupid but she had to say it.

'He said he felt a presence, the devil.'

Tom stared hard at her and nodded sarcastically. 'I see. Another reliable witness?'

'Isn't it yet another odd circumstance that the only known witness to Simon's death should himself me murdered later on?'

'So why didn't you report this before?'

'What, and have your lot frighten him away completely? He wanted to tell me more but was afraid to.'

'In case the bogey man got him?'

'The bogey man *did* get him,' Trevor interjected.

Tom stared at Trevor for a moment then returned his attention to Sam.

'He won't be telling anyone now will he? That explains

what Marcia was doing at his cottage though. Have you
been to see her yet?'

Sam was confused and cautious. 'Why should I?'

Tom glanced at Trevor Stuart. 'No one's told you then?'

Sam could feel a rising sense of panic.

'Told me what? What's happened?'

'Marcia was visiting Falconer's house and discovered
the fire. She made an attempt to rescue him and was caught
in a rather nasty explosion. She's in the burns unit at the
Park.'

'What! How bad is she?'

Tom shook his head. 'I don't know, but the paramedics
rushed her in after they found her lying on Falconer's lawn
with a door on top of her.'

Sam grabbed her bag and had reached her office door
before Tom Adams caught up with her. Her face was ashen
and bore a stricken expression.

'This is my fault, this is my bloody fault.'

Adams had to agree but didn't say so. Instead he offered
what help he could. 'Come on, you're in no state to go
anywhere, I'll drive you.' He turned to Trevor Stuart.

'I'll speak to you later Trevor.'

'Let me know how she is.'

Tom nodded and left the room, his arm firmly around
Sam.

They reached the Park quickly and Tom Adams stopped
outside the main entrance to the burns unit.

'Want me to come in with you?'

Sam shook her head. 'No, I'd rather see her on my own.'

'If you're sure.'

'Yes, thanks for the lift.'

'If there's anything else I can do, you know where I am.'

Sam nodded and stepped out of the car, making her way

quickly into the hospital. Following the seemingly endless lines of corridors she eventually arrived at the burns unit, made her way across to the reception desk and introduced herself.

'Doctor Ryan, I'd like to see Marcia Evans if that's possible.'

The nurse eyed her suspiciously. 'Are you her GP?'

Sam shook her head.

'No, I'm just a friend.'

'I'll have to check.'

The nurse wandered down the corridor and spoke to the ward sister, while Sam waited, scanning the desk for any notes that might refer to her friend. After a few moments the sister approached her. She was short and tubby with a stern and officious-looking face.

'Can I help you?'

Sam began again.

'Hello, I'm Doctor Ryan, I've come to see Marcia Evans who I understand is a patient here at the moment.'

The sister smiled self-importantly.

'I'm very sorry, but it's close family only at the moment.'

'But her family all live on the other side of London.'

'So I understand, but they have been informed and I'm sure they will be here as soon as possible.'

'But *I'm* sure, in the meantime, Marcia would like to see a friendly face.'

The sister failed to be moved.

'As I explained, family only.'

Sam suddenly lost any reserve she might have had, and staring firmly into the sister's face let go all her pent-up emotions.

'Now listen to me, you jumped up bloody nurse, I'm a senior member of medical staff in this hospital and unless you want me to bring more grief down on your head than you can possibly deal with you'll show me where Miss Evans's bed is now!'

Sam knew she was being unfair and unreasonable, and that the sister was only doing her job, but she wasn't in a reasonable mood. As Sam's face flushed with anger the sister took a pace backwards, convinced that Sam was going to attack her at any moment. She mustered all the dignity she could and, with a slight tremble in her voice, she nodded towards the apprehensive nurse hovering close by.

'Show Doctor Ryan to Marcia Evans's room. Please make it a brief visit, she needs to rest.'

Sam still wasn't in the mood to compromise and curled her lip.

'Thank you so much!'

She followed the nurse to a small side room and was let in. Marcia was standing by the wardrobe fully dressed with both hands and wrists bandaged. Much of the hair on the right side of her head had been singed away and the skin was blistered. As she entered, Marcia turned to face her, wincing as she did.

'Thanks for coming. Where are the grapes?'

'Thought you might have trouble eating them.' Sam was enormously relieved to find Marcia on her feet and apparently not seriously injured. They both hid the depth of their emotions with a show of bravado but each could feel the emotional tension just below the surface of their banter.

'You could have peeled me a few.'

'I will next time.'

Marcia looked astonished. 'Next time. God help me.'

'I'm so sorry, Marcia, I had no idea this would happen.'

'It wasn't your fault, it was mine for sticking my nose in too far.'

'What happened?'

'I'm not really sure, every time I think about it now it all seems to happen in slow motion. All I really remember is getting to the cottage and seeing it on fire. I ran across to it, boy was it bad, but I couldn't get too close because of the heat and flames. I remember thinking no one's got a chance if they're in there. Then there was this sort of scream from inside the cottage and I thought, Christ, there *is* still someone alive in there. So I put my jacket over my head to try and protect myself, and had a go at kicking the door in. All I remember then was this enormous bang and the next thing I know I'm in here covered in bandages.'

'How bad are your injuries?'

'Superficial, really. I was lucky. Hands and right side of my head mostly. The door I was trying to kick down protected me from the worst of the flames, otherwise you'd have been pulling me out of one of your fridges.'

'Don't, Marcia, I'll never forgive myself for putting you in such danger. You said you heard a scream, are you sure?'

'Yes, I know a scream when I hear one.'

'It couldn't have been an animal, cat, dog?'

'No, I don't think so, I'm pretty sure it was human.'

'What were you doing at the cottage anyway?'

'I met the old poacher on the hill, he was quite helpful but didn't want to know about the police. So I thought if I found him I might be able to use my enormous charm and get him to give us a statement. What caused the explosion by the way?'

Sam shook her head. 'No idea, they're still investigating it.'

'If it hadn't been for that I might have got him out. I take it the poor old sod's dead?'

'Before the fire started, I'm afraid.'

Marcia looked at her quizzically.

'What?'

'He'd been strangled. The fire was probably started to try and cover up the crime.'

'Like the Simon Vickers case.'

'Just like the Simon Vickers case. I hope our friend Tom Adams takes a bit more notice now.'

Marcia shook her head gently. 'I wonder who was doing the screaming then.'

Sam shrugged.

'Perhaps the killer, caught up in his own fire, who knows? What are you doing now?'

'Leaving.'

'Are you sure that's a good idea?'

Marcia grimaced. 'Probably not, but I've got to get into the lab.'

'Why?'

'I found a few things on the tree that might be helpful.'

'Marcia, you're incorrigible. Like what?'

'I took some samples of bark from the tree. They had a sort of smell about them.'

'Smell?'

'Yes, chemicals. I couldn't put my finger on it at first. I think it was the explosion that put me on to it. Ammonium nitrate.'

Sam frowned as if she didn't understand Marcia's point.

'It's an ingredient in making certain fertilizers but more importantly it's used to make bombs.'

Sam's eyes widened.

'What!'

'IRA have put it to good use over the years, and it was the main ingredient in the Oklahoma bomb, too.'

'Christ, have you told anyone?'

Marcia shook her head. 'No, not yet, like to be sure first. Don't want to look a prat if I'm wrong. I managed to dig quite a large splinter of metal out of the tree. If it was a bomb that should be covered in trace elements as well. Anyway, I want to get it analysed as soon as possible. I think it might be just what we're looking for.'

'Sure you're up to it?'

'I'm up to it, but only if you can do me a favour.'

'Anything.'

'My car is still down by the cottage. Could you bring it back to my flat? It's just that I don't think I'm up to driving right now.' She held her bandaged hands up to emphasize her point.

Sam nodded. 'Sure. I'll get you a cab.'

'There is just one other thing.'

Sam looked up.

'All the samples I took from the scene are in my murder bag.'

Sam still didn't understand so Marcia continued. 'Unfortunately the bag is still inside my car outside the cottage and I can't do a thing until I've got it.'

Sam smiled. It made a change for her friend to ask her a favour and as it would undoubtedly benefit Sam as well she could hardly say no.

'I'll pick it up this afternoon. Where do you want me to bring it, lab or flat?'

'Flat. I'll bum a lift home off one of the other technicians.'

'Better get that cab, then.'

'Sooner the better.'

Sam took a taxi to Jack Falconer's cottage. Despite only having a vague notion of its location all the driver had to do was follow one of the many police cars and vans that were heading rapidly for the area. The taxi dropped Sam close to the first police cordon. Despite Marcia's car being parked outside the cordon Sam decided to have a look at the scene anyway. She identified herself to the officer on the gate and was allowed through.

The cottage was completely gutted, wisps of fine ash were whipped up by gusts of wind and swirled around like smoke in the cold December air, disappearing into the woods which surrounded the back of the cottage. Only the chimney breast and part of one wall were left to show that there had once been a cottage there at all. The remainder lay blackened and twisted on the ground, contrasting starkly with the white snow all around it. White-suited SOCOs picked over debris, carefully bagging anything that looked even remotely interesting.

'Didn't know this was one of your cases, Sam.'

Sam turned to see the tall and gaunt figure of Colin Flannery looking down at her.

'It's not, well, not directly anyway, Trevor Stuart's dealing with it.'

He followed her gaze towards the cottage. 'Bit of a mess, isn't it? Don't know what they expect us to do after all this time. Scene's been well and truly contaminated by now. Still, I suppose you never know, we might just get lucky.'

'Do they know how the fire started yet?'

'Can't be sure until the fire investigation team gets here, but it looks like it might be malicious ignition.'

Colin Flannery was much given to using current phrases.

'You mean arson?'

He nodded and continued. 'I understand what was left of a petrol can was found inside the ruins.'

'Anything else?'

Flannery shook his head.

'No, not yet, but it's early days. How's Marcia by the way?'

'Bit sore, but she's managed to keep her sense of humour.'

Tom Adams suddenly appeared by her side. 'Fancy seeing you here. You're a bit late, the body's gone.'

Sam wasn't in the mood for Tom's sarcastic sense of humour.

'I've come to collect Marcia's car, she left it here.'

'I see. Don't mind if I have a quick look inside before you drive it away do you? Not that I don't trust you, just procedure.'

Flannery read the mood well and decided it was a good time to depart. 'I'll see you both later.' With a quick wave he was gone.

'It's arson, I understand?'

Tom looked after Flannery. 'I'll have to have a word with Colin. He's bit too loose with his tongue for my liking. Maybe, have to wait for the fire investigation team before we can say for sure.'

'You'll be seeing Rebecca again, that'll be nice for you.'

Tom ignored her, 'Looks like someone was determined to cover their tracks.'

'Until Trevor spotted he'd been strangled.'

'Our killer's not as good as he thought. Should make my job easier.'

'Or because he believed he'd got away with murder once by burning the body, he thought he could get away with it again?'

'Maybe, but that's yet to be proved. You'll be pleased to know that I've got Chalky and a couple of lads on it already.'

Sam stopped and looked up at Adams. 'Tell them to ponder on this. Simon Vickers left home at around midnight to visit Dominic Parr. He never made it. Instead he cycled to Cherry Hinton which would have taken him about an hour. He then stole a car, got drunk, drove the fifty minutes to Herdan Hill, crashed the car and killed himself.

The times don't add up Tom, they just don't add up.'

Sam was desperate to tell him what Marcia had told him about the ammonium nitrate but Marcia wouldn't have thanked her. Tom looked at her thoughtfully for a moment.

'I'll pass it on. Shall we inspect the car?'

It was unlocked and the keys still hung in the ignition. Tom pulled them out and handed them to Sam. 'Surprised she's still got a car to be picked up.'

Sam snatched them off him. 'I think she had other things on her mind at the time, like trying to save someone's life.'

Tom looked contrite, 'Sorry, out of order.'

Without saying more, he walked to the back of the car and opened the boot. Although it was a mess, with everything from old sweet papers and car park tickets to discarded clothes, there was nothing of real consequence and he closed it after a brief search. He then inspected the back seat and had a quick look inside the glove compartment. All proved negative. While Tom was searching the car Sam stood impassively outside, observing his progress. Finally, he pushed his arm under the front passenger seat and emerged with Marcia's bag.

'What have we got here?'

He looked across at Sam who shrugged and tried desperately to look innocent. Returning his attention to the bag he snapped it open and examined its contents. Not only did he find the samples of bark Marcia had discovered at the scene but also the piece of metal she had dug out of the tree. Adams's attention returned to Sam once more.

'Know anything about these?'

Sam shrugged and shook her head.

'No, nothing. Probably something Marcia's working on.'

Adams dropped them back into the bag and snapped it shut again. 'Think I'll hang onto this for a while, or at least until I've had chance to speak to Marcia about it, anyway.

Is she still in hospital?'

Sam shook her head. 'No she signed herself out.'

'She'll be at home, then?'

'Or the lab.'

'Right, I'll try her there. Car's all yours. Give Marcia my regards when you see her, won't you.'

Sam knew Tom was playing games, and almost certainly realized that her real mission to the cottage was to get hold of the contents of Marcia's bag. She wasn't going to give him the satisfaction of catching her out. She stared into his smug and smiling face contemptuously as she climbed into Marcia's car. Turning the engine over and pushing the gear stick into first, she raced off along the small dirt track towards the road, wondering what the hell to do next.

Instead of driving Marcia's car straight to her flat, Sam made a wide detour via Huntingdon and stopped off at the laboratory. Despite her injuries Marcia was working at her desk when Sam arrived at her office. She knocked quietly and let herself in. Marcia turned to face her friend, examining her empty hands.

'Where's the bag?'

Sam looked at her desperately. 'Tom Adams took it.'

'And you let him?'

'I didn't have a lot of choice.'

Marcia blew out hard. 'No. Sorry, Sam, I don't suppose you did.'

'Where does this leave us, back at square one?'

Marcia nodded.

'Just about, unless you can get some samples from the car?'

'Difficult. I've already been there once, and I can't really see them letting me take bits of it away with me. You could take some more samples from the tree.'

Marcia shook her head, dismally. 'It burnt down.'

'What!'

'Earlier today, it was on the news.'

'Covering his tracks with fire again.'

'Looks like it,' Marcia agreed.

'I was really hoping that we could have cracked it this time.'

'So was I.'

There was a stunned and awkward pause as if Marcia was considering something. Then, in an excited burst of enthusiasm, she said, 'I don't suppose you dug any bits and pieces out of Simon's body, did you?'

Sam nodded. 'Yes, quite a bit.'

'Where are they now?'

'Waiting to be analysed.'

'Could you get hold of any?'

'I expect so. You think they might still have some trace evidence on them?'

'It's worth a try, we've got nothing to lose.'

Sam nodded. 'And if we run into any problems…'

'You could dig a few more bits out.'

'Exactly.'

'Well what are you standing around here for?'

Sam leaned over, kissed her friend and disappeared from the lab as quickly as she had arrived.

Sam dropped Marcia's car off outside her flat before taking a taxi back to the hospital. The samples were still awaiting analysis so there was no need to spend Christmas Day rooting around inside Simon Vickers's charred and slowly decomposing body for bits of shrapnel. Despite a protest from the senior technician, she arranged for just over half the samples to be sent around to Marcia by special courier, even paying for the delivery herself. After that she picked up the computer disk she'd found concealed in Dominic Parr's sock and examined it. Although it had dried out it still looked jaded and worn and Sam wasn't sure how much good it was going to be. Immersion in freezing and polluted water for a few hours never helped. Fred entered the office, unexpectedly. 'Oh, it's you, Doctor Ryan. I thought we'd got an intruder. Either that or one of the customers decided that they had had enough.'

'Working late?'

'No, just left my jacket behind. Managed to get any action out of the police yet?'

'No, not yet, but I'm working on it.'

'I think you've convinced Doctor Stuart.'

'That's something, I suppose. Did you assist with Jack Falconer?'

'Was that his name? No one seemed sure when we were cutting him up. Doctor Stuart made a special check of his throat and found the hyoid bone broken. I don't think he would have if it hadn't been for the Simon Vickers case, and he knows it.'

Sam changed the subject. 'Thanks for the tip about Madam Wong, by the way.'

'Have you been to see her than?'

Sam nodded. 'Yep. A few days ago.'

'Any good?'

'Bit soon yet, I'll give it a few weeks and see. How long was it before you began to notice a difference?'

'Few days, I suppose, but it was a good month or two before the beer started to taste good again. Did she look into your soul?'

Sam looked at him for a moment looking for the cheeky smirk that usually followed that kind of comment. There wasn't one.

'Yes, she did. You too?'

Fred nodded. 'Weird isn't it?'

'Yes it was a bit.'

Fred changed the subject. He hated things getting too intense. 'Well, spring is on its way, I'm sure your nose will be full of smells by then.'

'I hope so, Fred, I hope so.'

'Course you will, works wonders does the inscrutable Madam Wong. Got to go, last minute Christmas shopping and only a few days left. See you tomorrow.'

As Fred disappeared, Sam looked at the date on her watch and sighed. Where did all that time go?

Although the temperature felt no warmer, much of the snow was clearing and now clung desperately to the verges, thawing slowly and sending cascades of water along the gutters to fill the drains and form large puddles by the side of the road. Sam was grateful for the thaw, as it made her journey home both easier and safer. It also gave her a view of the new potholes that had appeared menacingly in the track that led up to her cottage. When she finally got in Wyn was out, probably Christmas shopping, she thought. Sam made her way into the kitchen and put the kettle on. It had been one of the worst months she could ever remember. Christmas had always been such a good time for her; how could it possibly have all gone so wrong?

She made herself a quick mug of tea before heading towards her computer and switching it on. It took a few minutes before Sam was able to slip the disk she'd found in Dominic Parr's sock into the floppy drive. Although the computer attempted to read the disk, it was clearly having problems. Eventually a message flashed up on the screen. 'Unable to read disk. Cancel or retry.' Sam tried once more. Again the same message flashed up on the screen. She finally removed the disk, fearful of damaging her system.

If there was any information left on the floppy then her limited knowledge of the technology wasn't going to extract it. Sam dropped it back into its protective bag and locked it into her desk drawer. She didn't really know why she locked the drawer, she didn't normally, but there seemed to be something very precious about this particular object, which needed a little extra care.

7

SEEING EDMOND MOORE STANDING BY THE RIVERBANK
filming had disturbed Sam. She had considered confronting
him over it but decided against it. After all, he hadn't
actually done anything wrong, so instead she decided to
call on Peter Andrews and see if he could shed any light on
Moore's bizarre behaviour. She didn't have to wait too long
after knocking at the vicarage door before Peter Andrews's
smiling face appeared.

'Sam, what a nice surprise. Come in, come in. I take it
it's about the carol concert? I hope you can still make it,
we're relying on you?'

'I'll be there, don't worry, but that's not it.'

He looked at her, intrigued, and directed her gently into
the vicarage's large entrance hall. 'Tea?'

Sam shook her head. 'No, no thanks, I can't stay long,
just wanted a quick word with you.'

'About what?'

'Edmond Moore.'

The smile drifted from his face and he suddenly looked
rather grave.

'Shall we go into my study?'

Sam nodded and followed him into a small, dark, square room. The room looked as if it hadn't been decorated for years, and had an odd period feel to it. This feeling contrasted sharply with the large white modern computer and printer, which sat on top of the Victorian desk and dominated the room. Andrews directed Sam towards a chair before sitting down by his desk.

'So what's Edmond been up to now?'

The question made Sam feel slightly awkward, like a schoolchild telling tales to the teacher.

'He hasn't exactly done anything wrong, it's just that I saw him filming me the other day when I was dealing with a body in the Cam. It just seemed odd. I suppose I was wondering if it had anything to do with the film you are making together.'

Andrews shook his head.

'It certainly hasn't got anything to do with the small film we're making. There is only one location for that and that's here. I would think Edmond just took advantage of seeing something unusual when he had his video on hand.'

Sam wasn't convinced.

'Where does he work?'

'On the science park somewhere. He's a computer programmer or something like that.'

'He's got a car, I take it?'

Andrews nodded. 'A white Volvo.'

'So he has no reason to be on the riverbank in the early morning.'

'I don't know. He might have had a reason, I'll ask him if you like.'

'Discreetly.'

'Confessionally.'

'Thank you. What do you know about Edmond?'

Andrews shrugged. 'Not much. He came to the village just over six months ago from London because of his work. His hobbies seem to be computers and judo, he helps out at the club occasionally…'

'Ricky said.'

'And I think he's hoping to open a judo club in the village.'

'Ricky says he gives the students the creeps.'

'That's a bit hard,' Andrews frowned. 'He's a little intense, I'll grant you, and he's not the most attractive man I've ever been introduced to but that's all. Teenagers can be a little judgemental and cruel.'

Sam sat back in her seat. 'To be honest, Peter, I feel a little uncomfortable around him as well. Is he married?'

Andrews shook his head. 'No.'

'Girl friend?'

He shook his head again. 'I know what you're getting at, Sam, and I think you're wrong and even if you're not his private life has got nothing to do with us.'

'Unless he's using the club to get access to young boys.'

Andrews's mood suddenly darkened. 'I can't accept that. Have you any proof?'

Andrews sounded just like Tom. She shook her head.

'No, not yet, but let's hope that by the time I have, it's not too late.'

Andrews sighed deeply. 'Look, Sam, if you're really worried I'll try and keep a closer watch on things, but I really think you're barking up the wrong tree. He's just a bit awkward in company, that's all.'

Sam still wasn't convinced and knew she would have to persuade Tom to check his name against the criminal names index. For now, however, she let it go.

The following morning Sam was up early, having spent a

disturbed night running theory after theory through her mind. She was also finding it difficult to dismiss Moore's actions from her mind. When she finally staggered downstairs and into the kitchen she found Shaw brushing purposefully around her legs. Sam picked him up, stroking him gently behind the ears. It was normally her habit to leave him outside, collecting him only when she returned from work, but recently, with the freezing temperatures, she had given him the option of a warm kitchen and he'd taken it. She unfolded the paper that lay on the kitchen table and read the front page.

'Frozen body discovered under the Cam.'

The rest of the article outlined the discovery of Parr's body and the fact that a postmortem examination would be carried out to establish the cause of death. This was followed by a warning about crossing the Cam during the freezing weather. They'll have one hell of a headline soon, Sam ruminated.

'Morning!'

Ricky's cheerful voice broke through Sam's thoughts.

'Fancy some tea?'

'No thanks, I've just had one.'

'What are you up to today?'

'Packing. Ordeal by aunty Maude, remember?'

Sam nodded and smiled. 'I'm sure you'll have a great time.'

Ricky scowled at her as Sam folded her paper shut and walked across to him.

'I didn't know you worked with Simon Vickers at McDonalds.'

Ricky finished filling the kettle and plugged it in. 'I didn't really, he was only part time. When he was on I was normally off.'

'What about the computer club, did you have much to do

with him there?'

Ricky shrugged. 'No, not really. He spent most of his time with Dominic…'

'Dominic Parr?'

'Yes, that's him. He really didn't have time for the rest of us.'

'Was he good with computers?'

'Brilliant apparently, well, according to your mate Eric, anyway.'

'Why didn't you tell me you knew Simon?'

'Why should I?' he frowned.

'You knew I was dealing with his case.'

'So, what's that got to do with me?'

Sam picked up the paper and handed it to him.

'Seen the morning paper?'

Ricky took it and scanned the front page, shaking his head from side to side as he did.

'Bloody hell, who'd have thought it?'

He handed the paper back to Sam and continued to make the tea, trying hard to act indifferently to the news, but both his manner and mood had changed.

'Is that all you've got to say?'

He looked at her. 'I didn't know him that well. It's a shame but I'm not going to lose any sleep over it.'

'He called you cool.'

'Did he? Don't know why, we didn't hang together or anything.'

'What was Dominic like with computers?'

'He was okay, tended to follow where Simon led, though.'

'What about the Net, did he use that a lot?'

'All the time. It's what the club was all about really, and it was free.'

'Have you got a Net name, Ricky?'

He filled the kettle with hot water. 'Ant. Don't laugh.'

Sam was pleased that at least he'd been honest about it.

'I wasn't going to. Do you know what Dominic's and Simon's were?'

He shrugged. 'No idea but it will have been something to do with animals or insects.'

Now he was lying, and Sam didn't know why.

'Why insects?'

'Because those were the kinds of names Eric liked us to use. Don't ask me why, but he was paying the bills so we didn't argue. There was an odd bloke that used to come, he had a right weird one.'

He looked thoughtful for a moment, and Sam cut in. 'The Spider?'

Ricky hesitated for a moment before he answered. It was enough to let Sam know he was at least nervous about the question.

'No, it wasn't that. Grasshopper, something like that.'

'Do you know who the Spider is?'

Ricky looked away from her. 'Never heard of him.'

'It's just that Simon had various drawings in his room of insects,' Sam persisted. 'One of them was a giant spider. He seemed frightened of it for some reason.'

Ricky shrugged awkwardly again. 'Wouldn't know.'

As Ricky started to fill his mug Sam walked across to him and, turning his head towards her in her hands, stared deeply into his eyes.

'Listen, Ricky, if you know anything at all then you've got to tell me. I shouldn't really be telling you this but I think Simon and Dominic were murdered, and I think this "Spider" character might have had something to do with it.'

He pulled his head away from her grip and turned away from her but Sam continued. 'You might stop someone else being hurt, including yourself.'

'I told you, I don't know anything.'

Before she had time to pursue the matter further the phone rang. Sam walked into the sitting room and picked it up. It was an unfamiliar voice.

'Doctor Ryan?'

'Yes.'

'I'm sorry to bother you, Doctor, my name's Gary Mitchell, Marcia said I should call. I'm a colleague of hers.'

'Oh, right. What can I do for you?'

'She asked me to check out a whisky bottle and let you know what I discovered.'

'And have you discovered much?'

'A little. There are only two places locally which sell that type of whisky. One's close to the city centre and the other's in Hardwick, about four miles from the city.'

'They need to be checked out then,' Sam interrupted.

'I've already done it, I hope you don't mind.'

Sam was both pleased and taken aback by his efficiency.

'No, not at all, what did they say?'

'The city centre outlet hasn't sold a bottle for over three weeks, but the one in Hardwick has sold three over the same period.'

'That's certainly interesting, but how can we be sure it was even bought from the Hardwick store?'

'I took elimination prints from the man that ran the shop. They match the ones we found on the bottle. So I think we can be sure the bottle came from there.'

'That's disappointing.'

'Why?'

'I was hoping the prints might belong to our killer.'

'Oh, I see.'

'Can he remember who he sold it to?'

'No, unfortunately not, but he is sure that it wasn't a

young boy. He's quite strict about that sort of thing, apparently. He tells me it's a bit of a connoisseur drink. He only sells about twenty bottles a year.'

'But he has no idea who he sells them to?'

'Nope, sorry.'

'Well, thanks a lot. It's very kind of you to take the trouble.'

'That's fine, anything for Marcia. How is she, by the way?'

'Fine, I think she'll be out and about soon.'

'Good, because she owes me a big drink.'

'So do I.'

Sam put the phone down and returned to the kitchen. Ricky's steaming mug of tea was still sitting on the kitchen table but there was no sign of her nephew. She tried calling him but knew it was futile, he'd gone.

It was late afternoon when Tom Adams returned to Jack Falconer's cottage. Most of the previous day's frantic activity had finished and the place appeared deserted. As he pulled his car onto the grass verge by the side of the gate he noticed there was a new BMW Z3 sports car parked a few feet in front of him. He looked around but there was no sign of life. Picking up his radio handset he called in.

'Superintendent Adams to control, over.'

The reply came back immediately. 'Superintendent Adams, go ahead, over.'

'PNC check, please.'

'Wait one.' There was a brief pause while the operator logged into the Police National Computer.

'Go ahead, over.'

'Red BMW Z3 sports, registration number Papa, 735, Bravo, Tango, Delta. I'd like a lost, stolen and owner's check, over.'

The crackling voice returned.

'Wait one.'

There was another pause while the number was checked.

'Confirms as a Red BMW Z3. No trace lost or stolen. Registered keeper is a Rebecca Webber, 73 Adbolton Drive, Apple Hill, Cambridge. Will you require a printout? Over.'

'No, that's not necessary.'

Tom clicked the handset back into place and stepped out of his car. He moved quickly across to the garden gate, ducked under the tape and made his way towards the burnt-out shell of the building. Rebecca Webber was standing in the middle of the wreckage poking about in the ruins with a long stick. Occasionally she paused to crouch down and collect some sample that interested her, or take a photograph of something particular. Adams stopped at the edge of the ruin and called across.

'Morning, Rebecca.' He nodded towards the BMW. 'New car, very nice.'

She brushed some of the soot away from her white overalls.

'Women can have mid-life crises as well, you know.'

Adams smiled at her.

'I can't afford that kind of a crisis.'

Even in her protective suit and wellingtons she was still an attractive woman. Tall and slim with a bright young face and a crop of jet-black hair which, when not constrained in the hood of a protective suit, tumbled across her shoulders. Tom smiled at her as she made her way across to where he was standing.

'Found anything interesting?'

She nodded.

'Quite a bit actually.'

Without saying anything further she began to walk back

towards her car, several exhibit bags held tightly in her hand. Adams followed her impatiently.

'Well, what have you got?'

She put the exhibit bags down by the side of her car and began to pull off her overalls.

'You don't even give a girl chance to get undressed. Never heard of foreplay?'

Although he'd known and liked Rebecca Webber for some time, his dealings with her had been strictly professional and he wasn't prepared for her flirtatious mood. He found himself taking a step back and apologizing.

'Sorry.'

When she'd finished pulling off her overalls she straightened and looked directly at him.

'Right, what do you want to know?'

Tom found himself coughing awkwardly before replying. 'Are we dealing with an arson or an accident?'

'Arson.'

'Are you sure?'

'Positive, but we'll still have to go through the procedures to convince you, I suppose?'

'Try me.'

'Although I haven't had a chance to check all the possible sources of heat yet, fireplaces, electrical points, I think the seat of the fire was the sofa.'

'Where the body was found?'

'Yes. The fire damage to the skirting boards around the sofa and the ceiling above it were pretty centred and extensive. I'll be interested to see how quickly the various woods burn.'

'What difference will that make?'

'Different woods burn at different temperatures and speeds. Once we've worked that one out we can come to all sorts of conclusions. Time of fire, type of fire, causes. I found what's left of an old gas bottle in the ruin as well. It was probably that which caused the explosion. I think petrol was used to start it, though.'

'What makes you think that?'

'There were traces all over the place. The burn pattern in the carpet was consistent with petrol as well. Although I did notice that the carpets were nylon.'

'What difference does that make?'

'Unfortunately, nylon carpets have a similar burn pattern to that created by a petrol spill. So the labs will have to check, but I'm quietly confident. The rest of the team should be here after lunch then we can have a proper poke through the layers of debris. Should be able to establish a more accurate radius of error as well. I can tell you one thing with some certainty though, whoever started the fire came in through the back kitchen window.'

Adams looked at the blackened shell of the house.

'How the hell have you come to that conclusion?'

'When a fire starts the smoke blackens all the windows. So whether they're still in place or lying around the floor, the glass should be black. However, when the glass has already been broken, the debris that subsequently falls onto it protects it from the smoke, so it remains clear, like that from the kitchen window. The glass was also on the inside of the house, whereas it should have been blown outwards like the rest.'

'So you think he was murdered then?'

She shook her head. 'I didn't say that. That's up to the pathologist to establish, I'm only a simple fireman.'

'How long will your report take?'

'I can give you an interim one this week, but a full report will take a little longer.'

Tom nodded.

'I had a visitor the other day, a friend of yours I understand, although she didn't admit it.'

'Sam Ryan.'

Rebecca nodded. 'Yes that's her. Very attractive, for an older woman.'

'I suppose. Water under the bridge.'

Rebecca smiled quizzically.

'Really?'

Adams nodded.

'Yes, really.'

He turned and surveyed the charred remains of the cottage, mumbling to himself. 'Covering his tracks by starting a fire.'

Suddenly Sam's theories didn't seem so fanciful now.

Webber leaned forward slightly, unable to pick up what Adams was saying.

'Excuse me?'

He turned back to her. 'He was murdered, you see. Strangled.'

Webber shook her head.

'I've been doing this job for five years now and I've often wondered how many murders people get away with when the evidence is consumed by fire.'

Adams nodded. 'I think I'm about to find out.'

'Sooner you than me. See you later.'

Adams said politely, 'Fancy some lunch?'

She smiled and nodded. 'Perhaps you do understand foreplay after all.'

After extracting about half the samples from the hospital's laboratory Sam made her way across to the forensic science labs in Huntingdon and delivered them personally. Marcia was waiting when she arrived and started working on them immediately, leaving Sam to find her own way out. She decided to call at the hospital before making her way towards King's Lynn and the carol concert. There seemed little point in returning to the cottage until the concert had finished. Wyn and Ricky had left for Harrogate that afternoon and she didn't relish the idea of going back to the empty building alone. Besides, she was determined to keep on top of the paperwork before she finally retired for the few days off the holiday allowed. Christmas on her own wasn't a very pleasant prospect, but, as it was a matter of fact, she might as well lose herself in her work and hope it all passed quickly.

The hospital was almost empty with people heading home early to start the Christmas festivities. Even Jean, who was normally one of the last to leave, had gone. Sam made her way into the office and switched on the light before crossing to her desk. Instead of the expected pile of letters and paperwork there were two beautifully wrapped Christmas presents, one balanced on top of the other. She examined each of the presents in turn. The first was from Jean, and had a letter attached to it. Sam opened the envelope and read it.

'I've hidden all your mail so don't bother searching for it. There's nothing so important it can't wait until after Christmas. Have a happy one and I'll see you in the New Year. Merry Xmas, Jean.'

Sam smiled at the note before tucking it inside her handbag. Picking up Jean's present she shook it gently, but there wasn't a sound. She contemplated opening it but decided to wait until Christmas morning. The second parcel was from Fred. She looked at the card.

'Have a good one.'

Simple and to the point, she thought, just like Fred. It was certainly more than she had done for them, or anyone else for that matter. She still hadn't managed to buy a single present and would have to make it up to them all after the main celebrations were over. A party, probably during the spring, was her best bet. She could put up Christmas decorations and hand out presents; it could be very amusing. With all the mail and reports hidden there was little more she could do so she decided to lock up and head for home. She contemplated for a moment whether Tesco would sell pre-packed Christmas dinners for one; something she could stick in the microwave and have ready in a matter of moments. Her thoughts were disturbed by a loud knock on the door. She wasn't on her own after all.

'Come in!'

Trevor's face appeared around the door.

'Thought that was your car outside. Got you this.'

His arm suddenly appeared around the door holding a large present. 'Merry Christmas.'

Sam began to feel worse.

'Thank you, Trevor. I'm afraid I haven't managed to get you or anyone else anything yet.'

He smiled at her. 'Not a problem, it's the giving, not the receiving . . .'

'That's what they say, but is it true?'

He walked across the office and, putting his present down on the desk, held Sam gently by her arms and kissed her on the cheek.

'Of course it's true.' He looked down at the other presents on the table. 'And I'm clearly not the only one that thinks so.'

Sam leaned against her desk.

'Sorry about all the arguments over the Simon Vickers PM.'

Trevor looked at her. 'You've got nothing to apologize for. It was my fault. I'm afraid my ego got in the way of my objectivity, and not for the first time.'

Sam was sympathetic.

'Occupational habit, we've all done it.'

'I'm sure, but I've done it rather too often of late. So I've decided to leave.'

Trevor's revelation stunned Sam for a moment. She stared at him without speaking, without knowing what to say. He smiled at her, reading her mind.

'Before you say anything, the Simon Vickers case only helped to make up my mind. I've been thinking about it for a long time. And now with Emily, and the baby on the way...'

'Baby?'

One shock seemed to follow another.

'Didn't I tell you? No, I don't suppose I did. Well, we didn't know until the beginning of the week. She's only a few weeks gone so it shouldn't be too obvious as she makes her way down the aisle.'

'I thought you didn't want another family?'

'I didn't think I did, but now I've got used to the idea, I'm very excited about it. Nice to know I'm not firing blanks yet, as well!'

A thousand questions invaded Sam's mind. 'How are you going to support your new family?'

'Its all taken care of. I'm taking over from John Osbourne in March.'

Osbourne was the head of the department and had been for the last five years. With the job went a professorial chair. Professor Trevor Stuart. Sam wasn't convinced she could ever get use to the idea.

'So you see, Sam, you're not getting rid of me altogether, I'll still be hovering over you like an irritating swarm of midges.'

Sam was secretly envious and yet pleased for him at the same time. She had hoped one day to hold the position herself. No woman had yet managed to climb to that lofty academic height and she was hoping to be the first.

'Will I have to call you sir?'

'Absolutely.'

'Well, congratulations. New wife, new baby, new job. Mid-life crises dealt with.'

'I don't know about that, but it should calm me down for a year or two. What are you doing over Christmas?'

Sam shrugged.

'The usual, eating too much, drinking too much, falling asleep during the Queen's speech.'

'You'll have Wyn and Ricky with you.'

'They've gone away, I'm afraid, to see aunt Maude in Harrogate.'

'You'll be on your own then?'

Sam nodded. 'Looks like it.'

'Why don't you come and spend Christmas Day with us? We've more than enough of everything. It'll do you good.'

Sam wasn't convinced it would. Seeing Trevor and his new love together would probably depress her even more.

'No, thank you, Trevor, this is one Christmas when I think I would be more comfortable with my own company. Thanks for the offer, though, it's appreciated.'

He nodded understandingly. 'Well, if you change your mind just turn up, we'd be happy to see you.'

'I will. Thanks.'

Trevor changed the subject. 'Jack Falconer.'

He was finally coming around to the real reason for his visit. Sam looked up, interested.

'I've asked for you take over the case, if that's all right.'

Sam looked at him, slightly surprised, while Trevor continued.

'I think there is a link between the murders, and it seems silly to split the results between the two of us. This doesn't mean I'm losing interest, I'll support you in your findings. If anyone can get to the bottom of this mess it's you. All I can do is watch from the sidelines admiringly.'

'Thanks, Trevor, it's appreciated.'

'If there is anything else I can do to help, you know where I am.'

'Your Ivory Tower?'

'Exactly!'

Trevor began to make his way back to the office door and as he reached it Sam called across to him.

'You don't know anyone who's good with computers do you?'

Trevor turned. 'Why?'

'I found a floppy disc hidden in Dominic Parr's sock. If you remember he was Vickers's best friend. I've tried to read it on my computer but there's too much water damage. I think I need the help of an expert.'

'Have you told Tom Adams what you've found?'

'No, not yet. I'd like to see what's on it first. If it turns out to be something stupid then I won't have helped my cause, will I?'

Trevor nodded in agreement.

'There is someone. Works in the computer labs at Fitzwilliam. Brilliant with computers, never passed an exam in his life, but some people are just like that, I guess. If anyone can extract information from that disk then he can.'

'What's his name?'

'Russell Clarke, and you'll most likely find him working in the lab, he almost lives there. Failing that, he probably has rooms in college, the porters will show you.'

'Won't he have gone away for Christmas?'

Trevor shook his head. 'Not him, his idea of Christmas is an empty lab and that's just what he's got. See you soon.'

'Thanks, Trevor.'

With a final nod and half-wave he left the room, closing the door firmly behind him. Sam looked at her watch, it was six-thirty. Late, but she had the disk with her, and with a bit of luck she might catch Clarke in college, and still have time to get to the midnight mass she had promised to sing in. Sam raced towards the door.

Fitzwilliam was one of the more modern colleges in Cambridge, known unkindly by some of the students and residents as a 'redbrick'. As such, it suffered more than most from the snobbery which surrounded its more ancient counterparts. Its white and modern look said more about sixties architecture than about any ancient seat of learning. Despite that, however, the college had a first class academic reputation and was considered one of the better colleges in Cambridge. It took Sam half an hour to travel the six miles from the hospital to the college, along roads that were clogged up with last-minute Christmas shoppers, stripping the remaining gifts and food from the shops.

She parked in the Fellows' car park and quickly found the porters' lodge to ask directions. As the small and slightly built porter directed her through the college, Mr Enright, whose car had allegedly been stolen by Simon Vickers suddenly emerged from the porters' lodge. The fact that he was wearing the traditional grey uniform and ill-fitting bowler hat of a college servant indicated that he was a porter working at the college. He clearly recognized her but said nothing, retreating back into the porters' lodge quickly. Although Sam was surprised she wasn't unduly daunted.

The computer block was at the back of the college and Sam found it quickly. Peering through the glass she saw a solitary figure working at a computer which, she assumed, was Russell Clarke. He was hunched over the keyboard, lost in his work. Sam knocked gently and entered without invitation. She was in a hurry and didn't have time for the normal pleasantries. As she entered, he swivelled his chair to face her, a slight look of surprise and annoyance across his face. Sam wasn't put off.

'Russell Clarke?'

'Who wants to know?'

He wasn't at all what Sam expected. In his mid-twenties, he was tall and slim with a crop of jet-black hair and tanned features. His arms, like the rest of him, were broad and strong and his crystal blue eyes seemed to twinkle as he spoke. He looked more like a rock star than the thin, anaemic, bespectacled academic type she expected. Despite her initial surprise, Sam pressed on.

'I'm Doctor Samantha Ryan, Trevor Stuart suggested I come and see you, I'm after some advice.'

He smiled broadly at Trevor's name.

'Yes, I know Trevor. You're not one of his women, are you?'

Sam was taken aback for moment but recovered quickly. 'We work together.'

'You're a pathologist?'

Sam nodded. 'You look surprised.'

He shrugged.

'You just don't look the type.'

Sam did not respond to this comment in the prickly manner she might normally have adopted, acknowledging that she, too, had fallen prey to preconceptions.

'That's not an English accent.'

'Australian. I'm on an exchange with the Commonwealth Trust.'

'Enjoying yourself?'

'It's okay, bit bloody cold though.'

Sam sat down next to him and pulled the floppy disk

from her handbag. 'Trevor said you might be able to make something of this.'

He took it gently from her hand and examined it.

'Looks damaged. What did you do, drop it in the bath?'

'No, I took it off a dead body. The disk had been submerged with the body under the Cam for a few hours. I think there might be information on it that could be helpful to a murder investigation.'

He looked at her in astonishment.

'Really?'

Sam nodded.

'If it's that important why haven't the police come around to see me instead of you?'

'They're not convinced yet. That's where you come in.'

'I'm not going to get into trouble or anything am I?'

Sam shook her head reassuringly. 'On the contrary, they'll thank you for helping.'

She was lying but felt that on this occasion the end justified the means. Russell ran the disk through his fingers a few times as if undecided, then, making up his mind, he turned to his computer and pushed the disk into the machine. His hands moved quickly across the keyboard. But no matter what he did the same message appeared on the screen.

'Unable to read disk. The disk may be damaged, remove or retry.'

He finally gave up and turned his attentions back to Sam. 'More problems than I thought.'

Sam looked at him anxiously.

'Does that mean the information's gone?'

He popped the disk out of the machine and examined it closely.

'Maybe, it's hard to tell at this stage I need to do a bit of work on it first. Can I hang onto it for a bit?'

Sam nodded. 'When will you know?'

'As soon as I can. I'll get stuck into it tomorrow. Give us a ring in a few days.'

'Where will you be?'

'In here, I'm always in here. Ring the porters' lodge, they'll put you through.'

'You're going to work on it over Christmas?'

'One day's much the same as the other to me,' he smiled, 'not very religious, I'm afraid.'

'I see. Well, thanks.'

As he began to turn back to his computer, Sam asked him a final question.

'Just one more thing.'

Russell looked up, interested again.

'Do you know a porter called Enright?'

'Porky. We all know Porky.'

'What's he like?'

'A pain in the ass to be honest. I found him in here a few times.'

'He didn't seem the type to be interested in computers to me.'

Russell laughed. 'I don't think he is, but you can get access to some very dodgy sexual material on the Net. I think that's his game. He's a bit of a slime.'

Sam nodded.

'Thanks.'

'Pleasure. See ya soon then.'

He gave Sam a wave, turned back to his computer and was lost in his work once again.

After leaving Fitzwilliam it was a race against time to reach King's Lynn and the carol service. Her plight wasn't helped by the amount of traffic, which seemed to increase as she got closer to the town. Even at this hour people were still out and about. Attending Christmas parties, most of them, Sam mused. Christmas was always a busy time for pathologists, car crashes, over-consumption, and perhaps, more regrettably, loneliness. The mood of the season, for some at least, seemed to bring on a sense of melancholy and isolation. This could quickly turn to depression and, for some, lead to suicide. Old photographs and keepsakes of bygone and happier times surrounded many of the bodies she examined, as if they'd been having one last peep at a world they had once inhabited and then lost; they had not always been lonely, they had once loved and been loved. If the sum of a person's life is their memories then many of these had been good ones, but with only a few photographs to remember them by it could all seem so utterly pointless.

Sam finally arrived in the small market town and after asking several people for directions, discovered St Nicholas's chapel just off the ancient and attractive marketplace. It was an impressive and beautiful church, almost too impressive for such a small town. East Anglia was ittered with large churches, many of which seemed to have been built in totally inappropriate places by millionnaire cotton merchants trying to buy their way into heaven. After searching for a further twenty minutes, she finally managed to find a parking place and ran across to the chapel. Both Eric Chambers and the Reverend Andrews were waiting for her. Eric tapped menacingly on the surface of his watch.

'Come on, Sam, you're the last one, we start in ten minutes.'

'Sorry, sorry. I had all sorts of trouble with the traffic and parking.'

Slipping off her coat and handing it to Chambers, she took her place in the choir stands. The other members of the group looked at her sympathetically and there were a few reassuring winks as she mouthed her apologies to them. Ann Lambert, one of the older members of the choir leaned over and whispered in her ear.

'For what it's worth, I've only just arrived as well.'

Sam turned and smiled appreciatively. As she began to calm down she finally managed to look at her surroundings. The interior really was quite magnificent. As with most Christmas services, the church was crammed to capacity with many people standing across the back of the church and along each of the three aisles. The interior was lit entirely by candles, whose flames flickered and danced, creating their own distinctive smell and casting strange and haunting shapes across the darkened stonework. It was odd to consider that all these people were waiting for her and the rest of the choir to burst into song so that they could follow. She scanned the faces of the congregation, searching for Edmond Moore and his prying camera, but he wasn't there and Sam was relieved. Suddenly Eric Chambers was in front of them with his baton raised. The choir seemed to breathe in as one. He looked up and scanned his eyes across their faces, appearing to stop briefly at each of them with silent encouragement. Then he began.

The mass finished just before one, after which the Bishop and chapter thanked each of the worshippers in turn, wishing them a Merry Christmas. Eventually he turned his attention to the choir. He looked up and beamed at them.

'That was quite magnificent, I can't thank you enough. I just hope you now realize that all the hard work was worth it.'

Sam and the rest of the group smiled and nodded in agreement. He was probably just being polite but the compliments were appreciated all the same.

'Now I have arranged a little hot punch for you all before

I am forced to send you back into the cold Christmas night.'

Two members of the chapter brought in dozens of steaming glasses of red liquid and started to hand them out to the guests, who took them eagerly.

'They're all non-alcoholic, I'm afraid, don't want to upset the local constabulary, do we? So help yourselves to as many as you like.'

As Sam began to sip from her glass, both Eric and the Reverend Andrews joined her. Eric spoke first.

'It's not like you to be late.'

'Sorry,' Sam sighed, 'but I'm a bit busy at the moment, it's been a while since we've had three murders in such a short space of time.'

Eric and Peter Andrews looked surprised. 'Murders?' they said in unison.

Sam couldn't help feeling that they sounded like a double act. Eric shook his head. 'I haven't read about those.'

Sam sipped from her glass again. 'You will.'

Peter Andrews began to whisper, as if the conversation had become heretical.

'Dare we ask who?'

'Not yet, but I don't think you'll have to wait long.'

Andrews persisted. 'Can't you even give us a hint?'

Sam shook her head.

'Sorry, if it got out I'd find myself in trouble.'

Peter Andrews stood back, disappointed but accepting the situation. Eric, however, didn't give up quite so easily.

'It's not young Simon Vickers, is it?'

Sam shook her head and refused to answer the question.

'I respect your integrity, Sam, but I bet it is. Always thought there was something a bit fishy about that accident.'

Sam's attention was suddenly distracted by a slight whirring sound, which seemed to be coming from behind her. She turned her head to see Edmond Moore, video camera in hand, filming Sam and the rest of the choir. He was there after all. She felt slightly annoyed by this unwanted invasion of her privacy but kept calm. She looked across at Peter Andrews, who appeared awkward and embarrassed.

'How's the feature film coming along?' she asked.

'Very well, very well indeed. Last few days now before we go into the cutting and dubbing room. That bit should be great fun. So you won't have to worry about us for much longer.' It was a cryptic apology, but welcome all the same. Andrews continued. 'Looking forward to seeing the wasp attack on old Ted Landsden during last summer's fête. That should cheer me up if nothing else does.'

Sam smiled at the thought of the local vicar deriving pleasure at seeing poor old Ted Landsden getting badly stung by a rogue swarm of wasps. Finally, she put her cup back down on the tray.

'Well must go, or I'll never get to bed. Merry Christmas, everyone.'

The chattering group replied in kind as Sam moved away. Once outside, she looked up into the night sky. It was a beautiful, clear and crisp evening. Pulling her coat collar up around her neck and pushing her hands deep inside her coat pockets, she made her way to her car.

Sam took her time going home. As she drove along the darkened Norfolk lanes she could not rid her thoughts of the inquiry. She would also have to wait until Ricky got back before she'd have chance to talk to him again. Perhaps he might be a bit more co-operative by then. Christ, she thought, I hope he's not involved.

The roads weren't as busy as they had been earlier, so, despite her steady speed, she still managed to get home quite quickly. Pulling into the drive, she parked up in her usual spot and made her way inside. She had considered staying up for a while but waves of tiredness had begun to engulf her as she was driving home, so she decided to go straight to bed. As she made her way down the hall she noticed that the small reading lamp was still on in the sitting room. This surprised her, as she was certain it hadn't been on when she left home that morning. Could Wyn be back, she thought, puzzled. As she entered the room, Tom Adams looked up.

'Evening, Sam.'

For a minute she was surprised, then annoyed, and then pleased to see him.

'How did you get in?'

'I've still got my old key. I guessed you wouldn't have changed the locks. You can have it back if you want.'

He held the key between his two fingers and offered it to her. She crossed the room and snatched it out of his hand.

'How do I know you haven't got others?'

'You don't.'

'How did you get up here, I didn't see your car?'

'I came by taxi.'

Sam sighed angrily. 'You're not drunk are you?'

'No, but I'm hoping to be.'

He leaned down by the side of the settee and picked up a bottle of champagne. Sam crossed her arms defiantly.

'Oh you are, are you?'

He nodded while Sam continued to eye him furiously.

'Why are you here?'

'I was on my own. Wyn said that you were going to be, too, so I thought it might be nice to keep each other company for a while. Being the festive season and all that.'

'That's what you thought.'

Tom nodded.

'I was lonely, remembered a couple of past Christmases and found myself missing you. So I came round.'

'Well, in that case,' she paused for a moment before changing her tone, 'I'd better get some glasses out, hadn't I?'

Sam walked across to her drinks cabinet and pulled out two fluted champagne glasses while Tom eased the cork from the bottle. Sam returned with the glasses and Tom filled them carefully.

'Jack Falconer's cottage, it was arson, by the way.'

'And Simon Vickers and Dominic Parr were murdered.'

'That's yet to be proved.'

'And in the meantime you do nothing?'

'Well, not exactly nothing. I've already got Chalky putting a team together.'

'What, on Christmas Eve?'

'That'll teach him for telling Trevor about the PM, won't it?'

Sam smiled. 'Yes, it will. How's he doing?'

'Let's just say he's not as sceptical as he once was. Mostly thanks to the leads you gave us, though, it has to be said.'

'Flattery will get you everywhere.'

'Good. So until I go back after Christmas I've left it all in his capable hands.'

'And until then?'

'Until then, I'm all yours if you want me.'

Sam leaned down and, putting her glass onto the nearby table, kissed him slowly on the lips.

'I want you.'

Tom pulled her onto his lap and continued the kiss. When he'd finished Sam looked up into his eyes.

'You're not going to make me walk up the stairs, are you?

I'll understand, if you are, it's been a while, and you're not getting any younger.'

Pushing the champagne bottle under his arm and the glasses inside his jacket pocket, he lifted Sam off her feet and without another word, carried her up the stairs to her bedroom.

8

SAM AND TOM SEEMED TO SPEND MOST OF CHRISTMAS DAY making love. She had never appreciated before how novel sex in the kitchen could be, and was more relaxed and happy than she had been for months. Sex with Tom was certainly better than with any other man she could remember, not that her experience was extensive, but he seemed to suit her particularly well. Her problem was, as it had always been, that her love was conditional, and she wasn't sure whether Tom would ever be able to accept her under those circumstances. But, for now at least, all the passion of their earlier romance was back, and without the pressure and constraints of a binding relationship to sour it. This time marriage, commitment, or moving in together, were never mentioned. They were simply enjoying the moment. If only it could have been like this before, then they might well have remained together. If they could agree to settle for what they currently had, then perhaps it could still work.

The day wasn't entirely without its interruptions. Trevor rang in the early afternoon to see how she was coping and to remind her of his invitation. She reassured him, telling him that friends had turned up unexpectedly and she was being well taken care of; which, after all, was quite true. After that Sam took time to open her presents, which had been stacked neatly under her Christmas tree. She shook each of them in turn, putting her ear gently to the side of the parcel and trying to discover what was inside before opening them. It was a family tradition, maintained since she had been a small girl. Opening them carefully, she folded the paper and placed it neatly in a pile by the side of the tree. Tom watched with a combination of disbelief and exasperation at her concern over piles of waste paper. He knew there was no point remonstrating, Sam recycled everything. She was fond of saying, 'If everyone did a little, then a lot could be achieved' and he didn't need to hear a lecture right now. Instead he watched, as she paraded her gifts in front of him.

Trevor had given her an elegant pair of evening gloves with a note telling her that they might not have the same sensuous quality as latex, but looked nicer. Fred had bought her a book on aromatherapy, and Jean a rather attractive headscarf. She eventually arrived at Tom's presents. The first was a long oblong box. After shaking it, Sam opened it quickly. It was the board game, 'Operation'. To play it you had to remove various plastic organs from inside a cardboard figure. If you touched the side of the body while you were doing this a bell sounded and you lost. Tom suggested that they might play Strip Operation later. As each of them was wearing only one article of clothing, they decided it might be a very short game. Tom's second, and more serious gift, was a beautiful gold necklace. Sam was embarrassed by his generosity, but realized it would be insulting to refuse the gift, even though part of her desperately wanted to. Instead, she walked across to the mirror and fastened it around her neck. Despite her misgivings all she could hear herself saying was, 'It's beautiful. Thank you, Tom, thank you.'

Tom came up behind her and put his arms tightly around her waist.

'My pleasure, it looks good on you.'

Sam turned and kissed him long and hard on the lips as they slowly sank down to the floor.

During the late afternoon, and in the middle of a particularly passionate interlude, there was a gentle, and then loud, knock on the front door. Easing Tom to one side, Sam tiptoed to the window and peeped through the net curtains. It was Eric Chambers. He seemed to be holding a tray full of small plants half-wrapped in Christmas paper. Knowing how far he must have come, she felt awkward about not answering the door, but the situation was impossible. Tom crept up behind her and ran his hand along her back, making it arch.

'Who is it?'

'Eric Chambers, he's a neighbour.'

'I thought you didn't have any neighbours.'

'In the country, my boy, ten miles is a neighbour.'

'He's walked ten miles to see you? It must be love.'

'More like five. He comes across the fields.'

'He looks a bit old for long distance walking.'

'Don't be fooled by appearances. He's a tough old bird, former army special services, keeps himself fit.'

'I can just imagine him now going into the Iranian Embassy with his zimmer frame.'

Sam nudged him in the ribs as they watched Eric leave his present on the doorstep and head back across the garden and into the fields beyond. As soon as he had disappeared Adams spun Sam around, threw her over his shoulder and carried her, squealing, up the stairs and into the bedroom, kicking the door shut as he arrived.

By Boxing Day they were both exhausted and slept late. When they finally awoke they were extremely hungry. While Tom prepared a full English breakfast, Sam decided to check her Web message page. There were a few Christmas greeting notes from friends around the country but nothing more. She had hoped to hear from Russell Clarke at Fitzwilliam. After browsing through a few pages Sam finally gave up and shut her computer down. As she stood to leave, however, she noticed that all of Ricky's new equipment had disappeared. She was surprised that she hadn't realized before, considering how much of it cluttered her desk. He couldn't have taken it with him, so Sam ran up to his bedroom and searched through all his drawers and cupboards, but there was nothing. She made her way slowly and thoughtfully back downstairs to the sitting room, where Adams was waiting.

'Tom, you haven't had any large scale thefts of computer equipment recently, have you?'

He shook his head. 'Not that I know of, why?'

'It's Ricky…'

'Thought it might be. What's he been up to now?'

Sam shrugged.

'I'm not sure he's been up to anything. Just that he seems to have picked up a lot of expensive-looking computer equipment recently.'

'Working now, isn't he?'

Sam nodded. 'McDonalds. Not exactly City wages.'

'Perhaps he picked it up secondhand?'

'No, I don't think so. It all looked state of the art to me.'

'What's he got to say about it?'

'Reckons he's getting it cheap from a mate or something.'

'Cheap? I didn't know there was such a thing.'

'Nor did I, that's what's worrying me.'

'Have you talked to him about it?'

'I tried, but I didn't get very far.'

'Do you want me to talk to him?'

'No, not yet. I don't want him thinking his aunt is a grass. Besides, I'm not sure how much good it would do.'

'Shall I have a look at the stuff before I go? Make sure it's not marked up or anything?'

'I would have asked you to, but it's disappeared. I can't find it anywhere.'

Tom could see the concern written across her face and tried to soothe things a little.

'I'll check with the local intelligence officer, see if something's happened I don't know about. I'll run it through the computer, too. Maybe another force has reported something relevant.'

'While you're at it I don't suppose you'd consider checking a couple of names for me?'

'Why?'

'Just a couple of people I'm not happy with, that's all.'

'To do with Simon Vickers?'

'Yes.'

He nodded. 'Who are they?'

'Edmond Moody…'

'Date of birth?'

Sam shook her head.

'I don't know but he's in his late thirties, early forties.'

'Address?'

'Sowerby somewhere.'

'That's a lot of help. What about the other one?'

'George Enright…'

'The man whose car was stolen?'

Sam nodded.

NIGEL McCRERY

'Well, I can get his details off the crime report. Right leave it with me I'll call you tomorrow.'

'Thanks, Tom.'

He smiled, pleased at the effect his offer of help had had on her, 'Pleasure.'

Sam finished dressing before collecting Eric Chambers's present from the doorstep. It was a seedbox full of dormant tubers from his prize Dahlias. They were well insulated with garden fleece and plenty of newspaper and Sam felt both touched and delighted, as well as very guilty for having left them outside all night. Fortunately the porchway where they had been left was fairly well protected and she was hopeful that no damage would have been done. She brought the tray into the kitchen.

'Have you seen what Eric brought me?'

Tom glanced uninterestedly across at the package, which Sam opening. There was slight mockery in his voice.

'Oh, more plants, just what you need.'

Sam frowned at him. 'You are to gardening what Shakespeare was to spot welding.'

Tom smiled and shrugged before turning back to the breakfast.

'It was a very kind thought,' Sam insisted.

Tom turned the bacon for the last time. 'What did you get Eric?'

'Same as you.'

Tom smiled. 'Lucky man.'

'Do you know your trouble?'

Tom looked across at her. 'I've got a one-track mind?'

'It often helps a relationship when you've got similar interests. Just thought you should know that.'

Tom turned back to the breakfast, smiling secretly.

'He'll be after a few clumps of my Alstromeirias, he's been talking about those for ages,' Sam mused.

Tom nodded wearily and began to lay the table. 'Has he? Want some of this breakfast?'

Sam shook her head.

'No thanks, I'll go and sort these plants out.'

Leaving Tom to finish his breakfast and dress, Sam lifted several small clumps of tubers from a sheltered part of the garden and arranged them carefully in a wooden tray before wrapping them in old Christmas paper.

Dressed warmly against the cold, they set off across the fields towards Sowerby. Although most of the ground was flat, they tired quickly, due to the exertions of the previous day, and were glad when the spire of St Mary's church finally came into view. They struggled over the final stile and made their way along to Eric's cottage, which was situated at the far end of the village. As they reached the gate, Adams suddenly stopped and turned to Sam.

'What if he's not in, are there such things as taxis around here?'

Sam pushed the gate open and made her way along the path.

'He'll be in.'

Tom followed her but wasn't satisfied. 'We should have rung first, could have saved ourselves a long journey.'

Sam knocked firmly on the door. 'It's Boxing Day.'

Tom shrugged.

'So?'

'So it's one of the two days in the year that the Erics of this world don't go out.'

'What's the other?'

'Christmas Day.'

'He walked across to your cottage yesterday.'

'That was unusual.'

Tom shook his head. 'Let's hope this isn't one of his "unusual" days.'

As he spoke the door opened, and Eric stood framed in the doorway. Sam grinned at Adams triumphantly.

'Sam, what a nice surprise. I went to your place yesterday. Your car was there but no sign of life.'

Sam suddenly felt awkward. 'We went for a bit of a stroll to work off the Christmas dinner. You know what it's like.'

Sam pushed her cheeks out making herself look fat. Eric smiled.

'I do indeed, that's why I came across, and I felt much better for it.'

'Thanks for the Dahlias, I'll be in competition with you for the Dahlia cup at next year's annual fair now.'

'I look forward to the challenge!'

'I know you've had your eye on a few of these for a while so I thought I'd bring some across,' said Sam, handing over her offering.

'Wonderful, wonderful, thank you very much. Look, don't stand on the doorstep, come in, come in.'

Sam introduced Tom Adams, as the two of them entered the hallway.

'Eric, this is Tom, an old friend of mine.'

The two men shook hands. 'The policeman if I'm not mistaken.'

Adams nodded.

'"Thought so, you've got the bearing of a policeman. Spot them a mile off. Well, Sam seems to think you're all right, so you're welcome. Fancy a drink?'

Sam nodded. 'Tea would be nice.'

Eric nodded and turned his attention back to Tom.

'What about you? I've got a twenty-five-year-old malt in the cupboard if you'd prefer.'

Tom shook his head. 'No, tea will be fine, thank you.'

'Right, you two, make yourselves comfortable while I put the kettle on.'

Tom scanned the sitting room, taking in at a glance everything relevant and interesting about it. It was always the first thing he did when he entered a house or room. He couldn't help himself. Too many years doing the same job had created a system in his mind, where everything and everybody became suspicious or untrustworthy until they proved different, and at times that could be difficult. Almost all his colleagues, past and present, were the same. It was a wall they built over the years to protect themselves from emotional and physical harm. Unfortunately, sometimes that wall became so tall that it was difficult to look over it, without distorting the view.

Although dark and old fashioned, Eric's lounge was an interesting place, with a variety of pictures, porcelain figures and pots. A large black and white photograph that hung on the wall caught Tom's attention. He examined it closely. Although faded, it was quite clearly a photograph of a troop of soldiers; three were European, with a young and rugged looking Eric sitting at their centre, while the others looked Oriental. They were all carrying a collection of weapons, from sub-machine-guns to evil-looking machetes. He tried to distinguish the regiment from their cap badges, but it was difficult. As he continued to search the photograph for clues, Sam walked across to the French windows and looked out over the garden.

'Wish I could create something like this.'

Tom forced himself away from the photograph, having failed to identify the regiment, and joined her. He followed her idle gaze.

'I thought you had.'

Sam shrugged discontentedly. 'My effort's okay, but Eric's garden, well, it's just wonderful. Diversity of flowers and plants, full of colour and fragrance, interesting corners and secret places. I sometimes wish I could wrap it up and take it home.'

Eric returned to the room carrying a tray of tea and biscuits. Putting the tray down on the small coffee table he called across to Tom, 'Milk and sugar?'

Tom turned.

'Milk, no sugar, thank you.'

Eric poured the tea, followed by the milk, and handed it to him.

'Thank you.'

'Eric, the picture on the wall, where was it taken?'

Eric looked across at it.

'Burma, it was a few years ago now, though. I was with the Chindits. Had a go at the enemy behind their own lines. Fought alongside the Burmese, bloody fine fighters, best I'd ever seen, anyway. Attlee and the Labour government sold them out after the war. Bloody shame. Stopped the Japs almost single-handed. Thought we were a little special, too. Well, I suppose we were. The amount of blokes that didn't come back proves that. They didn't die easily either. All close-quarter stuff in the jungle, you know.'

Tom nodded, impressed. Eric might be getting on a bit now, he pondered, but he wouldn't have liked to take him on in his prime. He returned to the photograph, taking in a mouthfull of tea as he did. The taste of the whisky was both instant and overwhelming. This sudden and unexpected intake of alcohol made him choke and cough to such an extent that he was forced to put his cup down and lean against the fire place for support. Sam moved across the room quickly and patted him firmly on the back.

'Are you okay, Tom?'

Tom nodded, unable to speak for a moment. Eric smiled at Sam.

'I put a little bit extra in his tea, I think it caught him unawares, sorry.'

Sam stared back at him, annoyed. 'Yes, I think it did, Eric.'

Eric looked contrite.

'I'll make him a fresh cup.'

Tom shook his hand.

'No, really, it's fine. Just caught me by surprise, give me a moment and I'll be all right.'

He was as good as his word. A minute or two later he had cleared his throat, regained his breath and was sipping a little more carefully from the lip of the cup.

Eric turned to Sam. 'When are you back at work?'

'Tomorrow, I expect I'll have the normal list of over-indulgences. Stomach contents full of turkey, Christmas pudding and wine. I sometimes think that Christmas should come with a health warning: Christmas can seriously damage your health.'

Eric laughed. 'Got any further forward with your murder inquiry?'

Tom suddenly became interested.

'What murder enquiry is this then?'

'On the Vickers boy.'

Tom looked at Sam. 'News travels fast around here doesn't it?'

He stared across at Sam, but she refused to be intimidated.

'We're still in dispute about it, Eric, but fortunately I am hoping to change Superintendent Adams's mind very soon.'

Eric suddenly looked embarrassed.

'Look, I'm sorry, I've clearly spoken out of turn. I didn't mean to cause…'

'You haven't, Eric,' Sam cut in. 'Like I said, whatever problems there have been will be sorted out over the next few days, so stop looking so embarrassed.' Despite Sam's assurances, Eric still felt awkward. Sam glanced across at Tom, who had remained irritatingly silent during her exchange with Eric.

'Well, we'd better be off. Thanks for the drink, it should keep the cold out during the journey home.'

'My pleasure, you really should come around more often.'

Sam smiled and kissed him gently on the cheek.

'When the weather improves, I promise.'

'I'll hold you to that.'

As Sam and Tom made their way along the street towards the path that would take them home, Tom suddenly put his arm through Sam's.

'I've got a few questions I'd like to ask you when we get back to the cottage.'

'About what?'

'Releasing information on police business.'

'It isn't an ongoing case yet.'

Sam paused dramatically on 'yet'.

'You know what I mean, Sam.'

She smiled up at him cheekily.

'Are you going to punish me, sir?'

Tom looked down at her sternly. 'Absolutely.'

Sam raised an eyebrow at him.

'In that case we'd better get a move on, I'd hate to waste any time.'

Tom increased his pace and forged on across the frozen fields.

Sam had been right about her morning list. It was both long and full of people who had lost their spirit at Christmas. For a season supposed to be one of joy, it also contained more than its share of unhappiness and tragedy. Not that her

Christmas had been a bad one. Tom had made no demands, hadn't talked about long-term plans or marriage. She'd begun to relax with him again, enjoy his company and his lovemaking. Perhaps now, at last, they could start to arrange their lives around each other without challenging each other's motivations all the time. It was late afternoon before she finished. Fred was still on leave, and Sam was having to work with one of the other technicians. She didn't like doing this at the best of times, but Sid Halpern was famous for being the slowest technician in the department. There was nothing wrong with his work, he was meticulous about that, he was just slow. At times it was actually like watching someone work in slow motion. This frustrated Sam and inevitably ended in a row with Sid, who was also inclined to overreact and threaten to resign.

She decided to leave all the reports until the following day and made her way quickly to the car park and then to Fitzwlliam. Although she still hadn't heard from Clarke she felt he'd had long enough to come up with something. Sam left her car in the empty car park and made her way quickly to the computer room. Russell Clarke was already there, head down, shoulders hunched over the screen as usual, so lost in his work that he didn't hear Sam enter. She crossed the room and sat down in the chair opposite his. He didn't move for a moment. Sam started to talk but he raised his hand, silencing her, while he keyed in the last few instructions. Satisfied, he finally turned to Sam.

'Who upset Mr Enright then?'

Sam was confused for a moment.

'What?'

'Porky. He came to see me just after you left the other day. Wanted to know what you wanted. What I'd said to you. What you'd said to me.'

'What did you tell him?'

'That you were checking out a new program with me. I don't thing he believed me, though. Found him creeping around the block a few times since then as well.'

'Not frightened of him, are you?'

'Porky, no, he couldn't catch me.'

He gave Sam a cheeky smile and turned back to his computer. Putting Enright to the back of her mind for a moment she returned to the reason for her visit.

'So how did you get on?'

'Typical woman, only want me for my brain.'

He keyed in a number of fresh commands. 'Once I'd got the disk cleaned up properly, quite a lot. It took me a while to work out how to get into the disk but I managed it in the end. I divided it into different sections with about five hundred and twelve bytes of information per section. Then using a special tool...'

Sam was confused by the terminology.

'Tool?'

'Well, program, sorry, I'll try and keep it simple.' She felt she was being patronized, but kept silent while Russell continued.

'Anyway, using this program, I managed to read each section of the disk as I cleaned it up until I finally managed to retrieve the information you wanted.'

'Sounds simple enough.'

He laughed at her.

'It might sound it, but I can assure you it wasn't. Very few people in the country are able to work on this kind of technology, never mind develop retrieval programs.'

For all his good looks, Sam thought, he was still an anorak at heart.

'So, what did you discover?'

He returned to the screen.

'That's where it got really difficult. Whoever had the

disk really didn't want anyone downloading the information. He'd written it all in a computer code.'

Sam understood his personality by now and knew what to say.

'But you managed to crack it?'

'You bet I did. Obviously thought he was being clever, but he wasn't that good. He's still got a bit to learn before he starts to play with the big boys.'

Sam looked at him, a little tired of his arrogance.

'I don't think he'll ever be able to play with the big boys again, he's dead.'

The confident air seemed to drain from Russell as he turned back towards her. 'Look, I'm sorry, I didn't mean to cause any offence. I...'

Sam had got his attention, but didn't want to completely humble him. 'You haven't, don't worry, carry on.'

He turned back to his computer.

'Anyway they used an ASCII character set. It's what they call an "Xoring Exclusive". Sam gave him a distant look, so he qualified what he had said. 'It uses characters with a constant value.'

Sam nodded, but was in truth totally confused by the gobbledegook. Despite this she tried hard to keep up.

'How does it work?'

'You can use any number below 256 as your constant; once you know the constant the rest is quite simple.'

'For a computer genius.'

Russell smiled. 'Right.'

'So, once you'd cracked the code what did the messages say?'

Russell shrugged. 'Well, after all that not much really. Just notes from two mates to each other. His mate...'

'Simon?'

'Yes. Well, he was called "the Fly" and the other one...'

'The Bee.'

'You know already.'

'I've managed to pick up a few bits along the way.'

'They seemed to have a thing about insects.'

'They were into green issues.'

'Right. Anyway, most of the notes were about computers, some of it quite interesting, but mostly about meeting up and surfing their systems.'

'Notice any other Net names?'

'There were two more, the Spider and the Ant. The Spider's a good Net name. The Spider's Web, get it?'

Sam looked at him blankly as her thoughts suddenly and dramatically turned to her nephew. Russell continued, awkwardly.

'Anyway the Ant appears to be just a friend they meet up with at some club or other and exchange information, that sort of stuff. The Spider, however, is far more interesting. He seems to be some kind of cut-price computer salesman. His stuff was bloody cheap, too, and good quality, no rubbish. How he could do it for those prices I don't know. Some of it was lower than cost.'

'Ever come across the name before?'

Russell shook his head. 'No, only wish I had, could have saved myself a bloody fortune.'

'No idea who he could be then?'

'Sorry, can't help. I've tried to contact him, see if I can't pick a few bits up, but he hasn't responded.'

'You keep saying he. Why do you think it's a man?'

'I don't really, just assuming. That's the thing with the Net, you're never quite sure who's at the end of the line. Bit spooky ,eh?'

Sam nodded.

'Can I have a look?'

Russell changed seats, making way for Sam.

'Be my guest, but it's all pretty routine stuff.'

Sam took his seat and began to scan through the messages. Russell had been right, there wasn't much and most of what was there was boring. She found the pages where Dominic Parr mentioned the Spider, but there was no hint of his identity. All Sam knew for sure was that he was some sort of computer salesman with good quality and cheap equipment for sale. What was more significant, however, were the dates that he was mentioned. The last note from Simon to Dominic, sent on the night he was killed, read,

'Will be a little late tonight but should have a few surprises for you when I get there. The Spider's got some new tools; I'm going to have a look. Meeting in usual place.'

Sam scanned quickly through the rest of the notes until she found Dominic's last note. As she suspected it was to the Spider.

'Have the information you want. Meet by the pool, usual time.'

Sam was sure now that the Spider was her killer. The only thing she needed to find out now was *who* he was. She made a mental note of some of the items Dominic and Simon had mentioned. There were modems, scanners, microphones, in fact everything that the modern computer anorak would consider essential for his equipment. She decided that there had to be more. If not on this disk, then on others, or perhaps embedded into one of the hard drives. She would have to try and have another look through their work files. Finally, exhausted from looking at the screen and an endless stream of inane messages, she turned her attention back to Russell.

'Can you find out who this 'Spider' user is?'

He looked thoughtful for a moment, contemplating the request. 'Backtrack him to his Website you mean?'

Sam nodded.

'You'd have to be a bit of a genius to do that. So yes, I guess I could.'

'How are you going to do it?'

'Put out an enticing message first and see if he bites.'

Sam looked through Russell, lost in her own thoughts for a moment.

'Try describing yourself as an eighteen-year-old boy who loves the Net but is a bit short of cash and equipment. That should do the trick.'

Russell turned back towards his computer. 'Sounds good, let's see what we can do.'

'How difficult will it be to track him?'

'Depends how good he is.'

'There's a chance you might not be able to do it then?'

'I'll track him all right, got into the NATO system last year, they never did find me. Depends how many back alleys he sends me up. Anyway, let's see if we can contact him first. I'll see what I can do after that.'

Sam suddenly felt concern for Russell. After all, he was putting himself on the line for her and the operation wasn't without its dangers.

'If you do make contact you will let me know at once, won't you?'

Russell considered Sam's request carefully.

'I call and you come running? Sounds good to me, Doctor Ryan.'

Sam qualified her request.

'But only if you make contact with the Spider, is that understood?'

Russell smiled and nodded. 'Might get some cheap equipment.'

Sam took a firm hold on his arm.

'You might get dead as well.'

Russell looked at her, the cheeky grin vanishing from his face in an instant.

'Sorry, stupid remark.'

'It was. Now, with a bit of luck, and if you do exactly what I tell you, we might catch ourselves a killer.'

Russell looked uncertain. 'Unless he catches us first.'

Sam stood and looked at him for a moment, considering what he had just said. By asking Russell to do her this one small favour Sam knew she might have put his life at risk. But her desire to find the killer and justify her own theories took a selfish precedence over everything else, and she considered it a chance worth taking. Sam looked at him confidently.

'Then we'll have to be careful, won't we?'

Russell nodded back, trying to appear as confident as Sam seemed.

'We sure will.'

His eyes betrayed him, however, and it was clear to Sam that he was already unnerved.

Although Marcia's message wasn't altogether clear she sounded excited, so Sam knew it must be urgent and hopefully something to do with the shrapnel she'd dug out of Simon Vickers's body. Having parked in the nearest available spot she made her way quickly through the maze of corridors that formed the internal skeleton of the Forensic Science Laboratory in Huntingdon until she arrived at Marcia's office. Marcia was waiting for her. Eager for information, Sam dispensed with the niceties.

'Well, what have you found?'

Marcia grinned at her overexcited friend.

'It's nice to see you, too.'

Sam crossed the room, her excitement unabashed.

'Come on Marcia, what is it?'

'Ammonium nitrate, it was all over the samples you gave me. Must have been quite a bang.'

'Fertilizer bomb?'

Marcia nodded. 'It's the dual nature that makes it dangerous. You can spread it on your fields or blow up you neighbour.'

Sam nodded thoughtfully.

'I know, my father was killed by a bomb made of the stuff.'

Marcia wanted the ground to open up and swallow her. 'Oh Sam, I'm sorry, I didn't mean...'

Sam leaned across and squeezed her arm.

'No, it's okay, I know you didn't.'

'IRA?'

'Sam shrugged.

'Never found them. But it could just as easily have been one of the Protestant paramilitaries, they had no love of Catholic policemen, either.'

Marcia nodded sympathetically. She was lucky and still had both her parents, but dreaded the day when she might lose one or both of them.

'They used it to build the Oklahoma bomb, too. The government tried to ban it after that but failed.'

'Why?'

'America has some pretty powerful lobby groups and they managed to talk them around. Democracy at work, eh?'

'Well, whoever our bomber is, he certainly wouldn't have any trouble getting fertilizer around here. The place floats on it.'

Marcia laughed. 'I'm usually up to my bum in it.'

Sam gave a half-laugh, she knew exactly what Marcia meant.

'Well, at least Tom should be convinced now. I can't see him wriggling his way out of this one.'

Marcia shook her head earnestly. 'I don't think he was really trying to wriggle out of anything, he just has to be sure. There's a lot at stake, money, mostly.'

'It's what makes the world go around.'

Marcia looked at Sam seriously for a moment.

'No, Sam, it's what stops it.'

Sam could feel the situation becoming tense so changed the subject quickly. 'If only we could trace the source of the fertilizer, then maybe we could move on a bit.'

Marcia skipped off her stool, walked across to her bench and picked up an exhibit bag containing several pieces of shrapnel which she held up in front of Sam.

'I think I might just be able to help there. Ever heard of taggants?'

Sam shook her head as Marcia began to explain.

'Microtaggant. They're markers that help trace explosives.' Sam continued to watch her, silent but interested, as Marcia continued. 'It's a chemically stable material consisting of several layers of a highly cross-linked melamine polymer, each of which has a distinct colour sequence which can be translated to a numeric series according to the colour codes used. One is brown, two blue, three red and so on.'

'Sort of explosive fingerprint?'

'Just like an explosive fingerprint. The ultraviolet lamps should bring them out, then with a bit of luck we should be able to trace the manufacturer and from there where this particular batch of fertilizer ended up.'

Marcia's knowledge on all things forensic, and her

endless enthusiasm for her work, never failed to impress Sam.

'Do you think you'll be able to trace it?' Sam knew the answer before she asked the question but felt it had to be asked anyway.

'Absolutely.'

Sam gave her friend a hug.

'Then we'd better get on with it, hadn't we.'

There was an urgency about the situation when Sam arrived the following morning. A variety of officers, both uniformed and CID, darted quickly in all directions, carrying equipment from computers to filing cabinets, desks to drinks machines, in fact all the paraphernalia of a major crime inquiry. She was pleased to see that Tom was taking her theories seriously at last. She had taxied the analysis reports on the shrapnel across to him the previous day and then awaited developments. She didn't have to wait long for a reply inviting her to attend Cambridge's Police Force Headquarters, at her earliest opportunity. She had considered giving the report to Tom personally and watching the look on his face as he read it. But she wasn't sure that gloating was going to do her any good at this stage. Sam approached the constable on the front desk and identified herself.

'Doctor Ryan, I've come to see Superintendent Adams.'

The constable smiled.

'Yes, ma'am, he's expecting you. Do you know the way?'

Sam nodded. She'd been there so many times she was convinced she could have found her way to his office in the dark.

'Yes, I know the way, thank you.'

The constable pressed the security button and Sam

passed through the doors into the police station. After following the corridor for several yards she ascended various sets of stairs. On her way she passed what she thought at first was a member of Tom's squad. He nodded politely to her before moving on. Sam half-recognized him but couldn't quite place the name. Then she realized who he was. He wasn't a detective at all but the computer programmer who she had found working in her office a few weeks before. Whoever he worked for they must have some sort of local and undoubtedly profitable franchise. Jean had been right about one thing; he was certainly very attractive. After finding her way through the maze of corridors she eventually arrived at Adams's door. Before she had time to knock, Chalky White suddenly appeared at the entrance. On seeing her, he looked embarrassed.

'Morning, Doctor Ryan. Good job. Sorry about before, I was out of order.'

This unexpected apology took Sam by surprise for a moment, but she quickly recovered. She nodded a polite thanks but didn't speak, unwilling to forgive his previous attitude that easily. He looked back into the room.

'Doctor Ryan, sir.'

Tom's voice called from inside his office.

'Come in, Sam!'

Chalky stood to one side, allowing Sam into Tom's oversized office before closing the door quietly behind her. Before Adams had a chance to lift himself from his chair to greet her, the phone suddenly burst into life and he snatched it up.

'John, about bloody time. I want three SOU units at the scene. Has it been sealed off yet? I don't care how long it's been, I want it treated as if it had only just happened. How long before the SOCOs get there? Well, make sure they step on it. I want the other two scenes secured as well. Don't bother me with that right now, if we have to pay the overtime then we'll have to pay it!'

He slammed the phone back down onto the receiver, glaring at it as if he were trying to transport his thoughts along the line to the previous caller. He finally looked back at Sam.

'I take it you got my report, then?'

Tom nodded and spread his arms.

'What can I say?'

'Sorry?'

'I think you know that already. Did you bring the rest of the reports with you?'

Sam walked across to his desk and dropped a large green case file on it.

'There's your evidence. I think you'll find that not only are the Vickers and Parr cases linked, but so is the death of poor old Jack Falconer. As I said before, I think you've got a multiple murderer on your hands.'

Tom picked up the file and flicked through its contents.

'Not a serial killer then?'

'No, well not according to the FBI definition of one, anyway.'

'Three murders in three different locations on three different dates?'

'That's the one. No, I think we've just got your common or garden sadistic killer on our hands. There's nothing random about these killings. They're planned to perfection, possibly with some kind of sexual motivation. Our killer also has some limited knowledge of forensic science.'

Adams frowned.

'Why limited? Couldn't our killer be a scientist?'

Sam shook her head. 'I don't think so, he's made too many basic mistakes. He is well versed in computer technology, however, knows his way around the Web and may have access to cheap computer equipment.'

'What makes you think that?'

'It's in the report.'

'I'm sure it is but I'd still like you to tell me.'

Sam collected her thoughts for a moment.

'He contacted both Simon Vickers and Dominic Parr through the Internet. Once our killer had established that they were both male and young, he probably arranged meetings with the promise of selling them cheap computer equipment. I believe that he planned to kill Simon, possibly raping him first. Jack was killed for reasons of self-preservation because the killer thought that he had seen something that night which might give him away and once again the fire was used to destroy evidence. At this stage I can't guess why Dominic was killed. Whether our killer had already marked Dominic out, or whether he thought he was some kind of threat, I don't know.'

'How do you know about the Internet?'

'I found a floppy disk hidden in Dominic Parr's sock. It was waterlogged and damaged so I had it cleaned up and managed to extract some of the files…'

'When will you learn to stop interfering in police matters, Sam?' Tom cut in.

Sam turned on him. 'As I remember, it wasn't a police matter then. You were too busy counting the cost to take much notice of my findings.'

Tom eased back in his chair. Although annoyed at Sam's interference, he had to admit, even to himself, that if she hadn't interfered, there would be no murder investigation.

'Go on.'

'We managed to extract some coded notes. These were finally deciphered and we discovered that the two boys were in touch with a web site user called the Spider. Although I already knew about the Spider before that.'

'How?'

'There were references to him in both Simon's and Dominic's rooms.'

'Search those as well, did you?'

Sam nodded.

'With permission.'

'Not mine.'

'Parents'.'

'Who helped you with the disk?'

Sam stared at him without replying.

'It's okay, whoever it was isn't in trouble, it just might be handy to talk to them. You wanted a major murder inquiry, Sam, now you've got one. I think the least you can do is co-operate.'

She pondered the request for a moment.

'Russell Clarke. You'll find him in the computer block at Fitzwilliam.'

Tom nodded. 'Thank you.'

'Do me a small favour, though. Don't contact him until I've had chance to explain.'

'You've got until tomorrow morning, after that I'm going to have to send a team around, okay?'

Sam nodded.

'Deal. How did you get on with those two name checks?'

'Moore and Enright?'

'Yes,'

'Nothing on Moore, but Enright's interesting: he's got a couple of convictions for gross indecency.'

'With minors?'

'No, adults in local toilets. You know the kind of thing. Nothing recently, though.'

The information wasn't exactly what she'd hoped for but it was interesting all the same. Tom suddenly leaned forward in his chair. 'Now I think there's something you ought to know.'

Sam leaned forward expectantly.

'Remember you asked me to check the computers to see if there were any outstanding cases of computer theft?'

Sam nodded.

'Well, once we managed to get the computers back on line I did. There was nothing in Cambridge, as I thought, so I did a bit of digging in nearby counties...'

'And?'

'Two. A big one in Northampton and a slightly smaller one in Suffolk. Professional jobs, too. Managed to bypass the latest computerized alarm system, strip the place of most of its decent equipment and get out without being detected.'

'Did our thief only take equipment?'

Adams nodded. 'Yep, and only the good stuff too. Left thousands of pounds worth of computers behind.'

'Any leads?'

'None, they floated in and floated out without leaving a trace. Found some of the equipment, though.'

'Where?'

'Dominic's and Simon's rooms. Had to take most of it away. We upset Simon's parents, I'm afraid.'

Sam could imagine the effect having Simon's shrine disturbed must have had on Mrs Vickers.

'You didn't waste much time.'

'Can't afford to now, Sam, it's more serious than even you thought.'

Sam sat further back in her chair, increasingly intrigued by Tom's outline of the case.

'By the way, did you manage to find any of Ricky's equipment after I left?'

Sam shook her head.

'When does he get back, I'll have to talk to him about it,

you know that don't you?'

Sam nodded and prayed that Ricky wasn't too involved. She wasn't sure how far her friendship with Tom would stretch on this occasion. Sam dragged him back to the point. 'You said something about it being more serious than I knew?'

'When I was checking the unsolved crime files in Northampton I asked about any unsolved murders and unnatural deaths involving fire…'

Sam leaned further forward on her chair, eager for information.

'And?'

'There have been three . . .'

She could hardly contain herself. 'Murders?'

'One murder. Two, shall we say, suspicious deaths.'

Sam fell back in her chair. 'Christ. Over what period?'

'The past two years.'

'And the murder?'

'Still unsolved.'

'How old were the victims?'

'Late teens.'

'Cause of death?'

'Strangulation.'

'And the other two?'

'Burns. They were both glue-sniffers, stuck in some shed when it went up in smoke. They think it was a combination of glue and cigarettes.'

'And now?'

'I've applied for an exhumation order.'

'Do you want me to conduct the PMs?' Sam raised her eyebrows.

'No, I'm sure they're more than capable of sorting out their own problems. Especially now they know what they're looking for. There are others, too, I'm afraid.'

Sam was having trouble taking in the last piece of information and did not respond further.

'After the information from Northampton, I gave the Serial Crime Unit a call to see if they could dig anything up. They faxed this through to me about an hour ago.'

He handed Sam a sheet of paper which she snatched from his hand and read eagerly.

'Sixteen!'

Only three known murders. The rest are marked as suspicious or accidental deaths.'

'What were the profiles they fed in?'

'Male, late teens to early twenties, who were interested in computer sciences and whose bodies were burnt after death. They're still working on it.'

'Can I take it then the Serial Crime Squad will become involved?'

'They already are. They're sending a team down to assist tomorrow. I've a feeling your colleagues are going to be very busy over the next few months, though.' Tom looked at her thoughtfully for a moment. 'I need a big favour.'

Sam looked at him without speaking.

'This has to have been an ongoing police inquiry.'

Sam didn't understand for a moment.

'It has to have been the police who detected that Simon Vickers and Dominic Parr were murdered and not killed in an accident.'

Sam felt she should have been angry but instead felt rather flattered, even triumphant.

'Or the shit will fly everywhere?'

'No, just in my direction.'

Sam nodded.

'Okay, as long as you promise to take me a little more seriously next time.'

Tom held his hands up.

'Promise, and thanks. I hope there won't be a next time.'

'You'll have to clear it with Marcia as well.'

'I already have. She said it was fine by her if it was with you.'

Not the only one collecting favours, Sam pondered.

'Is there anything else I should know before I start to spend thousands of pounds of the taxpayers' money?'

Sam shook her head. 'As I said before, it's all in the files.'

'Well, if you do think of anything else, you will let me know, won't you?'

There was a sarcastic tone in Tom's voice and she decided to play him at his own game.

'If you're sure you'll believe me, fine.'

Before Tom could reply there was a knock on the door and Chalky White entered the room. He looked across at Tom.

'Miss Webber on the phone for you sir.'

'Tell her I'll ring her straight back.'

Although the question and answer seemed innocent enough Sam noticed Tom flush slightly and there was an awkwardness about the way he replied. Like a naughty boy caught with his hand in the biscuit jar. Sam looked at him.

'Miss Webber?'

Tom's awkwardness continued.

'She's the fire investigation office dealing with the Falconer case. I just need to go over a few notes with her, especially given today's developments.'

Sam nodded. She wasn't sure she believed him but perhaps, given the fun they'd had over Christmas, she was just being over-anxious and jealous. She decided to test him, just in case.

'I had a good time at Christmas. One of the best presents I can ever remember having. You'll have to wrap it next time.'

Adams gave a half-laugh and tried to change the subject.

'Can you get Marcia to send me anything she has, too?'

She hadn't expected such a sudden change. Now she really did feel concerned. 'I'll ask her today.'

'Thanks. Well, if that's it?'

He was dismissing her. No small talk, no discussion about Christmas Day or any future plans. Sam suddenly felt a wave of panic sweep over her body and she didn't like it.

'Right, I'll see you later then.'

'Sure.'

Sam left as Tom picked up the phone. As she closed his office door she was tempted to stop and try to listen in to his call. Finally she decided she was being stupid. He was beginning a major murder inquiry and the last thing he had time for was making dates or small talk. She decided to call him when things had calmed down a little and invite him around for a romantic dinner, that should do it. Until then she would have to allow him to be as professional as she liked to be. She turned and made her way out of the police station unconvinced by her own arguments.

9

SAM MET MARCIA IN HER CAR WITH A WARM FLASK OF tea, by the edge of the Cam, close to where Dominic Parr's body had been discovered. Marcia jumped in the passenger seat and felt the warmth of the car heater surround her body.

'I'm still supposed to be off sick you know.'

She showed Sam her bandaged hand as if to emphasize the point. Sam poured her a tea and handed it over.

'Here, you'll feel better after this.'

Marcia took it and sipped gratefully. 'The great British cure-all. What would we do without it? So what's the plan my captain?'

'Brought your wellies?'

Marcia nodded.

'Always.'

'We're going to try and collect some samples of diatoms from various locations along the Cam and see if I can match them against the ones I found in Dominic Parr's body.'

Marcia looked at her suspiciously.

'How many places?'

'Sam shook her head. 'Not sure yet but as many as we can.'

'Well, that's okay, then, there must only be a couple of hundred miles of river and tributaries to cover.'

'It won't be that bad. I can't believe he was drowned too far from where his body was found.'

'So I take it the diatoms are different from the ones in the water where his body was eventually dragged out?'

Sam nodded.

'Completely. I'm almost sure he was drowned elsewhere and his body dumped in the Cam at a different location.'

'Why? Why not leave the body where it was?'

Sam shrugged, unable to answer her friend's question properly. She could only surmise.

'To have taken so much trouble, there must be something significant about the location Dominic was drowned in. Our killer is trying to cover his tracks.'

Marcia sipped from her rapidly cooling tea.

'He's good at that.'

Sam smiled. 'He *thinks* he's good at that. But we know different, don't we?'

Marcia finished her drink and handed the plastic cup back to Sam.

'We do.'

Sam slipped into her wellingtons quickly and with Marcia by her side made her way down to the river. The tape surrounding the area where Dominic Parr's body was discovered was still in place and the two women ducked under it quickly. Marcia produced the first of the sterilized bottles and handed it to Sam. Although it was still bitterly cold, the river had finally thawed and was running freely once more. Sam waded slowly into the river until it was close to the top of her boots before crouching down and taking her sample. Marcia called across to her.

'Don't fall in, or we might be dragging you out later.'

Sam ignored the comment and continued to fill the bottle. Once it was full she replaced the top and dried it before handing it back to Marcia to label. As Sam reached the edge of the bank Marcia put her hand out and pulled her in.

'One down, three hundred to go.'

Sam looked at her.

'Are you going to complain all the way through this?'

Marcia nodded.

'Probably.'

Sam shook her head in exasperation and the two made their way back to her car.

The remainder of the morning was taken up with Sam collecting samples from various spots in the river and Marcia labelling and storing them. By lunchtime they were both ready for a drink and something to eat. Being close to Grantchester they decided to stop at the Rupert Brook. After ordering a couple of light snacks and a drink, they managed to find two seats at the far side of the lounge and settled down to await their meal. Marcia looked idly out of the window.

'What do you think the chances of us finding the right spot are?'

Sam shrugged.

'I don't know, and to be honest, even if we do find it, I'm not sure how much difference it will make to the inquiry.'

'So why are we bothering?'

Sam frowned. 'Just in case. The reason we follow most of the procedures, I suppose. Sometimes it pays off. Are you going to be all right on your own this afternoon?'

Marcia nodded. 'I'll be fine as long as you run me back to get my car.'

'Not a problem. Sorry about this, but if I don't catch up soon I'll have some very awkward questions to answer.'

Marcia nodded sympathetically.

'When can you let me have the results?'

'I'll start work on them straight away. If I burn a bit of the midnight oil I might be able to let you have something tomorrow.'

'Brilliant. Thanks for all the help, Marcia, it's really appreciated.'

'I've enjoyed it, let's just hope we get a result after all this effort.'

'Yes, lets hope so. And before someone else ends up in the Cam.'

After dropping Marcia off at the lab with the samples, Sam drove straight to the hospital to catch up with the mountain of work she had waiting for her. She had only just walked through the door when the phone rang. She decided to let the answer-phone take the call and listen to see if it was anyone she really wanted to talk to.

'Hello, Sam?'

It was Tom's voice. She waited to see what he would say.

'Sam, its Tom. Look, wherever you are can you get yourself across to Eric Chambers's cottage straight away, there's a problem.'

Tom's mention of Eric Chambers's name suddenly made her tense, and she snatched up the receiver.

'Hello, Tom, it's Sam, sorry I was in the other office. What the hell is going on?'

'Nothing I can really talk about over the phone. I'll bring you up to date when you arrive at the cottage. You'll need your murder bag.'

Sam wasn't satisfied.

'Eric's not dead, is he?'

Although it seemed like a stupid question, it wasn't. The only time anyone rang a pathologist, especially out of hours, was to tell them someone was dead and that her professional help was needed, and this sounded like a professional call.

'No, he's not dead, but we've got a couple of bodies all the same. Can you come?'

Sam was both concerned and intrigued. 'Yes, of course I can. I'll be about fifteen minutes.'

Grabbing her murder bag she moved quickly to the hospital garages where she had only just parked her car. The engine was still warm and it started easily. Pushing it into gear she raced off towards the scene.

When Sam arrived at Eric's cottage the place was buzzing with the usual array of uniformed police officers, SOCOs and detectives, as well as the wide variety of vehicles that follow a major inquiry around. Although a few local people had already gathered to try and discover what all the commotion was about, the press hadn't arrived yet, so Sam didn't have to worry too much about her appearance. However, she still made sure her brush and make-up were in her bag, just in case they arrived before she'd had a chance to finish.

The chaos that always surrounds the beginning of a murder inquiry seemed strangely out of place in this small, normally sleepy, hamlet. The scurrying blue and white overalls of the murder squad must have appeared like creatures from another planet to the villagers. Sam began to wonder exactly who had been murdered and wished Tom hadn't been quite so vague on the phone. He had made it quite clear that Eric was still alive, so, if it wasn't him, then who the hell was it? She parked close to the scene and walked across to the booking officer, who was standing by the garden gate and produced her identity.

'Doctor Ryan, pathologist.'

He took a brief look at his watch and noted down the time she arrived before opening the gate for her.

'Superintendent Adams is waiting for you, ma'am. He's over by the far bushes.'

He pointed Sam towards a group of detectives and SOCOs standing around a bush towards the back of the garden. Sam made her way across to them. As she finally reached the group, Tom turned and beckoned her over to his side. Sam joined him. He was looking into a large hole approximately four feet deep by six feet in width. As Sam peered down the hole, two burly Special Operations officers began to climb out. She looked past them deeper into the hole, aware that there was something lying at the bottom of it. As her eyes slowly became accustomed to the darkness, she began to make out first the skulls, and then the skeletal remains of two bodies. They lay side by side, their brown-stained skulls facing towards each other. The jaw on one of the skeletons had broken away and lay separately on the ground. The other had a grisly fixed smile, that only faces stripped of flesh can produce. Sam spoke without looking away from the remains.

'When did you find these?'

'This morning when we came to question Eric about the murder of Simon and Dominic.'

Sam was astonished. 'Eric! You've got to be joking.'

'Your friend Russell Clarke traced the Spider back to Eric's system.'

'I thought I asked you not to talk to him until I'd had chance to tell him what was going on?'

Tom turned to her. 'This is a major murder inquiry now, Sam, I had no choice.'

Sam looked away from him. 'Who did you send to do your dirty work for you, Chalky?'

He nodded.

'That's what he gets paid for.'

'Well I hope he didn't bully Russell, we might still need his co-operation.'

'No there was no bullying. When he realized the seriousness of the situation he was extremely co-operative apparently. I think it's best you keep away from him for a while as well. Don't want him getting confused about who's running the inquiry now.'

There was a sudden hardness about Tom's tone and attitude that Sam hadn't noticed before and didn't like.

'Anyway, Chalky called me and we paid Eric a visit.'

'Has he admitted it?'

Adams shook his head firmly. 'Not yet, but then they seldom do at first.'

'So how did you end up with a big hole in the ground?'

'Chalky suggested bringing dogs in to search the place, just in case there were other Simon Vickers buried under the lawn. To be honest I thought it was a waste of time...'

'But it wasn't?'

'No. Doesn't look like it.'

'Well, I suppose I'd better get on. What have you done with Eric?'

'He's been arrested on suspicion of murder. Trouble is, we're not quite sure whose yet. Hoping you might help us out with that one.'

Sam would never have believed Eric capable of murder. But there was the unpalatable proof smiling back at her from the bottom of the pit.

'Is Colin Flannery here?'

Adams pointed towards the cottage. 'He's in there I think. I'd better warn you he's not in the best of moods.'

'Why's that?'

'Apparently I didn't stick to *procedure* for cases of this sort.'

His imitation of Flannery's voice was excellent and for a moment Sam wanted to laugh, but managed to control herself. She understood Colin's objections though; he was a stickler for procedure and any deviation from the correct path was likely to get the rough end of his tongue. He was right, of course. Defence counsels would use any excuse to try and force through an appeal, and procedure was one of their favourite targets. You knew that if Colin was involved in a case, then there would be no procedural errors, or comebacks, and defence counsels would rarely waste their time searching for them once his name had been mentioned.

The cottage, like the garden, was alive with activity. SOCOs, uniformed and plain-clothed police officers were moving around with an urgency only an inquiry of this sort could achieve. They searched meticulously through cupboards and drawers removing a variety of objects, which were then packed carefully into various sized exhibit bags. Other SOCOs dusted for fingerprints or searched for fibres, while photographers took pictures of anything and everything.

Sam found Colin Flannery helping to pack a large quantity of magazines that had been discovered hidden inside a cupboard into a large clear exhibit bag. Sam picked one up. It was entitled *Gay Boys*. Eric was gay? It would certainly explain why he never married or showed any particular interest in women. It was strange, she pondered, that even when you think you know someone well, you don't really. After the bag had been sealed and labelled, Colin Flannery walked across to her flushed with anger.

'A right bloody cock-up, Sam. They'd already dug the hole by the time we got here. Photographs are all wrong, measurements haven't been taken properly, they didn't even bother contacting the Forensic Archaeologist. God knows how much evidence has been destroyed, moved, or disregarded. If you don't do things properly right from the start, you're bound to get yourself into trouble later. This would never have happened in Farmer's day. Now there was a police officer.'

Colin had always had a high regard for Farmer, and had been genuinely sorry when she had been forced to retire. Since then, despite having two other bosses, neither of them really compared favourably in his mind. Sam sympathized.

'How much can you retrieve?'

'I'm not sure. It depends how much damage their size tens have done.'

'I don't think its that bad.'

'It doesn't have to be. We're dealing with human remains, if they're knocked about, moved or crushed it can make a vast difference when we try and establish what happened to them.'

Sam allowed Colin his moment of anger while she waited patiently for him to calm down. As soon as he had, she continued. 'Found any fertilizer?'

He nodded.

'There are several bags of it in the shed.'

'Enough to make a bomb with?'

'A small but effective one, I should think.'

Sam sighed.

'Can you get it down to the labs as soon as you can for testing? Sooner we find out whether it's the same batch that was used to blow up Simon Vickers, the better.'

'It's already on its way.'

'Good. Have you got some spare overalls for me, Colin? I'll need to get into the pit as soon as I can.'

Flannery nodded. 'Yes, of course I have. I'm glad that at least someone's following procedure. I'll go and get you a pair.'

As Colin disappeared out of the cottage, Sam picked up the bag full of gay literature he'd just labelled. She sighed deeply, she had held Eric in high regard. It wasn't the fact that he was a homosexual that bothered her. She had always considered Eric, for all his bluster, to be an amiable character and one of the world's gentlemen. The sudden realization that her normally reliable judgement was wrong made her feel uncomfortable. Flannery returned after a few moments with her overalls, and she quickly pulled them on over her clothes. Once they had been secured, she made her way back into the garden, closely followed by Colin Flannery. She looked across at his concerned face.

'There's no need to worry, Colin, I won't get it wrong.'

'I know you won't, Sam, it's those buggers assisting you I'm worried about. They've made a big enough mess already, let's try and stop them making it any worse.'

Sam smiled broadly at him as they made their way towards the garden. She had to wait patiently for a few minutes while two members of Colin's team took photographs and video shots of the scene prior to her descent. Colin leaned across Sam's shoulder and whispered in her ear.

'Sorry about the delay, trying to catch up a little.'

Sam nodded, and continued to watched as the SOCO finished filming the scene. She couldn't help wondering if this would end up in the vicar's 'Year in the life' video. It would certainly make an interesting change from the normal pictures they would have to endure. When they had finished, Colin Flannery climbed into the pit and put footboards around the edges, allowing Sam to work around the remains without having to touch the bottom of the pit with her shoes. The scene was now preserved to Colin's satisfaction and he climbed out before Sam descended.

Once at the bottom, Sam crouched down, opened her bag, removed her dictaphone and began to examine the remains. From the size and shape of the pelvis on the right-hand skeleton, it was almost certainly female, while the one next to it was male. She began to dictate.

'Nine thirty-five am, 28th December 1998. Back garden of Rambling Cottage, Ewe Lane, Sowerby. I am about to examine the skeletal remains of two bodies. From the sizes of their pelvises I would conclude that one is male, and the other female, although further tests will be necessary to confirm this. Attached to the female skeleton are traces of what appears to be a yellow and blue dress. There is also a small quantity of what appears to be gold jewellery attached to the left wrist and neck.'

Sam gently picked up a small gold locket that was still attached to the skeleton's neck and opened it. Considering how long it had been under the ground it unclipped easily. Sam opened it carefully and peered inside. On the right side of the locket was the photograph of a young girl. She was very pretty, with long dark hair and wide eyes and appeared to be in her early twenties. On the other side of the locket was an older-looking man, perhaps in his late thirties or early forties. He was roughly handsome and reminded Sam of Eric. Engraved on the outside of the locket were the initials EE. Sam looked down at the pathetic remains and wondered if they were the two, once attractive, people in the photograph. She continued with her examination.

'The skeletal remains on the right appear to have what remains of a pair of trousers still attached to the lower part of the right leg. Both feet are also covered with rotting black leather boots of an old style.'

Tom's voice suddenly broke into her dictation. 'Any idea how long they've been down there?'

Sam shrugged and eyed both skeletons again.

'Not to the month, or the year for that matter, but a good many years. You'll have to wait until I get chance to carry out a few more tests before I can get it any closer.'

'Is there nothing you can tell us now?'

'Only that they're definitely dead.'

There was a humorous murmur from the SOCOs and detectives at the top of the pit, which was immediately silenced by an angry glance from Tom. Sam continued.

'One's male the other female. Hang on what's this?'

As she was speaking to Tom, a flash of light reflected off a sliver of metal protruding out of the ground by several inches suddenly caught her attention. She called to Flannery to ask if she could remove the object, before reaching across to dig the earth away from it with her hands. Finally, when she'd cleared enough of the dirt away she took hold of the metal and worked it clear. It was the blade end of what appeared to be a kitchen knife. The wooden handle had long since rotted away leaving the six-inch blade alone to tell its own terrible story.

Tom called down again. 'What have you found?'

'What's left of a knife.'

'Murder weapon?'

Sam shrugged. 'Who knows? I'll have a better idea later.'

'So are we dealing with a murder or not?'

Sam was evasive, unable to commit herself at this stage.

'As I said before, they've been here for some time and given the circumstances surrounding their burial, I'd say foul play was a definite possibility.'

She looked up at Colin Flannery.

'How long before you can get the remains to the mortuary?'

'Depends. I'd like each of the bodies to be removed individually, and as intact as we can. Try and keep the remains and their property separate. It's going to take a while if we're going to do the job properly.'

On the word 'properly' he glanced pointedly across at Tom who stared back unashamedly. Flannery continued.

'Best part of four hours to be safe, I would think.'

Sam knew it could be done quicker but Colin wanted to make his point. She looked at her watch.

'Shall we say after lunch, two pm?'

Tom and Colin Flannery nodded their agreement.

'Good. Can someone hold the ladder while I climb out?'

Once she'd stripped off her boiler suit and handed it back to Colin Flannery, Sam began to make her way from the scene. Adams followed.

'How much do you know about Eric Chambers?'

'Backbone of village life, Christian, decent man. Or so I thought. Where is he now?'

'Cell block.'

'Found anything else besides the magazines?'

'I think we know where he got his Web name from.'

Sam looked up, interested.

'Remember that photograph we saw of him in his sitting room?'

'The one of him in the army?'

'That's it.'

'Remember he said he was with Special Forces working behind enemy lines in Burma?'

Sam nodded.

'Well, I have to admit I was quite impressed, so I did a little bit of digging into what their role actually was.'

'And what was it?'

'Let's just say I wouldn't like to have been at the other end of one of their knives.'

'This is all very interesting, Tom, but where's it getting us?'

'Sorry. Their army insignia. It was a large black spider.'

'Sounds like you've just about got him wrapped up.'

'Just about. I think that, combined with the fact that it looks like he's gay, knew both of the boys, has an intimate knowledge of computers, and has killed with his hands before…'

'A long time ago.'

'Like riding a bike, I should think. He was probably as good at finding his way around woods as Jack Falconer, and,' he finished triumphantly, 'given his training, could quite easily improvise a crude bomb from the fertilizer we found in his shed.'

Sam wasn't as impressed as she felt she ought to be. She didn't know why. The evidence, although mostly circumstantial, was compelling. She just didn't believe Eric Chambers was capable of murder. She challenged Tom's opinion.

'All a bit circumstantial, isn't it?'

'Oh, and of course we found two bodies in his back garden, fancy me forgetting that. Pretty solid evidence, I would think.'

Sam hated his cocky attitude, especially given his previous opposition to the very idea that the two boys were murdered. She allowed him to continue for a while longer, however.

'I can't help thinking we've got our man, Sam.'

'We'll see. Coming to the PM?'

'Wouldn't miss it for the world.'

As they reached the gate Sam turned to him.

'Fancy some dinner on New Year's Eve? I've got a couple of recipes I'd like to try out on you.'

Tom shook his head. 'Sorry, sounds great, but I'm already committed.'

Sam was disappointed.

'Something you can't put off?'

'No, sorry, I'm away for a couple of days with friends. It's been planned for months. Not much I can do about it now.'

Sam thought it odd that he hadn't mentioned it before, but wasn't willing to give up that easily.

'Fancy some companionship?' she smiled invitingly at him. 'You won't be sorry.'

'Sorry, Sam, it's too short notice. Plans have been made, one extra at the last minute, well, you know.'

Sam was sure he was lying but decided to let it go for now.

'Okay, then. I'll see you when I see you.'

Tom nodded nervously.

'I'll give you a call, we'll try and fix something up.'

Sam gave him a wave of acknowledgement as she walked back to her car, but something told her he would not call. She was confused and hurt by his attitude after their time together over Christmas. They had seemed so close and Tom had made all the running. Why was he now distancing himself so rapidly?

Sam spent the rest of the morning making up for lost time. There was no morning list, so she managed to get through a pile of old paperwork by herself. Progress was slower than usual because Jean wasn't there to sift out the important files from the unimportant. Both Fred and Jean were still on leave, and Sam felt lonely and abandoned. She glanced at her watch, only two hours before she would have to carry out the postmortem examination on the two bodies found in Eric's garden. She wasn't looking forward to doing them with yet another stranger to assist. Until he wasn't there, Sam hadn't realized how well she worked with Fred. They had sort of grown together since she arrived at the Park and now she felt uncomfortable working without him. She had tried ringing him at home but there was no reply. Probably away with some girl, making the most of his break, before coming back to another year of blood, guts and brains. Most people were still off enjoying their Christmas and New Year. She found, as she sat alone in her office, going through yet another prosecution report, that she resented them. Resented their happiness and contentment. The phone suddenly burst into life and stopped her sliding any further into the depths of depression and self-pity. She snatched up the receiver.

'Hello, Doctor Ryan.'

Sam recognized Tom Adams's voice at once, and hoped he'd changed his mind about the New Year.

'Sam, it's Tom, listen I've got a bit of a problem.'

'Just the one?'

Tom ignored Sam's sarcasm and continued, 'Eric Chambers is refusing to talk to anyone…'

'Solicitor's advice?'

'No, he refused to see a brief initially. He says the only person he will talk to is you.'

'Me?'

Although she knew Eric well she was still surprised.

'Given the circumstances, I'm quite happy to allow you to interview him about the murders in my presence, if you're willing.'

'Are you sure that's legal?'

'Despite his refusal to see one, I've called the duty solicitor in. He reckons it's fine as long as Eric's aware of his rights and agrees to it willingly.'

'And is he?'

'Mr barrack-room lawyer, I think so.'

Sam thought hard about what she was about to commit herself to. It was way outside her normal remit. She felt she ought to call Trevor as the new head of the department, but decided against bothering him over Christmas. There was no one else to clear it with so she made up her own mind.

'Okay, I'll come down.'

'How long?'

'I'll be about half an hour.'

'Thanks, see you shortly.'

Sam spun around in her chair and stared through the window across the freezing Cambridgeshire countryside. She had hoped Tom would call, but it wasn't the kind of call she had expected. She began to wonder if perhaps it was time to become more committed to one person and put her career on the back burner for a while. After all, she had achieved all she was likely to for the time being. Trevor was going to be head of the department for the foreseeable future and by the time he came up to retirement, perhaps administration might seem more appealing. She really would have to set things straight with Tom as soon as possible. In the meantime however, she was still annoyed and suspicious about New Year's Eve.

Half an hour later, Sam found herself backing into a reserved space at Cambridge Central Police Station. A young, fresh-faced constable was waiting for her and took her to Tom Adams's office. On arrival he knocked on Adams's door sharply.

'Come in!'

The young man opened the door, allowing Sam in, before closing it quickly and quietly behind her. Tom stood as she entered the room.

'They get younger all the time,' Sam observed.

'And more useless. Thanks for coming so quickly.'

'You wanted me here early, didn't you?'

'Yes, but I didn't want you breaking your neck to get here either.'

Sam wanted to get on. 'So, where's Eric?'

'Interview room number one.'

'Shouldn't we be there then?'

Sam had decided to play it cool just to make it clear how annoyed she was with Tom over New Year's Eve.

'I thought we'd have a talk first.'

Sam shook her head.

'I haven't the time. I've got the two PMs in an hour and a half, and given the state of the bodies, if you want me to make any kind of identification or establish their cause of death, I'll have my work cut out.'

Tom looked at her intensely. 'Look, although I'm not saying the PM won't be necessary, Eric might have already told us everything we need to know before you start.'

Sam scowled at him.

'First of all, the PM is always necessary. He could be lying or mistaken. Secondly, even if he does tell us everything we want to know now, he might change his mind later, especially after a clever lawyer gets hold of him and discovers he's entitled to legal aid.'

Tom was irritated by her attitude.

'I realize all that, Sam, all I'm saying is that it might help to have a few facts before you start. I doubt very much that he's asked to see you just to lie about what happened. He could have done that to me just as easily.'

'Did Colin Flannery and his team find anything else in the house?'

'About a thousand pounds worth of computer equipment.'

'From one of the robberies?'

'Oddly enough, no.'

'Where from then?'

'We're still checking. But with all the other evidence I think it will be enough.'

The conversation didn't seem to be getting them any further, so Sam stood up impatiently.

'Let's get on with it, shall we? I don't want to waste any more time than I have to.'

Sam knew the feelings of anger she had towards Tom Adams were personal and nothing to do with the situation. She was probably being paranoid but she was beginning to feel cheated, even used. Although she had no evidence, all her instincts told her there was someone else. And although she knew she had no right to, she hated him for it. Adams stood and walked across to the door.

'You'd better follow me, then.'

Sam walked along the brightly lit corridors that made up the new and improved station, down three flights of stairs and into interview room number one. Eric was sitting on the opposite side of a small wooden table. By his side was Mr John Gordon, who had advised Mr and Mrs Vickers to come and see her in the first place. Sam looked across at him.

'What goes around comes around, eh, John?'

He gave her a brief smile.

'We don't know that yet, Sam.'

And you'll make money out of everyone, Sam pondered. Tom cut in.

'Have you fully informed your client of his rights, and explained to him what's about to take place?'

Gordon nodded.

'He's been fully informed.'

Eric Chambers nodded in agreement.

'You realize, Mr Chambers, that you are still under caution?'

Eric nodded again, this time more impatiently than before.

'Yes, yes. I'm fully aware of all my rights, now can we please get on?'

As Sam and Adams sat down opposite Eric Chambers, he reached out and squeezed Sam's hand.

'Sorry about all this, Sam. Sorry you had to be dragged into it. But right now you're the only one I can trust.'

Sam smiled a little awkwardly. She wasn't sure quite how to handle the situation yet and couldn't decide what would be an appropriate response at that moment.

'I'm not sure I do understand yet, Eric. But I'll do my best for you.'

Tom and Gordon glanced at each other briefly. It was one of the more bizarre interviews they had attended.

'Is there anything you want…?' Sam continued.

Tom suddenly intervened and stopped her.

'Just a moment, Sam.'

He leaned over and turned on the tape recorder which was situated on the side of the table.

'One oh-five pm, Monday, December 29. Interview with Mr Eric Chambers. Present are John Gordon, Mr Chambers's solicitor, Detective Superintendent Adams and Doctor Samantha Ryan, the county pathologist. Doctor Ryan is going to conduct the interview with the permission of all present.'

He leaned back and nodded to Sam, who started her interview again.

'Eric, I'm here to talk to you because you wanted me to. Is that correct?'

Eric Chambers nodded and Adams's firm voice cut in. 'For the tape please, Mr Chambers.'

'Yes.'

'Is there anything you want to tell me?'

He nodded.

Adams interrupted again. 'The tape.'

'Yes, sorry, I keep forgetting.' His attention returned to Sam. 'I suppose you want to know about the bodies?'

'Are you sure you feel like telling us?'

'After sixty years it's quite a relief. God knows what the good people of Sowerby are going to think, though. Biggest thing that's happened in the village since the Domesday Book, I shouldn't wonder.'

Sam gave a sympathetic smile.

'So what happened?'

'It was my mother, really. She was a cold, dominating figure. Looked after me well enough, well fed, clean behind the ears, that sort of thing, but not much time for love. She was the same with my father. I think she took her churchgoing a bit too seriously. You see the problem was my father wasn't a Christian, well, not a practising one, anyway, and my mother despised him for that.'

'Did she know he wasn't a Christian before she married him?'

'Oh yes, but like all women she thought she could change him. Thought she could make my father see the light, come to God. You know, the kind of thing the doorstep preachers spout. He wasn't a bad man, my father, provided for us very well, he just wasn't a good Christian and my mother couldn't stand that.

'Sex was another thing. I think father rather enjoyed it, but mother certainly didn't. When she wasn't listening he used to call her the iceberg. God alone knows how I was ever conceived. More luck than judgement I shouldn't wonder. She didn't much like me, either. Not because I wasn't a churchgoing Christian, I was, she made sure of that. But because I was his, and I think she thought she could see his wickedness in me.'

Eric drifted into silence as if reminiscing on the past. Sam gently pulled him back.

'So what happened?'

'The inevitable, I suppose, he met someone else. Bound to happen. Local girl called Kate Edwards. Pretty little thing, she was, about twenty as I remember. Anyway, a lot younger than my father. She was always full of life. She used to work at the local manor with her mother, downstairs maid or something like that.'

'Did your mother know about her?'

'Not at first, although I think she suspected. He started to go out more, stay out late, some nights he didn't come back at all. When he did, there used to be terrible arguments. Anyway, in the end he told her he was leaving, running off with Kate and setting up home in another part of the village.'

'What did your mother have to say about that?'

Eric shrugged. 'She was furious.'

'It must have hurt her?'

'Yes. It was bad enough that he had committed adultery, never mind setting up home with his mistress in the same village. I'm not sure she could have lived with the shame.'

Adams spoke for the first time since the interview had started.

'Who was responsible for killing them?'

Eric looked across at him.

'That was my mother. Don't forget I was only fifteen and brought up in a sheltered environment.'

'How did it happen?'

'I don't think it would have happened if my father had just left, but all the anger and vindictiveness that had built up over the years came pouring out and she set about him with her vicious tongue. Then he seemed to change his mind about moving out. He said he was going to throw her and me out and move Kate in. Anyway, I'm not sure what happened next, I think my mother must have snapped. All I heard was a sort stifled scream followed by a gurgling sound, then a thud as my father fell to the floor.'

Tears began to form in Eric's eyes as Sam reached out and took his hands again.

'Where were you when all this was happening?'

'In my bedroom, listening in the doorway.'

'Did you go and see what had happened?'

'Mother called me down and forced me to look. She'd stabbed him, the knife had passed clear though his neck, there was blood all over the floor and it was still flowing from the wound so I think he must have still been alive, well, for a while, anyway. I've never seen so much blood, it seemed to cover everything, it ran across the floor in great rivers.'

'What did your mother say?'

'Mother? She was totally unrepentant. Grabbed me by the neck and told me that was what happened to evil ungodly people, and that if I ever spoke a word about what happened I'd end up the same way. Comments like that make quite an impression on you when you're fifteen, I can tell you.'

'I think they'd make quite impression on you no matter how old you are,' said Adams. 'What happened to Kate?'

'Mother gave me a note, told me to take it to Kate.'

'What did it say?'

'It told her to come to the house at once and not to tell anyone that she was coming, and it was signed from my father.'

'Wouldn't she have recognized the writing?'

'That's the odd thing, really, she couldn't read very well. When I eventually found her I had to read the note to her. She came back with me.'

'And your mother was waiting?'

Eric nodded.

'Yes. I had to show her into the dinning room, my father had been murdered in the kitchen, you see. So I did. As she walked in, my mother called her a tart and stabbed her straight away. Then mother seemed to go mad and just kept stabbing her, God knows how many times, she went on and on. The poor girl screamed for mercy, asked for my help, but I just stood there petrified, couldn't move, couldn't do a thing, it was horrifying. She seemed to take ages to die.'

'And after she had.'

'Mother made me help her to dig a grave in the back garden, it took us all night. We managed to drop the bodies in as dawn broke. Funny thing is, when it was all over, she insisted on saying prayers over their grave, asking God to forgive them. We spent the rest of the day cleaning up the cottage. In fact my mother spent the rest of her life cleaning up the cottage. Like Macbeth's queen, always trying to get the spots out. Swore they were still there, even years after she had killed them.'

'Why didn't you tell anyone?'

'I couldn't, while she was alive, then I didn't want her memory dishonoured after she was dead.'

Sam nodded understandingly.

'Public and private faces?'

'Precisely. Old-fashioned values, I suppose. Not that they're much use these days. Besides, I was involved, too, and I wasn't sure how much trouble I would be in. My mother said if I ever told anyone they would hang me, and that if they didn't she would. She used to say, 'There's room for three in there you know.' Used to frighten me to death. Still have nightmares about it now.'

'She doesn't sound like a very nice woman.'

'My mother? No, she wasn't, devil incarnate, despite all her godly ways. When she died I remember laughing, laughing until I cried.'

'How did you explain your father's disappearance?' Adams cut in again.

'That was the easy part. With both my father and Kate gone everyone thought they had run off together. Mother burnt all his clothes. People in the village were very kind and understanding, except Kate's mother, she never believed her daughter had run off. She knew there was something wrong. I used to see her watching me for years after they died. Made me feel very uncomfortable, I can tell you. I was more upset when she died without knowing the truth about her daughter, than when my mother died. I hope they can be buried properly now, in the graveyard.'

'What about Simon and Dominic,' continued Sam, 'did you have anything to do with their disappearance?'

Eric suddenly leaned back in his chair and glanced across at his solicitor.

'Of course not, what's that got to do with anything?'

Adams cut in. 'We believe they were killed by a Website contact called the Spider. I understand that's your Website name.'

Eric shook his head.

'I'm afraid you've got that wrong, it's Beetle.'

'We traced the Website user called Spider to your location. I also understand that the Spider was your battalion insignia during the war.'

Eric suddenly sat up straight, full of indignation. 'It might well have been the battalion's insignia, but it's certainly not my Website name. Beetle is. You can check.'

'We will.'

'Are you a homosexual, Mr Chambers?'

Eric Chambers suddenly looked deflated and sat back in his chair, casting an embarrassed eye at Sam.

'Yes.'

Sam suddenly felt defensive for Eric.

'There's no need to feel ashamed of your sexuality, Eric.'

He gave her a quaint smile. 'Not now maybe, but in my day, well, that was a different story. These things die hard, Sam.'

Adams interrupted again. 'Where do you meet your partners?'

'Boots and Saddles.'

'Where?'

'It's a club for aging poofs on the outskirts of the city.'

'I don't think I know it.'

'Probably not.'

'Did you ever have sexual relations with your students?'

Eric looked at him aghast. 'No, never. That would be unethical, certainly not proper.'

'How well did you know Simon Vickers and Dominic Parr?'

'They were both students of mine. Simon was brighter, but Dominic worked harder to keep up. Saw them both once a week at the church hall, that was about it.'

'Did you kill them?'

Eric looked at John Gordon, who instructed him, 'You don't have to answer that if you don't want to.'

Eric turned his attention back to Tom and looked him straight in the eye.

'No, I didn't.'

Adams stared hard into his face, trying to judge whether or not he was telling the truth. Eric broke his concentration.

'What have you done with my dogs?'

The question caught Adams off guard for a moment. 'They're in kennels, I think.'

'Which ones?'

Adams wasn't sure; he hadn't actually dealt with it himself.

'I'll find out, let you know.'

'Please do, they've never been away from home before.'

Adams returned to the point. 'Have you ever killed?'

'Yes, when I was in the army, you had to, it was you or them.'

'Have you killed with your hands?'

'When necessary.'

'How did you do that?'

'With a knife, normally.'

'What about strangulation?'

'Couple of times, if I thought it was necessary. Harder than it looks though.'

'Is that how you killed Simon and Dominic?'

Gordon stepped in again. 'You don't have to answer that.'

Chambers nodded his understanding.

'I didn't kill them, I've already told you that.'

'What about making bombs. Could you do that as well?'

'Yes, it was all part of the training.'

'Did you blow up Simon Vickers's car after you murdered him?'

Gordon stepped in once again.

Eric looked sideways at his solicitor. 'Thank you, John, you've already outlined my rights and I appreciate it. But I always thought police stations were places for truth. Where the guilty were found out and the innocent released.'

Gordon shook his head gently at his client. 'Whoever told you that, Eric?'

Eric returned his attention once more to Tom Adams.

'I didn't make a bomb and I didn't kill the two boys. You can continue to ask me questions all night, the answer will remain the same.'

This time, Gordon looked across at Adams. 'I hope that clears matters up for you, Superintendent?'

Adams continued. 'We found a large quantity of

computer equipment concealed in your garage. Can you explain where it came from?'

Eric Chambers sniffed, annoyed at the accusation and full of self-righteousness.

'Firstly, it wasn't concealed, except perhaps from burglars. Secondly, I buy the equipment from a warehouse in Ipswich and get decent discounts from the company because I buy in bulk.'

'Do you pass the equipment on to the boys at knock-down prices?'

'Depends what you mean by knock-down. I charge them what I paid. There's no profit in it, if that's what you're getting at.'

'What's the name of the warehouse?'

'The Computer Warehouse. It's a huge place that sells cheaply for bulk orders.'

'What about receipts?'

'You'll find them in a large green box in my bureau, if you haven't rooted them out already.'

Adams leaned back in his chair and attempted to change his tack.

'Mr Chambers, look at it from our point of view. We have already found two bodies in your garden. You have told us they were killed by your mother, but that is yet to be confirmed. I am dealing with the murder of three more people, at least two of whom were well known to you. One of those boys, Dominic Parr, had anal intercourse, was probably raped, before he was murdered. A Net user called the Spider which I understand, despite your denial, is your Net name, contacted both boys. This so called Spider offered to sell them cheap computer equipment. We found a vast array of computer equipment in your house. Simon Vickers and Jack Falconer, both fit men, were strangled, then their bodies were burnt to try and hide the evidence.

Simon Vickers's car was also blown up with a home-made bomb. Now, considering everything I have just told you, I think you would have to admit that it makes you a prime suspect. So I ask you again, did you murder Simon Vickers, Dominic Parr and Jack Falconer?'

Eric became more upright than normal.

'No, I didn't.'

Gordon suddenly put his hand on Eric's shoulder, and stared at Adams.

'Mr Chambers has answered all your questions directly and honestly, and I don't see what more this repressive questioning will achieve.'

Adams glared at him. 'I think I'm the best judge of that.'

'No, I think I am. Mr Chambers is an elderly and much respected member of his community, and I think he has been questioned long enough. It appears to me, Superintendent, that your so-called evidence is all circumstantial...'

'Like the bodies in the garden?'

'That is another, and entirely different, matter and one that Mr Chambers has been open and frank about. As I said, when it comes to the matter of the other murders, I think your evidence is purely circumstantial and lacks any reliable substance.'

Adams thought for a moment. Then, turning to the tape recorder, he said, 'Interview terminated at one twenty-six pm.'

He switched off the machine and returned his attention to Eric Chambers.

'I think that will be all for today, Mr Chambers.'

'Does that mean I can go?'

'No, sorry, you will have to stay with us for a little bit longer. We will probably want to talk to you again about the murders.'

Eric looked nervously at John Gordon.

'Don't worry, Eric, they won't talk to you unless I'm here.'

Adams pressed a button by the side of the table and a tall police officer entered the room. Adams nodded to him, and the constable took Eric by the arm and led him to the door. As he reached it, Eric turned to Sam.

'I'm very sorry you've got mixed up in all this, but I really wasn't sure who else to call.'

'That's fine, Eric, don't worry, I'm sure Mr Gordon will look after your interests very well.'

He nodded.

'I'm quite innocent, you know.'

Sam nodded encouragingly, then as Eric was finally being led back to the cells a question suddenly came to mind. She didn't know why she hadn't thought of it before.

'Eric, have you ever heard of anywhere called the pool?'

'Chambers looked at her thoughtfully for a moment before shaking his head.

'No, sorry, Sam, never heard of it. Is it important?'

Sam shrugged. 'I don't know Eric. I don't know.'

Sam arrived back at the Park later than she had hoped. The team had already assembled, and Colin Flannery tapped his watch in annoyance.

'Sorry everyone, unavoidably detained.'

She changed quickly before dashing into the dissecting room. The two skeletons had already been unwrapped and lay on separate tables. Sam moved across to the female skeleton and looked down at the pathetic remains of what had once been a vital, young woman. After a few moments, she glanced across at Colin Flannery.

'Is she all here?'

He nodded. 'As much as we could find, and I think that should be most of it. They were buried pretty deep.'

Sam looked back at the remains.

'Okay, let's get on with it.'

She pulled the overhead microphone closer to her mouth and began the commentary.

The two postmortem examinations took all afternoon and ran into the early evening. When Sam had finally finished, she was exhausted. She walked across to her mortuary office and collapsed into a chair. Tom followed closely behind and sat down opposite her.

'Well?'

Sam looked up at him.

'Everything Eric said was true, as far as I can tell. The female skeleton is that of a woman in her late teens or early twenties. From the injuries to her ribcage she has been stabbed repeatedly, probably with the knife we found inside the grave...'

'Probably?'

'The grooves in the bone match the edge of the knife, so it's more than likely. After this long I can't give you many definites. I think they have been there anywhere between forty and sixty years. The other skeleton is that of a man in his late thirties or early forties who was probably stabbed to death as well. I haven't been able to find any evidence to confirm that, though, so I think we'll just have to take Eric's word for it.'

'Murder weapon?'

'Probably the same knife.'

'Anything at all that doesn't add up?'

Sam shook her head. 'No, not really. The stab marks seem a little low, but then people weren't very tall in those days. Other than that, nothing at all.'

Tom remained thoughtful for a moment. 'Do you think he killed the two boys?'

Sam hesitated.

'The evidence all seems to point to that, but my gut reaction says no.'

'Gut reaction, eh? I remember a time when the whole bloody force worked on gut reaction.'

'Why did you stop?'

'Kept locking up the wrong people,' he smiled.

'Did you find the receipts for the computer equipment?'

Tom nodded.

'And the warehouse. He was at least telling the truth about that one. Who else do you think could have done it?'

'That's your job not mine,' Sam shrugged. 'All I would say is, don't be too blinkered just because you've already got Eric in.'

'No, I'll keep the inquiry active for as long as I can. Think I'll probably charge Eric though.'

'Even though you think he's innocent?'

'I didn't say that. I think he *probably* is. Just don't want to close my mind to other possibilities.' He gave Sam a smile, 'Don't want to be made to look a fool twice on one inquiry.'

'What about his Net name? Found out about that then?'

'He was telling the truth about that, as well. Officially, at least, it's the Beetle. Doesn't mean he couldn't have another, though.'

'Do you think someone else could have got access to Eric's files? I mean used Eric's network and his own name? He's not very security conscious, is he? Key under the third rock from the right and all that. Anyone could have walked in, used his machine and walked out again.'

'I think, from talking to your friend, it was all a bit more sophisticated than that.'

The phone on the mortuary wall suddenly rang. Sam snatched it up quickly. She recognized the voice at once, it was Russell Clarke.

'Can you hold on for a minute?' She looked across at Tom Adams. 'If that's all, it's private.'

Tom nodded understandingly.

'See you tomorrow.'

Tom left and Sam returned to the call.

'Russell, what can I do for you?'

He sounded excited, almost hysterical. 'I've had another message, Doctor Ryan.'

'What?'

'From the Spider. I've had another message.'

10

S AM DECIDED NOT TO SAY ANYTHING TO TOM ABOUT
the call just yet. She reasoned that it might not be anything
of importance and didn't want to burden him with
additional trivia in the middle of a major inquiry. In truth,
although the police had taken over the inquiry, Sam still felt
close to it and was none too pleased at the way she was
being treated. She parked a short distance from Fitzwilliam
and made her way to the college on foot. She was
concerned that Chalky White, or one of his team, might still
be lingering in the college and catch her lurking around the
computer block. She took the back route into the college,
thus avoiding the porter's lodge and the owners of any
enquiring eyes who might decide to ring their friends in the
constabulary, particularly friend Enright.

Russell Clarke was sitting by his machine, engrossed in
his work as usual, but this time he heard her enter and
turned to greet her.

'Doctor Ryan, I wondered how long it would be before
you showed up. Thought it might be another one of your
police friends for a moment.'

Sam smiled warmly at him and sat down by his side.

'They're no friends of mine. They've already been to see you, then?'

He nodded. 'I'm afraid so.'

'Sorry. They said they'd give me chance to talk to you first.'

'But they didn't.'

'No. They're rather good at that. Didn't give you too hard a time, I hope?'

He shrugged.

'Most of them were all right, but that Detective Inspector White, he's a bit of a...'

'Bastard?'

Russell nodded.

'Right.'

Sam smiled at him. 'What did you tell him?'

'Just about everything. Sorry, he was very persuasive.'

'He didn't do anything to you, did he?'

He shook his head.

'No, but he described what he could do most vividly. That was enough.'

'Yes, he would. You said just about, so I take it you managed to hold some information back.'

He raised his eyebrows at her. 'I'll show you, it will be easier.'

He turned back to his computer and tapped in a series of instructions.

'Have a look at this.' He moved to one side while Sam examined the screen.

'Received your call. That's fine. Meet me at the usual place by the pool. 11pm tomorrow.'
SPIDER.

When she'd finished reading the message she looked up at Russell.

'When did you get this?'

'A few minutes before I called you.'

'Was it sent to you?'

He shook his head. 'No, I just picked it up.'

'How?'

'I'm not sure, really. I have been scanning for messages to and from the Spider but I wasn't scanning when the message popped up, odd, really.'

'Have you managed to trace it back yet?'

He shook his head.

'I've tried, but whoever it is has been very careful this time. He keeps leading me up blind alleys.'

'It's not Eric, then?'

'I'm not sure, as I said, I couldn't trace it back. Besides, isn't he already locked up?' Sam nodded, as Russell continued. 'Whoever it is, he really seems to know what he's doing. It's going to be tough.'

'What about the person he sent it to, any clues there?'

'Nothing. Not even a caller name. That's still our best chance, though.'

'How do you mean?'

'If the receiver calls back and confirms the meeting I might get a lock.'

'Why?'

'Chances are the receiver isn't as clever as the sender and we just might be able to trace the Website.'

'Any chance of the police experts having picked up the message as well?'

'Shouldn't think so, they're not that good. If they were they wouldn't be working for the police, would they?'

Sam smiled at his arrogance.

'Have you said anything to the police about this?'

'Like I said, Inspector White didn't get everything out of me.'

'Can you keep it to yourself for a little while longer?'

'In case the receiver calls back?'

Sam nodded.

'Okay.'

'Thanks.'

She leaned across and kissed him on the cheek. 'You've got all my numbers, haven't you?'

He nodded.

'Call me any time of the day or night if you get a breakthrough. Okay?'

'I understand. You're not thinking about going after this guy on your own are you?'

Sam shook her head vigorously. 'No chance, he's far too dangerous, but I'd like to be the one that tells Adams who the killer really is.'

'Any chance of me being there when you do?'

Sam smiled at him broadly.

'I'll see what can be arranged. By the way, has Enright been around recently?'

'No, not for a few days. I think he must be ill or on leave.'

'Right, thanks.'

Sam turned and left the room.

The following morning Sam was up early, determined to make a prompt start. Both Jean and Fred were due back, so Sam hoped things would have pretty much returned to normal. It was only when they were missing that she realized how much she missed them. They were familiar and comfortable with each other's ways, and that was important in any profession, but especially to her. She valued the easy working environment they provided for her, which allowed her to devote the whole of her attention to the forensic pathology, rarely distracted by the tedium of overseeing and regulating the basic practicalities of running such a department.

As she entered her office Jean stood quickly and pointed towards her room with an outstretched finger.

'Superintendent Adams is here. He's been waiting about a quarter of an hour.'

Sam nodded. It must be something important to drag Tom away from his lair, she reasoned. Especially at a time like this.

Tom Adams was standing at the far side of her office, looking out of the window. He turned as she entered.

'Afternoon, Sam, been off on your own inquires again, I hear.'

Sam moved across the room to her desk. 'Whatever makes you think that?'

'My spies at Fitzwilliam actually.'

Sam winced inwardly. She obviously hadn't been as careful as she thought.

'So, why visit Russell Clarke?'

'To apologize.'

If Sam was good at one thing it was thinking on her feet. Tom looked a little taken aback.

'For what?'

'Chalky White's behaviour.'

'First I've heard of it.'

Sam dropped her briefcase by the side of her desk and sat down.

'There's a first.'

There was a sarcastic edge to Sam's voice that Tom didn't like.

'So what's he done now?'

'Besides putting undue pressure on a person who, up to

now, has been nothing but helpful? He also went to see Russell before I'd had a chance to explain to him what was going on, as you promised.'

'Sorry. Breakdown in communications.'

'Like the one allowing him to tell Trevor what my PM findings were?'

'I'll talk to him.'

'I think someone should before he really upsets another friendly witness.'

'I'll see to it.'

Sam leaned back in her seat. 'By the way, I don't know if it's relevant but Enright hasn't been into college for the last few days, apparently.'

Tom shrugged.

'I'm not surprised.'

'Why?'

'Because he's legged it.'

'What?'

'It was you that put us onto him. After you mentioned his name I did a bit more digging. The vice squad was already taking an interest in him with regard to supplying pornographic material. So they turned up at his house bright and early yesterday morning and turned it over.'

'And Enright?'

'Gone.'

'Did they recover much?'

'Quite a stash, apparently. Mostly gay stuff.'

'Where was he getting it from?'

'They're not quite sure yet, but he was downloading quite a bit from the Internet and then copying it. His house resembled a TV studio.'

'Any connections to Simon or Dominic?'

Adams shook his head. 'Other than the fact that it was his car that Simon stole, nothing.'

'Bit of a coincidence, though, don't you think?'

'That's all it is so far, a coincidence.'

'Any other information on Moore?'

Adams shook his head.

'Nothing. Not even a parking ticket. He's squeaky clean according to our records.'

'And they're infallible?'

'No, but they're all we've got to go on.'

Sam sat back in her chair thoughtfully trying to make sense of the information Adams had just given her. He interrupted her thoughts.

'Your friend Eric Chambers has been released pending a decision by the DPP.'

'He hasn't been charged then?'

'No, he's been free and frank about the skeletons in the garden and doesn't pose a threat to the community at large. His solicitor's words, not mine.'

'Its probably true, but all the same, I'm still surprised they allowed him bail.'

'For what it's worth, so were we. I've got a couple of my lads on him so he should be okay for now while we try and collect some more evidence.'

'Good luck.'

'Thanks, I think we're going to need it.'

'When was he released?'

'Yesterday afternoon.'

'Where did he go when he got out?'

'Gordon took him straight back to his cottage. There now, as far as I know.'

'Has he got all his computer equipment?'

'He's still got his own; we had no grounds for removing that. We just took away the stuff we thought might have been stolen. It wasn't, by the way...'

'What?'

'Stolen. Everything he said checked out. Had receipts for everything as well.'

Given Eric's methodical nature that didn't surprise Sam at all. 'He still has access to the Web then?'

Adams nodded.

'Suppose so.'

'Are you monitoring it? I mean, considering that's how we think he contacted his victims.'

'We have been since he went back home.'

'Did he use it yesterday?'

'I've no idea,' Adams shrugged, 'but I can find out, why?'

'Just a hunch.'

'Woman's intuition?'

'Pathologist's actually.'

She moved the conversation on, not wanting to risk a bout of verbal fencing over chauvinist attitudes.

'You said there was something else.'

'I need to see Ricky. Can you bring him down to the station today?'

'Yes, sorry, I should have let you know. They didn't get back until late last night so I haven't had a chance to talk to him yet. I'll bring him down about three. Will that be okay?'

Adams nodded awkwardly.

'Fine. I'm sorry about the heavy hand but you understand?'

Sam grimaced.

'We'll be there at three.'

What started as a day of good intentions finished with Sam having done little, if anything, to catch up with her workload. She had tried to concentrate after Adams had gone, but couldn't. She was far too concerned about her nephew and his part in recent events. Finally, she gave up and decided to take the rest of the day off. She couldn't really afford the time but was far too stressed to give the reports her best attention and decided they would be better left until she was in a improved frame of mind. En route to her cottage, Sam decided to call on Eric Chambers and see how he was coping. She wasn't sure whether a visit of this sort compromised her or not, considering her role in the investigation, but as Eric hadn't actually been charged with anything and Sam was convinced of his innocence, so she finally persuaded herself that a visit would not be harmful.

The street outside Eric's cottage seemed busier than normal. The cottage was situated at the far end of the village away from the shops and amenities and, as a consequence, few people normally passed by. Now, however, since the discovery, there were several people walking their dogs, couples out for a stroll, and gangs of children on bikes trying to look over the hedge into the back garden. Incidents like this seldom happened in a small hamlets, and would undoubtedly be the topic of conversation for some months, if not years. After locking her car door and staring out a couple of sightseers, Sam progressed down the drive and knocked on Eric's door. After a few moments, a voice called anxiously, 'Who is it?'

Sam called back.

'It's Sam Ryan, Eric.'

He opened the door.

'Should you be here, Sam? Adams has two men across the road watching my every move.'

Sam nodded.

'Yes, I know. But at least you're out of prison. Can I come in?'

Eric stood gratefully to one side.

'Yes, yes, of course you can. Come in, come in.'

He looked urgently along his garden path and then back at Sam.

'Had the press here for most of the day. I think they've gone now.'

'They'll be back.'

Eric directed Sam into the sitting room and she made her way to the French windows at the back of the house. The hole and most of the garden were still taped off. Eric stood by her side. 'Made a bit of a mess of it haven't they? It'll take me years to put it all back together again.'

Sam looked across at him.

'No. A couple of seasons should do it. I'll come and give you a hand if you like.'

Eric smiled at her.

'That's very kind, Sam, but I've decided to leave. Set up somewhere else.'

Sam was surprised. Eric had lived in the village most of his life and really didn't know any other place or people.

'Where? Why?'

'North Devon. I have a cousin there, and why? My life here will never be the same again. Kids are already calling me names. I can't imagine going into the village and being stared at or whispered about behind my back. I might as well get out and start again where I'm not known.'

'I don't think it would last long, people move on to other things and other events.'

'That's a big city person talking. Around here this *is* the big event, the only one that's ever likely to happen. They won't forget, I've already been given my sentence.'

Although Sam wanted to dissuade him she knew that he was probably right. For a man like Eric this situation and the associated loss of his good name within the community would be intolerable.

'When are you thinking of going?'

'When this mess has all been cleared up. I think the police will be keen to keep me around until then.'

Sam nodded.

'Yes, I'm sure you're right. Is there anything I can do, anything you need?'

Eric shook his head.

'No, I'm fine for now.'

'If there is anything, you will ask, won't you?'

'Of course I will.'

Sam knew he wouldn't, but it made her feel better to know she had at least offered to help. There followed an awkward pause, which was relieved by a loud knock on the front door. Eric approached it cautiously.

'Who is it?'

'Peter Andrews!'

Eric turned to Sam and raised his eyebrows. 'Probably come to cleanse my soul and hear my confession.'

He opened the door and Reverend Andrews entered.

'Hope you haven't brought your video camera with you, reverend.'

'No, I haven't, Eric. I just thought you might be in need of a friend right now.'

He looked up at Sam.

'I see I'm not the only one who's had that thought. Hello, Sam.'

'Peter. I was just leaving.'

'Not because of me, I hope. I haven't disturbed anything important have I?'

'No, I was about to leave anyway,' Sam reassured him. 'I won't outstay my welcome.' She turned to Eric. 'Just remember what I said.'

'I will, and thank you.'

Sam turned to the Reverend Andrews.

'I expect I'll see you soon as well.'

'If you're there on Sunday you will.'

As she stepped onto the pavement, she noticed Adams's men sitting in a car opposite the cottage. As she glanced across at them one picked up his radio and called in. She couldn't imagine who they were talking about.

Sam arrived home shortly before lunch to find Wyn's car missing and the cottage apparently empty. She hung her coat in the kitchen and made her way into the sitting room. It was then, through the silence of the sitting room that she heard the faint tapping of fingers on a keyboard. The sound was coming from her office. At first she was tempted to call out but decided against it and instead made her way slowly and carefully towards the half-open door. When she reached it she gripped the door handle firmly and pushed it open. Ricky turned sharply and looked at her. There was no look of pleasure in his face, just surprise, even fear.

'Aunty Sam, what are you doing here?'

Sam looked at him, surprised.

'I could ask you the same question.'

'Just catching up on the Web, seeing if there are any outstanding messages, that sort of thing.'

Sam's face remained expressionless. 'And are there?'

'No, nothing all, a bit boring, really.'

He turned his attention back to the computer, pressing both the 'send' and 'off' switches. He tried to act as matter of factly as possible, but Sam could feel the panic within him. She decided to take advantage of the situation and press home her initiative.

'Where's all that new equipment I saw you with earlier in the month? It seems to have disappeared.'

Ricky shrugged. 'Wasn't working properly so I took it back.'

'Took it back where?'

'Framers, in town.'

'I thought you got it cheap?'

'I did, they were having a sale.'

Sam paused for a moment searching her nephew's face. She knew he was lying.

'How deeply involved are you in all this, Ricky?'

He looked down, unable to meet Sam's stare.

'I think it's time for the truth, don't you? Now where did you get all that equipment from, the Spider?'

Ricky shook his head vigorously. 'No, not him, I never met him, never.'

'Who, then?'

'Simon and Dominic, they got it for me. They got it for everyone.'

'And where did they get it from?'

'No idea. I just know that it was cheap.'

Sam was beginning to feel exasperated.

'For Christ's sake Ricky, they're dead, murdered. Now where the hell did they get it from?'

'The Spider. I think it was anyway, they said it was.' He looked close to tears.

'And who's the Spider?'

'That I don't know.'

'Ricky!'

'I don't, honestly I don't.'

'Is it Eric Chambers?'

'I don't know. All we did was give our orders to either Dominic or Simon and they got the kit for us. That's all I know.'

'And you never asked any questions?'

'It was cheap.'

'It was bent! So where is it now?' Sam spoke furiously.

'In the shed.'

'What were you going to do with it?'

He shrugged. 'No idea, just wanted to get rid of it.'

'And lose all that money?'

'It wasn't that much.'

'And you've no idea who the Spider is?'

'No, I really never got that close. Like I said, it was all done through Dominic and Simon.'

The phone rang in the sitting room, breaking the moment. Sam walked back into the room and picked it up.

'Doctor Ryan.'

A familiar voice was on the other end. 'Sam, it's Tom Adams. Eric Chambers made two calls from his Website yesterday.'

'Did you manage to trace them?'

Yes. One was to a friend in King's Lynn and the other to his cousin in Bath. All quite innocent, I'm afraid.'

Sam was relieved at the news. It would have been a weight off her mind to have the identity of the killer known, but she was glad that it wasn't Eric.

'Thanks for letting me know, Tom. Looks like it might be back to square one.'

Tom sounded more optimistic than that.

'I'm not sure I'd have gone quite that far Sam. There's still a lot of evidence against Eric, I haven't written him off yet. Are we still on for three o' clock?'

'Yes, I'll be there. See you then.'

She put the phone down and returned her attention to her nephew.

'That was Superintendent Adams, he'd like a word with you at the station about three o'clock.'

Ricky nodded.

'Right. Will mum find out?'

'Yep.'

'Shit. I'm not sure who I should be more afraid of, me mum or Superintendent Adams.'

Sam smiled at him. 'My money's on your mum.'
Ricky's head dropped.
'Shit, shit, shit.'

Sam wasn't happy about leaving Ricky but felt she needed to see the Vickers again before matters went any further. She arranged to collect him at two-thirty from the cottage and Ricky had agreed to look smart and have all the computer equipment, which had been languishing in the shed, packed in the box she left out for him. Sam hadn't seen the Vickers for some time and wondered how they were coping with all the pressure now the truth had finally been revealed.

The street was quiet as she drove slowly along it. No press or gawpers here, thank God. She pulled up outside the house, and made her way to the door, ringing the bell and waiting. Mr Vickers appeared a few moments later, his serious expression changing to one of delight upon seeing her.

'Doctor Ryan, what a nice surprise.' He called back into the house, 'Edna, Edna, it's Doctor Ryan,' then turned his attention back to Sam. 'Come in, Doctor Ryan, come in.'

He directed her into the dining room, where his wife was just emerging from the kitchen. She looked at Sam nervously.

'Have you got some more news?'
Sam shook her head.
'No. It's in the hands of the police now. They'll keep you informed of developments, I'm sure.'

'They've already arrested someone, you know,' said Mr Vickers eagerly. 'Didn't take them long once you'd convinced them, did it?'

Sam shook her head.
'No, no it didn't.'

She wasn't sure if they knew Eric had been given bail or that she was unconvinced of his guilt. For now she decided to keep both pieces of information to herself.

Mr Vickers continued, 'They've been here, took statements. They were very kind, left a policewoman with us for quite a while. Nice girl, kind-hearted.'

'Good, I'm glad they're keeping you up to date. I was just wondering if there was anything else I could do.'

Mr Vickers shook his head.

'I think you've already done more than enough and we're grateful. There is something I can do for you, though, I'm just sorry it's taken so long.'

He walked across to the cabinet situated on the back wall of the room and opened a drawer, pulling out three sheets of paper which he handed to Sam.

'It's that list you asked me to get. Not that it will be much use to you now but just to show that I did it.'

Sam looked confused.

'All his friends and aquaintances, remember? I wasn't sure whether I should have given it to the police or not. But then, as it was you that asked first and got the inquiry started, I thought I'd hang onto it for you.'

Sam glanced across the list of names on the front sheet. She recognized a few of the names from the computer club, and a couple she was slightly surprised to see, Edmond Moore and Peter Andrews. But still, they were all associated with Eric's computer club so she shouldn't have been that surprised. She folded the sheets and pushed them inside her handbag.

'Thanks, but I will hand them on to the police. They've got more resources, they'll be able to check the names off quicker than me.'

Mr Vickers nodded. 'As you like, Doctor Ryan, they're yours to do what you want with.'

'How are you coping?'

'Bit better since they arrested that man for murdering Simon.'

'You haven't been bothered too much by the press and neighbours?'

'No, not really. Press were a bit of a nuisance for a while, but that policewoman saw them off. Haven't bothered with us since.'

'Good.' Sam stood. 'I'll have to go, it was just a flying visit to see if you were both okay.'

Sam looked down at Mrs Vickers, who had hardly said a word since she arrived. Just sat watching proceedings, looking pale and depressed. Sam smiled at her.

'I'll see you both soon then?'

Mrs Vickers nodded and Sam began to leave the room. As she reached the door Mrs Vickers called across to her.

'Make sure he doesn't get off, won't you, Doctor Ryan, make sure he doesn't get off. Don't let anyone else suffer like us.'

Sam nodded sympathetically, torn by her own doubts, and left.

After her encounter with the Vickers, Sam made her way to the Forensic Science Laboratories in Scrivington in the hope that Marcia might have already got somewhere with the diatom analyses. She pulled into the laboratory car park, and after identifying herself, made her way to Marcia's office. She knocked and Marcia waved her in, knowing what she'd come for.

'You were quick, I've only just left the message on your answerphone.'

'I've been out for most of the morning.'

'Happy coincidence, then.'

'You've finished the analyses?'

Marcia nodded. 'Yep.'

'And got a positive result?'

'Yes. Have a look in here.'

Marcia pointed to one of the many microscopes sitting on top of the clean white work surfaces in the lab. Sam pressed her eye to the top and peered inside, examining the small but distinctive organisms.

'Brilliant. Where did the diatoms come from?'

'Grantchester, of all places. It was one of the samples we took just before lunch.'

Sam stood up and gave her friend's arm a gentle and affectionate squeeze.

'I knew I could rely on you. Exactly which location is this from?'

'Byron's Pool. It's about ten minutes away from the pub.'

Sam became very alert.

'Byron's Pool?'

'Yes. Don't you remember? It's at the back end of the village. Its got a right history as well. All sorts of naughty goings on took place there apparently. I was talking to the landlord after…'

Although Marcia continued with her history lesson about Byron and his Pool, Sam was lost in her own thoughts. Why she hadn't considered Byron's Pool more seriously before, she didn't know. She'd visited it often enough. Even had a nude midnight swim on one occasion, although she had carefully avoided swallowing any of the water. The river wasn't as clean as it might have been when the Bloomsbury lot were cavorting there towards the beginning of the century. It always seemed to take someone else to point out the obvious.

Marcia's voice finally managed to penetrate through Sam's thoughts. 'You're not listening to a word I'm saying are you?'

Sam turned abruptly to face her friend, who was pacing up and down her lab, annoyed at Sam's apparent lack of interest.

'You've discovered the pool.'

Marcia was a little confused by Sam's enthusiasm for the location.

'I think it was discovered a long time before I got there.'

Sam shook her head. 'Sorry, the Pool is where this Spider character seems to set up most of his meetings. There's one there tonight at eleven.'

'Are you sure?'

'About the meeting?'

'And the Pool.'

'As sure as I can be. Got the information about the meeting from the Spider's Web page. He wants to meet at the Pool, and it's been mentioned a few times before on other messages. Added to that, we've got the information about the diatoms. I think it's a fair bet.'

Marcia considered. 'Certainly seems to make sense. Are you going to tell the police?'

Sam nodded.

'If we're going to have any chance of catching him tonight I'm going to have to, it's all become a bit too dangerous. Besides, now they're officially involved I promised to hand on any relevant information to Tom and I don't want to upset him any further.'

'He rang today.'

'Tom?'

Marcia nodded. 'Yes. He wanted the diatom results as soon as possible as well. How did he know what we were up to?'

'He's got spies everywhere.'

'Shall I send them to him?'

'We'd better do everything through proper channels

now, I think. You've stuck you're neck out too far for me already.'

'Treading on police toes doesn't normally bother you.'

'Only when there's something to be gained by it, and I need their help right now.'

As Sam spoke the phone rang. Marcia picked it up quickly. 'Marcia Evans.' She listened for a moment before handing it over to Sam.

'Jean. It's urgent apparently.'

Sam took it off her eagerly. 'Jean?'

Her secretary's voice was clear at the other end of the line.

'I'm sorry to bother you, Doctor Ryan, but I've had a man called Russell Clarke from Fitzwilliam on the phone, he says he needs to see you urgently. Something about being contacted on the Net by the receiver, whatever that means. I'm sure I don't know what he…'

Sam was almost beside herself with excitement.

'Is he at the college now?'

'Yes I think so. He said he'd wait for you there.'

Sam slammed the phone down quickly and stood.

'Got to go. That obvious link I was looking for, it's just come up.'

It took Sam just over an hour to reach Fitzwilliam. She pulled her car into one of the Fellows' spaces and raced across to the computer labs. Russell Clarke was sitting in his normal place awaiting her arrival. Sam didn't bother knocking, just burst straight in and sat down beside him.

'Well, what have you got?'

Clarke looked surprised for a moment before a broad grin stretched across his face.

'Christ, you don't hang about, do you? Your secretary told me you weren't around.'

'She found me,' Sam said impatiently.

'Sorry I'm late calling you but I had Inspector White and his friends around here earlier bollocking me for talking to you again and asking me all sorts of difficult questions.'

'Did you tell them anything?'

'Just blinded them with science. It wasn't hard, he's not too bright when it comes to new technology.'

'Well done. So what have you discovered?'

Clarke turned back to his computer and executed a few nimble key strokes.

'I got this message last night.'

The screen was suddenly filled with a three-line message.

'Spider. Sorry it's taken so long to get back to you but I've been away for a short break. Yes I can meet you by the Pool at eleven. I will have goods please have cash ready. I've got . . .

Sam scanned the message quickly.

'Sounds like someone's negotiating to buy another load of equipment to me,' said Russell.

Sam nodded.

'Maybe. The message seems to have been cut short for some reason.'

'Yes, don't know why that was so I couldn't pick up his Net name, which might have helped. Not that it made any difference because I still managed to trace him.'

'That didn't take long, when did the message come through?'

'Few hours ago.'

'So where did you trace it to?'

'I can't give you a location but I can give you a Net address, its HTTP colon, back slash, backslash, WWW dot body dot UK dot UK dot.'

For a moment the number didn't completely register with Sam. She wasn't sure whether it was because she didn't believe it or didn't want to believe it.

'Are you sure about the address?'

'Yes, absolutely sure. Why?'

'It's my address.'

Sam's car screeched to a halt inside the courtyard at the front of her cottage, sending showers of gravel crashing against the neatly whitewashed side of the house. After fumbling about in her handbag for a few moments searching for her front door key, she gave up and raced around to the back of the cottage, bursting into the kitchen and confronting her bemused sister.

'Where's Ricky?'

For a moment Wyn was stunned by Sam's aggressive arrival but managed to blurt out, 'He's gone out on his bike.'

'How long ago?'

'Couple of hours. He was just leaving as I arrived. I shouted after him but you know what he's like, he threw a deaf one.'

'Was he carrying anything?'

'Only his old scout rucksack, although God knows why, he hasn't used it in years.'

'Did it look full?'

'Didn't really notice. Look, Sam, what's this all about? You're beginning to make me nervous.'

Without replying, Sam turned and hurried up the garden to the shed. The door was wide open, which was unusual in itself. As she reached the edge of the door she turned on the light and scanned the interior carefully. Lying on its side on the floor was a large cardboard box, which Sam had previously used to store bulbs. She crouched down and turned it the right way up. Lying at the bottom was a short black computer cable, all that was left, Sam surmised, of the equipment Ricky had hidden there. Wyn suddenly appeared at the door.

'Would you please mind telling me what the bloody hell is going on, Sam?'

Sam stood still holding the cable she had retrieved from the box and faced her sister.

'I think Ricky could be in serious trouble.'

Wyn looked confused. 'With the police?'

'I wish it was only the police. I think it might be far worse than that.'

Wyn shook her head.

'You're beginning to scare me, Sam, what the hell is going on.'

'He was involved with Simon Vickers and Dominic Parr.'

'The two boys that were killed?'

Sam nodded. 'Yes.'

'And you think Ricky might be next, don't you?'

Although she knew she should be protecting her sister, she couldn't see the point in lying.

'If we don't find him quickly, yes.'

Tears began to well up in Wyn's eyes 'What are we going to do, Sam, what are we going to do?'

Sam put her arms tightly around her sister.

'I'll call Tom, he'll find him I'm sure.'

It took Tom less than an hour to arrive at the cottage. He came alone and for once, not surrounded by the usual pack, or even his shadow, Chalky White. Wyn answered the door and took him through to Sam's office. For the moment, anyway, Wyn had managed to calm herself and, despite a little reddening of the eyes, was holding back the tears. Tom sat down opposite her and leaned forwards. His own face had a taut appearance.

'Has he turned up yet?'

Sam shook her head. 'Unfortunately, no.'

'How long has he been missing?'

'A few hours.'

'Not long for a teenage boy.'

'He's taken all his computer equipment with him.'

'The stuff you couldn't find over Christmas?'

Sam nodded. 'It was hidden in the shed. I never thought of looking there.'

'Any idea where he might have taken it?'

'To see the Spider.'

'That's a bit speculative isn't it?'

Sam shook her head.

'Not really.' Sam decided that total honesty was now her only option despite the anger she knew it would induce from Adams. 'Russell Clarke intercepted a message from the Spider arranging a meeting tonight at the Pool at eleven o'clock.'

'Why didn't you tell me what you had going on?' Adams interrupted.

'I didn't want to come to you half-cocked. I was going to tell you everything I had found out when I brought Ricky to see you at three, but then events overtook me.'

'Wouldn't I have been a better judge of what was half-cocked?'

'In retrospect, yes. But remember what a battle I had just to get you to treat the deaths as murder in the first place. I wanted to present you with sound information or I was afraid you would just dismiss it.'

Tom smiled and nodded. He couldn't see the point in being too angry with Sam. If it wasn't for her unorthodox and inquisitive nature he wouldn't be heading up a major murder inquiry.

'So what's happened since?'

'Russell Clarke interrupted a reply from the person the Spider had sent the message out to, confirming all the details for their meeting. Russell managed to trace this call…'

'He didn't trace the original call then, the one from the Spider?'

Sam shook her head.

'No. He tried but the Spider was a bit too devious, I think.'

'So where did he trace the other call to?'

Sam looked earnestly into Tom's face. 'They traced it to here, to my computer.'

Tom breathed out deeply, but remained calm.

'Right then, if we're going to catch this bastard, we need the time of the meeting and the location.'

'Eleven pm at Byron's Pool in Grantchester,' said Sam triumphantly.

'Where did you get that information from?'

'Russell Clarke for the time and Marcia for the location. The diatom samples we took from Dominic matched samples we took from Byron's Pool. It's not a hundred per cent certain, I know, but it's a damned good bet that's the location and we've no better suggestion.'

Tom sat back in his seat, impressed despite himself.

'What do I need with a murder squad when I've got you and Marcia?'

Sam was unable to appreciate the compliment under the circumstances.

'Have you any idea where Ricky could be at the moment?' Adams continued.

Sam shook her head desperately. 'No. We've tried all his

friends, not that they would tell us much anyway, far too loyal.'

'Let me have a list of them and I'll send a couple of lads out to do the rounds. That should shake them up a bit. Any other ideas?'

'Not one.'

'Is there any chance that Ricky or the Spider might realize you know about this meeting?'

Sam wasn't sure what he was getting at and shook her head, 'I don't think so.'

'Good, in that case we're going to have to make a few arrangements of our own.' He smiled across at Sam and winked. 'How much do you know about computers?'

'Enough.'

'Enough to send a message to the Spider?'

For a moment Sam was stunned by the request, and flustered.

'No, I wouldn't trust myself. Russell Clarke would be a better bet.'

Adams nodded and leapt up.

'Okay, Russell it is. I'll get a car over to Fitzwilliam to pick him up.'

'Wouldn't it be easier for us to go there?'

Adams shook his head. 'I don't think so. If the Spider is as clever as we think he is, he might trace the call back to the college and become suspicious. If he traces it here we should be okay.'

It was so obvious that Sam realized how ridiculous the question must have sounded and cursed herself for asking it. Her confusion quickly turned into her normal inquisitiveness.

'Can I ask what all this about?'

'We need to change the time of the meeting if we can. Make it a little later.'

'Why?'

'Because we need time. Time to grab Ricky and set up our own trap for Mr Spider.'

'And the location?'

'No, we'll leave that as it is. If it's the place he normally has his "meetings" he'll feel comfortable, relaxed, off guard. Which should make him easier to grab. Right, I'd better send a car for young Mr Clarke, then. Can I borrow your phone?'

Sam nodded.

'Do me a favour, Tom, will you?'

Adams stopped by the door and turned back into the room.

'Don't send White. Russell's frightened of him and we need him to be in the best possible mood if he's going to help us.'

Adams smiled and nodded. 'I'll send Jim Clegg, he's a bit of a social worker, he'll do fine.'

'Thanks.'

Adams made his way quickly into the sitting room, keen to get started.

Russell Clarke looked decidedly apprehensive when he finally arrived at Sam's cottage. Wyn met him by the door and took him through to the sitting room. As he entered, Sam and Adams stood and he shook hands with each of them in turn.

'Sorry to call you out like this, Russell, but we need your help just one more time,' said Sam.

Clarke nodded and shrugged his shoulders. 'Why not, if it's the last time? It's just that it's getting in the way of the old PhD at the moment.'

'It will be the last time, I promise.'

'Thanks for not sending Inspector White to pick me up,

by the way.'

'We weren't sure you'd come if we did.'

'I wouldn't have.'

Sam glanced across at Adams, who smiled knowingly at her. Russell broke the moment.

'So, what do you want me to do?'

Adams cut in before Sam had chance to respond.

'We want you to try and contact the Spider for us.'

Russell Clarke didn't seem at all concerned by this request. In fact he was almost offhand about it.

'Why?'

'The meeting tonight, the one you picked up on the Net, we need to try and alter a few things.'

'You know I haven't got his Website number?'

Sam nodded. 'We know. We're just going to have to put the call out like we did before.'

Russell seemed uncertain.

'It's a bit risky. How long have we got?'

Adams looked at his watch; it was seven-thirty. 'Three-and-a-half hours, three if we allow for a bit of travelling time.'

'Now, that's not very long, is it? I'll see what I can do, but no promises.'

Sam smiled at him.

'That's all anyone can ask.'

Sam showed Russell into the office and he made himself comfortable in front of her computer. Turning it on he clicked his way into the Internet, waiting for a few moments for a line to become free. He didn't have to wait long. He brought up the message board and awaited further instructions.

'So, now we're in, what do you want me to write?'

Sam contemplated this request for a moment before replying:

'Spider. Unable to make eleven o'clock meeting can we put it back to . . .' Sam turned to Adams, 'What time do you want it to be?'

'One am. That should give us plenty of time to get things sorted out.'

Sam looked back at Russell who was already typing the information in.

'Is there a reason you want the meeting put back. He might want to know.'

'Tell him you were having problems with your aunty,' Adams cut in.

Sam scowled at him as Russell typed in the information.

'How do you want me to sign it, Ricky?'

'No, sign it Ant. Its Ricky's net name, the one he would use.'

Russell tapped in the final few lines and pressed 'send'.

'That's it. It's cross your fingers time.'

Sam looked at Adams. They could only wait.

After two hours of waiting, any optimism they might have felt at the beginning had evaporated. Tom paced up and down through the house like a caged cat, mumbling to himself about the right decision and correct procedures. Meanwhile, Sam, Wyn and Russell made a half-hearted attempt to relax by playing Scrabble. It didn't work, but at least it helped pass the time. Finally, his patience exhausted, Tom made his inevitable decision.

'I think we've waited long enough, it's back to plan 'B' I think.'

Sam looked across at him. 'I'll grab my coat.'

Russell looked across at her, disappointed.

'Sorry, did my best.'

Sam smiled at him. 'You've got nothing to be sorry about, you've done more than enough.'

Wyn walked across to Tom and helped him pull his smart black Crombie on over his suit.

'You will watch out for Ricky, won't you? Don't put him in any danger or anything.'

He squeezed her arms gently and affectionately.

'He'll be our first consideration, promise.' He looked across at Sam, who had pulled her own coat on and was coming out of the kitchen. 'Coming?'

She nodded and crossed the room quickly to hug and kiss her sister, who was finding it difficult not to burst into tears.

'He'll be fine. I'll look out for him, you know that.'

Wyn nodded.

'I know, I know.'

'I'll leave Russell here to keep you company until we've got some news. That will be all right, won't it, Russell?'

He nodded.

'Yes, sure. We can finish the game.'

As the sight of Adams's impatient face caught the corner of her eye she pulled herself gently free of her sister's grip. As she did, the sound of the 'message received' audible alarm suddenly emanated from Sam's office. For a moment nobody moved, almost thrown into a state of shock by the sound. Russell was the first to react, jumping off his chair and dashing into the empty office. This sudden and violent movement energized the rest into action and they quickly followed him. Russell pulled the chair up close to the computer and, after tapping several keys, brought up the message as the rest of the group leaned over and waited.

Ant. Thank you for your message. Please
call to rearrange. Spider.

Russell scanned the message and the page with increasing excitement.

'He's given us his user number. Look.'

They followed his pointing finger to the top of the message where the user number was clearly displayed. Adams cut in quickly.

'Can we trace the caller from that?'

Russell nodded. 'Yes, just like a phone.'

Adams noted the number down quickly before turning to Sam.

'Is this the only phone line you've got in the house?'

Sam shook her head. 'No, it's a dedicated one. You can still use the phone in the sitting room.'

Adams nodded his understanding and rushed out of the office towards the sitting room phone. Russell began to reply to the Spider.

'Spider. Is time and location no longer possible? Ant.'

They waited. After a few moments the message came back.

'Ant. Location is still good but time bad. Can you make it for midnight?'

Russell looked up at Sam.

'Well, can we?'

Sam rushed through into the sitting room where Adams was just finishing his call.

'He wants to know whether he can make it midnight.'

Tom contemplated this for a moment. 'Same place?'

Sam nodded.

'Okay, midnight's fine.'

They moved back into Sam's office and nodded to Russell, who began to type out his reply. Despite the situation he was obviously enjoying every moment.

'I just love this real time stuff.'

*Spider. Midnight fine, looking forward to
meeting you then. Ant.'*

Watching a killer speak within inches of her reach and yet not being able to touch him sent shivers up Sam's spine. Voices without form; it was almost supernatural. The Spider's final message came back.

'I look forward to meeting you then, Ricky. We've so much to discuss.'

Wyn let out a slight scream.

'Christ, he knows who he is. How does he know who he is?'

Sam put her arm around her sister. 'I don't know, I just don't know.'

Adams was more upbeat about the whole situation.

'He's gone for it, he's only bloody gone for it.'

As he spoke the phone in the sitting room rang. Sam answered it. She recognized the monosyllabic voice at once, it was Chalky White.

'Is the boss there?'

She handed it over to Adams. 'It's Chalky.'

'Did you get a trace? Good. Where was the call from. Where? Are you sure? Bloody hell. Well, let's get a team around there at once. I'll see you there in fifteen minutes. What? No, don't stand the operation down yet, you never know, we might still miss him.'

He slammed the phone down and scanned the expectant faces.

'Well, we know where the call came from. The vicarage at Sowerby. It's the Reverend Peter Andrews's line.'

Chalky White and his team were already waiting just

outside the vicarage by the time Sam and Adams arrived. Adams climbed out of his car and strode across to his bagman.

'What have we got, Chalky?'

'Nothing yet, sir, thought I'd wait for you to arrive. There's several lights on, so I assume someone's in.'

Adams turned to Sam.

'Is the reverend married?'

His voice came out in waves of grey vapour against the darkness.

'No.'

'Girl friend?'

Sam shrugged. 'I don't know.'

'Is he gay?'

Sam shrugged again.

'Not that I know of, but then I don't know him that well. He's got a housekeeper if that's any help.'

Adams nodded and turned back to White. 'Get a couple of the lads at the back of the house.'

'Already done, sir.'

'He turned to Sam. 'I'd like you to come; it might help to have a friendly face with us.'

Sam caught a glimpse of Chalky's disapproving stare.

'Fine by me.'

'Good. Let's get on with it, then.'

With Sam by his side Tom and his team made their way quickly down the path that led to the front door and knocked firmly. After a few moments the hall light clicked on. Adams looked at Sam confidently.

'Looks like there is someone in.'

As he said it the front door opened and a plump, middleaged woman stood framed in the doorway. Her welcoming smile was quickly replaced by a frown when she saw all the men packed into the porch. Sam took the initiative.

'It's all right, Mary these gentleman are police officers. They'd like a quick word with Peter, if that's possible.'

She eyed the policemen suspiciously before replying. 'I'm afraid he's out at the moment, Doctor Ryan.'

'When are you expecting him back?'

'He wasn't sure when. Some time after midnight, he said.'

'What time did he go out, Mary?' Adams cut in.

She looked at Adams then back at Sam. 'Look, I'm not sure I should be telling you these things, I mean, what would the reverend say?'

Sam smiled sympathetically at her.

'It's okay, Mary, he wouldn't mind, I'll have a word with him later.'

'Well, if you say so, Doctor Ryan, I suppose that's okay.' She paused for a moment as if trying to get her facts right, 'He left about half an hour ago on his motorbike.'

Sam knew the next bit was going to be difficult.

'Where does he keep his computer, Mary?'

'In his office.'

'I'm afraid these gentlemen are going to have to take a quick look at it.'

Mary suddenly stood back inside the hall as if Sam had pushed her hard.

'Have they got a warrant? Otherwise they're not coming in here without the reverend's permission.' She crossed her arms and looked at them defiantly.

Sam looked up at Adams.

'Wait here a minute.'

She stepped closer to the housekeeper. 'Listen, Mary, I wouldn't ask this if it wasn't a matter of life and death, you know that. But I really must look at Peter's computer.'

She looked at Sam for a moment as if she was making up her mind. 'Life and death, you say?'

Sam nodded. Mary paused for a moment thinking about the implications of her next decision.

'Well, all right, you can have a look, but I don't want their size tens walking all over the house.'

Sam looked back at Adams who nodded his approval. She turned back to the housekeeper.

'Can you take me to his study, Mary?'

Mary turned and Sam followed her to a small office at the back of the house. The computer sat on a desk in the centre of the room. Sam walked across to it and felt the back; it was cold. So she turned it on and waited. After a few moments it kicked into life and the Windows icons appeared on the screen. Sam first established that the user number was in fact Peter Andrews's, but to her surprise, it wasn't. Following this unexpected revelation she clicked into the program manager and examined the last time the computer was used. It gave the previous day's date and a time of five-fifteen pm. Sam turned to Mary.

'Are there any other computers in the house?'

'She shook her head. 'Only in the church hall where he has his little computer club for the kids, like.'

'Is it open?'

'No, but I've got the key.'

'Can you let us in, Mary. As I said, it's very important.'

Having let Sam into the house, letting her into the hall wasn't such a big decision.

'I'll get the keys.'

Ten minutes later Sam, Tom, Chalky and two other members of the team were inside the hall. There were four computers, which were kept on trolleys and stored in a secure cupboard. They were wheeled out one at a time and placed in the centre of the hall. Adams looked down at the housekeeper.

'Do you know if this all of them, Mary?'

She nodded. 'As far as I know.'

They plugged in the computers quickly and switched them on, examining each in turn. It was White who finally discovered the one they were looking for.

'I think I found it, boss.'

Adams and Sam joined him. The user number was the same, and it had been used only fifty minutes before. Adams was slightly confused.

'How come this computer is registered to Peter Andrews?'

Sam shrugged. 'If he pays the bill and ordered the line, his name will be on it. Probably on all of them.'

Adams's attention returned to Mary.

'Did the reverend come in here at all this evening?'

She shook her head. 'Not that I'm aware.'

'Have you been with him over the past hour?'

She nodded.

'Oh yes. He was in his study working on his sermon for Sunday. I took him a drink in.'

Adams nodded thoughtfully. 'Chalky, have a look around, see if there's any sign of a break-in.'

White nodded and began to examine all the windows, doors and skylights. He returned to Adams.

'Nothing, boss, the place is clean.'

Adams turned back to Mary. 'Who else has keys to the hall?'

Mary stopped and looked down at her feet, lost in deepest thought.

'Only one other person that I know of. That's the verger. Oh, and Mr Moore who helps out at the club.'

Sam sat in Tom's car, looking out into the cold night. A slight mist was rolling off the river towards them, surrounding everything it touched and covering much of it from view. She glanced at her watch; it was ten-forty.

They had been there almost two hours. She looked across at Tom, who was leaning back in his seat with his eyes closed.

'You're not asleep are you?'

He didn't move but replied gently, 'Just resting my eyes.'

'Is it always like this?'

He nodded. 'Mostly, you get used to it. Depends what the takeaway's like, really.' He opened one eye and smiled.

'Are you sure your man will spot Ricky when he arrives? What if he takes a different route? He might not be easy to see with this mist.'

'We won't miss him. There are no routes which I don't have covered and my lads will spot anything that moves.'

'Who have you got on standby?'

Sam had suddenly become talkative and Adams realized he wasn't going to get any rest, so he sat up.

'We've got two Special Operations units and an armed response team, as well as half the murder squad, a chopper on standby and most importantly of all, me.'

Still not completely satisfied by his reassurances, she let it go and started to stare out of the window again. Suddenly the radio crackled into life, making her start and causing her heart to pound.

'Charlie Two to Charlie One, over.'

Adams picked up the handset to his radio quickly.

'Charlie Two, go ahead, over.'

'Suspect sighted cycling into the village with a large haversack on his back. Do you want us to pick him up, over?'

'Affirmative, Charlie Two, get him out of sight as quickly as possible. Bring him across to me when you've got him, over.'

'Ten-four, sir.'

Sam looked across at Tom, relief flooding her face.

'Suspect, I'm not sure I like the sound of that. I thought he was a witness.'

Adams smiled. 'It's just police speak, Sam, nothing to worry about.'

Sam didn't really care, Ricky was out of danger and that was all that mattered.

Half an hour later a white Special Operations van pulled alongside Tom's car and two burly uniformed officers got out, holding Ricky by the arms. Adams wound down the window to speak to them.

'Put him in the back, will you?'

'Right, sir. What do you want us to do with this, it's full of computer kit?'

'Put it in the back with him.'

As Ricky stepped into the back of the car, he saw Sam for the first time.

'Oh God, aunty Sam, I'm sorry. Thought I could sort it out on my own. Stupid.'

Although she was glad to see him and wanted to throw her arms around his neck and thank God that he was safe, she controlled herself.

'Have you any idea how worried everyone's been about you, especially your mother? She's beside herself.'

'Sorry.'

'We're not dealing with a small-time thief here, Ricky, we're dealing with a bloody serial killer, the most dangerous form of life there is, and you were almost certainly the next on his list. What were you thinking about?'

'I thought if I could find out who he was I might get myself out of trouble over the knocked-off gear.'

Sam nodded. 'You did, did you?'

'Yes.'

'If you really want to help, Ricky,' Adams interjected, 'there is something you can do, but it's going to take some guts.'

He looked across at Adams.

'Anything.'

'I want you to keep the appointment with the Spider...'

Sam was astonished at this previously unannounced decision. Ricky looked at his watch.

'It's a bit late now, its gone eleven.'

'We've changed the time.'

'You've contacted the Spider?'

Adams nodded. 'On the Net this afternoon.'

Sam forced herself into the conversation. 'I'm sorry, Tom, but there is no way I'm going to allow Ricky to act as bait in this game. Wyn would never forgive me. Sorry.'

'Aunty Sam, I'm nineteen now, I don't need anyone's permission anymore. Stop treating me like a child.'

Sam's eyes flashed at him.

'I will when you stop behaving like one.'

Ricky fell back in his seat, shaking his head, while Adams spoke up for him.

'Sam, he's in no danger. We'll make sure he arrives at the scene before the Spider. He'll be under observation by at least three coppers at all times. Christ, he'll be better protected than the Queen.'

'Things go wrong.'

'Not when I'm in charge they don't.'

Ricky was still obviously keen, 'Come on, aunty Sam. I'll be fine, and if things do start to go a bit wrong I can always run, I'm good at that.'

Sam turned to Adams.

'If anything, *anything* happens to him, I'll hold you personally responsible. Do you understand that?'

Adams nodded. 'Completely. Now shall we retire to the Rupert Brooke? I've arranged a quick briefing for half past.'

Tom Adams knew that it was imperative the operation was not only kept a secret but that it was planned to perfection. The fact that it was being carried out during the winter helped. During the summer months Byron's Pool was full of tourists. Now, however, they were few and far between. Hides had already been carefully prepared along all the main exits and entrances, containing at least two Special Operations officers in each one. Parked out of sight on the edge of the village were two further units, positioned so they were close enough to get to the scene quickly but far enough away not to cause suspicion if they were spotted. The Tactical Fire arms unit based themselves inside the Rupert Brooke with their cars hidden in the private car park at the back of the pub. The briefing only took ten minutes and then, as police officers scurried off in all directions, Sam stood in the large empty car park with her arm over her nephew's shoulder. Adams helped Ricky on with his haversack.

'Now, remember what you've got to do. Cycle up to the edge of the Pool, drop your bike off and walk the rest of the way until you reach the Pool itself, then wait. Understood?'

Ricky nodded. 'Understood.'

Sam pulled him around to face her.

'Now listen, just do as we've told you and you'll be fine. There are police officers all over the place...'

'Like I said,' Adams cut in, 'you'll be under surveillance by at least three officers at all times, so you'll be quite safe.'

Ricky looked at them both and nodded confidently.

'Fine, I'll get off then.'

He leaned across and kissed Sam gently on the cheek.

'No worries, aunty Sam, I'll be fine.'

Sam nodded, trying desperately to be reassured but failing miserably. She watched as Ricky set off on the short cycle from the pub to the Pool, wondering what the hell she would say to Wyn if anything went wrong.

Tom looked at her, almost reading her thoughts.

'Nothing will go wrong. It's in the hands of professionals now.'

Sam continued to watch Ricky disappear along the darkened street.

'I just want him to do a bit more growing, that's all.'

Tom turned and walked back to the car, followed by Sam, to take up their position with the Special Operations units just outside the village.

As Sam waited by the door to one of the vans she could hear the operation as it progressed, through the whispered instructions of the officers at the scene. They had all tuned to a channel which couldn't be picked up by outside bodies, so their lines of communication were as secure as they could make them. Ricky had already reached the Pool and was waiting. Sam glanced at her watch, it was eleven fifty-five. Suddenly one of the observation units called in a message.

'Target arrived in Pool car park. He is on a 500cc Yamaha motorcycle registration number Lima, 156, Alpha, Tango, Mike.'

Adams turned to one of his officers.

'Get that PNC'd.'

He returned to the radio, listening intently.

'Can't see his face yet its still covered by a helmet. Suspect is about six three and slim. He is wearing a black and red all-in-one leather motorcycle outfit with calf-length black leather boots.'

There was silence for a moment.

'He's removed his helmet and hung it onto the cycle but it's still too dark and misty to see him clearly. He's now making his way along the path towards the Pool.'

The officer Adams had asked to do the PNC check reappeared with a slip of notepaper, which he handed to Adams. He scanned it quickly before handing it to Sam.

'Recognize the name?'

There was a hint of sarcasm in Adams' voice that Sam didn't like. She read the information.

'Yamaha 500cc motorcycle registered to Reverend Peter Andrews.'

Sam suddenly felt sick. Here was the proof staring her in the face, but she couldn't get her mind around the full implication of what she was reading. All that time she had been working with him, thought of him as a friend. She hadn't even the slightest inkling that it could have been Peter. He had never aroused any suspicion. As normal, Adams wasted no time in taking action. Pulling Sam along with him he jumped into the SOU van and they sped off at high speed towards the scene, Adams shouting his instructions down the radio.

'Do not move in yet unless Ricky is in danger! My ETA is approximately two minutes!' He looked across at Sam, who was hanging onto the back of the van as it sped through Grantchester. 'I want this bastard myself.'

The van finally came to a halt in the small car park that led down to the Pool. Tom jumped out and began to run along the darkened path, followed by four burly uniformed officers from the unit. Sam did her best to keep up but quickly lost them ahead of her in the dark. After around two hundred yards, Tom sighted Andrews and quickened his pace further. When he was about ten yards from his quarry he finally and almost involuntarily called after him.

'Stop, police!'

The place seemed to suddenly fill with police officers. The figure turned calmly and faced the oncoming rush. Adams could see his face now, blue and luminous in the moonlight. It was indeed the Reverend Peter Andrews. As Tom reached him, figures who up until then had appeared to make up the flora and fauna on each side of the path suddenly seemed to come to life and surround the surprised man. Tom Adams finally reached him and took hold of his arm.

'Reverend Peter Andrews?'

Andrews nodded, looking surprised and bemused as Adams continued. 'Can I ask you what you're doing here, sir?'

'I was asked to come here.'

Between heavy breaths, Adams panted. 'Can I ask by whom?'

He pointed to Sam, who had finally caught up and arrived at the scene.

'By Doctor Ryan. I got a message on my computer yesterday. Something secret she wanted to discuss with me.'

'What, here?'

'Yes, well, I thought it a bit odd, but she was so insistent.'

'How did you know it was Doctor Ryan, sir?'

He shrugged. 'The message said so, how else?'

Adams and the rest of the squad turned as one to Sam, who shook her head vigorously.

'I sent no message except the one to the Spider today.'

Adams turned back to Peter Andrews.

'Peter Andrews. I am not satisfied with the explanation you have just given me and am arresting you on suspicion of murdering Simon Vickers and Dominic Parr.'

Tom then went through the routine of cautioning Andrews. For a moment Andrews was struck dumb. He just kept glancing around himself at the various officers in disbelief.

'You've got it wrong, superintendent, I was asked to be here. The message is still on my computer, you can see for yourself.' He glanced desperately across at Sam. 'For goodness sake, Sam, tell them. I'm no killer, there's been some terrible mistake.'

Tom looked into his face. 'Yes, and it was you that made it.'

He was handcuffed quickly and pulled back down the road by two of the SOU officers. Adams called across to Chalky White.

'Chalky, go with them. Make sure all his clothes are bagged and get a team down to his house, I want it sealed. Better seal the church until the SOCOs have had time to have a look, as well.'

Chalky nodded and disappeared into the night in the same direction as Andrews had just gone. Adams turned to Sam.

'You'd better go and get your nephew. Bet he's frozen by now. I'll see you in the car park.'

Sam nodded and began to walk away. As she did Adams called after her. 'You can be a pain in the butt sometimes, Sam, but we'd have never got a result without you.'

Sam gave him a tired smile, turned and made her way towards the Pool.

Lost in her thoughts about having failed to spot Peter Andrews's guilt she quickly arrived at the spot. She scanned the bank but failed to spot her nephew. She wasn't unduly concerned, it was dark and the mist was thickening. He was probably sheltering below one of the trees, he would be impossible to spot without the help of one of the unit's night glasses. She called out.

'Ricky, Ricky, it's Sam, where are you?'

Still there was silence.

'Ricky, this is no time to be playing stupid games. I'm cold and the police are waiting for us in the car park!'

There was still no movement and other than the night calls Sam would have expected, not a sound. She began to wonder if he hadn't already started to make his own way back to the car park after hearing all the commotion and she'd just missed him in the dark.

Suddenly, to her right and just in front of her came a loud splash. It was too noisy to have been a fish, and moving closer to where she had heard the commotion, Sam strained her eyes to try and see what it was. It took her a few moments to adjust to the darkness but when she did, she could quite clearly see the shape of two figures struggling in the water together. As she watched, she could feel a rising tide of panic sweep through her body. Despite the dark, her own fears, and unfamiliar terrain, Sam began to run headlong towards them. Every instinct in her body told her that Ricky was in mortal danger.

As she neared the figures she could see that one of them was her young nephew. His clothes were as distinctive as ever. He appeared to be struggling with a much taller man, who was clearly trying to force his head under water. Sam was unsure what to do at first but as she reached the edge of the bank the solution seemed obvious and she sprang from the muddy surface and landed on the man's back, wrapping both her arms and legs around him tightly and pulling for all she was worth. The figure finally lost his balance and fell backwards into the water, trapping Sam underneath him and forcing her body under the water as he fell. Despite this, she was determined to hang on for as long as she could, giving Ricky plenty of time to pull free and escape. She wasn't sure how long her grip lasted, but it seemed like hours. Finally exhausted, she was forced to let go and as her captive was release he quickly disentangled himself and was gone. Sam scrabbled and thrashed in the mud and water as she pushed herself towards the surface. As she emerged from beneath the murky waters her mouth opened wide, and she drew in great gulps of air.

Realizing how much danger she was still in, Sam twisted her head this way and that quickly, looking for the figure. Before she had time to look behind, however, she felt her head being forced back below the black waters of the Cam. Fighting against the pressure, she managed to take in a lungful of air before her face hit the water. Kicking wildly, she managed to free herself from the grip the figure had on her neck and lift her head up again. She had no idea what had happened to Ricky and, for the moment at least, he was not her main concern. Suddenly her right arm was levered high up her back, forcing her body down and her head back beneath the waters. This time there was no escape. Sam thrashed around as much as possible but she was tiring and the cold water was draining her strength. She could feel herself becoming exhausted, the air she had collected deep inside her lungs was depleted.

Finally Sam could feel her body begin to let go as her lungs screamed for air. She had heard that drowning was an easy and gentle way to die, but there was nothing easy or gentle about this. This was terror. Suddenly, and without warning, the vice-like grip was released and Sam was pulled to the surface, spluttering and waving her arms as she emerged. The first voice she heard was Ricky's.

'Are you okay, are you okay?'

He was half-pulling, half-dragging her towards the riverbank. Sam tried to splutter out reassurances.

'Fine I'm fine, who the hell was it?'

Ricky laid her gently onto the bank and lifted her head, nodding towards the water. Lying face down was the limp and unconscious figure of their attacker.

'I hit him across the head with a rock. I think I must have killed him.'

Sam looked up at him. 'You've got to get him out.'

Ricky shook his head.

'Not me, he's in deep water. I'm too tired.'

'How the hell did he get past all the police checks?'

'He swam, swam across the river. He must have been bloody mad, it's freezing.'

Sam shook her head. Across the river, the one place they hadn't secured.

'Did you get a look at him?'

Ricky shook his head. 'Not a good one. He was bloody strong, though. Thought I'd had it until you came along.'

Sam managed a forced smile.

'Me, too.'

Sam fell back onto the bank, breathing deeply and unable to move further. As she lay there the familiar voice of Tom Adams cut through darkness.

'Sam, Ricky, where the hell are you?'

Sam was too exhausted to call but her nephew managed one shout before collapsing back next to her. Tom Adams and Chalky White ran across to them and Tom was quickly kneeling by the side of Sam.

'What the hell is going on?'

Sam, still unable to speak, pointed to the body, which was just beginning to drift downstream. Adams looked across at Chalky.

'Get it before it disappears.'

Chalky looked at him for a moment unable to believe the order he had just been given. Adams repeated it.

'Well, don't just stand there, pull it in.'

Chalky did as he was ordered and waded out into the Cam. The water was chest height before he finally managed to grab the body and pull it in. Sam had recovered a little but was shivering violently. With Tom Adams's help she managed to sit up and watch as Chalky emerged from the water and turned the body over. She couldn't see at first, as water from her hair dripped into her eyes. Finally she managed to wipe the worst away. The mist drifted around the group of figures on the bank and as it thinned briefly, the moon emerged and the face of Eric Chambers was clearly illuminated. Sam looked at Adams and then back to Eric. Adams's arms tightened around her as they all took in the truth of what they saw.

'The one thing that I have learned over the years in this job, Sam, is that more often than not it *is* the obvious.'

He looked down at Chalky. 'Is he dead?'

Chalky nodded.

'I think so.'

Sam crawled down the bank to Eric Chambers's body and placed her fingers on the side of his neck. There was a visible wound by his temple where Ricky had hit him with the rock. She still searched for a pulse, but there was none. Whether it was the blow from the rock or drowning would be established later, what was certain was that he was dead. Sam looked up at Adams again.

'Why, why would he do it? He seemed such a gentle man.'

Tom shrugged.

'Who knows. We've only got his word that it was his mother who killed his father and his girl friend. Perhaps some people are just born evil. He must have sent the message to Peter Andrews to draw us off. Whatever else he was, he was a clever old sod.'

Sam looked back at Eric Chambers's half-open eyes.

'I don't suppose we'll ever really know what motivated him now.'

'No, I don't suppose we will,' Adams agreed.

He put his arm around Sam and lifted her from the ground. Chalky and Ricky had set off ahead of them, Ricky swathed in Tom's jacket, and both figures trembling from head to toe.

'Come on, we've got to get you all warmed up, and there's one very frightened vicar back at the van. Let's put him out of his misery.'

Sam nodded and, with his arms tightly around her for warmth and support, they made their way from the Pool.

EPILOGUE

THE PROBLEM WITH LOSING YOUR MAIN SUSPECT IS THAT it leaves so many questions unanswered. Tom Adams, together with the Serial Crime Unit, was already dissecting Eric's life and trying to connect him to as many of the unsolved murders around the country as he could. It was going to be a long, thankless task with no guarantees of an answer at the end of it. Sam wasn't even sure whether Eric's story regarding the murder of his father and his mistress was true. She now thoght it was more likely that it had been Eric, and not his mother, that had committed the murders, and that his mother had protected Eric, not the other way around. It would certainly explain the reason for the stab marks being so low on the skeletons. Tom had already established that the murders, the ones they knew about, started shortly after Eric's mother died. So with his safety net gone the evil had been unleashed. In truth, however, it would only ever be suspicion, no one would ever know the real truth. After the PM, which Trevor kindly agreed to do, Eric Chambers was finally laid to rest next to his mother in Sowerby churchyard. There were a few local objections but these were dismissed by Peter Andrews, who felt it was up to God and not the people to judge him now.

As for the rest, Enright was eventually picked up in London with a large quantity of pornographic material, and is awaiting trial on several charges. Ironically, John Gordon is defending him. Why Eric had chosen to steal his car the night Simon Vickers was murdered Sam didn't know, but it did seem an odd coincidence. Despite being interviewed by Tom Adams for some time he denied being involved with Eric, but most people had their doubts. Peter Andrews and Edmond Moore finished their film and it was a great success, even getting a showing on the BBCs *Video Diary* programme. The new boiler was installed and the choir was eventually able to sing without the necessity of thick coats and warm hats. Despite Sam's continuing reservations about him, Moore remained an important member of both the church and the village, taking over where Eric had left off.

It was probably the speed that eveything returned to normal that made Sam turn down a very lucrative deal as head of department at Barts. The idea of moving back to the crowded indifference of London didn't really appeal, either.

Ricky recovered quickly from his ordeal at Byron's Pool and decided to continue his education in computer studies at one of the local further education colleges. Wyn and Ricky also decided to move out of Sam's cottage. Wyn was working and felt like having a little more of her own space, so she purchased one of the new two-bedroom flats in town that overlooked the Cam. Although Sam was pleased for her, she also knew she was going to miss her sister and nephew very much and dreaded the loneliness that she knew was to come.

It was probably Wyn's and Ricky's move that finally convinced Sam it was time to change her lifestyle a little. Life with Tom, she considered, wouldn't be so bad. He clearly loved her and she had strong feelings for him, so that was as good a start as any. Besides, she was ready to settle down and couldn't think of anyone she would rather settle down with. Perhaps, she pondered, it wouldn't only be Trevor getting married this year. To this end the Sunday after Wyn and Ricky moved, she picked up the best bottle of champagne she could find, and early one Sunday morning made her way around to Tom's house fully intending to get him drunk over a champagne breakfast, and see what developed from there.

The red Z3 sports car was parked on Tom Adams's drive. She knew who it belonged to, there weren't that many Z3s around yet. She could also see from the early morning dew that covered the windscreen that it had been there all night and probably for many other nights before that. Part of her was tempted to march up to the front door and confront him with her discovery. But then, she asked herself what good that would do. She just about managed to hold off the tears as she pushed the gear stick into first and pulled off along the long road that eventually led to her empty cottage. All of a sudden the position at Barts Hospital seemed very appealing.

POCKET
B O O K S

SILENT WITNESS

A Doctor Samantha Ryan Mystery

Nigel McCrery

When forensic pathologist, Dr. Sam Ryan, is
called out to a murder scene, she is far from
pleased. Tramping around a graveyard in the
dark is not how she'd planned to spend her day
off. And then another, related, death is
discovered, and Sam is under pressure to come
up with evidence the police desperately need. By
now, though, the killer has decided that Sam is a
threat and must be removed . . .

Silent Witness is the brilliant debut of a major
talent in crime fiction – tautly written, it will grip
its readers right to its breathlessly tense
conclusion.

ISBN 0 671 01780 2

PRICE £5.99

POCKET
B O O K S

STRANGE SCREAMS OF DEATH

A Doctor Samantha Ryan Mystery

Nigel McCrery

The body of a young woman is discovered in a
disused shed at an American airbase just outside
Cambridge. She has been raped before being
viciously murdered.

The police investigation begins, and suspicion
falls on an American airman who had been seen
dancing with the woman earlier that evening.
Home Office pathologist Doctor Samantha Ryan
arrives on the scene and is immediately absorbed
in the case. When two FBI agents arrive on the
scene, the investigation suddenly becomes more
urgent. Could the murder be linked to a number
of horrific killings both in the United States and
Europe over the last few decades?

ISBN 0 671 01781 0

PRICE £5.99

POCKET
BOOKS

THE INFILTRATOR
E.A. MACDONALD

John Stockart is an ambitious man. He knows
that when you are toying with people's lives,
playing God with human genetics, potentially
making a fortune from creating 'designer' babies,
you keep it a secret. So when some critically
sensitive information goes missing, he is not a
happy man.

As freelance journalist Sasha Downey begins to
pick up the threads of a devastating story – the
clandestine experiments of a genetic scientist . . .
the collusion of one of the country's most
powerful government ministers . . . an
undercover operation ready to silence all
intruders – she knows she must expose the
perpetrators. But the killer net is tightening
around her and a deadly race has already begun,
as Stockart's agents close in on Sasha . . .

ISBN 0 671 85268 X

PRICE £5.99

**SIMON &
SCHUSTER**

THE KEEPER
E.A. MACDONALD

Investigative journalist Kirsten Cooper doesn't
take long to succumb to the charms of enigmatic
religious cult leader David Norton who, for nine
years, has been dedicated to preparing the world
for Christ's Second Coming.

Alerted by Kirsten's disappearance and her own
suspicions, researcher Jane Carlucci begins to
piece together some disturbing facts about the
Fellowship. Desperate to find evidence to
support her theory she goes into the very heart of
the cult group, but soon loses contact with her
links to the outside world. And now, in a move
that threatens the safety of millions, the
countdown to the moment Norton has been
waiting for has begun . . .

ISBN 0 684 84053 7

PRICE £16.99
Available November 1999

SIMON &
SCHUSTER

RESURRECTION
KEN McCLURE

A young Iraqi student at the Institute of
Molecular Science in Edinburgh kills himself for
no apparent reason, and Adam Dewar stumbles
on the horrific possibility that the student had
been under pressure from the Iraqis to
reconstruct the smallpox virus . . . and then
smallpox breaks out on the Muirhouse Estate.

The priority is to contain the virus, but with the
death toll rising, riots breaking out on the estate
and the continuing presence of the Iraqi secret
service in the city, Dewar is in a race against time
to discover the source of the disease and prevent
it falling into the hands of a hostile nation. A
nation that would be only too willing to hold the
world to ransom.

ISBN 0 684 85128 8

PRICE £16.99

**SIMON &
SCHUSTER**

WE'LL MEET AGAIN
MARY HIGGINS CLARK

Dr Gary Lasch is found dead at his desk and his
beautiful young wife, Molly, is arrested and
charged with his murder.

Six years later, on Molly's release from prison,
she reasserts her innocence in front of reporters
gathered at the prison gates, among whom is
investigative reporter Fran Simmons.
Determined to prove her innocence, Molly
convinces Fran to research and produce a
programme on Gary's death.

But Fran soon finds herself enmeshed in a
tangled web of intrigue and menace and, as her
investigation proceeds, there are those who
know they must make a choice: face ruin, or
eliminate Fran.

ISBN 0 684 82131 1

PRICE £16.99

POCKET
B O O K S

YOU BELONG TO ME
MARY HIGGINS CLARK

Regina Clausen was forty-three, successful in her
career but insecure and unfulfilled in her personal
life. Travelling alone on the luxury liner Gabrielle,
she disembarked in Hong Kong saying she would
rejoin the ship when it docked in Japan. She was
never seen again.

Five years later, radio presenter Susan Chandler does
a series about vanishing women on her radio talk
show. When a caller, who refuses to identify herself,
tells of meeting a man on a cruise who gave her a ring
inscribed 'You Belong to Me', but then disappeared
when she refused to leave the ship with him, she
thinks little of it. But then Regina's mother appears at
Susan's office with a ring bearing the same inscription
which was found amongst her daughter's belongings,
and Susan begins to suspect that they are on the trail
of something dangerously sinister . . .

ISBN 0 671 01037 9

PRICE £5.99

SIMON & SCHUSTER
A VIACOM COMPANY

ORDER FORM

This book and other **Simon & Schuster** titles are available from your book shop or can be ordered direct from the publisher.

☐	0 671 01780 2	**Silent Witness**	*Nigel McCrery*	£5.99
☐	0 671 01781 0	**Strange Screams of Death**	*Nigel McCrery*	£5.99
☐	0 671 85268 X	**The Infiltrator**	*E. A. MacDonald*	£5.99
☐	0 684 84053 7	**The Keeper**	*E. A. MacDonald*	£16.99
☐	0 684 85128 8	**Resurrection**	*Ken McClure*	£16.99
☐	0 684 82131 1	**We'll Meet Again**	*Mary Higgins Clark*	£16.99
☐	0 671 010379	**You Belong To Me**	*Mary Higgins Clark*	£5.99

Please send cheque or postal order for the value of the book, and add the following for postage and packing: UK inc. BFPO 75p per book; OVERSEAS Inc. EIRE £1 per book.

OR: Please debit this amount from my:

VISA/ACCESS/MASTERCARD ....

CARD NO...

EXPIRY DATE..

AMOUNT £...

NAME..

ADDRESS...

....

SIGNATURE...

Send orders to:
Book Service By Post,
PO Box 29, Douglas, Isle of Man, IM99 1BQ
Tel: 01624 675137, Fax 01624 670923
http://www.bookpost.co.uk or
e-mail: bookshop@enterprise.net for details
Please allow 28 days for delivery.
Prices and availability subject to change without notice.